PERFECT PREY

Helen Fields studied law at the University of East Anglia, then went on to the Inns of Court School of Law in London. After completing her pupillage, she joined chambers in Middle Temple where she practised criminal and family law for thirteen years. After her second child was born, Helen left the Bar. Together with her husband David, she runs a film production company, acting as script writer and producer. The D.I. Callanach series is set in Scotland, where Helen feels most at one with the world. Helen and her husband now live in Hampshire with their three children and two dogs.

Helen loves Twitter but finds it completely addictive. She can be found at @Helen_Fields.

Perfect Prey

HELEN FIELDS

avon.

AVON
A division of HarperCollins*Publishers*
1 London Bridge Street,
London, SE1 9GF

www.harpercollins.co.uk

A Paperback Original 2017

3

First published in Great Britain by
HarperCollins*Publishers* 2017

A catalogue record for this book is
available from the British Library

Paperback ISBN-13: 978-0-00-818158-1
Trade Paperback ISBN: 978-0-00-822004-4

Set in Bembo by Palimpsest Book Production Limited,
Falkirk, Stirlingshire

Printed and bound by
CPI Group (UK) Ltd, Croydon, CR0 4YY

MIX
Paper from
responsible sources
FSC www.fsc.org **FSC™ C007454**

For Brian and John – the dads and grandads – reading their newspapers in the great beyond, and wondering what all the noise down here is about. With love from those who will never forget you.

Acknowledgements

Let me start by thanking the good people of Edinburgh. Forgive me for making it the murder capital of Europe for one hot summer in this book. The truth is that I've rarely felt safer in any other city. Likewise to the men and women of Police Scotland who do such a great job, and who put up with my queries with endless patience. Edinburgh City Council likewise, and I doubt it's possible to find a friendlier bunch of people answering phone calls anywhere in the world. Thank you Paul Murrell for your help with researching Edinburgh's School Crossing Guards and getting my facts right. Also, BBC Scotland – I have to tell you about the gentleman who answered my call regarding the news team, who feature in this book in a brief but unforgettable moment – you made me laugh, you listened, and were so supportive I forgot that you and I had never met.

And to those people without whom these pages would still be a figment of my (fairly overactive) imagination, I am grateful to you every day. To Caroline Hardman – my agent – and Joanna Swainson for providing backup, if you hadn't believed in me I'd still be writing, but it wouldn't be anything like this much fun (and no one would have read any of it)! And a mention for Emily Hayward-Whitlock at The Artists Partnership, so much fun and a wonderful outcome.

Helen Huthwaite – soother of egos, calmer of nerves, beautifier of words and all round top banana – you have made this an absolute joy. And as for the Avon team, what can I say? Helena Sheffield, Phoebe Morgan, Rosie Foubister, Hannah Welsh, Rachel Faulkner-Willcocks, Oli Malcolm, Victoria Gilder (on loan) and Louis Patel (until recently), there really is never a dull moment. Also, to the mothership – HarperCollins – the marketing, design, sales and support teams, it's you who get books on shelves and in hands, and I appreciate your support more than you know.

A book is a non-stop process. Once this manuscript leaves my hands it goes to my first readers. Perfect Prey took its tottering preliminary steps in the imaginations of the lovely Andrea Gibson, Allison Spyer, Jessica Corbett and Amanda Patchett. They saved me from endless typos, plot failings and character weaknesses. More than that, they told me the thing I needed to hear – that it was all going to be okay – these are the sorts of friends who understand how to temper criticism with kindness, and that is no mean feat.

My gratitude to the staff at the McDonald Road Library in Edinburgh, who answered my ridiculous questions and showed me around their stunning building. What a vital and wonderful job you all do.

To the Banshees – Emma Bailey, Gareth Hollingsworth, Joe Marston, Nick Pritchard, Federico Rea, Andrej Srebrnjak and Katy Ward – for the film, the website, the good-natured mickey-taking and the general fabulousness of you all, I will buy doughnuts.

Then to this. My family have kept me sane in spite of everything. My mother, Christine Fields, who I still cannot allow to read my books (just not appropriate) thank you for the constant emotional and practical support. To Gabriel, Solomon and Evangeline – never stop throwing your dirty clothes, plates and apple cores around the house at random points – that's what family really is, even if I moan at you. I know these years will go too fast. When a future you reads these words, know that every second I spend writing is a gift you gave me. I was not with you at the park. I was not reading with you. I was not baking cupcakes or talking about your day. Words are not enough.

And to David Baumber, champion of my books and dismisser of self doubt, I'm not sure you could have given me a single second more of your time, your support, one ounce more of your enthusiasm. (Also many, many cups of tea). Kiss me.

PART ONE

Chapter One

There were worse places to die. Few more terrifying ways of dying, though. It was an idyllic summer backdrop – the cityscape on one side, the ancient volcano Arthur's Seat silhouetted in the distance. The music could be felt before it was heard, the bass throbbing through bones and jiggling flesh. Sundown came late in Edinburgh in early July and the sky was awash with shades of rose, gold and burnt orange. Perhaps that was why no one noticed when it happened. Either that, or the cocktail of drink, drugs and natural highs. The festival was well underway. Three days of revellers lounging, partying, loving, eating and drinking their way through band after band, bodies increasingly comfortable with fewer clothes and minimal hygiene. If you could take a snapshot to illustrate a sense of ecstasy, this would have been the definitive scene. Washing through the crowd, jumping as one, as if the multitudes had merged to create a single rapturous beast with a thousand grinning heads.

Through the centre of it all, the killer had drifted like smoke, sinuous and light-footed, bringing a blade to its receptacle like a ribbon through air. The slash was clean. Straight and deep.

The extent of the blood loss was apparent on the ground, the wound too gaping for hands to stem the flow. Not that there had been time to get the victim in an ambulance. Not that anyone had even noticed his injury before he had almost completely bled out.

Detective Inspector Luc Callanach stood at the spot where the young man had taken his last breath. His identity had not yet been established. The police had pieced together remarkably little in the hour since the victim's death. It was amazing, Callanach thought, how in a crowd of thousands they had found not a single useful witness.

The young man had simply ceased his rhythmic jumping, crumpling slowly, falling left and right, forwards and backwards, against his fellow festival-goers, finally collapsing, clutching his stomach. It had annoyed some of them, disrupted their viewing pleasure. He'd been assumed drunk at first, drug-addled second. Only when a barefooted teenage girl had slipped in the pool of blood did the alarm ring out, and amidst the decibels it had taken an age for the message to get through. Eventually the screams had drowned out the music when the poor boy had been rolled over, his spilled entrails slinking closely in his wake like some alien pet, sparkling with reflected sunshine in the gloss of so much brilliant blood.

The uniforms hadn't been far away. It was a massive public event with every precaution taken, or so they'd thought. But making their way through the throng, police officers first, then paramedics, and clearing an area then managing the scene, had been a logistical disaster. Callanach looked skywards and sighed. The crime scene was more heavily trodden than nightclub toilets on New Year's Eve. There was enough DNA floating around to populate a new planet. It was a forensic free-for-all.

The body itself was already on its way to the mortuary,

having been photographed in situ for all the good it would do. The corpse had been moved so many times by do-gooders, panicked bystanders, the police, medics, before finally being left to rest on a bed of trampled grass and kicked-up dirt. The chief pathologist, Ailsa Lambert, had been unusually quiet, issuing instructions only to treat the body with care and respect, and to move him swiftly to a place where there would be no more prying cameras or hysterical caterwauling. Callanach was there to secure the scene – a concept beyond irony – before following Ailsa to her offices.

In the brief look Callanach had got, the victim's face had said it all. Eyes screwed tight as if willing himself to wake from a nightmare, mouth caught open between gasp and scream. Had he been shouting a name? Callanach wondered. Did he know his assailant? He'd been carrying no identification, merely some loose change in his shorts, not even so much as a watch on his wrist. Only a key on a piece of string around his neck. However swiftly death had come, the terror of knowing you were fading, of sensing that hope was a missed bus, while all around you leapt and sang, must have seemed the cruellest joke. And at the very end, hearing only screams, seeing panic and horror in the sea of eyes above. What must it have been like, Callanach wondered, to have died alone on the hard ground in such bright sunlight? The last thing the victim had known of the world could only have been unalleviated dread.

Callanach studied the domed stage, rigged with sound and lighting gear, and prayed that one of the cameras mounted there might have caught a useful fragment. Someone rushing, leaving, moving differently to the rest of the crowd. The Meadows, an expanse of park and playing fields to the south of the city centre, were beautiful and peaceful on a normal day. Mothers brought their toddlers, dog walkers roamed and joggers timed

5

the circuit. Strains of 'Summer is A-Coming In' sounded in the back of Callanach's mind from a screening of the original version of *The Wicker Man* that DI Ava Turner had dragged him to a few months ago. He'd found Edward Woodward's acting mesmerising, and the images of men and women in animal masks preparing to make their human sacrifice had stayed with him long after the projector had been switched off. It wasn't a million miles away from the circus in the centre of which this young man had perished.

'Sir, the people standing behind the victim have been identified. They're available to speak now,' a constable said. Callanach followed him to the edge of the field, leaving forensics constructing a temporary shelter to protect the scene overnight. Leaning against a tree was a couple, wrapped together in a single blanket, their faces tear-stained, the woman shaking visibly as the man comforted her.

'Merel and Niek De Vries,' the constable read from his notebook. 'A Dutch couple holidaying here. Been in Scotland ten days.'

Callanach nodded and stepped forward for quiet privacy.

'I'm Detective Inspector Callanach with Police Scotland,' he said. 'I know this is shocking and I'm sorry for what you witnessed. I'm sure you've explained what you saw a few times now, and you'll be asked about it many more. Could you just run over it for me though, if you don't mind?'

The man said something to his wife that Callanach couldn't follow, but she looked up and took a deep breath.

'My wife does not speak good English,' Niek De Vries began, 'but she saw more than me. I can translate.'

Merel rattled off a few sentences, punctuated with sobs, before Niek spoke again.

'She only noticed him when the girl screamed. Then Merel bent down to shake him, to tell him to get up. He was on his knees, bent forward. We thought he was drunk, sick maybe. When Merel stood up again her hand was covered with blood. Even then, she says, she thought maybe he had vomited, ruptured something. Only when everyone stepped back and we laid him out, did we see the wound. It was as if he had been cut in two.' Niek put one hand across his eyes.

'Did you see anyone before he fell, near him, touch him, push past him? Did anyone seem to rush away from the area? Or can you describe any of the people standing near you in detail?' Callanach asked.

'Everyone was moving constantly,' Niek answered, 'and we were watching the stage, the band, you know? We don't have any friends here so we were not really looking. People were jumping up and down, screaming, going this way and that to get to the bar or the toilets. We were just trying not to get separated. I hadn't even noticed the man in front of us until he fell.'

'Did he speak at all?' Callanach asked.

Niek checked that question with Merel.

'She thinks he was already unconscious or dead when she first spoke to him. And anyway, the noise was too much. She would not have heard.'

'I understand,' Callanach said. 'Officers will take you to the police station to make full written statements and then transfer you to your accommodation.'

'Not British?' Merel stuttered, addressing Callanach directly for the first time.

'I'm French,' Callanach replied, 'well, half French, half Scottish. I apologise if my accent's hard to understand.'

'*Le garçon était trop jeune pour mourir.*' The boy was too young to die, she said, continuing in French although Callanach found he was hearing it in English, so fast had his translation become.

Merel De Vries recalled one other thing. Above the music, a woman laughing in the crowd, so loud she could hear it even as she'd bent down to help the victim. What struck Callanach as odd was Merel's description of it. That it wasn't a happy laugh. In her words, it had echoed of malicious.

Chapter Two

'The cut came from a single weapon, but the implement would have been customised by skilled hands,' Ailsa Lambert said. 'Two perfectly paired scalpel blades must have been bound together with a spacer between them creating a gap of four millimetres. The combination would have rendered the wound impossible to close or suture, even had he been in hospital when he'd been attacked. The twin incisions are . . .' she paused as she picked up a flexible measure, 'twenty-eight centimetres in length. They have pulled apart substantially, causing a gaping wound resulting in massive trauma. His organs then moved, sliding down and forward, so that much of what should have been in his abdominal cavity exited his body as he fell and rolled. Some of it even has identifiable shoe marks from those around him. Blood loss caused his heart to stop.'

'I get it,' Callanach said wearily. 'Not much doubt over cause of death. Anything else I need to know?'

'Tox screen will be a while. He has no other visible injuries, seems superficially healthy, his lungs tell me he wasn't a smoker, good boy,' she patted the corpse's hand with her gloved one and smiled grimly. 'But this weapon, Luc, this weapon wasn't designed for self-defence. And you can't pick it up at the hardware store either. Someone crafted it, adored it. The cut was deep, even, and yet very little force seems to have been required to puncture far into the abdominal cavity. Whoever did this took pride in it, thought about efficiency, understood the mechanics of it. This was no impromptu stabbing or weapon grabbed in the heat of an argument.'

'An assassination then?' Callanach asked, bending over the body and taking stock.

'More like a ritual, if you ask me,' she said. 'This was dreamed up, practised and perfected.'

'How old is he?'

'Between eighteen and twenty-two, I think. Five feet, eleven inches. Active, no spare fat, good muscle mass but not one of those types who live at the gym. Size ten shoe. Brown hair, hazel eyes. No defence wounds. Never saw it coming.'

'So he didn't recognise his attacker as a threat when they came for him?'

'Most unlikely. You don't look well yourself, Luc. Are you sleeping?' Ailsa asked as she peeled off her gloves and made notes.

'I'm sleeping just fine,' he lied.

'Eating properly? You're pale and you have broken blood vessels in your eyes.'

'I'll phone you tomorrow for the tox results,' he evaded. 'Anything before that and you have my mobile number.'

'Give my regards to DI Turner, would you? I haven't seen her for an age. I used to catch up with her mother regularly at an opera appreciation group but I haven't bumped into her recently either,' Ailsa said, stretching her back. In her mid-sixties, tiny and birdlike, she was a force to be reckoned with.

'I'll pass that on,' he said, stripping off his own gown and dropping it into the bin outside the door.

On his return to the station, a grim welcome party sat around in the incident room. Callanach looked directly to Detective Constable Tripp.

'Just following up a lead from a phone call, sir,' Tripp said. 'Young woman called in to say she and her boyfriend got separated at the festival. He hasn't turned up yet. I've sent a car to pick her up.'

'Did she give his name?' Callanach asked, grabbing coffee as he sat at a computer.

'Sim Thorburn,' Tripp replied, pressing a couple of keys and waiting for a photo to load, one step ahead as ever. Some new social networking site popped up in seconds with a multitude of larger than life photos. In each one, the lad was smiling, laughing, his expression carefree and guileless. In the last, he was hand in hand with his girlfriend. Without a doubt, it was the same hand that Ailsa Lambert had been patting a short while ago.

'That's him,' Callanach said. 'So what do we know?'

'At the moment, everything that's on his home page. He didn't bother with privacy filters, so it's there for the world to see. He's twenty-one, Scottish, lives in Edinburgh.'

'Police record?'

'Not that we can find.' A phone rang behind Tripp and someone passed him a note. 'The girlfriend's here, sir. And DCI Begbie wants to see you as soon as you're done.'

'Of course he does,' Callanach said, standing up. 'Do you have any idea where DI Turner is, Tripp? Only Ailsa Lambert was asking after her.'

'Off duty,' DC Salter shouted from the corridor. 'Said something about maybe being in late tomorrow too. Did you want me to get a message to her, sir?'

'No thanks, Salter,' Callanach shouted after her. 'It's nothing that can't wait.' Unlike Sim Thorburn's girlfriend, no doubt already suspecting the worst but who'd be downstairs holding out for a miracle. She would be imagining some mistake, hoping perhaps that in spite of the evidence, her boyfriend had met some friends and wandered off without telling her. Any number of excuses for his disappearance would be going through her mind. Until she saw Callanach's face, he thought. People knew the second they looked at you.

'I'm sorry,' he said, as soon as he saw her. Introductions were pointless. She wouldn't remember Callanach's name in a few seconds' time, anyway.

'You can't be sure that it's him yet,' she whispered. 'You haven't even asked me about him.'

'We found several photos on an internet site of the two of you together.' He held out an example that Tripp had printed off in anticipation. 'Is this Sim?'

She sobbed and took a step away from the photo as if the paper itself was a weapon.

'Have you seen him?' she asked. Callanach pulled a chair out for her and she sat.

'I have. I'm sure it's him.'

'What . . . what . . .' she couldn't say the words.

'He received a knife wound. It proved fatal. It would have been very fast. The ambulance didn't have time to get to him.'

'A knife wound? I thought maybe a ruptured appendix or a blood clot or . . . he was stabbed? It's not him. No one would do that to Sim.'

'He wasn't in any trouble that you knew of? It might be something as simple as a family feud, money problems, someone settling an old score?'

'Don't be so stupid!' the girl snapped. It was an understandable reaction given what she was going through. What she didn't understand was how cold the trail would get with every passing minute. 'He was a charity worker. He earned minimum

12

wage and still spent every spare moment doing extra unpaid voluntary service.'

'Can you tell me more about that?' Callanach asked.

'He worked in the homeless shelters, ran the soup kitchens in the city, organised fundraising. Sim was the gentlest, kindest person you could ever meet. He gave away every last penny. It was the only thing we ever argued about.'

'And you didn't see anything strange yesterday? No one following him?'

The girl shook her head, shock taking hold. Callanach knew he'd got all he was going to get from her by then. He handed over to Tripp to organise the formal identification of the body and obtain family details. Callanach had to get a lead, and fast. Somewhere, the man or woman who had slaughtered Sim Thorburn had undoubtedly already hidden the weapon and neutralised any incriminating forensic evidence.

'Salter,' Callanach shouted on his way towards the incident room. 'Find out who's controlling the footage from the concert. I want it available tonight. And try to keep the Chief off my back for a while, would you? I've got work to do.'

'So have I, Detective Inspector,' DCI Begbie said, appearing in the doorway. Lately he seemed larger every time Callanach saw him. It wasn't healthy, putting on weight that fast. The Chief hadn't been exactly slim when Callanach had joined Police Scotland, but now he was working his way towards an early grave, for no apparent reason. 'Is something wrong, DI Callanach?' Begbie asked. He realised he'd been staring at Begbie's straining shirt buttons.

'No, sir, just distracted.'

'Frankly, that's not very reassuring. What leads have we got?' Callanach tried to find a way to express the completely nega- tive nature of the case so far, and struggled to answer. 'That good, huh? Well, somebody must have seen something.

Thousands of potential witnesses and we're stuck. Bloody typical. Have media relations organise a press conference. Might as well do it immediately. We can't have people scared on the streets. There'll be a rational explanation for this. No one walks up to a complete stranger and slashes them. Get answers, Callanach. I want someone in custody in the next forty-eight hours.'

'Chief . . .'

'Got it. You don't like doing press conferences. Duly noted.' Begbie walked off, puffing as he went. Callanach considered following to ask if his boss was all right, then recognised that for the career-ending move it would be and made his way back towards the incident room. He was starving, but the idea of a fish and chip supper being consumed straight from newspaper was making him queasy. There was no prospect of getting home for twelve hours and the healthiest food at the station was probably an out of date packet of crackers abandoned at the back of a cupboard. Callanach was getting his thoughts together to lead a briefing when someone thrust a carrier bag into his hand.

'Stop looking at everyone else's food as if they're eating poison. It's off-putting. You're not doing anything to help your reputation for French snobbery,' DI Ava Turner said, pushing a fork into his free hand. 'Prawn salad. Not home-made, so you're safe from my pathetic efforts.'

'I thought you were off duty and not coming in until late tomorrow. Have you been demoted to the catering division?'

'You can always hand it back,' she said, checking her phone and frowning.

'Too late.' Callanach ripped open the packaging and tucked in. 'Ailsa Lambert was asking after you. Do I take it that Edinburgh's elite social circle is not functioning properly?' he smiled.

'How do you tell someone to shut up in French?' she

responded without looking up from her phone. Ava had spent much of her career trying to distance herself from the privilege she was born into. The expectation that she would become a doctor, lawyer, actuary or similar – at least until she settled down and produced grandchildren for her eager parents – had spawned a rebellion landing her in the grimy world of policing. But even at work she couldn't escape the fact that her family's closest friends included the upper levels of Police Scotland brass, politicians, CEOs and even the city's chief forensic pathologist.

DC Salter interrupted, handing over two pages of A4 and checking her watch. 'DCI Begbie said he knew you were busy so he's organising the press conference for you.' Salter was trying not to smile. Turner ruined the effort by laughing out loud. 'I've written out some notes for you, sir. Media will be gathered in about an hour.'

'Wow. Reduced to using the media circus already? This time tomorrow morning women will be swooning over your face on the front cover of every paper. So Police Scotland's pin-up detective is getting back out there, is he?' Ava said. Callanach had been with the Major Investigation Team in Edinburgh for eight months, and in that time Ava had never missed an opportunity to make fun of him. His distant career as a model made him a particularly easy target.

'It wasn't my idea,' Callanach muttered. '*Merde!*'

'Language,' Ava admonished.

'I thought you couldn't speak French,' Callanach said.

'You've been mistaking my ignoring you for failing to understand you. It's a different concept,' Ava said.

'Do you not have work to do?' Callanach asked, shaking his head at her, watching the grin spread across her face. Ava was the sort of woman who left men wrong-footed. She looked innocent enough, her long brown hair a tangle of curls, with grey eyes that shifted colour depending on the light. But she could cut to the chase in a second. Being direct seemed to be the only way she knew. When he'd arrived from France his head had been a mess. Too much had happened for him to walk away unscathed emotionally. The last few months had been curative, and Ava had played a large part in that, mainly because with her he could just be himself.

'Earth to Callanach,' Ava said, waving her hand in front of his face. 'I was only teasing. It's that bad then? You've really got nothing to go on?'

'Less than nothing,' Callanach said.

'DI Turner!' Begbie shouted from the corridor.

'I'm off duty, sir,' Ava shouted back. 'In fact, I'm not even in the building. You're imagining me.'

'Too bad for you I have such an active imagination. Get a squad over to Gilmerton Road. There's been another murder.'

Chapter Three

The house in Gilmerton was an unpretentious semi-detached, with a plain but carefully tended garden and a Mini in the driveway. A high wooden gate allowed access to the rear garden. The upper windows of the property were small, but at one corner, presumably where the internal staircase ran, an unusual slit of window spanned both floors to look out over next door's driveway. Two uniformed officers had been posted at the gates and the circus of forensics, pathology, and photography had yet to properly begin. The area was peaceful, the streets asleep.

'What happened?' Ava Turner asked the officer guarding the front door.

'A neighbour heard some loud banging followed by a couple of screams, phoned it in. There was no answer when we knocked so we went round the back and found the kitchen door open. Body's in the bedroom, ma'am. Do you want me to come in with you?'

'No, stay put. And keep people off the garden. Who's the victim?' Ava asked.

'Mrs Helen Lott, mid-forties, lived alone as her husband passed away a while back, apparently. Neighbour was quite friendly with the deceased. We haven't told her what we found yet . . .'

'Good. Where the hell are the rest of the team?'

'All still over at The Meadows dealing with the murder at the festival. No one was expecting a second murder on the same night,' the officer said, rubbing his hands together. Even in July, Scotland was no place to stand outside in the small hours.

'Bloody right. That's Edinburgh's murder quota for the whole year. God almighty, the press will have a field day,' Ava muttered, already making her way along the narrow path to the rear of the property.

The lock on the back door had been sliced through. If it was a burglar, then it was a highly professional job as opposed to the usual smash-and-grab, taking whatever was nearest to the window. The perpetrator had paid a lot of money for decent tools, and must have known what he'd need. Ava pulled gloves and shoe covers from her bag and made her way in through the kitchen door, careful not to disturb anything as she went. The lock had been broken, although there hadn't been any chain or secondary security. She cursed how cheaply people valued their lives.

The house was dark, as it would have been when the intruder crept through. Ava kept the lights off, imagining how the killer had moved and navigated the property. There was enough light from a street lamp to make it easy. None of the stair floorboards were squeaky. There was every chance the killer had got all the way to Helen Lott's bedroom without disturbing her at all. Dark smudges on the stair carpet and a glistening trail on the handrail were an insight into the scene that was about to unfold.

The smell of vomit was noticeable from halfway between floors, beginning as a sharp twang, growing riper and more meaty as she got closer. Something else, too, when Ava pushed open the door to the main bedroom. A rotten smell. Human faeces.

In the bedroom, she turned on the light to allow a detailed view, taking an involuntary step back from the carnage on the floor. The body was difficult to see at first, hidden as it was by a wooden chest of drawers. Clothes had tumbled out everywhere, hiding all but the woman's right foot and right arm. Ava tiptoed across and peeled the corner of a jumper away from the face. Blood had erupted from her mouth, nose and ears. The vomit was already crusting on the carpet and in the wrinkles and folds of her skin. The victim's eyes, a vivid and unusual shade of blue, bulged in their sockets, and stared somewhere over Ava's shoulder as if watching, terrified, for her attacker to return. There was very little white remaining in her eyes, the haemorrhaging like crazing on an antique vase. Her neck and face were swollen solid, a deep shade of purple. It was as if she had been painted from the neck up by an angry toddler in all the colours of fury.

The chest of drawers, a broad, weighty piece, lay across her body. Its position there was no accident. Ava looked carefully at the damage. The chest's back panel, which now faced the ceiling, had been smashed in, the sides caving inwards. Faint bootprints marred the floral pastel bed linen. The attacker had jumped from the mattress onto the chest, adding to the murderous crushing pressure that had squeezed the breath from the victim's lungs as she'd lain terrified beneath it. Helen Lott's visible leg was twisted to an unnatural angle, and the nails of her free hand were bloodied and hanging. Ava folded the hand upwards to where the nails would have made contact with the chest of drawers. Sure enough, corresponding scratch marks ran down the polished surface. The poor woman would have been conscious then, enough to have done all she could in those last desperate minutes to fight her way out. Death would have been the only kindness, Ava thought. Mrs Lott would have been grateful when the darkness finally swallowed her.

'Oh, my dear,' a small voice came from the doorway, 'what on earth is this, now? I was just saying to Luc earlier how I was missing you. I certainly didn't mean to see you under these circumstances.'

'I need as much as you can tell me about the killer. Single assailant or a gang, was there a weapon? Just give me enough to get started, Ailsa,' Ava said.

The pathologist, covered head to foot in a white suit, making her appear smaller than ever, opened her bag and withdrew a thermometer and a variety of swabs.

'It's a difficult scene, not much room. Keep your squad out until I'm done. Get me some decent lighting and I'll need the photographer immediately.'

'That's fine,' Ava said, as Ailsa knelt next to the body.

'She's still quite warm, so the attacker, singular or plural I can't say, hasn't gone terribly far yet,' Ailsa said, photographing with her own tiny camera as she went, shining a light in Helen Lott's eyes, ears and mouth. 'Death was within the last forty-five minutes, that's the best I can do for now. I'd put money on the perpetrator – if it was one person acting alone – being male and very large. This took an absolutely extraordinary amount of strength and overwhelming rage. No weapon other than this furniture was required to cause these injuries. Whoever it is must be covered in blood though. They'll be keeping out of sight until they've cleaned up. This blow to the face, you see the swelling and discoloration here,' Ailsa pointed to the side of Helen Lott's head, 'probably fractured the cheekbone, maybe the jaw too, and would have put her on the floor so that the furniture could be pushed on top of her. The weight of the furniture forcing the air from her lungs, combined with the fractured jaw would have prevented her from screaming. That might have been incidental or planned, no way of knowing. It's an unusual crime scene. Very personal. I've never seen a crushing death outside of a car or industrial accident before. And these blood spatters here and here,' Ava followed Ailsa's eyeline outwards from the chest of drawers along the carpets to the walls and wardrobe, 'suggest to me that the crushing wasn't a single continuous force.'

'Meaning what?' Ava asked.

'Meaning, I'm afraid, that whoever did this jumped again and again, causing individual injuries and almost explosive bleeds each time they landed. When we've moved the furniture and the body, we'll see a star shape coming out around her.'

'Bastards,' Ava said, hands on hips, hanging her head.

'I bet you don't let your mother hear you speak like that,' Ailsa said, smiling gently. 'Now let me take care of Mrs Lott.'

Ava went back down the stairs, turning each light on as she went, issuing orders through her radio. Technicians were carrying lights and sheets in before she'd even reached the kitchen door. Ava walked out onto the street and looked around. It was a quiet residential area, devoid of CCTV and not wealthy enough for any of the residents to have invested in their own surveillance systems. It would have been obvious that the house was occupied, so late at night with a car on the driveway. The burglar – if it was a burglary gone wrong – would have been cautious about the residents.

'Officer,' Ava called to the uniform she'd spoken to on the way in. 'Is there anything obvious missing or any sign of ransacking?'

'Handbag with purse in it still on the kitchen table, ma'am. Other than that we didn't want to disturb too much.'

She went back to her car and dialled Begbie's number.

'Turner here. It's a bad one, Chief. Female victim, living alone. Crushed to death with a piece of her own furniture.'

'You've got to be bloody kidding me,' Begbie sighed. Ava could almost see him scratching his head as he tapped his pen on the desk. He sounded exhausted. 'Sexual assault?'

'No idea. And we won't have confirmation until Mrs Lott has been taken in for a full autopsy. The torso and two limbs have been pretty comprehensively flattened.'

'Suspects?'

'Nothing yet. Pathologist's still with her. Everyone was over at The Meadows so it's taken a bit longer than usual to get going. Almost certainly a male attacker. Not sure if there's more than one. It's brutal, a lot of force. We have a bootprint. Officers are with the neighbour taking a statement. After the incident at The Meadows, the press will—'

'I know, I know,' Begbie said. 'But they'll have to be told. They'll find out soon enough anyway. Better from us.' Ava could hear the Chief's heavy breathing down the phone. His chest sounded as if it was chugging between words.

'Sir, nothing else will happen tonight. Maybe you should just go home. Callanach and I are both available to take calls.'

'Don't you start too, Turner. If I wanted another woman nagging me, I'd have committed bigamy long ago. Just seal off the scene and bring back some useful bloody info. The very least I expect is one hundred per cent more than Callanach's turned up from The Meadows. Not that that's setting the bar very high, mind you.'

Chapter Four

Callanach sat with an expressionless video editor, and tried to avoid the pile of newspapers that some helpful person had left on his desk. What he needed to do was sift through the footage from four different cameras and see if anything recorded might resemble a lead. Thankfully the timelines were such that the job, initially at least, was a limited one.

The first two tapes were from static cameras, no operators. They both covered the front areas of the crowd, and the place where Sim Thorburn had been standing was a distant blur. The remaining footage was more difficult to navigate. One camera operator had been moving around on the stage, intermittently filming the band and looking out at the crowd. The second camera operator had been on a cherry picker crane to give more dynamic angles. It was painfully slow to sit through, but finally the first glimpse of the thankfully tall Niek De Vries emerged amidst the masses.

'Stop it there,' Callanach said, leaning forward and peering hard at the screen. 'That area, can you make the section larger?'

The editor pressed a few keys and leaned back, hands behind his head.

'Is that it?' Callanach asked. 'It's too blurry.'

'Yeah, you know that stuff in films where they can suddenly zoom in and it all goes super-sharp and you can see inside people's pockets and read what's written on a note? That's all bollocks,' the editor said. 'There's one picture, it consists of a certain number of dots. You can see closer but then it gets less sharp. If I had a pound for every time I've had to explain that.'

'Zoom back out then, left a bit,' Callanach said. 'That's Sim,' he said. 'Play it from there.'

As the screen came to life, Callanach could see Sim bouncing up and down, in and out of the line of sight. It was sketchy, but unmistakably the victim. He was bare-chested, like many of the men in the crowd, having presumably shed his T-shirt in the heat of the sun and the crowd. Sim was singing along, one arm in the air pumping in time to the music. He looked relaxed and happy. Behind him and slightly to the right stood Merel De Vries.

'He has absolutely no idea what's coming,' Callanach said to himself. The camera began to shift to the right, and Sim's face edged towards the far side of the screen. 'No,' Callanach shouted. 'It's just about to happen. Freeze the frame or something.' The editor tapped the space bar. Callanach searched the picture but found nothing new. 'Let it play,' he said. Another tap and away slid Sim's face, about to shift fully out of frame as he seemed to bump into the body of someone passing in front of him. 'Stop! Right there. That's it.'

Callanach's mind filled in the blanks. The subtle shift of a body through the crowd, slipping the knife out of a pocket, pulling off the sheath, sliding the razor-sharp blade along Sim's naked stomach as they passed, ready with a cloth to clean up and avoid bloodying anyone else. Slipping quietly away before the victim had hit the floor. They would have moved in a

24

zigzag through the crowd. Taking a straight course through the masses, directly out of the area, would have been too obvious.

'Play it back again,' Callanach ordered. On a second view, it was clearer that Sim's head hadn't even turned. There had been no distraction, no conversation, no recognition. Had there not been the movement of a few blurred pixels, dark in colour, vague in shape, passing just in front of the lower half of Sim's face before he'd fallen, it might have been murder by ghost. 'You're going to tell me we can't improve that section of the picture, aren't you?' The editor simply raised one eyebrow. 'I need the best quality print-off you can get of all the frames when his face and that blur are in sight.'

Tripp entered, holding a document that he was reading as he walked.

'Forensics, sir. Just came through by email. Nothing on it.'

'What do you mean nothing?' Callanach asked.

'Only what you already found out at the autopsy. Victim had no drugs in his system, trace amounts of alcohol. Healthy, no previous injuries except what looks like a childhood broken leg. He was clean. Cause of death as you'd expect,' Tripp said.

'Any new information since the press conference?' Callanach asked.

Tripp looked edgy. 'You've not heard, sir? You turned your mobile off again, then, did you?' Callanach's hand went to his pocket and came out again clutching a black screen. 'Someone started a media site, people have been uploading every bit of festival footage from their phones. There are thousands of hours to view. Other than that, no useful leads. Then there's the public outcry. I think DCI Begbie may have barricaded himself into his office. Media relations have been trying to get hold of you. Some journalist wants an interview.'

'Do you think it will help?'

'Not my call, sir. But I think one of the papers dubbed you

Police Scotland's answer to Brad Pitt, so maybe you won't want to . . .' Tripp's voice faded out.

'That'll be all, thank you Tripp. Is the DCI available?'

'He said only for people with good news,' was Tripp's parting reply.

'Seems like we're all going to have a disappointing day then,' Callanach muttered.

He walked into Begbie's office to find the Chief handing a bundle of files to a plain-clothes officer he hadn't seen before.

Begbie pointed to a seat which Callanach decided not to bother taking.

'No idea how long we'll be here, I'm afraid,' the plain-clothes officer continued, ignoring Callanach's presence. 'Obviously we'll be working with your regional squad. We may also need a few of your men for on-the-ground inquiries.'

'I'm afraid that as of yesterday all my lot are taken,' Begbie growled, eyes closed. 'Unless Callanach here has some unexpected news for me.' Callanach stared out of the window. 'Well then, you can have what office space you need, all the facilities, local knowledge to your heart's content. Manpower is your problem.'

The officer made a non-committal noise, which Begbie ignored as he flicked the switch on the small kettle he kept in his room, presumably to minimise the need to walk the few yards along the corridor to make tea. Callanach took the opportunity to study the newcomer. The accent was recognisable as upper-class English, and the corresponding attitude was clear from the tone of his voice plus the slight upward angle at which he held his head.

'Right, I'll be getting along then. We'll review our requirements and revisit the manpower issue at a later date, DCI Begbie.' He left without a thank you, not quite bothering to ensure the door was shut. Callanach finished the job for him.

'Anything I should know about, sir?' Callanach asked.

'Not today,' Begbie muttered. 'Got a suspect yet?'

'Dark hair. Short, slight build, but that's a guess as the crowd wasn't disturbed by the murderer passing through. Could be male or female. My best description would be something along the lines of Professional Grade Murderer.'

'Thank you Detective Inspector, be sure never to repeat those words in front of another living being. DI Turner is currently in her office trying to organise an investigation into a man she has, much like yourself, already named inappropriately. You may have a Professional Grade Murderer on your hands; Turner has The Crusher. Almost certainly male, heavy, strong, brutal and a raving psychopath if the autopsy details are anything to go by.'

'Two in one night? Isn't that unusual for this area?'

'Unusual? It's a disaster of monumental proportions, is what it is! Do you know what the headlines said this morning?' Callanach still hadn't braved the papers. 'No? Well, let me halve my burden by sharing it with you. "Not safe on the streets, not safe in our homes. Edinburgh's Night of Monstrosities". Not catchy but pretty bloody appropriate, don't you think?' Begbie threw himself into the chair behind his desk so hard that it skidded backwards half a metre. 'And I don't have the money in the budget to pay for any overtime for the remainder of the year! Do something about it, man. I've got two bodies in the morgue and I daren't so much as answer the phone.'

Callanach didn't wait to have Begbie vent any further. It sounded as if Ava was having an even worse day than him. He wandered in the direction of her office for some mutual bemoaning of fates, not bothering to knock. As he opened the door there was a sudden parting of bodies, Ava stepping quickly backwards and banging her hip on the corner of her desk, the man she was with looking more annoyed than embarrassed to have been interrupted. Callanach recognised him as the plain-clothes officer who had recently departed the Chief's office.

'Begbie didn't introduce us. Seems he's having rather a busy day. I'm DCI Edgar,' he said.

'Callanach,' he replied, holding out his hand and shaking the detective chief inspector's. 'I interrupted. Apologies.'

'No, you didn't. What was it, Luc?' Ava asked, brushing hair away from her face.

'Thought I'd just see how you're doing. The Chief said you've picked up a rough one.'

'That's the best kind, isn't it?' Edgar chipped in.

Ava made her way to the other side of her desk and sat down.

'Joseph's here from the National Cyber Crime Unit in London. An attack is imminent and there's intelligence that it's being organised from Edinburgh.'

'Probably best to limit the spread of the information, Ava. I gather Callanach has matters of his own to worry about.'

'I do,' Callanach said, 'so I'll catch you later. Good to meet you.' He closed Ava's door, grimacing, and wiping the palm of his right hand on his trousers as he went.

Chapter Five

'Some bastard leaked the autopsy summary!' Ava yelled, slamming Callanach's door and throwing herself into a chair. 'Which means either someone in Ailsa's office or a police officer here is responsible, as if this wasn't bad enough already.'

'Have you slept?' Callanach asked.

'Listen to this.' Ava ignored his question, tearing open the newspaper she was clutching and beginning to read. '"Helen Lott, a forty-six year old palliative care nurse, was deliberately crushed to death in her own bedroom." Of all the monsters I've ever dealt with, who would want to kill a nurse who looks after terminally ill patients? "Injuries included multiple fractured ribs and sternum, a collapsed windpipe and severe damage to internal organs, resulting in internal bleeding and asphyxiation. A neighbour alerted police after loud noises were heard coming from the property late at night. The autopsy report suggests that the murder was torturous and orchestrated to cause as much pain to the victim as possible. Mrs Lott will be sadly missed by work colleagues and patients alike, who have described her as nothing short of an angel who had dedicated her life to nursing." Did you know there's graffiti about the murders emerging on walls across the city? God only knows who started that off. And we've just been notified that concerned citizens are planning a Take-Back-The-Night-style protest march. Like we don't have enough policing to do already. What the fuck is going on?'

'Have you reported the leak?' Callanach asked.

'Of course I have. We've got two officers interviewing anyone with access to the information at the city mortuary, and a member of our technical services team is checking the digital route the document took from there to us to make sure the breach didn't come from Police Scotland's end. On top of that, all the usual media outlets have been contacted to see if anyone approached them offering the article for money. No joy there so far. Why is the first thing that happens always the last thing you need?' Ava huffed.

'You want coffee?' he asked.

Ava shook her head. 'Sorry about yesterday. With Joe. It was . . .' her voice dwindled.

'None of my business,' Callanach said.

'Joe and I were friends at University. He phoned me a few weeks ago to say he was likely to be posted here. You know how sometimes you just pick things up where you left them as if no time had passed at all . . .'

'Forget it. You want to get something to eat on the way home? If I don't get a shower soon my clothes are going to sue me for hygiene abuse.'

Ava looked down at her hands.

'It's fine,' Callanach said, Ava's unspoken plans hanging in the air between them. 'I'll catch you tomorrow. And don't worry about the papers. New story every day, remember?'

That turned out to be good advice. In spite of the endless coverage afforded by two murders in one night, the media headlines the next day focused on an altogether different target.

The largest incident room was taken up with an array of well-dressed plain-clothes officers, freshly washed and scrubbed, who obviously had not been up all night watching endless mobile phone footage and scanning photos with no results.

'Something happen overnight?' Callanach asked Sergeant Lively as he passed by.

'Fuckin' snobby idiots strutting around, acting like they own the place. Hunting a bunch of nerds no one in their right mind gives a damn about. Makes you look almost like a frigging native.'

'Look almost like a frigging native, *sir*,' Callanach reminded him. Lively sniggered.

'Aye, whatever.' Lively wandered off, stuffing a sandwich into his mouth. Callanach and he hadn't hit it off since day one. A long-in-the-tooth sergeant with decades in the job, Lively had his own preferred candidate pegged to fill the role of Detective Inspector when Callanach had transferred in. It was a fair assumption that Lively had overseen a campaign of piss-taking posters and nasty rumours that had undermined Callanach until he nailed his first case with Police Scotland. He and the detective sergeant had finally progressed from coming close to blows, to tolerating one another, although the verbal abuse hadn't stopped. At least the influx of Scotland Yard's finest had provided a favourable comparison.

Callanach's phone was ringing as he reached his office. He took the call as he threw his jacket onto the desk. It was too hot for any sane person to be wearing more than shorts and a T-shirt. Shirts and ties were one of the drawbacks of promotion.

'Callanach,' he said.

'DI Callanach, I've left several messages for you,' was the opening line. 'This is Lance Proudfoot. I'm the editor of an online news and current affairs blog. I was hoping to get a statement about the festival murder.'

'How did you get this number?' Callanach asked.

'Switchboard put me through.'

'That'll be a career-shortening decision then,' Callanach said, imagining the conversation he'd be having later with the idiot who had answered the phone. 'No statements. You had everything we're giving out at the press conference.'

'To be fair to the young lady on your switchboard, I may have given the impression that I was a family member,' Lance said. Callanach sighed. 'And your media office occasionally forgets to invite the online press to your conferences, hence the need for a certain level of . . . inventiveness about sourcing information.'

'I'm not sure you and I are equally content to supplement the word inventiveness for the term lying, Mr Proudfoot. And I'm afraid I have to get on with some work,' Callanach said.

'So you can't comment on last night's hacking scandal either then? Only I heard that Scotland Yard had sent a crack team of investigators to Edinburgh.' The last phrase was heavily laced with sarcasm. It was all Callanach could do to stop himself agreeing. Instead, he opened a news site on his mobile and scanned the headline. A group calling themselves The Unsung had hacked into the accounts of various bankers and investors recently awarded some jaw-dropping bonuses, and transferred the funds. 'Brilliant bit of anti-establishmentarianism,' Lance continued.

'Looks like plain old theft to me,' Callanach replied.

'I beg to differ. The hackers transferred the funds into the accounts of several good causes, anything from children's hospices to animal shelters. Only took twenty-five per cent of each bonus, too, so they weren't even greedy about it. They were just making a point about the obscenity of the highest paid compared to the desperate underfunding of non-profit-making causes,' Lance said.

'Well, it's not a Major Investigation Team case, I'm afraid, so yet again, no comment,' Callanach said, itching to put the phone down, only the journalist on the other end was proving remarkably hard to get rid of politely.

'Ah, so they have called in the cavalry. Doesn't surprise me at all,' Lance said. Callanach mentally kicked himself for his indiscretion. 'Take benefits away from single mums and the disabled and there's not one politician available for comment. Nick some cash from a load of fat cats and the government mobilises.'

'It's still a criminal offence. We don't get to make judgement calls about the morality of the crimes we investigate,' Callanach said.

'You've got to admit it was clever though. Now the losers have to report each unauthorised money transfer as a crime, which is how the press gets the details of the offences. Then the so-called victims have to ask for their money back from each charity. What would you do, DI Callanach? Say you got a four million pound bonus on top of already inflated wages, three million is still in your bank account. You going to make a spectacle of yourself and insist that the local war veterans' society gives you your million back? Named and shamed doesn't even start to describe how little love the public have for these guys. Quite some stunt, isn't it?'

Callanach didn't answer. Quite some stunt indeed. It certainly explained the peacocking going on in the incident room.

'Anyway, I'm just after one comment on the record,' Lance continued. 'The public want to know that their city is safe. Will you not take the opportunity to reassure them?'

'This is a murder investigation,' Callanach said. 'Not a game and not a publicity opportunity. Have some respect.'

'Listen, I do this because I care about getting news stories out. I don't work for a paper that'll edit my words to meet the owner's political agenda, or to maximise advertising revenue potential. I'm my own boss and I take responsibility for what I write. Do me a favour. Just one line. We're not all bad, you know.'

Callanach brought up Lance Proudfoot's online profile. His news blog had nearly one hundred thousand followers and it looked as if his feed was picked up by some of the bigger media outlets. He sighed. It was worth keeping the popular press onside. And there was always the possibility that it might actually prove useful.

'Fine,' Callanach said, feeling resigned. 'But unnamed. An anonymous source inside the police. The festival attack appears motiveless. Whilst the majority of murders are committed by persons known to the victim, this does not appear to be the case. We ask the public to remain vigilant and for anyone with any information to come forward as soon as possible.'

'That's all?' Lance asked.

'Don't push your luck,' Callanach said. 'Use my name and we never talk again.'

'Does that mean I can call you if I have more questions?'

'No, it doesn't. And the next time you lie to switchboard to get put through, I'll have you arrested.' Finally common sense kicked in and Callanach hung up, flicking back to the news headlines and reading the hacking story more thoroughly.

Ava's friend DCI Edgar was going to have his work cut out wading through the mire of public relations mud about to rain down. The Unsung may have committed grand scale fraud and theft, but it was hard to imagine many people condemning them. And it was a big enough story, just about, to deflect the media's attention and provide some breathing space while they made headway on the murders. Couldn't have happened to a nicer guy, Callanach thought, wondering how long Joe Edgar would be using Edinburgh as an investigative base. He reached for his coffee and for an unlit Gauloises cigarette to suck.

Chapter Six

DC Christie Salter wished Callanach a quiet goodnight and went home to her new husband. She'd put off taking her sergeants exam for her wedding and honeymoon. When Callanach had advised against making the sacrifice, she'd laughed. Max Tripp went home to his twin brother with whom he was flat-sharing. The Chief went home to a wife who had tolerated him for no fewer than thirty years. Even miserable Sergeant Lively had someone waiting for him to get home so they could share a meal and stare at a mutually chosen television programme and forget the outside world.

Callanach retreated to an empty flat.

Scotland had been a new start for him, returning to the land of his long since dead father. But it had meant shedding the social circles and family comfort that had been at the centre of his world. He was trying, certainly. There was the gym, work, a good wine shop, places where people knew his name and greeted him with a smile. Beyond that, replacing old friends with new was time-consuming and soul-destroying.

He fired up the computer, waiting for his emails to appear and hoping desperately for contact from his mother. There was also the matter of checking that Astrid Borde had not been in touch. Since she'd falsely accused him of rape when they'd worked together at Interpol, then followed him to Scotland, he had worried every day that the nightmare might begin again. It hadn't mattered that the rape allegation was entirely a figment of Astrid's twisted imagination and a symptom of her obsession with him. The stigma of it had stuck. People he'd worked with for years avoided him. His closest friends grew guarded, then distant, finally disappearing altogether. Innocence, he had learned, was a technicality when sexual assault was involved. However many times he told himself to live in the moment, there was little escape from the impact of the past. Not when it still affected him as physically as it did.

Too restless to sleep and too tired to go out, Callanach checked out Lance Proudfoot's online news blog again. He found a brief section outlining Proudfoot's career history with publications in the US and Canada, as well as some of the larger British newspapers. His news coverage wasn't bad. Less sensational than the tabloids, and less prone to navel-gazing than some of the broadsheets. There was an interesting editorial piece on the hacker thefts, with a side piece on the National Cyber Crime Unit, largely highlighting how far behind the offenders' capabilities the police were, given the budget constraints and compared to the sort of money the gifted could earn in the private sector. DCI Joseph Edgar's name popped up briefly and Callanach checked him out for something to do. Public school, followed by a law degree, chair of the debating society, with interests in cricket and rugby. Never married, steady career path. Callanach picked up his mobile to text Ava. He was halfway through it when there was a knock at his door. It was late, much later than he was used to being disturbed. Not that anyone ever knocked on his door.

'Who is it?' he called as he walked slowly through his lounge.

There was no reply. Callanach peered through the spyhole. In the corridor he could hear banging then rattling, but no visible person. Searching for a blunt weapon, he selected a knife sharpener from the kitchen and made his way back to the door. More frantic noises came from the area just out of the visual field of the spyhole. Callanach slid the bolt back as quietly as he could and stepped out, weapon raised.

'Please don't hurt me!' the girl in the corridor screamed, arms raised, falling backwards against the wall.

Callanach dropped the sharpening steel and raised his own hands.

'It's all right,' he said. 'I'm a police officer. Are you hurt? Was it you who knocked my door?'

The woman began to laugh, breathing fast, somewhere between terrified and amused.

'Yes, that was me. You didn't answer, so I assumed there was no one in. And no, I'm not hurt. I just moved into the flat opposite yours,' she said, pointing at the only other door on the same level as Callanach's in the converted house. His new neighbour was tall and slim, with blonde hair tied up in a ponytail and a broad smile. 'All my fuses have blown. I've absolutely no idea where the fuse box is so I was trying the loft hatch in case the box is up there. I figured, if your layout was the same as mine you might be able to help me. I'm so sorry. I obviously scared you.'

'No, I'm sorry. Just being overcautious. Of course I'll help. The fuse box will be in your airing cupboard. I'll fetch a torch.'

A few moments later he was inside the flat opposite his own, reaching into the top of the cupboard, flipping open the plastic cover, and there was light.

'Nice to meet you,' she said, thrusting a hand out towards Callanach. 'I'm Bunny. My real name's Roberta, but my little sister couldn't say that when we were growing up. She called mc rabbit, hence the nickname, and it kind of stuck. Thanks for helping. And I'm talking too much. Listen, I haven't got much in, but can I at least get you a beer? Plenty in the fridge.'

'I should go,' Callanach said, glancing at his watch. 'You should really get a chain put on your door.'

'I will, especially living alone. What about you?' Bunny asked.

'I have a chain . . .'

'No, I meant do you live alone?'

Callanach paused as Bunny opened the fridge door. By the time he'd figured out how to answer, she was pushing a cold bottle into his hand.

'Yes,' he said. 'I live alone. But I'm not at home very often, so you should really make sure that you have proper security in place.'

'I'll remember that. Feel better knowing you're just over the corridor though.' She waited for him to say something and Callanach realised he hadn't introduced himself.

'Callanach,' he said. 'Luc.'

'That's foreign, right?'

'French,' he said.

'Oh my God. My mates are just going to die when they meet you. Well, slàinte, good health, Luc Callanach,' she said, clinking the neck of her bottle against his. 'Here's to many an evening spent with a beer in hand and a friend to share it with. So tell me about you. Lived here long?'

'Not that long,' Callanach replied, looking around. The apartment was full of boxes, most overflowing with clothes, electrical gadgetry and accessories. Unpacking was going to take a while.

'Messy isn't it?' she said, following his eyeline and kicking a couple of boxes shut. 'I'm so busy with work I couldn't stop to unpack properly. I'm a hair and make-up artist. Anything from weddings to films. You should be an actor with that face.'

'The police service doesn't approve of moonlighting,' Callanach said quickly. 'And I've got to be back on duty in a few hours so I really should go now. Thank you for the beer.'

'Being a policeman must be exciting. And those poor people killed this week. Awful, wasn't it?' Callanach made his way back out into the corridor. 'Listen, we're neighbours. Let me give you my number, in case you need anything.' Before he could stop her, she grabbed a pen from her pocket followed by his hand and began scribbling on it. Callanach fought the urge to pull away. 'There's my number. I'm a terrible sleeper so call any time. It's going to be fun living here, I can already tell.' It took another ten minutes to get away.

There was an email from Tripp when he got back into his own flat. 'Sir, on my way over. Couple of video files you might want to see tonight.' It was timed fifteen minutes earlier. Callanach threw dirty plates into the dishwasher and closed some doors. He was waiting for Tripp to knock when he heard voices in the corridor. Evidently Bunny hadn't shut her door since he'd left and had found Tripp before he'd had a chance to reach Callanach.

'Constable,' he said, sticking his head out. 'I gather this is urgent. We should get on.'

'Sorry, Luc,' Bunny shouted. 'We got chatting. He's sweet, he is.'

Tripp looked like he didn't know which way to run.

'In you come, Tripp,' Callanach instructed. 'And you should shut your door, Bunny. It's late.'

Safely inside, Tripp was a shade of beetroot.

'New neighbour then, sir? She seems very, um, enthusiastic.' Tripp raised his eyebrows and seemed to be struggling to control a grin.

'Was there something important, detective constable? Only I was hoping to get some sleep for the first time in several days.'

'Of course, yes. Couldn't send the files over the internet. No time to securely encode them. Here you go.' Tripp opened a laptop, and clicked on a folder in which two items sat. As the first played, Callanach could hear the now familiar song that the band had been playing when Sim Thorburn had hit the floor. The footage was taken from a few rows in front of the victim, on a mobile phone whose owner was obviously taking a selfie of herself singing along. For a split second, in the background, a shadow passed across Sim's face. As the shadow cleared the screen, Sim could be seen slightly out of focus, looking down towards his stomach, his face registering confusion. Then he lurched to one side, out of shot.

'Is that all?' Callanach asked. 'It doesn't tell us any more about the attacker.'

'One more piece of footage,' Tripp said. 'Top right-hand corner of the screen.'

Tripp pressed play. More mobile footage, this time obviously designed to show the scale of the audience, mobile held high in the air, turning around in a three-sixty loop. After a few seconds, Tripp pressed pause and pointed.

'There,' he said. 'Only in shot for a second, but it's clearer than in the previous footage.'

Callanach looked more closely. Sim Thorburn was hidden from view, but he could see Merel and Niek De Vries. To the left of them, walking in profile, was an adult with dark brown hair flopping over their face. The attacker was wearing large, dark sunglasses. Tripp let the video play to show the person's sudden change of direction away from the camera and into the crowd.

'Male or female?' Callanach asked.

'Can't be sure,' Tripp replied, closing the lid of the laptop. 'But not that tall, slim and therefore able to move about relatively unnoticed. Caucasian. Hair could be natural or dyed.

41

Might even be a wig. Clothes didn't stand out to anyone, so no help there.'

'Perfect camouflage,' Callanach said, leaning back on the couch and closing his eyes.

'Could it be someone from one of the homeless shelters, do you think?' Tripp asked. 'Sim would have come into contact with plenty of people suffering mental health problems. No one keeping tabs on them, no one to recognise them.'

Callanach shook his head.

'I wish I believed that, Max,' he said. 'Because sooner or later the person you're describing would get arrested for something else, have a breakdown and confess, get drunk and show someone the knife. This took planning. It needed care and consideration. More than that, it needed nerves of fucking steel. Can you imagine the psyche of a person who can walk through a crowd of thousands, take out a weapon, cut hard and deep and precisely, then not rush away? To walk on slowly through the crowd, certain you've done such a good job that you have the time to get out of there, whilst putting the knife out of sight, making sure you don't emerge from the crowd covered in blood. This person knew how to cut. They may be a psychopath but they're not mentally ill, not in the way we think of it. This is someone who feels nothing at all. No panic, no fear, no sense of danger. Nothing at all.'

'How do we catch them then, sir, if they're that good?' Tripp asked.

'You know what, Tripp? I don't have a fucking clue.'

Chapter Seven

Begbie's complexion was waxy and grey. Callanach saw Ava's expression as they went in for a briefing, and knew she was worried too. Ailsa Lambert joined them seconds later.

'For Heaven's sake, what have you been eating, man?' Ailsa screeched, walking over to the chief and staring closely at his skin, suffering none of Ava and Callanach's reticence.

'Don't start on me, Ailsa,' Begbie said. 'It's not as if I've got time to get on the running machine.'

'You've enough time to consume high levels of fats and sugars by the looks of it. How much are you drinking?'

'Can we not do this in front of my detective inspectors, if you don't mind? We've other matters to discuss,' Begbie grumbled.

'You won't be discussing anything unless you make some changes. The next conversation we'll be having will take place with you lying motionless on a slab and me speaking into a voice recorder,' Ailsa said.

'You've had your say. Now would you take a seat?' Begbie pointed to a chair.

Ailsa mumbled to herself but sat anyway, pulling a tablet out of her bag and tapping it furiously. 'Morning, you two. Seems like we've been here before. Who wants to go first?' Neither of them had time to answer before she continued, 'Helen Lott. Crying shame. I know some doctors she'd worked with. Great loss to the city, this one. There aren't many who can do her job. Vast amount of force used, trauma unlike anything I've ever seen deliberately caused. Horrible way to die, she'd have felt all of it. The good news is that we believe we have his DNA.'

Ava muttered what might have been thanks to some unidentified deity, then cut in, 'Has it been run through the system?'

'It has. No hits I'm afraid, but we can tell you that it's from a male Caucasian. At least if you arrest any suspects, we'll be able to confirm a positive identity. Other than that the crime scene was clean. No fingerprints. Gloves were definitely worn. No hairs that we've found,' Ailsa said.

'Where was the DNA?' Ava asked.

'On her forehead, just at the hairline. There was a droplet of saliva mixed in with a little blood. At some point, he leaned over her face, was obviously overexcited, and dribbled or spat, possibly whilst talking to her or watching her. I suspect he'd bitten his tongue or cheek, hence the blood cells. Definitely wasn't from the victim and it was fresh, so it was from someone in the room with her as she died.' The pathologist pulled out duplicate copies of photographs and handed one bundle to Ava and another to Begbie. 'You can see from the photos that it was a frenzied attack, but I'd say planned in advance. Killer probably lost control in the middle of it. Initially, she received a blow to the face, hard enough to cause her to fall and prevent her from defending herself. Then the chest of drawers was placed on top of her, and I mean placed rather than randomly pushed. It was central to her body, well balanced, stopped her from getting up. The positioning caused maximum damage to her vital organs. Looks as if her ribs broke first, then her sternum was fractured when additional weight was applied. The pressure to her stomach made the poor woman vomit, adding to the asphyxia she was already experiencing from being unable to draw breath into her lungs. She had a variety of other limb fractures, and body-wide contusions. One of the broken ribs pierced her right lung, speeding up death and by then she was probably grateful for it. Her internal organs were fatally damaged at that stage. Internal bleeding was extensive, as you'd expect. She lost control of her bowels pretty much as she died. Just moving the drawers would have taken a tremendous amount of strength. You're looking for someone very large, possibly who weight trains, works out regularly. Someone who was there for the specific purpose of making his mark.'

'I'm not sure this one could be much worse,' Ava said, rubbing a hand over her eyes.

'I'm inclined to agree with you,' Ailsa noted.

'So no good news at all?' Begbie asked.

'In case you hadn't noticed, I'm a pathologist. When I walk through your door, I'm never bringing good news.'

'I meant in terms of identifying a suspect,' Begbie said.

'It's someone so physically large that they won't blend into a crowd, if that helps. And he'd have had her blood, and probably vomit on him as he left. He didn't leave any clothing or gloves at the scene, so somewhere there is very damning evidence. If you're willing to risk the public response, you can ask if anyone's husband, son, brother, landlord, whatever, arrived home stinking, exhausted and bloody on the night in question. I guarantee there's an evidence trail,' Ailsa finished.

'And the festival death?' Begbie asked, quiet again. He was slumped in his chair, his chin almost to his chest.

Ailsa took another long look at him before answering.

'Only confirming what you already know. The incision was just above the waistline of his shorts, which were, I think the phrase is, low-slung. He wasn't wearing a T-shirt, so the flesh was accessible. Incredibly skilled work, if you'll forgive how extraordinarily distasteful that is as a concept. The attacks are polar opposites of each other. Odd on one night, but isn't it true that the least likely coincidences are always bound to happen? That one's going to take some old-fashioned boots on the street police work.'

'And with one less person than you normally have on your team, Callanach,' Begbie added. 'DCI Edgar needs a detective with local knowledge to work with his men. They're stepping up the investigation since the cyber attack.'

'Sergeant Lively,' Callanach responded immediately. Finally Ava gave a tiny smile. 'He knows the city better than anyone.'

'He's also the least tech-savvy member of the squad. Even I'd have more chance of understanding the cyber crime unit briefing than him. I'm moving Max Tripp over. You said yourself you've no leads at present. You're all just sitting around waiting for divine intervention. And Tripp gets all this digital stuff. You can do without him for a couple of weeks.'

'Sir, not Tripp. He's a good DC. I need him.' Tripp was Callanach's go-to detective constable, arriving early, leaving late, who even managed to signal exhaustion with a bright smile. He was occasionally wearying to be around, but a welcome antidote to the older officers' cynicism.

'It's done, Callanach. Get some results and you can moan to your heart's content. Under those circumstances I might actually listen. And the media department is up in arms that someone gave a statement to the press yesterday without going through them. Find out who it was and bollock them for me.'

Begbie's phone rang and as one, they took it as their cue to leave.

Ailsa caught Ava's arm in the corridor as they were parting. 'How are you doing, dear?' she asked.

'Getting on with it,' Ava replied.

'And your parents? I'm dreadful about keeping up with old friends. Not enough hours in the week and all that. You'll apologise for me, will you?'

'Not necessary, Ailsa, they know how busy you are. Which is why I'd better let you go.'

'Forgive me, Ava, but you know how people speculate.' Ailsa took a step closer, dropping her voice a notch. 'Your mother has missed several of the clubs she usually attends. Our mutual friends are concerned. Some have contacted me to ask if I know why.' She let the question hang, her face showing nothing but compassion and care.

Ava wanted to lie, knowing that the truth was the opening of a gate that meant she would have to talk about what was happening to increasing numbers of people. And talking about it meant having to think about it even more than she already was.

'She has cancer, Ailsa. She's getting treatment. Everyone has been wonderful.'

'Poor her,' Ailsa said softly. 'And poor you. I won't ask you any more. Not here. But I'll be thinking of you all. And if there's anything I can do . . .' she finished.

'I know that. And I won't hesitate, I promise,' Ava said, closing the conversation down as politely as she could.

'All right then. Now call if you have any questions. And be careful with this case. Whoever killed Helen Lott is operating beyond the extremes of violence that even we are familiar with.'

Ava was dealing with a terrible case, Callanach thought. Close-up police work, dealing with levels of extreme brutality, could be too much for anyone. He pretended to be busy looking through the Sim Thorburn autopsy photos that Ailsa had left for him, but studied Ava peripherally. She was tired and not herself. Her best friend Natasha was away, spending a semester at a university in the States as a guest lecturer. Ava didn't have her usual support network available and Callanach had been too distracted to notice. If he was honest with himself, avoiding Ava might be closer to the truth. He waited until Ailsa left.

'We still haven't christened that fishing rod you gave me,' Callanach said. 'When this is over and you and I finally get some time off, how about I take you up on your offer of showing me the lochs?'

'I'm not sure I can think about that now,' Ava said. 'Too much going on.'

'I understand,' Callanach said. 'Then how about a movie tonight? We could both do with thinking about something else for a while.'

A figure appeared beside them. Callanach hadn't been aware of being watched whilst he'd been talking to Ava, but DCI Joe Edgar had obviously caught the gist of their conversation.

'That's nice. Always good to see work colleagues supporting each other. I'm afraid Ava and I are having dinner with her parents tonight though. I haven't seen Percy and Miranda for years. Can't wait to tell them what I've been up to,' Edgar said. 'And I've moved that young DC of yours over to my incident room. He'll do better mixing with my team full-time. He'll have to buck up though. We keep pretty high standards. Hope it won't be too much of a shock for him.'

'He'll be fine,' Callanach said, a tiny muscle at the corner of his lower jaw flexing. 'You shouldn't underestimate Tripp.'

'Good, we need them bright and on the ball for the stuff we have to deal with. See you later, darling,' he said, giving Ava a pat on the shoulder. 'Callanach,' he nodded on his way out.

Callanach shoved his hands in his pockets and took a deep breath as he watched Edgar leave.

'He's just a friend,' Ava said, shaking the shoulder Edgar had touched.

'Dinner with your parents? Thought you couldn't stand that sort of thing. Or them, for that matter.'

'What the hell would you know about me and my parents? God, could you just not comment? For once? You know, Luc, you're the most closed-off person I've ever met and you're lecturing me on my family relationships. You've got some nerve.' She paused, staring at him. 'I've got work to do.'

Callanach stood still until she'd walked round a corner. Keeping a steady smile on his face and his pace measured, he went back to his office and shut his door. Then he slammed one foot hard into the base of his desk. The wood splintered. His toes ached. He grabbed his coat and headed out into the city.

It was a long way to The Meadows from the station but he needed the air.

There was a greater uniformed police presence on the streets than usual. Understandable in the circumstances. Of course, if there was another attack, the chances of the police being in the right place at the right time was still highly unlikely, but people felt better when there were uniforms around. The reality was that for all the protests and outrage, life went on. Though not for Sim Thorburn's girlfriend, not for a while, anyway. And not for Helen Lott's extended family, who'd made statements on the news about her terrible passing.

Perhaps the most visual scar left on the city was the graffiti. It had started with one scrawling that an eagle-eyed news reporter had captured the day after the first murder. Callanach made his way to it – a pilgrimage of sorts. Near the centre of the city, where Guthrie Street emerged onto Cowgate, on the curved wall of a hostel in bright blue paint had been left the immortal words, 'A Charity Worker!' The fact that the enraged graffiti artist had bothered to punctuate the phrase spoke volumes. The press had embraced the simplicity of expression and adopted the image as their own banner of social indignation.

Sim Thorburn wasn't a drug dealer who'd sold one tab too many. This was no illegal immigrant with an unpronounceable name, or prostitute long since unrecognisable to friends and family. This was a symbol of Scotland's heart and soul. The very innocence of the victim was a crime in itself, the press had made that clear. Callanach walked until he found the tag. Below it was the statement, 'A hospice nurse', no punctuation this time and the writing was smaller, in red.

From there the copycats had taken over, using the walls in every part of the city to vent their fury at the violation of their peaceful lives. Callanach couldn't blame them. Such violence was shocking. He'd investigated many terrible cases – child sex trafficking, drugs tested on Eastern European orphans, weapons experiments dressed up as religious wars – they had all come down to money. But this felt like something else. Perhaps just the sheer hell of it. That was what he saw in the words left on the city walls. Futility.

Chapter Eight

At home, a note had been stuck under his door.

'Knock for me. Made way too much sausage casserole. Will keep it warm. Bunny.'

Callanach contemplated slipping into his apartment silently, before realising he'd spend the whole evening feeling guilty and rude, and opted for the path of least resistance. Bunny opened the door as he was knocking it.

'Brilliant timing!' she said. 'I was just coming to see if you were home yet. Did you get my note? Of course you did, silly me, that's why you're here. Come on in. I was opening a bottle of red. Much nicer not to be drinking alone.'

Callanach murmured something noncommittal about how tired he was feeling but by then Bunny was pulling out a chair for him at a small table and putting a glass in his hand. The wine was cheap but drinkable. He was a grape snob – part of the French culture he'd inherited from his mother – but the food smelled good and he was hungry after walking miles around the city.

'So I finally tidied up, thank goodness. Still got a few boxes to go, but it's looking more like home. There's tomato sauce if you want it. I can't eat without it.'

'I'll pass,' Callanach said. 'So you're settling in then?' he managed, remembering his manners and the need to make small talk.

'Oh yeah, been at it all day. And I'm having a flat-warming party next Saturday. I can introduce you to my friends. You free?'

'I'm not sure,' Callanach said, deciding to be at work whether he was needed or not. 'I'm pretty much always on call. Never know what's going to come up. Sounds like fun though.'

'Oh, but I've told them all about you,' Bunny said, piling more sausages in a beefy tomato sauce onto Callanach's plate, and telling him every detail of her best friends' lives as they made their way through dinner. 'God, I nearly forgot. Some woman was at your door earlier. I did wonder what was going on, as she didn't knock or anything, just stood there like she was trying to figure something out. She jumped a mile when I put my head out.'

Callanach's stomach tensed. He put down his fork. If Astrid had reappeared he'd have to move. There was no way he could face being constantly followed again.

'Did you catch her name?' Callanach asked Bunny.

'She didn't really say much. Muttered something about how it wasn't important. She'd see you tomorrow.'

'Can you describe her?' Callanach asked.

'Sure, average height, longish brown curly hair. Grey eyes. Size eight to ten. I was wondering if it was your girlfriend.'

'I don't have a girlfriend,' Callanach said, regretting the admission as soon as he'd made it.

'I'm single, too,' Bunny said, holding out her glass to be chinked. 'That's good. We can keep each other company.'

'I should find out who that was at my door,' Callanach said, already sure it was Ava and wondering what had prompted the visit. 'But thank you for dinner, although you shouldn't have worried about me.'

'Oh, it's no bother. We should make it a regular thing.'

'I'm out a lot,' he said. 'Regular doesn't work for me. I'll bump into you occasionally though.' Bunny's face dropped and Callanach felt clumsy. He could have been kinder about it, not that kindness was necessarily the best way to put women off.

Back in his flat, he checked his mobile for messages. There was nothing. If Ava had been calling round about an urgent police matter she'd have left a text or voicemail. He glanced at his watch. Presumably she'd be at dinner with her parents and Joe Edgar by now. Still, Callanach thought, if she'd come looking for him it must have been important. He kicked off his shoes and dialled her number.

Her mobile rang only twice before she answered. He could hear conversation in the background, and a distant high-pitched voice making their disapproval of the fact that she was taking the call obvious to everyone.

'Turner,' Ava said. 'Hold on please.' A door closed and foot-steps echoed on wood.

'Ava, it's Luc,' Callanach said. 'Is everything okay?'

'Everything's fine,' she was terse. 'Has something happened I need to know about?'

'No,' Callanach felt like he was treading through mud. 'I just . . .'

'Oh, right, the girl told you I'd been round,' Ava said. 'It was nothing. Just wanted to have a word with you about . . .' she paused momentarily, 'the Chief. I'm worried about him. Nothing that can't wait until I next see you.'

'Was that it?' Callanach asked. 'Sorry, I went to The Meadows to walk the scene again.'

'No need to explain, and I apologise if I made things awkward with your neighbour. She told me she was waiting for you to get home for dinner.'

Callanach rolled his head backwards from one shoulder to the other.

'She just moved in. I think she's lonely. I really don't . . .'

'Well, I'm at my parents as you could probably hear, so I can't chat. Catch you soon.' Ava hung up. Callanach threw his phone onto the sofa and poured himself a more palatable glass of wine.

'Fuck,' he said, stripping off his suit and going to shower, running the water as hot as he could bear and climbing in with his glass still in hand, held just out of the stream.

He should have been able to walk away from work and relax. He wound back the clock inside his head and replayed memories of easier days in Lyon. He'd lived in an apartment he'd loved, with a terrace overlooking the park near Interpol's headquarters. There had been girlfriends. Not that he'd flitted from one to another, but always someone to share a good meal, to hop in a car for a weekend away, to travel to the coast and waterski or sail. And there had been sex. Not like his early twenties when the fever to sleep with women had, at times, consumed him. When he'd used his model looks and intellect to charm and then entice any woman he'd wanted. Easy sex, without the emotional noose that tightened when he thought about it now. Astrid Borde and her false accusation of rape had finished him, both as an Interpol agent and as a man.

He turned his face up into the steaming spray of water and slid a hand down to his penis, willing it hard, trying to remember the last time he'd been with a woman. He conjured images of days and nights he'd spent intent on nothing but physical pleasure – sex on sand dunes, in planes, on boats, in hotels across the world. But now there was nothing. It was as if the muscle he'd once taken so much for granted had simply ceased to exist, leaving a useless flopping length of pitiful flesh to taunt him.

Then there was a flash of another face in his mind, a woman he'd tried not to think about. With it came the jolt of a feeling he'd all but given up on, his muscles performing no more than a spasm in his hand, a quickening inside before it evaporated.

Callanach grabbed the handle of the shower door, squeezing the metal as if he could crush it, growling aloud with the effort of trying to drag the life back into himself. But it had gone. That fleeting hope that he could be normal again.

'*Merde!*' he shouted, smashing a fist into the shower glass, getting nothing in return except bruised knuckles and a dull thud. '*Je suis pathétique.*' He reverted to French as he always did when he lost control, although the message was the same in any language. He was pathetic. But his muscles had flared into life, if only for a second. It was proof, as if he'd needed it, that there was no physical damage. 'Enough,' he said, snatching a towel and throwing it over his shoulders.

As he walked through his bedroom, he paused to stare in the mirror. He was still in good shape, rarely going more than two days without punishing himself at the gym, naturally eating cleanly, always aghast at the piles of chips, pastry and white bread that seemed to flow through the doors of the station. He hated to feel bloated and heavy. His mother had lectured him about diet from before he could talk back. Fruit, vegetables and protein. Everything else was just excess. She'd long since stopped lecturing him. Had not communicated with him at all since his brief spell of incarceration before he'd been bailed pending trial. He got his olive skin from her, and his dark hair. No matter how long he lived in Scotland, his skin was never going to pale enough for him to pass as a native. It was as if his father's Scottish genes had passed him by.

He ran a hand through his hair, pulling his shoulders back and inspecting his muscle tone as if he were buying a piece of meat. He'd let his head rule his body for too long, trying everything except therapy, save for those few embarrassing obligatory sessions with the Interpol psychologist before he'd served his notice.

Determined to move on, he opened his laptop and skipped through a variety of websites until he found one that looked vaguely professional, then he pulled his wallet from his jacket. In less than a minute he'd purchased a drug without prescription and left his credit card details online. It wasn't clever but it wasn't going to get him in serious trouble, even if he was caught. What worried him more, having finally made the choice to buy the drug that might offer him relief, was finding someone with whom he could use it.

Chapter Nine

Three weeks had passed since Sim Thorburn's murder. Twenty-one days when each morning was marked by the increasing quietness and frustration of Callanach's team. Today the atmosphere was different. Not in his incident room, but certainly across the hall. A body of men and women was massing at the station. The way they were dressed and the palpable excitement could mean only one thing. Callanach realised they were on a pre-raid briefing. DC Tripp caught his eye, and Callanach managed a nod in response before his purloined detective constable looked back at the whiteboard where DCI Edgar was pointing at the blueprint of a building and barking instructions. However much money the hackers had stolen, or 'relocated' as The Unsung had released a statement to explain, was enough to justify a huge public expenditure to ensure they were caught. Callanach wondered what the difference in governmental financing was between the hackers' case and his investigation into Sim's murder. Probably best not to know, he thought. That way lay only bitterness and disillusionment.

He had begun to accept that the trail to Sim's killer had run from lukewarm to cold. It seemed more likely than ever that it was just some random attack, perhaps mistaken identity, perhaps someone Sim had crossed unknowingly. Since the funeral, his girlfriend had left Edinburgh and returned to her parents' house in Newcastle, leaving only a forwarding address and a message to say how disappointed she was that there had been no progress. Callanach could sympathise.

Since then, he'd lost two more squad members to an attempted rape outside a nightclub, and even Begbie hadn't asked for a progress report for a couple of days. Callanach watched as DCI Edgar's team trotted out of the incident room and down the corridor like an army squadron given the go for a secret mission, albeit carrying warrants and laptops instead of guns. Tripp looked half-embarrassed, half-bored as he kept pace in the line towards the stairs.

'Sir,' Salter said, coming up behind him. 'We've had this passed on from the uniformed team on duty. An elderly gentleman, missing all night. Wife is distraught. He's never failed to come home before.'

'The Major Investigations Team is doing missing persons now, is that right?' Callanach sighed.

'Seems likely to be more than that. His mobile and wallet have been found on a park bench on top of a pile of books. Name is Michael Swan. This morning he missed a community awards ceremony. He was due to be recognised for the child literacy programmes he's set up across the city. Wife said he'd been looking forward to it for weeks.'

'Sounds more like he's had a breakdown and run away. Come on then, Salter. That's if DCI Edgar has left any vehicles for the rest of us.'

They headed east across the city towards Craigentinny golf course. The expanse of greenery would have been visible from Michael Swan's bedroom window, Callanach realised, as his wife described how her doting husband had always dreamed of retiring next to a golf course. Ironically, he'd then become so consumed with what began as a part-time librarian's post that he'd barely picked up a club since.

'Has he been unwell, or acting out of character at all, Mrs Swan?' Salter asked, sipping the coffee that had appeared courtesy of an adult daughter who was comforting her mother.

'No. My husband was a creature of habit. He came and went at certain times. Had clothes for work and clothes for the weekend. He always told me if something was bothering him. And I could tell, you know. It's like that once you've been married long enough. But to leave his wallet and phone in a public place? He'd never be so careless.' The daughter handed her mother more tissues from the box rapidly being used up and Callanach checked his watch. The library wasn't normally open until later but the caretaker had agreed to meet them there and open up. If Michael Swan had left a note anywhere, it was likely to be on his desk.

At the library it was confirmed that Michael Swan had checked out with his swipe card at 8.37 p.m. the previous day. Salter immediately radioed through to the station for a CCTV check of the route he'd have taken to the point where his wallet and mobile had been abandoned. Callanach moved forward at the caretaker's beckoning and looked through the documents left on a modern reception desk.

'Is this where Mr Swan would have spent most of his time?' Callanach asked.

'Aye, here to check books in and out. The building is on two levels. Library down here, meeting rooms upstairs, used for educational programmes and whatnot. Sometimes authors come here to talk about their books. Other evenings it's used for community meetings, you know, the local historical society, a dieting club,' the caretaker leaned down to whisper in Callanach's ear, 'and the local alcohol and drug addiction service is in on a Wednesday, but we're not supposed to talk about that. Bit sensitive for those attending, you know.'

'And this is everything? He has no employee locker, no personal area?' Callanach asked.

'There's a little staff area behind that glass there. Used for administration, but also for coats, mugs, a place to concentrate without being pestered.'

The caretaker unlocked another door into a thin room at the side of the main library hall, half wall and half obscured glass, with desks lining one side, and full of the sort of mess that busy, hard-working people leave in their wake.

'Here you go, laddie. This was Mr Swan's mug. I'm sure it's all just a terrible mistake. He's a good man. No harm'll have come.' The caretaker picked up a well-used, slightly chipped mug bearing the legend, 'Eat well, drink well, read well', clutching it to his chest rather too tightly.

'Thank you,' Callanach said. 'We'll have a quick look round and let you get on with your day.' Across the main hall of books was the entrance hall where they'd come in. Steps leading upwards were signposted to education rooms. Another side door bore no marker. 'What's through there?' Callanach asked the caretaker.

'That goes down into the basement. Holds books not currently on the shelves, ones that need mending or replacing, old posters, redundant furniture. More of a storeroom than anything.'

'Did Mr Swan have a key to that as well as to the front door?' Callanach asked.

'Not on his own set, although there's one kept on the keys in the desk so the staff can get in if someone asks for a book that's not on display.'

'Could you get it for me please?' Callanach asked.

'I'm not sure why he'd have left anything in there, particularly. But I'll open up anyway.'

The caretaker walked ahead and Callanach followed, checking the time. He was due in a meeting with the press liaison officer to give another useless update on the Sim Thorburn case, but he should at least phone and say he'd be delayed. The heavy door swung open and the caretaker reached around the side to flip on the lights. Nothing happened.

'Fuse box?' Callanach asked.

'I'll go and see,' the caretaker said. 'Give me a moment.' He wandered off back into the main hall as Callanach stepped inside, taking the few steps down into the basement. The door had been heavier than he'd anticipated and it swung shut behind him. The area was effectively windowless, with a dim pane of glass glowing green-brown with moss and mud from decades of a lack of cleaning, and only the faintest vein of light from beneath the door at the top of the steps. Something rotten hung in the air, as if the basement had been built too close to a sewer pipe, polluting with its sulphurous putrescence.

Callanach took out his mobile and switched on the torch app that would drain the battery in no time, but it would do for him to get his bearings and stop wasting any more minutes. He walked between rows of books, all neatly stored, with boxes at the end of each line containing the expected jumble and junk. Children's toys, some costumes, ageing furniture that no one had decided what to do with. He turned a corner, letting his phone shine at the floor, sensing rather than seeing obstacles as he walked away from the neat rows of books. There was a noise behind him. He spun round, disoriented. One foot flew out from beneath him and he threw a hand to the side to grab what he could to stabilise himself. His other foot followed the same fate, slipping on the floor, and his free arm shot up rather than out, clutching at the first thing it touched. It was a textile, smooth and slippery, wet on one side. Callanach shouted as he fell, landing on his back as whatever his hand had found loosened in his grasp. He closed his eyes as pain shot through his coccyx. A few moments later he repositioned his mobile and shone the light upwards.

Above him was, without a doubt, the body of Michael Swan. He had been suspended horizontally from a metal structural beam by his neck and his bound ankles. Callanach could only see fragments as the beam of torchlight moved, shakily, along the length of the corpse. Whoever had hung him had almost entirely skinned Swan's face. Callanach had read numerous articles about it but never seen a case where it had been done. An incision had been made around the outer circle of facial skin, starting at one side of the lower jaw, heading up around the cheekbone, across the forehead and back down the other side. Finally, like a perfectly skinned rabbit, his face had been peeled.

Callanach felt the stickiness in his palm and knew that the resulting flap of skin had been what he'd grabbed as he'd slipped. He didn't need the torchlight to confirm the pool of blood he was lying in.

'Police officer, put down your weapons,' Salter shouted from the doorway, no doubt assuming an assault and possible injury.

'I'm all right, Salter. There's no one else here.' He may not have checked every inch of it, but Callanach was sure the assailant had left the building the night before, taking Swan's mobile and wallet with them.

'The fuse box is fine, the light bulbs must all have blown.' Callanach could hear the caretaker's voice getting closer.

'Salter, get everyone else out of here right now. Close down the scene. Contact the pathologist immediately and call forensics in. Do not enter. I've already compromised the evidence.'

He could hear urgent instructions being given and the sound of footsteps disappearing away.

'You sure you're not hurt, sir? It sounded bad,' Salter called.

Callanach unlaced his boots and left them where he'd trodden so as not to spread any more evidence around the room.

'Missing person confirmed deceased. I'm uninjured. It's going to be a difficult crime scene to process. I want an absolute lockdown on communications going out of here.' Callanach moved gingerly towards the door, feeling his lower back as he went. He'd cracked it hard as he went down and parts of his legs were numb.

'What the fuck?' Salter said before she could stop herself. She started forwards to grab him, but Callanach raised a warning hand.

'Don't touch me,' he said. 'If there were trace fibres or evidence on the floor, they're on me now.'

'God, sir, you're covered in it. Are you sure you didn't injure yourself? Only that looks like too much blood . . .' her voice trailed off.

'Take a breath,' Callanach said, 'then call Begbie for me. He needs to see this for himself. I want the whole building sealed off. No one touches anything. Make sure the caretaker doesn't re-enter this part of the building.' He could hear his own voice shaking.

'How bad is it, sir?' Salter asked. Callanach just stared at her. 'Will I send uniforms round to notify Mr Swan's wife?'

'That'll be our job, I'm afraid, but this will take a while,' he said. Sirens were approaching at a pace. Salter made her way out of the building to ensure that the scene was protected from the outside of the building in.

Callanach stayed as still as he could, knowing every item of his clothing would need bagging and testing. He tried not to think about the gore dripping from his trouser legs and hands. He had witnessed horrors before, but the gruesomeness of this was its staging, the dreadful dramatic love with which it had been conceived. Even to the point of smashing the light bulbs, he now realised, so that the full effect of the killer's creation could only be witnessed in torchlight. Michael Swan's face reduced to a horror mask, still dripping with bloody gore, would forever be a scream in his memory. He felt dizzy, sick, made himself take air and get a grip.

Technicians appeared carrying swathes of plastic sheeting and battery lights by which to work. They said little as Callanach described the scene so that they could properly equip themselves, both practically and mentally.

Ailsa Lambert arrived looking concerned, issuing businesslike orders.

'You're holding your back,' she said, looking Callanach up and down.

'I'm fine,' Callanach said. 'Just a slip. Ailsa, this may be the worst . . .'

'I'm going to organise a car to take you home, Luc,' she said, pulling out her mobile.

'There's no time,' he said.

'Then you'll have to consent to a paramedic assessing you for shock. If you try and drive in the next two hours I'll have you disciplined myself. Understand?' Callanach considered arguing but didn't. 'Good,' Ailsa said. 'Now this. Is it torture?'

'Yes. Not sure if it was pre or post mortem. He's strung up parallel to the ceiling.'

'My job would be easier if human beings had evolved without imaginations. Right, strip off – I'll have someone bring you a suit. They'll have to swab your hands and face as well. We'll need every fibre,' Ailsa said.

'What happened to you?' Begbie roared, storming towards them, almost bursting out of the crime scene coveralls he was wearing. 'Has this whole city gone mad?'

'You'll achieve nothing like that,' Ailsa told him gently. 'And my crime scene needs minimal disruption so go in easy, if you don't mind.'

'And we've no idea who we're looking for, is that right?' Begbie aimed at Callanach.

'Not as yet, sir,' Callanach responded. The Chief was already pushing himself through the doorway into the basement that was still in the process of being lit.

Callanach heard a string of expletives bellowing from the storeroom in an ever more guttural and breathy Scots accent. Begbie was both furious and bewildered, a combination of emotions with which Callanach could sympathise. There was a pause, a loud groan, then a thud. Other voices called out. Ailsa and Callanach went running. DCI Begbie was on his side on the floor, one hand clutching his chest, feet paddling furiously against the pain.

'Call the paramedics,' Ailsa shouted to the nearest scenes of crime officer. The Chief's breathing was more reminiscent of a marathon runner than someone who had recently made a trip of a few hundred yards from a car, hauling air in and chugging it out. Ailsa removed his tie and loosened his shirt while Callanach grabbed a torch from a passing officer. The additional light showed Begbie's face as ashen but slick with sweat. His jaw was clenched tight, eyes wide. Callanach took hold of Begbie's right hand, half expecting rejection. The Chief squeezed Callanach's in silent reply, gripping hard, holding on. Blood trickled from his knees and hands where he'd hit the floor and he looked unexpectedly like a victim. Confused, scared, helpless.

'Help me sit him up,' Ailsa said to Callanach. They sat the Chief with his back against a stack of boxes while a technician fetched a blanket. 'George, these are aspirin. I want you to chew them slowly,' she said, pushing two small pills into Begbie's mouth. He grimaced but made the effort, his hands shaking as he steadied himself. 'By God, man, I'm not supposed to be here looking after you. Have I not got enough to be getting on with? Quite the shock you gave me!'

Begbie did his best to issue a response, but managed nothing other than a breathless wheeze, and went back to chewing. Ailsa checked him over for other injuries, wiping her face when the Chief closed his eyes for a moment. If Callanach didn't know better he'd have thought she was wiping away tears.

The paramedics were inside before anyone could get crime scene suits on them or even shoe covers. It took only a couple of minutes for them to get Begbie onto a stretcher with an oxygen mask covering his mouth and nose, but in that time Callanach saw the look on Ailsa's face turn from deep concern to complete frustration. Bloody footprints ran all the way across the floor. Begbie had fallen into the middle of the key forensics area, followed out of necessity by the men saving his life. Everyone stopped, hands on hips, shaking disbelieving heads at how much more complicated and unlikely to yield results their tasks had just become.

'I'll follow him to the hospital,' Callanach said. 'Would you mind calling Ava, please Ailsa? She's friendly with the Chief's wife. Someone ought to pick Mrs Begbie up.'

Chapter Ten

Callanach's mobile rang just as he arrived at the Royal Infirmary.

'How's the chief?' Ava asked.

'I don't know yet. We won't get anything out of the doctors until they've run tests.'

'What the hell happened? Where were you?'

'At a crime scene,' Callanach said.

'You're kidding. Must have been one hell of an incident to have got the chief that worked up.' There was an empty silence. 'Right, I'll be there in twenty minutes. I've already had the superintendent on the phone asking what's going on. She's on her way too, so make sure everything's under control.'

Callanach's lower back flared into a ball of agony. 'Got to go,' he said, grabbing a door handle to keep upright and breathing hard.

'Sir, are you feeling all right?' a nurse asked. Callanach tried to nod, thinking he should make a joke to reassure her so she could move on. What came out was a wail as he finally lost control of the pain. 'I need a bed,' the nurse shouted. An orderly came running, taking Callanach's weight, slipping one arm around him as the nurse pulled back a curtain to reveal an unused cubicle.

A doctor was with him in moments, stripping him and rolling him onto one side to press gentle fingers down the length of his spine.

'Could you just give me some painkillers?' Callanach snapped. 'I'm with the man who's just come in with a heart attack. And the superintendent is due any minute. I really can't be on my back when she arrives.'

The doctor wrote a couple of notes whilst managing simultaneously to look completely bored.

'Have you had a bad fall?' he asked.

'Yes,' Callanach said. 'I slipped, but it wasn't that dramatic.'

'It was dramatic enough that it appears to have fractured your coccyx. You must have landed on the edge of it pretty hard. The injury won't limit normal activities, but it's going to be painful for six weeks or so,' the doctor said.

A voice that was authoritative and impatient in equal measure echoed down the row of cubicles.

'I appreciate the fact that I am not family but I do have an amount of authority here. DCI Begbie became ill at a crime scene for which I am responsible, in the capacity of his immediate superior representing his employer. And where's Detective Inspector Callanach?'

Callanach rolled his eyes and gritted his teeth as the doctor pressed more firmly against the base of his spine to complete the diagnosis.

'Sorry, who?' a nurse beyond the curtain asked.

'Ugh,' Superintendent Overbeck groaned. 'Police officer, French accent, tallish, popular with the ladies.'

'Oh, I know,' the nurse replied. 'He's with the doctor, too. Just in this cubicle. You can visit him once the doctor has finished.'

'Finished like hell,' Overbeck said, ripping the curtain aside and walking in.

'I'm with a patient,' the doctor said. Callanach frantically but ineffectually tried to cover his backside with the edge of the sheet he was lying on.

'Discharging him will solve that problem,' Overbeck snapped. 'Begbie's having a heart attack and you're in here getting a free back massage, Callanach. Get some clothes on, man. Unless you're actually dying I want a debrief immediately.'

'This patient has a fractured coccyx. It's badly damaged and he's in a lot of pain. I need to ask you to leave,' the doctor said.

'It's all right,' Callanach muttered. 'I'll be straight out, ma'am.' The nurse handed him a gown.

'You need medication, rest and further investigations. There's no way you're fit for work,' the doctor said. 'I'm signing you off from duties.'

'Am I right in thinking there's another body on its way to the mortuary, Detective Inspector?' the superintendent asked. Callanach nodded. 'Then are you fit for duty, or shall I have someone wheel you out in a nice comfy blanket?'

'That won't be necessary,' Callanach said.

The doctor stared at him. 'I'll give you a shot to kill the pain. You'll need a prescription to get you through the next couple of weeks. Avoid sitting for too long. No cycling, rowing, weightlifting or other sports that put a strain on your tailbone.'

'What's happening?' Ava asked, appearing around the corner of the curtain. Callanach sighed.

'Apparently the detective inspector needed a nap,' the superintendent said. The doctor threw her a look that would have shamed most people. Overbeck seemed to take it as a compliment. 'I'm going to express my sincere concern to Begbie's wife. What's her name again?'

'Glynis,' Ava said.

'That's right. You two, with me in five minutes.' She stalked off, leaving the doctor to fill a hypodermic syringe. Ava turned her back as it was administered.

'How's the chief doing?' Callanach asked.

'Stable. It was more of a warning than full-blown cardiac arrest. He won't be going home tonight and his wife's very upset, but he'll live.'

'I'm sure the Super will make the Begbies feel much better,' Callanach muttered. Ava smirked. The doctor cleared the room and pulled the curtain across to give them privacy. Ava kept her back turned as Callanach put the forensics suit back on.

'You decent now?' Ava asked after a minute.

'More than I was when Overbeck walked in without any warning. She didn't even break stride. Just stood there with me half-naked.'

'Some day you're having,' Ava said. 'Listen, Ailsa phoned me back. She told me what you walked into. It's no wonder the chief reacted the way he did. Are you okay? Only I can make your excuses with Overbeck, get a car to take you home . . .'

'I don't think I'd have a job to come back to in the morning,' Callanach joked. 'A drink after work would be good though, if you're not busy. It'll be more fun than just taking painkillers.'

Ava paused before meeting his eyes. 'That sounds like a good idea. I'll meet you back at the station. We can go on from there.'

It was two in the afternoon before Callanach left the hospital, and his next stop was the mortuary. Ailsa was waiting for him with coffee as he walked into her office.

'You're walking strangely,' she said.

'I fractured my arse,' Callanach replied.

Ailsa burst into a fit of laughing he hadn't expected.

'I'm sorry, dear, I shouldn't be laughing. Alternate hot and cold compresses. Make sure you have a soft enough mattress. It's painful. Was that when you slipped under poor Mr Swan's body?' He nodded. 'I needed the laugh. It's been quite a day and I'm afraid it's not over yet. Drink the coffee. Take some painkillers if you need them. We have to go and spend some time with the body.'

Callanach had known he wouldn't get away with simply being given an oral report. He'd viewed hundreds of dead bodies in his time, witnessed scores of autopsies, but this one was going to leave an indelible memory. He did as suggested and swallowed tablets before getting a gown and going in.

'Has Mrs Swan been in for a formal identification yet?' Callanach asked.

'She has indeed, although I wish we could have spared her that,' Ailsa said. 'I replaced the skin over his face and did my best to make her husband look as he had in life, but there was very little softening the blow. I think Tuscany would be nice to retire to, don't you? Warm climate, olives trees, good food. Have you been there?'

'I have,' Callanach said. 'But I didn't know you were retiring, Ailsa.'

'Neither did I, Detective Inspector. But today, for perhaps the first time, it occurred to me that there is more to life, to what's left of mine anyway, than this. Now, here we are. Look closely at the incision marks around the face. We pulled the edges of skin back together and took some photographs to make it easier to see. These are the marks close up.' She moved back from the corpse to a computer and pressed a button. Immediately an image filled the screen that would have been impossible to understand had Callanach not been told what he was looking at.

The skin was grey either side of the wound, the central gash

71

a line of black. The skin on the right-hand side of the incision was smooth, but on the left there were minute tags regularly along the path of the cut. Ailsa pointed along the uneven side.

'Caused by the blade,' Ailsa said. 'The weapon was extremely fine and extremely sharp. What you're seeing wouldn't have been visible to the naked eye. We had to enlarge the image multiple times to pick this up.'

'Why only along one edge of the wound?' Callanach asked, walking away from the screen and back to the body to see if he could detect the difference on the skin itself.

'Think of it like a bullet, with micro detail that links it to having been fired from a specific gun,' Ailsa said. 'All blades leave different impressions if you look closely enough. Find me that blade and I'll be able to tell you if it's a good match for this incision.'

'That helps with evidence at trial but it doesn't identify the attacker,' Callanach said. 'So who am I looking for?'

'Someone who knows their way around the human body, who is not the least bit squeamish. A person who enjoys the spectacle. But that's not why I got you here. Look at this.' She tapped a key and another image popped up. The same smooth line ran down one side, a microscopically jagged edge along the other.

'I see the same markings.' Callanach walked back to look down at Michael Swan's face. 'Which section of the wound is that picture from?'

'None of it,' Ailsa replied. 'You'll be needing to look at Sim Thorburn's injuries for that.'

Callanach stood still and let it sink in.

'But that was a double blade. It can't have been the same weapon as was used on Thorburn,' he said.

'Not the same weapon, but possibly scalpel blades manufactured in a single batch, all with the same minuscule flaw. The first two blades were used to home-craft the weapon that killed Thorburn. The next one became part of a more traditional knife. Without seeing the blades themselves I couldn't swear to this in court, but between us, I'd say whoever killed one, killed the other. And there's more than that. Come here,' she said, beckoning Callanach over to Michael Swan's body. 'The scalpel's point of entry is at the left lower jawbone and the victim needs to be lying down for this to work. The only way to get such a clean cut would have been for the killer to have been sat at the crown of the head, like so.' Ailsa positioned herself behind the top of Swan's head and held her pen as if it were the knife. 'Starting at the left jaw and pulling backwards means the killer was using their left hand. It didn't occur to me with Thorburn until I was doing this autopsy today, but the draw of the blade on Sim was from his right to his left. The video footage you have shows the perpetrator passing in that direction. I think the killer chose the direction of walking specifically to allow them to use their left hand.'

'Anything else?' Callanach asked. His mind was full of possibilities. The links between Thorburn and Swan. The description of the killer from the festival who was short and light, hardly a good candidate for hauling a grown man up to a ceiling beam. A growing sense that this was a beginning and that there was worse to come. 'What could be worse than this?' he asked aloud.

'If you want the worst,' Ailsa answered, assuming the question was for her, 'then you'd best have it all at once. It was the loss of blood that caused heart and brain function to cease for Michael Swan, just as for Sim Thorburn. Swan was alive when he was skinned. And he took a while to die. It was torture of a degree that I find difficult to describe adequately. I see no evidence that he was drugged to make him compliant whilst the procedure was undertaken, although the toxicology screen will take a couple more days. Who'll be taking DCI Begbie's place while he's on sick leave?'

'We're answering directly to Superintendent Overbeck on the current open murder cases,' Callanach said. 'She'll need to be copied in on the autopsy report.'

'She'll have it tomorrow. You'll be needing to rest your back now. No point aggravating it any further.'

'It's potentially a serial killer getting started then, Ailsa, that's what you think?' he asked quietly.

'It's a possibility we cannot afford to ignore. You and I have seen enough to recognise the signs. When people enjoy killing to this degree, there's very little that stops them until they're captured or dead.'

'Ailsa, about the leaking of the autopsy report on Ava's investigation into Helen Lott's death . . .' Callanach began.

'I know what you're going to say and I agree it would be disastrous for that to happen here. But it was no one in my department, Luc. If you find that I'm wrong, I'll take full responsibility, but my staff respect what we do here, no matter how long the hours they work and how difficult the circumstances. No one does this job for the pay or the glory, and those who don't like it leave pretty damned fast. Everyone my end has been interviewed about the leak and our procedures have been security-checked for weaknesses. We're clean.'

'I can't believe it's anyone at the station,' Callanach said. 'No one could have accessed it who didn't have proper security clearance. I don't see what there was to gain.'

'Don't get too distracted with it now,' Ailsa cautioned. 'I'd say you have more than enough on your plate. I believe you have two dead by the same hand.'

'Even so,' he said. 'Would you keep this offline? Do it the old-fashioned way. No emailing of reports, typed-up paper versions only. I can't take the risk of this getting into the public domain.'

'If you feel that strongly about it, then of course,' Ailsa said. 'Now off you go and protect the good people of this city. They're having a very bad month indeed.'

Chapter Eleven

'Tripp!' Callanach yelled as he limped down the corridor towards the briefing room. He stopped. Tripp wasn't there, of course. Borrowed to become one of DCI Edgar's hacker hounds, Tripp was no use to him now. He found DC Salter and waved at her to come to his office once she'd finished her phone call. He bundled up his coat to act as a cushion and sat down very slowly indeed. His fractured coccyx was producing a stabbing pain that made concentration difficult.

'What's the news?' Salter asked as she came through the door.

'All bad. There must be some CCTV footage between the McDonald Road Library and Regent Gardens where Michael Swan's belongings were found. Find something. I know it was probably dark, but I need you to compare it with the footage from The Meadows killing.'

'But that was a totally different thing, sir. Surely you don't . . .' Salter stopped. Callanach met her stare with a direct look. 'Oh shit. All right, then. I'll get on it.' She looked pained. Callanach felt the same way.

'Not a word to anyone else yet, Salter. Get started. I'm calling a briefing for this afternoon but this cannot get out.'

As Salter left his office, DCI Edgar entered.

'Sir,' Salter greeted him, with a polite nod of her head.

'Fetch me a cup of tea if you're not busy, Constable. Strong. No sugar,' the Detective Chief Inspector added.

Callanach gritted his teeth and stood up, feeling the fractured halves of his coccyx grate as he moved. He fought the desire to notify Edgar that DC Salter was, in fact, very busy indeed and that the addition of the word please would have made such a request more palatable.

'Can I help you, sir?' Callanach muttered, reaching in his pocket for another dose of painkillers.

'Came to see you about DC Tripp. He's not got the training my squad have, but all the same he's a worker. Thank you for the temporary transfer.'

Callanach wondered what he was supposed to say, and more importantly, when he'd be able to sit back down.

'How did your raid go, sir? I gather you had a firm lead on your hacker,' Callanach said when it was clear Edgar was in no mood to disappear.

'It was a useful exercise. Cutting off his exits, reducing his options. He knows now that we've discovered one of his bases. He'll find it increasingly hard to get into his system without us realising he's online and picking up a trace.' Edgar picked a non-existent piece of fluff off his sleeve. 'You know, I think you're putting DI Turner in a somewhat difficult position, phoning her when she's not at work. She needs to be able to switch off. I encourage my team to find friendships beyond work colleagues.'

Callanach sat down. He obviously wasn't going to be invited to sit. Nor was he prepared to be given a lecture on how to choose his friendships whilst standing to attention.

'I'm surprised DI Turner finds herself incapable of making that plain to me in person,' Callanach said.

'I'm surprised you want her to suffer the humiliation of having to do so,' Edgar said, straightening up. 'She and I go back a long way. We're extremely close. Intimate friends, you might say. You'll appreciate she's been able to confide in me about her need to distance herself from certain . . . aspects . . . of her work life.'

Callanach wasn't in the mood for DCI Edgar's little chat and he certainly didn't have time for any more prevarication.

'Meaning me?' Callanach asked.

'Ava thought you might get aggressive about it. Perhaps that's why she hasn't mentioned this herself. I don't know if it's a French thing, Detective Inspector, or an Interpol thing, but women here like to have their personal distance respected.'

The gloves were off then. Callanach stood back up, determined not to let the pain caused by the move show in his face.

'And I don't know if that was a racist thing or a jealousy thing, Chief Inspector, but I have nothing other than respect for DI Turner and she knows it. So it seems to me that perhaps you're following your own agenda here, more than acting on her behalf.'

'Careful now,' Edgar said, leaning across the desk and into Callanach's face. 'You wouldn't want me feeling the need to speak with your superior officer about insubordinate behaviour.'

'Go ahead. DCI Begbie knows me well enough, even if I haven't been here that long. I'm sure he has no more desire to have Scotland Yard's away team here than I do,' Callanach replied.

'I'm sure you're right, but Begbie's not here. He'll be lucky to get declared fit this side of Christmas. I think you'll find that Superintendent Overbeck and I see eye to eye on most things. Certainly, she wouldn't want one of her DIs claiming sexual harassment against another of her DIs. Can you imagine what a public relations nightmare that would be?' Callanach laughed out loud. DCI Edgar waited until Callanach had finished, then walked to the door. 'Laugh all you want, but a man with your past should be more prudent about his future.' Edgar waited for his point to hit home, his gaze drifting down to Callanach's hands which had involuntarily rolled themselves into fists at his sides. Edgar rewarded himself with a grin before exiting.

Callanach stared at the wall ahead, breathing hard. Ava would never make such an allegation. She'd know how much that would hurt him, from her more than anyone else given how much he'd confided in her about the false rape allegation. But then he wouldn't have expected her to have shared the details with her new boyfriend, either. He wondered how that conversation had come about. Not in the office, he was sure. That was a late-night intimate discussion, conducted in low tones with no one else around to interrupt. He picked up a stapler and lobbed it at the far wall.

A uniformed officer walked in with a large, overly bright greetings card in one hand and a pen in the other.

'Did you want to sign the chief's get well soon card, sir?'

'Out!' Callanach shouted, slamming himself back down into his chair. 'Fuck,' he yelled, standing straight back up, the pain a firework shooting through his backside. He grabbed the painkillers he'd been preparing to take, threw them into his mouth and chewed them dry. The bitterness was good.

Of all the people Ava could have told about his past, why DCI Edgar? Callanach had never asked her to keep quiet about it, and the bare bones of the story had already reached some ears at the station, but it could have been left to fade into history. Was it possible that she really felt he was pursuing her? They'd seemed to have become friends, spent time together, sometimes with other people, occasionally alone. If Ava felt intimidated by him, how come he'd never sensed that from her?

Salter appeared holding a cup of tea.

'Oh,' she said. 'DCI wanted a cuppa. Is he coming back, do you know?'

'Not into my office, he's not,' Callanach said. 'I'll take the tea.'

Salter handed it over carefully, taking a few quiet paces over to the wall and picking up pieces of broken stapler from the floor. 'Er, did you maybe want some biscuits with that?' she asked.

'No,' he said, slamming the cup down onto his desk, 'but thank you,' he managed. 'Come on Salter, get someone else to carry on where you've left off with the CCTV. You're coming back to the McDonald Road library with me. And phone Ailsa Lambert, see if she's got some free time to meet us there. Tell her it's urgent. I'm sick of waiting. Let's see if we can't figure out a bit more about our killer.'

'All right, sir. Give me five minutes. I'll drive,' she said. 'Doesn't look to me as if you'll be up to using the clutch.'

Callanach glared at his laptop screen. He was angry. Fed up with fighting a past he hadn't asked for and that wouldn't let go. Perhaps it was finally time to draw some lines under it all. Maybe that's what it would take to move on. He had a couple of minutes before Salter would be ready. More than enough time to write the one email he'd thought he'd never have the heart to write.

'*Maman,*' he began, writing in French, speaking English in his head, forcing himself to move forwards and adopt the country of his birth as the place to build a future. He didn't allow himself the luxury of emotion as he wrote. There had been too much of that. Too many months of grief and regret. His mother had slowly removed herself from his life as the months passed when he was awaiting trial in Lyon. Finally, with the trial date just days away, she had disappeared. His efforts to contact her had ended in changed mobile numbers and letters returned unopened. There had been no attempt by her to explain her reasons. Her absence alone was enough content for a novel. She had no faith in him. It had been too great a test even for a mother's love. 'Mum, It seems you've decided to have no more contact with me. I will leave you in peace. Luc.' He clicked send, shut the laptop, and put on his jacket.

Chapter Twelve

By the time Callanach and Salter reached the McDonald Road library to the north of Edinburgh city centre, Ailsa was outside waiting for them, eyes on her watch.

'I wasn't sure you'd be at work today,' she said, greeting Callanach with a pat on the shoulder. 'Is it sore?'

'Haven't noticed it,' Callanach lied, looking up over the building's exterior.

'I do like a bit of creative stoicism,' Ailsa smiled. 'I'll be down in the cellar seeing what sort of shape the crime scene is in. Meet me down there, and don't be too long about it. My clients may not be able to complain, but I still don't appreciate keeping them waiting.'

The library was a stunning old three-storey construction, with a round turret on the corner. 'None of the windows were broken and no locks were forced. The ground level doors were alarmed. So how did the killer get in?' Callanach asked Salter.

'Maybe they hid,' Salter said. 'Waited until everyone else was out and then reappeared.'

They walked past the police officers still protecting the crime scene, ducked the crime scene tape, and entered. Callanach studied the layout with fresh eyes. Beyond the front door was a foyer with a staircase to the right leading up to community rooms. The door past the stairs led into a large studio area. Straight ahead was the central section of the library. Extraordinarily light, with architectural glass ceilings and tables for reading and working, the main body of the library had notices that proclaimed the watchful eyes of its CCTV system. Callanach called over one of the CSIs working onsite.

'What's the last you found of Michael Swan on the CCTV?' Callanach asked.

'I can show you,' she said, opening up a laptop. A fuzzy black and white picture came into view. 'This is the victim here. He leaves the central library room from the staff area and walks towards the front doors. We're assuming that was him intending to leave for the night.'

'Run it back a bit,' Callanach said. The footage reversed for a couple of seconds at high speed and Callanach hit the space bar to stop it. 'Play it from here.'

Michael Swan could be seen from the camera at the rear of the main room walking towards the staff area at the right-hand side of frame. He paused once, turned his head. Walked out of frame, then came straight back, walking out towards the main doors. The latter part was the shot they'd watched initially.

'He's not carrying anything,' Salter said.

'Actually, if you look carefully you'll see he has his keys in his hand when he walks back across. That's what makes it obvious that he's about to leave,' the CSI said, sighing as she spoke.

'How often do you leave work after a whole day with nothing in your hands?' Salter responded.

'It's summer,' the technician replied, brushing hair out of her eyes and adopting a tone of voice midway between stroppy and defensive. 'He hardly needs a coat. I don't see how this is evidentially important.'

Salter clearly had more to say. She looked at Callanach before continuing. It wasn't like her to get involved in an argument, but he could see she wasn't done yet.

'Have you had another member of the library staff show you Mr Swan's personal effects?' Salter asked, ignoring the challenge and following her own line of thought.

'Of course. There's the usual work paraphernalia, mugs, pens, notes, a book he was in the middle of reading. Some other random personal correspondence. We've followed procedure. Everything's been bagged and tagged.'

'Could we see it, please?' Salter asked. The tech called a uniformed officer over, who promptly disappeared then returned with a large clear plastic bag containing several other smaller plastic bags, each containing a single item. Every bag had a label with a unique reference number, time, date and location on it. Callanach and Salter looked through each one.

'Here,' Salter said, holding up one particular bag with a thick piece of card, bearing gold leaf edging and italic printing. Michael Swan's name was written in pride of place. Salter read it out. '"You are hereby invited to attend Edinburgh City's Community Achievement Awards." This was being held the morning after his death. And it says very clearly that the invitation must be produced at the door for entry.'

The tech officer had stopped looking stroppy and was fiddling with her laptop instead.

'So he forgot it,' she snapped.

'I don't think so,' Salter addressed Callanach directly. 'His wife told us he'd been looking forward to that. It would have been on his mind all day. I don't believe he was ready to leave when he went towards the door.'

Salter rewound the CCTV footage again and hit play.

'You see here, sir,' she said, pointing at Michael Swan's face as he turned mid-walk. 'He hears something or is distracted by something. We know then he picks up his keys and goes towards the front door. I reckon he opened the door for someone else to come in. Not for him to get out. That's why he hadn't picked up the invitation yet.'

Callanach watched the footage one more time, then looked back at Salter.

'Remind me again why you missed the last round of sergeant exams, DC Salter,' he said.

'I was on honeymoon, sir,' Salter said.

'Make sure you're available to take them next time. That's an order,' Callanach said.

'I might be too busy in six months' time,' Salter said. 'I could get talent-spotted by a Hollywood agency or appear on *Masterchef* and end up opening my own restaurant.'

'I doubt that,' Callanach said. 'I've tasted your toasted sandwiches. Seriously. You'd have passed the exams at the last sitting. Don't let it wait.'

'Detective Inspector,' Ailsa Lambert shouted from the doorway. 'You only have me for another few minutes. There are reports of an incident across the city. My team will hold the scene for me briefly, but it's now or never. I've a full day ahead.'

They walked down into the basement, hastily donning white crime scene overalls, shoe covers and gloves. The scene was entirely different to the snapshot Callanach had of it from when he'd fallen. The area was now lit from all angles. Michael Swan's body had, of course, been taken down but he was still suspended there in Callanach's mind.

'Two questions,' Callanach said. 'How did the killer get Mr Swan to come down here, and how did they get him into position hanging from the overhead metal beams?'

'If he let the killer into the building voluntarily,' Salter said, 'it must either have been someone he recognised or someone who seemed non-threatening.'

'Okay, assuming either case, once in the building they persuaded him to open the basement and come inside.'

'Easy enough if they were armed,' Ailsa noted, pulling a thick wad of A4 photos from a folder. 'Showing a knife or a gun would have the desired effect. Getting the man seven feet into the air makes less sense. The killer would have had to put down their weapon. No way of tying these knots without two hands.' Ailsa paused to point out close-ups of the knots. Both were tied in the same way, one binding the hands, one binding the ankles, then another rope had been passed through the ankle knot, through the hand knot and looped around his neck.

'What damage did the rope around his neck do?' Callanach asked.

'Very little in real terms, and it certainly wasn't strangulation that killed him. The rope would have been useful to keep him still whilst his face was skinned. Of course, he'd have been on his back whilst that was being done. Other than that, once he was hoisted up to the ceiling, it simply held his head in place until he was found. There's virtually no internal damage to the neck or throat area, only external bruising and chafing of the skin.'

Callanach moved to stand in the area where he'd fallen, directly below the space that Michael Swan's face had filled.

'So he stood still whilst his hands and feet were tied. The killer at that point holding no weapon. Mr Swan is then restrained by the additional rope fed from ankles to neck, and is laid on his back and skinned whilst still conscious.'

'No drugs in his system, no blow to the head. I'm as sure as I can be that he was conscious when it started. I would guess he blacked out from shock and pain at some point, but he might well have come round again prior to blood loss stopping his heart and starving his brain of oxygen.'

'So he must have been hoisted up,' Callanach said.

Ailsa handed him a different photograph. This one showed

Michael Swan in his final position, tied to the metal structural supports that ran across the ceiling, and facing down towards the floor. Somehow the photographer had managed to get high enough to capture the scene from parallel with the body. The image was ghoulish and dizzying.

'So the end of the rope that ran the length of his body was then slung over the metal beams that ran perpendicular to the corpse, formed a final loop by passing back through the ankle knot to get his legs off the floor, and tied off at ground level at the base of the bookshelf.' Callanach pointed to an old metal bookstand that must have weighed tons given the amount of paper on it. 'Easily enough ballast to have stopped his body from crashing down. How much did Michael Swan weigh, Ailsa?' Callanach asked.

'A fraction under eleven stone. He was fairly slim so that would've helped. Still a lot of weight to lift that high though,' she said.

'Not necessarily,' Callanach mused. 'If the killer attached a weight to the free end of the rope it would have worked like a pulley system, the hanging weight hoisting the body up using gravity and thereby reducing the amount of pulling force required to lift him. Any reasonably fit adult would have been able to haul him up. It's clever.'

Ailsa pulled her mobile out and tutted.

'I've got to go. All I would add is that Mr Swan was pulled up there immediately upon the cut to the facial skin being completed. His legs were slightly higher than his head, helping the continued bleed from the facial wound. That's why there was so much blood on the floor directly below the face. Keep that copy of the photos for reference.' She handed them over as her phone beeped repeatedly. Ailsa swiped at the screen. 'God knows what's going on, I've got a hundred messages a minute coming into my phone.'

'Thanks Ailsa,' Callanach muttered, staring hard at the photos of Michael Swan's face. The pathologist was nearly at the door when Callanach called back to her. 'Ailsa! Is it possible that the killer cut round the edge of his facial skin, then hoisted him up to the ceiling, climbed on a chair or desk then pulled the skin flap down when he was already suspended?'

Ailsa stood still a moment. 'Entirely possible,' she said eventually. 'It would explain the relative lack of blood on his clothes and the rest of his body. Unfortunately it also probably means that he was conscious after the cut and before being hauled up there. He might well not have passed out by that stage.'

'Meaning Mr Swan might have watched his own blood pouring onto the floor, suspended there, waiting for death?' Salter asked.

'Whoever committed this crime is evil, and that's not a word I use lightly. I think you should assume the very worst. If nothing else, it will give you more incentive than ever to catch the perpetrator,' Ailsa said.

'I think that image is rather more incentive than I need to do my job properly,' Salter said as Ailsa left quietly.

Chapter Thirteen

Callanach's phone buzzed, displaying a number he didn't recognise. Sending the call to voicemail, he walked slowly around the basement, getting a feel for how the killer and Michael Swan would have moved around and how complex it would have been to set up such an elaborate tableau. That was how it felt. As if the killer had been creating something akin to an art installation. Of the sickest mind and most foul imagination, but an installation it was. And about as far from an impulsive killing as it was possible to get.

Even with the bright crime scene investigation lighting it was hard to see clearly beneath the book shelves, between the stacked boxes and unused piled-up furniture at the sides of the room. Callanach set his mobile to torch and flashed it down at floor level as he crawled stiffly along, wincing at the pain in his lower back. It was always possible that the scalpel had been dropped and not yet spotted or that some tiny object had spilled out of the killer's pocket whilst taking out gloves or a knife. The basement was a galaxy of DNA, passed across from chairs once sat in, books borrowed, shoes that had traipsed in and out over more than a century. The chances of the forensic team being able to isolate any evidence relating to the killer's identity were lottery-worthy, which might well have been part of the attraction of the kill-site.

Salter looked washed out. The edge of her hairline was visibly damp and she was half covering her mouth with one hand. None of them were immune to the shock of such barbarity, no matter how long they'd been on the job.

Callanach stood up, suddenly feeling ridiculous for thinking he could magic evidence out of thin air. He took another look at Salter who didn't seem to be recovering and pointed towards an old chair pushed against the wall.

'Take a seat for a minute,' he said. 'Begbie's out for the foreseeable future and I'm injured. I'm not prepared to take any more risks with my squad members.' Salter plodded towards the chair, breathing hard. Callanach knew the sound of someone trying not to throw up when he heard it. His phone began buzzing in his pocket again.

'Sir,' Salter said.

'Unrecognised caller again. Who the hell got hold of my mobile number? Those idiots on switchboard need—'

'Sir!' Salter repeated, pointing towards the wall.

Callanach looked up. His DC was pointing at an old corkboard that had been leaned against it. It contained ageing posters about library fun days, an advert for a meet the author event, some personal notices – people selling, buying, offering services – and, near the top, a photo. Nothing dramatic, just a woman walking towards the car in her driveway. Callanach disconnected the phone call and stepped closer to the photograph to pick out the detail. He sighed as he realised he recognised the tan-coloured bungalow with the wrought-iron front gate, and the woman in her sixties, face slightly obscured as her grey hair flew sideways in the breeze.

'Michael Swan's widow,' Salter whispered.

'Taken when she had no idea she was being watched. The killer knew the address, knew who his wife was, who knows what else,' Callanach said. 'Pinned there as a reminder to the victim throughout his ordeal. I guess it's not hard to imagine why he didn't fight.'

'He had children and grandchildren,' Salter said. 'The killer would have known that too, if they'd done any research. How could anyone do that? Not just kill, but literally deface a man.'

'Mrs Swan had no idea she was being watched,' Callanach repeated, peering closer at the photograph. 'That's what makes it so scary. The killer could have been there hours, or watching for days. Get it logged as evidence, then have a copy taken. I need you to go directly to Mrs Swan's house. If she can tell us when it was taken, maybe we can understand how long this was going on.' Salter's phone rang. She answered the call and walked a few steps away to talk, as Callanach proceeded to the exit to strip off his suit.

As soon as his feet hit the pavement, Callanach's mobile began to ring too.

'Yes,' Callanach snapped.

'This is Lance Proudfoot, we spoke before. I'm from the online news blogging site?'

'I thought we'd concluded our conversation, Mr Proudfoot. I'm busy, so . . .'

'Do you have a comment about the latest body, Detective Inspector? We've got the photos already, so if you could just give me a line or two about how Police Scotland plans to investigate, or what reassurance you can give the public?'

'How the hell did you get photos of Michael Swan's body?' Callanach snarled. 'You release those and I'll have you in a cell before you can reach your door.'

'Not Michael Swan. The young woman in the dumpster. The

photos of her were emailed to me embedded in a download-able file this morning. Me and the rest of the popular press, unfortunately. It's not exactly an exclusive. Did you not know? A huge part of the city has been closed off. The police are everywhere.'

'Salter, what have you got?' Callanach shouted over to her.

'Caucasian female murder victim, early twenties, probable strangulation. Body left in a large bin. Must be what the pathologist was called to, sir,' Salter responded, putting her own hand over her mobile mid-conversation to answer. 'DI Turner is at the scene and heading it up. They want us back at the station. Superintendent's called her own briefing.'

'Right Mr Proudfoot, no comment, but I'm sending officers over to your offices to inspect your computer. I want those files. Back up what you need. You've got about ten minutes,' Callanach said.

'Oh, for heaven's sake. At least give me something I can print before you destroy everything,' Lance moaned.

'Police Scotland have no comment at the present time,' Callanach said. 'Print that.' He hung up and shouted enough details to enable uniformed officers to find Lance Proudfoot and seize his hard drive. 'Get the car, Salter. We'll stop at the scene on the way back to the station.'

Twenty minutes later they arrived as close as they could get to Valleyfield Street. The crime scene boundary extended well beyond the two entrances of the road. Leven Street and Glengyle Terrace were both sealed off, and across Leven Terrace, where a footpath led into The Meadows, a police cordon enclosed a huge section of parkland.

Salter disappeared in search of other members of the squad. Callanach made directly for Ava who was deep in conversation with Ailsa Lambert, under the shelter of a temporary white awning designed to keep out prying eyes. Not that it would make much difference now, if photos really had been leaked to the press.

Ava saw him approach and beckoned him in. Within the confines of the tent was a blue dumpster. Callanach was handed a crime scene suit with accessories. He really shouldn't have bothered taking the last ones off, he thought.

'Cause of death?' he asked Ailsa as he brushed past her to get a better look.

'Barring us finding something more at autopsy, almost certainly strangulation,' Ailsa said.

'I need more officers down here, Luc,' Ava said. 'Can you tell the superintendent when you get back to the station? And the overtime restrictions will have to be lifted. This'll take more man-hours than they're paying for.'

There was a screech from the end of Valleyfield Street, a loud scuffling of feet, then a man could be heard shouting. Callanach drew his gaze away from the twenty-something young woman lying in the dumpster, the lower half of her body still concealed in a rough sack, as Ava stepped out of the tent and took control.

'Stop right there,' she ordered. 'Officers, get control of those people.'

A woman barged through, frantic, wailing. Ava tried to grab her but momentum made her unstoppable. She pushed Ailsa aside and launched herself towards the dumpster, hands gripping the edge, peering inside. All the noise she'd been making instantly ceased. She sank to the floor. A second later and a man appeared behind her. He took one look at her face and stumbled, his knees hitting the pavement hard, falling into the woman's side. They stayed there like that, rocking and shaking, until Ava sat down beside them.

'Can you tell me who she is?' Ava asked.

The woman tried to speak. Her mouth worked itself open

and shut but nothing came from it. Uniformed officers appeared, Ava looking at them in a way that made it clear they should never expect promotion after letting members of the public burst onto a crime scene.

'Move these people to somewhere private and secure. Look after them. Make sure they have access to medical assistance if required and ascertain their relationship to the deceased, please,' Ava said. The uniformed officers wrapped blankets around the shoulders of the two obviously grieving people, and persuaded them gently towards a vehicle.

Ava pinched the bridge of her nose between finger and thumb, grinding her teeth.

'Can we not get a frigging break? Bodies are piling up and we seem to be the last to find out what's happening,' she muttered. 'How in God's name did they know where to find us?'

Callanach pulled out his phone and internet searched the terms 'body', 'Edinburgh', and 'breaking news'. It took just seconds. Various pages popped up with the story. As yet, not one news agency had been stupid enough to risk prosecution by posting the shared photos of the dead girl, but there was a clear description of both the girl and the crime scene, right down to the details of what she'd been wearing.

'A young woman has been found dead in a Valleyfield Street dumpster,' the first article began. 'She is believed to be in her twenties, with long blonde hair and wearing a scouting uniform. Of particular note is the multicoloured, knitted scarf around her neck. Police have not yet issued a statement or confirmed her identity.'

'Ma'am,' a uniformed constable said, keeping his distance from Ava. 'That's Mr and Mrs Balcaskie. They've confirmed the deceased is their daughter, Emily. She's twenty-four years of age and attended a scout meeting here last night in that building over the road. When she didn't come home they assumed she'd decided to stay with friends in the city. It was the description of the scarf on the news reports that made them realise it was her.'

'Thank you, Constable,' Ava said. 'I'll be over to speak with them personally in a moment.'

Ailsa took photos as Ava and Callanach stared in at the corpse. The knitted scarf was wrapped several times around the girl's neck, pulled so tight that the fibres were straining, the ends of it shoved hard into her mouth. Her eyes were bulging, the whites stained dark red from haemorrhaging.

'What's happening, Luc? Four murders in two weeks? It's as if a pack of wild animals has been let loose in the city.' Ava wiped a tear away, keeping her back carefully towards her squad. Callanach hadn't known her long, as friendships went, but he never thought he'd see her emotional at a crime scene. She was a career police officer – a fiercely tough, professional one. He wanted to stretch a hand out, to give some comfort, but DCI Edgar's words squirmed in his guts. Perhaps Ava did need some space, want to keep the boundaries of their friendship rigid and clear.

'Sometimes these things all happen at once. There's rarely an explanation,' he said. 'I'll report to Overbeck for you. There'll have to be a press conference soon and a lid needs to be put on media coverage. How did they get hold of photos of the body so quickly?' he asked.

'Didn't you hear?' Ava asked. 'It was the press who reported the body. They alerted us. Even gave us the address. Someone wanted her found, and with as much media circus as they could rouse. Tell Overbeck I'll call later to update her in person. And if you bump into Edgar, explain that I'll be busy for the next twenty-four hours, would you?'

'Sure,' Callanach said, taking a step away, his mind made up about whether or not it was appropriate to offer support beyond the procedural or administrative. It was clear that DCI Edgar was already filling that gap. He left Ava making her way towards the couple who should never have faced the tragic indignity of hearing the news of their daughter's death via the media, regrouped with Salter and headed back to the police station.

Callanach headed straight for Begbie's office where Superintendent Overbeck had temporarily set up shop. She was on the phone when he entered, cooing a mixture of 'yes sir' and 'no sir' into the mouthpiece in a reassuringly soothing manner. Five minutes later, she put the phone down and looked up.

'Sit down, Callanach. I've got gridlock across a square mile of the city, the press want to hang me out to dry and I'm being chased by a team of American fucking documentary makers who want to do a two-hour special on the murder craze sweeping out of control on Edinburgh's streets.'

'Ma'am, I've just—'

'Don't speak, Inspector,' she said, taking out a mirror and lipstick. 'Your current job is to accompany me and not to bollocks anything up. We are going down to give a press statement now. The ladies and gentlemen of the media are to be regarded as our friends – the sort you exchange Christmas cards with but are always too busy to actually see in person. We will appear obliging whilst giving them precisely nothing. We have an opportunity with these cases. We can solve them quickly, providing justice and relief to the families of the deceased, and come out of this acclaimed and heroic. Or they will continue to blight Scotland, in which case you and DI Turner can take an endless vacation in the back of beyond as I scapegoat you for incompetence. Either way, I will not be made the whipping girl for any monumentally shit-storming failure to protect the general public from the lunatic killers currently rampaging unchecked. Do you get it?' She applied liberal lipstick, raising one appraising eyebrow in her mirror. 'Good. Off we go then.'

The conference room was buzzing. It was hard to imagine how any more cameras, microphones or bodies could possibly have been shoe-horned in. Unlike past press conferences with the well-worn figure of DCI Begbie at the helm, when Overbeck stalked in with her high heels, perfect hair, and an attitude you could use to cut sheet metal, there was an immediate silence. Introductions and format announcement done, the superintendent began spinning.

'I'm personally overseeing the Major Investigation Team in the absence of DCI Begbie, and I shall be relying heavily on Detective Inspector Turner and Detective Inspector Callanach to bring these cases to a swift and successful close. Rest assured that I will not allow my officers to sleep until these killers are behind bars. As you know, we now have four open murder cases and I will not tolerate anything but the highest of standards being applied. We owe that to the deceased and their families and loved ones, who are constantly in our thoughts. In the meantime, we appreciate your continuing support and may, at times, ask for your understanding and discretion. I've worked closely with many of you before,' Overbeck managed a suitably sad-looking smile, 'and I hope you know that where I can release information, I will.'

'Superintendent, can you confirm the identity of the latest victim?' the question was shouted across the sea of journalists' heads.

'Emily Balcaskie was found dead this morning. As you all know by now, her body was found in Valleyfield Street. She was a primary school teacher at Bonaly. Last night, in her capacity as a scout leader, she attended a meeting and failed to return home afterwards. We believe, although the investigation is in its most preliminary stages, that she was walking through

The Meadows towards her car when she was approached. It seems likely that she was killed in the park and then her body was returned to Valleyfield Street.'

'Are all four killings the work of one serial killer, Superintendent?' a different voice yelled. Overbeck didn't even blink, Callanach had to give her credit for that. Nor did she pause before answering in a silky smooth voice that wouldn't have been amiss in a chocolate advert.

'The methods used in the murders of Sim Thorburn, Helen Lott, Michael Swan and Emily Balcaskie have all been wildly varying, as have the places and times of death. We see no pattern between the four cases currently under investigation. Please do not disturb your readers with talk of serial killers. There are a number of possible explanations for these murders occurring so closely in time. As you know, drugs often play a part in violent murders and the variety of parties, celebrations and festivals throughout the city in the summer necessarily attracts some less wanted elements. We have yet to rule out whether or not any of the victims knew their attackers, as statistics tell us is the most likely scenario in cases of this sort.'

'Why hasn't Police Scotland released the details of how Michael Swan was killed yet?' a man near the front asked. Callanach recognised him from an online search as Lance Proudfoot. He was balding, tall and sporting a T-shirt that proclaimed him an avid Rolling Stones fan.

'We're still liaising with Mr Swan's family and there are some highly technical forensic issues. We hope to have a statement with you in the next forty-eight hours,' Overbeck replied.

'Was the police raid on a warehouse in Newington linked to the murders?' a woman near the front asked. Callanach wondered how much more successful the investigation might be if all the journalists worked for the police instead of the media. They certainly knew more than he did about what was going on around the city at the moment.

'Whilst I can't give you any specific information about that, I can tell you that the raid you're referring to was part of an ongoing investigation by a specialist team from Scotland Yard and nothing to do with any of the murders.' That would be DCI Edgar's hacker then, Callanach thought. That case didn't seem to be progressing at any great pace either. He needed DCI Tripp back. Callanach would have to talk to Edgar about when that was likely to be possible. 'And now I'm afraid I'm required elsewhere,' Overbeck went on. 'Any other questions should be directed through the media liaison office and you all have the crime-line numbers to encourage the public to come forward with information. Please do remember to add them to your releases. Many thanks for your patience and your efforts to assist us.'

She stood up, pausing almost imperceptibly whilst the cameras caught her best side, then nodded to Callanach who followed her out, wondering why he'd been paraded through such a time-wasting farce.

'Well done,' she said, once they'd cleared the public area. 'Always good to present a united front and let them see us working as a team.'

'Talking of teams, we're going to need more officers. Could you lift the restrictions on overtime? I suspect we'll have to outsource some of the forensics to other areas. Ailsa Lambert's team is flooded. We'll get a bottleneck on return of crucial evidence if there aren't more resources available.'

'Submit requests in writing via email,' Overbeck said, drifting away. 'And I want a written update every twelve hours. Arrest someone, Callanach, or get on a plane back to Paris. And find a reason to delay releasing the details of Michael Swan's murder, or there won't be a hotel room in the city that's not full of gutter press trying to turn Edinburgh into the horror capital of the world.'

Callanach returned to his desk. It was chaos. Not the physical wood and metal structure before him, but the random pieces of information he was pushing around. He grabbed a clean sheet of paper and a pen, and wrote the names of the four victims currently in limbo at the city mortuary. Death by strangulation, facial skinning, stabbing and crushing. The Meadows was the only location any of the killings had in common, but even that was different areas of the park. He added each victim's age, job and address next to their name. Save for the use of related blades on Thorburn and Swan, there were no obvious links. It seemed to be a dead end. If forensics couldn't bring them a lead through the national database then he'd have to find a different way.

Chapter Fourteen

Callanach used his mobile call log to dial Lance Proudfoot's number.

'Detective Inspector! Goodness me, I hadn't expected you to call. Are you phoning to gloat about the seizure of my hard drive as evidence? Only I'm having a bad enough day as it is.'

'Tell me about the email you received with the photos this morning,' Callanach said.

Lance sighed. 'The email came in early. Initially I assumed it was one of those viruses hidden inside junk mail, you know? Then a mate from a newspaper phoned to check if I'd been sent the same thing they had. One of their interns had opened it, completely contrary to instructions, but seventeen-year-olds – what can you do? Anyway, the photos were in a down-loadable file, return address didn't work. No sender details. They were in colour, looked like they'd been taken using a phone camera. Horrible. And they'd been sent to every press outlet you can name. Three photos of the girl's body from different angles, all taken once she'd been put in the dump-ster, one of the outside of the dumpster, one of the road sign. The lighting is blown out, the edges are dark, so I'd say they were taken using flash at night rather than first thing this morning.'

'Do you know who was first on the scene?' Callanach asked.

'No idea. Wasn't me and you can be damned sure it wasn't a police officer either. Whichever journalist downloaded them first would have made sure they got the story before calling it in.'

'Leeches,' Callanach hissed as he scribbled notes.

'Can I quote you on that? Only your delightful superintendent may think that's not a good example of promoting the police/press supportive working relationship,' Lance laughed.

'Do you ever want to get your hard drive back?' Callanach asked.

'Come on, Inspector, I was joking. For what it's worth, I agree with your assessment that sometimes my colleagues' ethical code is not all it should be. However, I'm running a different angle. Seems to me there's not much left to explore from the victim perspective. That horse has well and truly left the stable. I'm covering the graffiti angle, gauging public outcry. I've been photographing the sites across the city. Do you have a comment on the words left on the wall in High School Wynd, near the junction with Cowgate?' Lance asked.

'I've got more pressing things to worry about than graffiti, Mr Proudfoot. Call the city council if you want something done about that,' Callanach said.

'Really? Only I took your call to me as a sign of desperation.' Callanach had no response to that, other than to remind himself why he usually avoided private conversations with journalists. The experience most often resembled wrestling a snake. Had Proudfoot not been made a part of it by virtue of the emailed photos, Callanach would never have made the call. 'I was on my way to photograph the High School Wynd graffiti when your boss called that last press conference. I went there afterwards, and what I found is deeply confusing. Concerning even. And I think it might just turn out to be important. Meet me there? I want to see what you make of it,' Lance said.

'Just tell me what—' but the dead line tone was already an indication of how useless finishing the sentence would be. Callanach looked at his watch. He could be there in a few minutes and wouldn't lose more than half an hour, and although he didn't want to admit it, he was curious. Against his better judgement, he went to find Lance Proudfoot.

Callanach hadn't thought about the address before he'd left, but it made sense now. High School Wynd was the short stretch of road from which you entered the mortuary car park. Cowgate ran through a stretch of the old city, from Grassmarket to Holyrood, and housed those historically uncomfortable bedfellows – extraordinary wealth and extreme poverty. The wall there had become one of the many sites of an ever-expanding canvas of graffitied social commentary since the killings began.

As he approached, an ancient, battered motorcycle pulled up beside him and the driver dismounted. He tugged off a helmet that looked held together more by stickers than substance, and greeted Callanach with an unexpectedly friendly slap on the shoulder.

'You came,' Lance said. 'I've got to say, I wasn't entirely expecting that. Quite refreshing to meet an open-minded copper.'

'Truth is, I can combine this with a visit back to The Meadows. Also, it's a first and final act of tolerance. I generally dislike people who try to win mystery points by putting the phone down while I'm speaking,' Callanach said, staring with something that felt rather like envy at the old BSA Bantam. He hadn't been on a bike in years. Suddenly, it looked and sounded like the definition of freedom.

'Then let me show you why I've got you here, and you can leave me feeling like a prize idiot when I turn out to be wrong. What do you see?' Lance asked, pointing at the middle of the rainbow of outraged comments.

'Really?' Callanach asked.

'Ach, come on man, will you not engage in conversation? All right then. You see that blue spray paint to the left of the main section?'

Callanach could see it all right. The latest in a string of horrified bystanders expressing their disbelief at the victims falling prey to such brutality. 'A PRIMARY SCHOOL TEACHER!' the capital letters screamed. It was much like all the other graffiti adorning the brickwork in the city – simple, brief, outraged. And directly across the road from where the victims ended up. Appropriate.

'What about it?' Callanach asked.

'I left the press briefing before the rest of the media crowd. There might have been one or two people ahead of me, but that was all. Then I came straight here to get a couple of photos for today's blog. I had the piece nearly finished. When I got back to the office to publish it, I noticed that comment.'

Callanach's brain was struggling with the day's overload, but even he was starting to feel the disjointedness.

'The graffiti was already here,' Lance emphasised. 'And to the best of my knowledge, no one in that room knew the dead girl was a teacher, let alone what grade. A scout leader yes, you could just about make out the uniform in those god-awful stills we were sent, but that was it. So I looked again, double-checking, and noticed this.' Lance took a couple of further steps forward, pointing up at the wall. 'Here, here and here. No fewer than three different places where other people have sprayed or painted over the top of the words teacher, primary and the exclamation mark.'

'It was there before the press conference,' Callanach said, drawing out his mobile and readying his camera.

'I might be mistaken,' Lance continued, 'but looking at the stuff written over the top, I'd say it appeared quite some time before that lassie put on her uniform to go to her scout meeting yesterday.' Callanach looked at the evidence for that. The journalist was right. The paint over the top was from different contributors, left at different times, and some of the graffiti appeared weather-worn. 'So have you got a comment for me now, Detective Inspector?' Lance asked.

'I have a question,' Callanach said. 'What's it going to take for you to keep this quiet?'

Lance stared at him. 'Something's not right, is it?' he asked.

Callanach shook his head. It made no sense. If the killer was announcing their next target for attention, or to create a sense of fear in the community, then why not do so more publicly? Had the journalist not worked out what had happened, it would almost certainly have gone unnoticed. And why risk getting caught for the sake of making your mark?

'I need to close this place off for a while,' Callanach said. 'And I need absolutely no one to figure out why. Can you give me that at least?'

'We're not all bad, Callanach,' Lance said. 'I want this bastard caught just as much as you do. You never know who could be next. Of course I'll keep it quiet, but could I ask a return favour? Not much, but just something to print. Need to do the whole wolf/door avoidance thing. The only way my blog feed makes money is through advertising and that means readership numbers.'

'I'll get you something,' Callanach promised. 'I owe you that. Can I ask you to send me your photos of the wall taken earlier, just in case anything's changed since then? In the meantime, we need to get away from here before anyone realises we're staring.' He walked the journalist back to the motorbike and offered his hand. 'I'm grateful, Mr Proudfoot.'

'You can call me Lance, Detective Inspector,' he said, shaking Callanach's hand warmly. 'Let's keep in touch.'

Chapter Fifteen

An hour later the area was coned off while a team of passably believable would-be engineers inspected the pavement and drains along High School Wynd. Officers arrived in unmarked cars and questioned every member of staff at the mortuary about anyone they'd seen taking an interest in the wall. There was CCTV footage around the outside of the mortuary for security purposes but none focusing on that particular area, although any graffiti artists would have had to pass through a section of road covered by cameras. That amounted to hundreds, perhaps thousands, of passers-by, with no means of filtering out persons of interest.

Photographs were taken. The street area below the graffiti was swept for DNA, fibres, and random items, making Callanach feel that they were literally clutching at straws. Notes were made about paint layering to ascertain more about the order in which the markings were made. Then the pseudo-engineers left. Without fuss, without sirens. Hopefully without anyone noticing much at all.

Callanach sent teams to the two other largest known areas of graffiti to photograph and detail the impressions on those walls too. His return to the police station was met with an impatient crowd in the incident room. There were now four distinct areas set up – Thorburn, Lott, Swan and Balcaskie. The teams were overlapping out of necessity. Even Callanach was beginning to forget where one case ended and the next started. More uniformed officers were being shipped in from Glasgow and Aberdeen to keep boots visible on the streets, protect crime scenes and follow up avenues of investigation. As soon as Callanach walked into the briefing room, Ava stood up.

'Let's get started,' she said. Callanach hadn't really noticed her public school English accent before, but after such close proximity to DCI Edgar, it was more striking. Ava always bemoaned the fact that although she was as Scottish as the lochs themselves, her family had done their best to ruin any chance she had of fitting in by sending her south of the border to school. She tucked a stray curl behind her ear and pressed some keys on her laptop. 'An update,' Ava announced. 'Emily Balcaskie was immediately recognised by family and friends when the press released a description this morning of the deceased wearing a scout uniform with a brightly coloured, striped knitted scarf. Her primary school class knitted it for her earlier this year as a well done present for being nominated in a teachers' association awards tribute. She's been a teacher for just two years, still lives with her parents in Bonaly to the south-west of the city centre. They were not aware of anyone harassing her or following her. The school reports that she was happy, uncomplaining and, in their words, "had everything to look forward to". Overall, Miss Balcaskie was confident, outdoorsy and popular. The forensic pathologist has confirmed death by strangulation, using the scarf described. One of Emily's shoes has been found in The Meadows, not far from the path that leads there from the eastern exit of Valleyfield Street. By the time she left the scout meeting it was dark. All the scout leaders stayed late for a leadership meeting followed by a social event. No one noticed her go. I think it's safe to assume her attacker followed her into the park and pulled her into the bushes where she was killed. He waited until the area was clear to carry the body, concealed in the sack in which she was found, back to the dumpster.'

Detective Sergeant Lively raised a hand. Callanach hadn't seen him around much. He'd been posted into Ava's squad on the Helen Lott murder.

'You said "he", ma'am. Do we have any reason to assume that?'

'Three things,' Ava said. 'The strength it would have taken to have strangled Emily with her scarf, given the stretch in the fabric. Her windpipe was completely crushed but there were no fingermarks. The pattern of the knitting was ingrained into her skin. Second, the physical effort of carrying her body back to the dumpster. Emily was five foot six. It would have taken an extreme amount of effort to have moved her dead body. And finally, thank God, we have a witness.'

There was an audible release of breath from the assembled group. Ava waited for silence before continuing.

'A bulky figure was seen carrying a sack on his shoulder out of the park at around 2 a.m. The figure was dressed in dark, scruffy clothes, wearing a hat, face pointing downwards presumably from the effort of hauling the sack on his back. Best guess on height is six foot three. Large build. The witness assumed it was a homeless person carrying their sleeping bag and possessions, coming out of the park and looking for shelter for the night. He crossed Leven Terrace from The Meadows, entered Valleyfield Street and that's where the witness lost sight of him. She was just entering her flat further up Leven Terrace after a night out.'

'So the man wasn't all that careful not to be seen?' DS Lively continued. 'How can we be sure it was him?'

'Simplest explanation, Detective Sergeant. Unless there were two men hauling sacks that size along the same route at that time of night. Time of death is estimated to have been about 11 p.m., meaning her killer remained concealed in the bushes for a number of hours before braving the street. I think that counts as being careful not to be seen,' Ava finished.

Lively was playing devil's advocate with his usual charm and sensitivity. Ava turned away from him, flicked onto a map of the roads surrounding Valleyfield Street and began allocating door-to-door checks.

Callanach slipped out. He felt as if the reality of the situation was slipping away from them. Ailsa's warning that two of the deaths might have been caused by blades forged in the same batch was pinballing around his brain. Photos and autopsy reports were being leaked to the press and the resulting investigations had drawn nothing but blanks. No two deaths were the same. Police Scotland resources were being pushed to the absolute limits.

Not just closing, but locking his door, Callanach barricaded himself inside his office and switched on his laptop.

'Too many deaths,' he said to the blank screen as it fired up. 'That's not a coincidence. It's a campaign.'

He chose a search engine and typed in Emily Balcaskie's name. Inevitably, the first couple of pages were flooded with the reporting of her death, but Callanach found what he'd been looking for on page three. Here there were personal details. Her graduation results listed in a standard university page. An article relating to her father, a wealthy banker, in which Emily was mentioned, accompanied by a photograph in the society pages of some magazine. Finally he found a link to a video posted by the school where Emily had worked. Callanach clicked play and waited.

The video was a rough recording of a television interview. The shot was framed to show Emily in the midst of her classroom surrounded by cherubic faces, some tugging at her sleeves or peeking out from behind her, grins alight with the overwhelming excitement of having a camera present.

'I'm amazed,' Emily said, her eyes shining under the portable lights, 'and so honoured that my pupils wrote the letter nominating me for the Teacher Awards.'

'And we're told they have one more surprise for you,' the off-screen interviewer said. 'Something they've made themselves.'

A boy and a girl, aged six or seven, appeared in shot holding up the scarf. From the look on Emily's face, they might just as well have been handing her a winning lottery ticket. Her eyes filled with tears, exactly as the interviewer had presumably been hoping they would, Callanach thought. She gave each child a hug before wrapping the scarf repeatedly around her neck and proclaiming that she would wear it every single day.

Callanach pressed pause. Emily Balcaskie had been cruelly robbed of her life. Above and beyond that, the children who so obviously adored her would never be able to fathom how the world could be such a barbaric place. The killer couldn't have chosen a more archetypally perfect human being.

Returning to the search engine, Callanach cleared the box and typed in 'Michael Swan'. This time, he found what he'd been looking for much sooner, in the form of a newspaper article from Edinburgh's local press.

'Mr Michael Swan of Craigentinny Ave, Edinburgh, has been nominated in recognition of his many years of support for the city's child literacy programme. He is a volunteer librarian at the McDonald Road library and a keen golfer. Mr Swan is described in his nomination as one of our community's finest assets who works tirelessly to improve the prospects of those in our poorest areas.' A photograph of Michael Swan was included, standing with one arm around his wife, holding up a silver cup at the golf club directly behind his house.

Callanach went back to the search engine, omitted Emily Balcaskie's name, and simply wrote, 'Edinburgh primary school teacher'. This time the first article listed was the link to the footage he'd already watched of Emily's nomination for the Teacher Awards. He was in the process of typing, 'Edinburgh librarian' when there was a knock at his office door.

'Not now,' Callanach shouted.

'It's DC Tripp,' a voice came back. 'The superintendent said I should see you, sir.'

'Fine, come in,' Callanach shouted, misspelling his search terms and starting again. Tripp tried the door and ended up simply rattling the handle. Callanach marched over to unlock the door.

'Sorry, sir, I didn't know it was such a bad time,' Tripp said.

'Wait there,' Callanach barked, racing back to his screen. 'I've fucking got it,' he said, reading the first entry. It was the article he'd just been reading about Michael Swan and the child literacy programme. 'Tripp, what was Helen Lott's job title again? Her nursing specialisation.'

'Palliative care. Linked to one of the city hospices, I think. I didn't have much to do with that one. It was about when I got transferred to DCI Edgar's team. Actually that's what I've come to talk to you about, sir . . .'

'Helen Lott was given a long service medal. If you type in her job description and add the word "Edinburgh", you get a few job adverts and some general information, but the first press piece you get is about her, even without typing in her name.'

Tripp followed where Callanach was pointing and skim-read down the screen.

'And the relevance?' Tripp asked.

'Same goes for all of them,' Callanach said, 'except Sim Thorburn, I haven't checked him out yet. But there's prominent,

112

recent media coverage of Lott, Swan and Balcaskie. Easy to find. Enough information for them to be located and stalked. A kid could have done it.'

'Okay, that's the how, but it doesn't explain why they were chosen as targets in the first place,' Tripp said. 'Were all the press pieces written by the same writer, same paper?' Callanach shook his head. 'Same awards ceremony?'

'No, but the connection is the victims' roles in the community. They all do jobs that benefit other people, work that requires a caring attitude. They're all good people and because of that they've each come to the attention of the media. The murders aren't impulsive. They require a knowledge of each victim's movements, interests, where they work, where they live. Not one of them has been randomly grabbed off the street, not even Emily Balcaskie. The scarf she was strangled with meant a lot to her. The fact that it was used to kill her was symbolic. It was part of the defilement.'

'Do you want me to get working on it, sir? Maybe there are more articles that will give us better information . . .'

'You're on loan to DCI Edgar, Tripp. I have no say in it. Even with us short-staffed, the superintendent still wants Scotland Yard to be given whatever assistance they ask for.'

'The superintendent released me. The cyber crime unit has made enough progress that it was felt you needed me more. They've obtained information on an internet security company it's thought may employ a key suspect. DCI Edgar said that was all the local help they needed, so I'm free to go.'

'Patronising bastard,' Callanach muttered, typing furiously on the laptop.

'I'm not sure I'm allowed to comment on that, sir. He doesn't seem to have made a lot of friends here though. Except DI Turner. They've been disappearing off together almost every evening after work.'

'Every evening?' Callanach asked, turning around to look at Tripp.

'Well, every evening I was still around to notice . . .' The computer binged loudly. 'There you go,' Tripp said, looking over Callanach's shoulder. 'Confirms what you thought.'

Callanach turned his attention back to the screen where a large rainbow graphic was loading with text running down the centre. More blog entry titles were listed on a menu to the left, with links to a Twitter account, Facebook page and Instagram. The writer was tirelessly committed to blogging and campaigning for human rights, charities and social injustice. Callanach scrolled down. At the very bottom of the page was a photograph of the writer. Grinning broadly in what looked like an African village, bare-chested in life as he had been at the point of death, was the author, Sim Thorburn.

'What did you type in?' Tripp asked.

'Charity worker, Edinburgh,' Callanach said, reaching out for the graffiti photos sitting on his desk. 'I used exactly the words that were painted on the wall. And the last blog on his page was about the music festival he was due to attend.'

Chapter Sixteen

Ava was at her desk at midnight when Callanach finally got through the queue of people needing her attention. Tripp had already given her the relevant internet searches and graffiti photos. There were bags under her eyes and her clothes were crumpled. Callanach handed her a large bag of salted popcorn from a nearby newsagent, and sat down with a coffee.

'Why the popcorn?' she asked, even that failing to bring a smile to her face.

'I'm guessing all cinema trips for the foreseeable future are cancelled. You must be having withdrawal symptoms by now.' Ava set it aside unopened. Callanach looked at the baggy sleeves of her shirt and at the way her jawbone and cheekbones were showing in the harsh electric light. 'You're losing weight,' he said.

'Who's got time to eat?' she asked, lining up the graffiti photos along her desk.

'Are you ill?' Callanach asked.

'What I am is busy. Tell me about the photos,' she said.

Callanach recapped.

'I've already contacted a handwriting expert regarding the

graffiti but there's nothing they can do without an imprint made on paper, plus it's in capitals and spray painted, so the usual handwriting rules don't apply. All the paint types are common enough to be found in any DIY store. I think it's the way the victims are being sourced that's the link between them,' Callanach said.

'But it's not one killer,' Ava replied. 'Sim Thorburn was killed by someone short and slight, we know that from the video footage at the festival. The only reliable witness we have in Emily Balcaskie's case made it clear that we're dealing with someone taller than average who is heavily built and strong with it. I take it you're no further forward with the Michael Swan investigation?'

'Ailsa Lambert suspects that the blade used to kill Thorburn might have been taken from the same batch of blades used to skin Michael Swan's face. There are similarities in the scoring pattern along one edge of the incisions.'

'Great,' Ava pushed the photos away and threw her head back, closing her eyes. 'So we have either two or three killers. We're not sure which. But definitely not just one.'

'Would one be better?' Callanach asked, taking a sip of coffee.

'Don't be flippant,' Ava said. 'You know that's not what I meant.'

Callanach took a breath. He wasn't there to get into conflict with Ava. Everyone was fighting for the same team and yet it seemed as if none of them could pull together to make progress at the moment.

'Have we got anywhere on the leaking of photos to the press? They must have been taken by the killer. Tracing his phone or computer may be the only direct link we'll get,' Callanach said.

'You know what the police digital technology department is like. We're always a step behind because we can't afford to pay the rates available in the private sector. The kids who can crack this stuff don't want to work for the Government on basic pay structure,' Ava sighed again. 'It was an encrypted file routed through multiple machines, outside of the UK. That's as much as we're going to get.'

'That's not all we've got,' Callanach said. 'There's the leaked autopsy report from Helen Lott's death. That sort of data leak leaves a trail; we just need someone with the right skills to follow it. More importantly, it looks as if one of the graffiti comments referencing a primary school teacher was written prior to Emily Balcaskie's body being discovered.'

Ava looked confused. 'That's not possible.'

'There were photos taken immediately after her identity was made known at the press conference. There wasn't time for that graffiti to have been left and then for other people to have painted over the top.'

'Are you suggesting that having murdered Emily, her killer went straight to some wall and wrote her profession on it? Like some new take on a trophy?'

'All the evidence is circumstantial,' Callanach said, 'but actually I think the victim's job description was posted before she was killed. Quite a while before, looking at the state of the graffiti painted over it.'

Ava shifted her shoulders up and down, exercising out the hours spent at her desk. 'Spell your theory out for me, Callanach, because it's late and I'm just not following.'

'I think Emily's killer left a clue about his next victim, possibly days in advance. Figure out how, when and why, and maybe we can stop this. Until then, all we can do is watch the walls and stay a step ahead.'

Ava's door opened and Edgar walked in. He said nothing as he passed Callanach, going directly to Ava's desk and setting down several cartons of food, pulling a bottle of wine from another bag.

'I'd invite you to join us, Detective Inspector,' Edgar said, 'only I'm sure you've somewhere you'd rather be than here. Did your constable report back to you? I released him. Seems the Major Investigation Team is struggling somewhat.'

'Lay off, Joe,' Ava said, ripping off a lid and tucking into a steaming pile of rice.

'Darling, do you mind? We have to maintain the system of rank while we're at work.'

'Luc, I'm sorry. That was really helpful. Can we pick up here first thing in the morning?' Ava asked.

'Sure,' Callanach said, getting to his feet. 'In the meantime, we have concealed CCTV cameras set on all the known areas of graffiti, with twenty-four hour surveillance. How's your hacker investigation going, sir? Have those bankers and share-holders got their money back from the charities yet?'

DCI Edgar finished pouring a glass of wine and handed it to Ava.

'There should be arrests in about two weeks. We've established some contacts, made covert enquiries. My team is gathering intelligence without making our presence obvious. Careful, planned, professional work, DI Callanach. The people we're dealing with are some of the finest minds in the world. You can't rush in and blunder around. That's why I was sent up here. Local forces just aren't equipped for this level of work,' Edgar said, standing up to face Callanach directly.

'That would be my local force, and honestly I think it's equipped to deal with just about anything that's thrown at it. I seem to have lost my appetite,' Ava said, pushing the largely untouched cartons away and draining her glass. 'So I'm off. I think that's about all the bullshit I'm prepared to tolerate for one day.' She put on her coat and picked up her car keys. 'I'll see you two tomorrow.'

'Are you not staying at mine?' Edgar said. 'I had housekeeping come in especially.'

Ava paused briefly at her door, with a backwards half glance at Callanach.

'I think I need to be alone,' she said.

Callanach arrived home at 2 a.m., starving and exhausted, to a note pinned on his door. Unlocking the door as soundlessly as he could, he stepped inside before opening the note.

'Hey Luc, got some pals coming over for a few bottles and some pizza. I'd love it if you joined us – they're dying to meet you. Bunny xxx.' Callanach screwed it up and threw it away. He wasn't in the mood for his enthusiastic neighbour, and he certainly wasn't in the mood to meet any of her friends. It was entirely possible that they were still across the corridor, so he decided to forgo cooking, showering or any other giveaways signalling his presence, and fall directly into bed.

Between the sheets he shifted from side to side, throwing the covers off then pulling them back over, realising his brain wasn't as tired as his body. Trying to read was futile. His eyes wandered over the same words a few times before he admitted defeat. Finally, he picked up his phone and began trawling the internet again, looking for articles he'd missed that might link the victims.

After a few failed searches, he ended up reading a piece about The Unsung's recent hack. Most of it was standard factual reporting, but some keen journalist had gone to Edinburgh's leading internet security company, CyberBallista, for a comment about how such a breach would have been organised and the complexity of unscrambling the hack in order to find the cyber attackers. CEO of CyberBallista, Ralph Hogg, had given a predictably tech-heavy, complex response designed to keep their clients believing they were getting good value for the vast amounts they were paying to remain unhacked. As uninteresting as DCI Edgar's efforts to recoup very rich people's

119

spending money were, the article gave Callanach an idea. He dialled Tripp's number.

'This is Max,' a muffled voice said.

'Callanach here,' he replied

'Oh shit, I mean, sorry sir. God, what time is it?' Tripp asked.

'Go into the other room, Max. I've got to get up for work in three hours,' another deeper voice rumbled in the background. Callanach hadn't stopped to consider either the hour or his detective constable's private life.

'Listen, Tripp, I apologise, it's 3 a.m. I'll call back in daylight.'

'That's all right,' Tripp whispered. In the background, Callanach could hear footsteps and a door open and close. Tripp's voice gained some normality. 'What do you need?'

'You've been working with DCI Edgar's unit. I need access to someone inside CyberBallista who can get to the source of the Emily Balcaskie photo email and the autopsy leaks. Do you have a name? Only I'd like to get on it first thing tomorrow morning.'

'I'm not supposed to talk to anyone about that investigation, sir. DCI Edgar was very clear that it was beyond normal security remit. No emails, no texts, nothing that could be traced online if the hackers were following our investigation. Specifically, no discussing it with anyone else at the station.'

'That's ridiculous. We're all working to the same ends. I'm a senior officer and all I need is a heads-up about the best person to talk to. You must have some idea.'

'I'll lose my job, that's what DCI Edgar said. Told me to forget any previous loyalties and understand the value of what we were doing.'

'Four people are dead. Westminster's interest in protecting its international finance industry has to take second place. The investigation's at a standstill.'

Tripp was silent on the other end of the phone. Callanach

had never known him be anything other than at his most helpful. It was the way he was built – endless enthusiasm, absolute devotion to the job. It was unthinkable that he wouldn't be motivated to help.

'Sir, it's difficult enough in my situation. I do my best to work hard and keep everyone off my case. I don't want any more attention than is necessary.'

It took Callanach a few seconds to figure out what Tripp was talking about, before remembering the voice in the background when he'd phoned. Being a gay man in the Scottish police force, in any police force for that matter, wasn't easy. In spite of much greater tolerance than the previous generation had experienced, there was still an amount of macho inanity to wade through each day. Tripp managed it by being something else – the good lad, slightly geeky, always first to volunteer – now it made sense. Better that, than people focusing on other aspects of his personality.

'That's all right, Max,' Callanach said. 'If you've been told to prioritise confidentiality then that's what you should do. Get some sleep. I'll see you at the station.'

'Sir,' Tripp whispered, 'CyberBallista are the best in Scotland, possibly in the whole of the UK, but you can't talk to them. DCI Edgar wants absolute distance between police and industry professionals.'

'I get it,' Callanach said, moving his mobile away from his ear.

'No, sir, I don't think you . . .' Tripp was saying as Callanach ended the call. DCI Edgar was a control freak. The only way Callanach could approach CyberBallista on the record would be with Edgar's permission and Callanach was damned if he was going to crawl to him.

He brought up the CyberBallista website, trawling through the 'Our People' section until he found Ben Paulson, head of Deep Web Navigation Systems. Paulson had an impressive CV.

Callanach recognised the names of most of the companies he'd worked for, even if he didn't seem to stay in one place very long. More important than that were the press reports the search engine brought up. A trade magazine from the tech sector two years ago called Paulson, 'a programmer with a once-in-a-generation intellect that makes the rest of the team useful for nothing but filling up seats at the table'. His industry peers had voted him, 'Most Likely to Change the Future of Tech' when he was just nineteen years old. There was another article which detailed exactly how Paulson had prevented the hacking of a global pharmaceutical company's database, leading investigators directly back to a Russian gang. Callanach had glazed over before reading to the end of the paragraph defining how that had been possible, but Paulson sounded like exactly the person he needed. Someone who could find their way around parts of the internet hidden to the vast majority. If he couldn't approach Ben Paulson directly, then he'd find a way to ask for his help privately. Edgar would never need to know, and that meant keeping it from Ava as well. It wouldn't be fair to ask her to keep secrets from her bedfellow.

Chapter Seventeen

At 9 a.m. Callanach headed over to Leith Street. He knew the building he was searching for by its proximity to Ava's favourite cinema. The modern glass and steel construction housed multiple companies. The one claiming the prestigious top floor, overlooking Leith Street to the front and Greenside Row at its rear, belonged to CyberBallista. Approaching through the front door was asking for trouble so Callanach drove into the multi-storey car park below, buzzed security who were conscientious enough to go down and check his badge, then made his way up to reception level.

From there, rather than going on record with the receptionist, Callanach headed for the toilets and dialled CyberBallista's number, asking for Ben Paulson. There was a pause as the receptionist tried to connect him, then came back on the line.

'Mr Paulson's busy at the moment. I can take your number and ask him to call you back.'

'I need to speak with him immediately,' Callanach said. 'It's regarding his vehicle. If I can't talk to Mr Paulson I'll have to telephone the police to follow it up.'

'One moment,' she said.

'I haven't been involved in any incidents, so I strongly encourage you not to try to scam me. You've chosen the wrong guy,' was the opener. Ben Paulson was American, something Callanach hadn't anticipated. West coast drawl, slightly gravelly. It was a complete contradiction of all the stereotypes he'd drawn up in his head, expecting something more precise, academic. It may not have been fair, but that was the image he'd always had of computer experts.

'Mr Paulson?' Callanach checked.

'Obviously,' came the response.

'I'm in the ground floor reception area of your building and I need to talk to you. There's no problem with your vehicle but I am a police officer. This is off the record, so I'd rather not sign in and come up, if you don't mind.'

'If this is a company matter you'll need to speak to the CEO. All enquiries go through him.'

'It's a private matter,' Callanach said, ready for the stonewalling. No one wanted to speak to the police who didn't have to. 'I need your help with an ongoing case.'

'That doesn't explain the cloak-and-dagger approach. What is it that's keeping you from getting in the lift and coming up to the top floor?' Ben asked.

'Internet security has been getting a bit of bad press lately. Your CEO was on the news talking about it.'

'Two minutes,' Ben said, putting down the phone.

Callanach had expected more of a fight or at least a request to be more convincing. In exactly the time specified, his mobile rang again. The call was from a withheld number.

'Car park, two floors down. Silver Audi in the far corner opposite the lifts,' Ben said. Callanach found the car complete with occupied driving seat. Approaching the driver's side, he found the window wound down a couple of inches. 'Show me your identification,' Ben said. Callanach took out his badge and held it to the window where Ben photographed it before checking Callanach out online. 'Get in,' Ben said, unlocking the front passenger door.

Callanach slid in, ill at ease with the level of suspicion his visit to Ben Paulson had elicited. If he'd made Ben too uncomfortable, there might be a complaint to the superintendent.

'I'm recording this conversation, Detective Inspector Callanach, so we're going to confirm at the outset that you're not showing me any warrant, that I'm not under arrest and that I've not been read my rights,' Ben said. The photo on the company website hadn't done him justice. He was blond, tanned in spite of the Scottish weather, and in good physical shape. Overall, he presented as more likely to be at home on a beach carrying a surfboard, than at a desk worrying about protecting company databases.

'I agree,' Callanach said. 'All of the aforementioned is correct. But I'm here unofficially and I was hoping you'd agree to keep this quiet, too.'

'So you're not here about any hacking allegations, then? Let's just be clear about that.'

Callanach cursed. The conversation was being recorded and he was way off limits. Everything DCI Edgar's team was doing was supposed to be under wraps. Saying nothing about it at all seemed to be the only way forward.

'I'm here about the recent murders in the city. You must have heard about them.'

'Even my distant relatives in San Diego have heard about them. Never thought America would be the safer option compared with Scotland.' Ben was joking but his face was hard, unreadable. 'So you'll confirm that nothing you're going to ask me in any way involves the recent internet security breaches? Only it seems odd that you need help on a murder case but you can't approach CyberBallista directly.'

Callanach was stuck. This man wasn't stupid enough to be fobbed off.

'There are obviously investigations underway into the hacking – not that I'm anything to do with that – but there's evidence I need expert help to understand, and I won't get permission to engage CyberBallista directly at the moment. I can't say anything more.'

'Why me?' Ben asked.

'You're CyberBallista's head of Deep Web, and by all accounts there's no one better than you at your job. I need to trace a pathway that an email took and identify the sender. It's too well encrypted for our internal department to unravel. You looked like my best chance. If I have to go elsewhere it's just additional time, more costs we don't have the budget for, and red tape sending away confidential hard drives.' Ben said nothing. 'I know I'm asking a lot. I can pay you something, not as much as your firm would charge, and it'll be from private funds, but I need you to look into two discrete incidents. It shouldn't take long.'

'You have no idea how long it could take,' Ben said, switching his phone off and sitting back in his seat. He glanced at his watch. 'Sum it up for me.'

Callanach took a breath. He was about to disclose sensitive information to a man he had no basis for trusting. True, he must have been vetted by CyberBallista as he obviously had access to some highly confidential data, but that didn't mean he was beyond corruption. The real question was what other options did he have? There wasn't enough money to engage CyberBallista's services as a company, someone was leaking information, which meant he wasn't sure who could be trusted any more, and every other pathway on the investigation seemed to be blocked. It was proper procedure versus practicality. Practicality won.

'This is confidential information,' Callanach said. 'I need you to promise me I can trust you with it.'

'I'm still sitting here listening,' Ben said. 'Don't push your luck.'

Callanach sighed. 'Photos of Emily Balcaskie's dead body were leaked. They must have been taken by the killer. He wanted the press to get them before we could get a lid on it. All too well encoded for us to trace. Then there was a leaked autopsy report, only I can't believe anyone from either the mortuary or the police would have done that, and our internal investigation has reached a dead end. I think someone from outside went into the computer system and gained access to the report illegally.'

'Why should I help you?' Ben asked, but it wasn't bluster. His shoulders were down and his tone was enquiring rather than angry.

'Because you can,' Callanach said. 'And because I can't understand anyone not wanting to help if it was within their power. So will you?'

'I can't do it from work. Everything we do here is trackable. And my place is private. Get me access to one of the email accounts the photos were sent to. We'll start from there. Don't expect miracles. I'm a long way ahead of Police Scotland's abilities, but there are ways of cloaking these things that are foolproof.'

'Give me your mobile number,' Callanach said. 'I'll text you an address later. I just need to check it out first. There's someone who should be able to help.'

Ben took a second mobile from his pocket and transferred Callanach's number into its memory. A second later, Callanach's mobile buzzed.

'There you go,' Ben said. 'You can use that number for messages. I don't take calls or emails on it though, so don't try. And it's not traceable, triangulation has been disabled.'

Ben's guard was up again. He hadn't wanted to give out his mobile number and Callanach couldn't blame him. It hadn't exactly been a normal morning, and getting involved in tracing a now globally notorious murderer was enough to make anyone feel defensive.

An hour later, Callanach arrived back at the station. He walked into the middle of a conversation, as only DS Lively could conduct it.

'Oh, he's back in the fuckin' building, is he? Hard to believe he's bothered turning up at all . . .' Lively was mouthing off in the incident room.

'Right behind you, Sergeant,' Callanach said, well aware how little good it would do to discipline the veteran officer who had something of a fan club amongst the older generation of Police Scotland's finest. 'Opinions on your own time.'

'We've been waiting,' Lively said, not the least bit concerned at having been overheard.

'Good for you. Presumably there was a reason for that. Would you like to share it?'

'CCTV of the route the killer took between the McDonald Road library and dropping off the books and Michael Swan's belongings at Regent Gardens. Watch.' Lively hit play and the screen showed a blurred image of a person crossing a road, then walking off into the distance. They were clutching a large bundle to their chest, and wearing a floppy-brimmed hat covering all but nose and mouth, hair tucked up inside.

'How do we know that's our suspect?' Callanach asked.

'Early hours, first light, walking alone. Apart from that, there's this,' Lively said. 'It's not great quality but you can definitely make it out.' He pressed play again and a different camera showed the same person further up the same road from a different angle. Almost no part of the walker's face showed, but they dropped an article and bent down quickly to pick it up. 'We can't change the resolution of the shot,' Lively said, 'but the tech boys have been able to enlarge the image. What they got was this.' Lively switched to a closer, blurry still image of the article that had been dropped. On the cover, Callanach could just make out a large green squiggle with a red oval on the end, and the letters 'terpillar'.

'Tell me,' Callanach said.

'It's from *The Very Hungry Caterpillar*, sir,' Lively said. 'Probably not a required text for you geniuses at Interpol, but every kid in Scotland has read it. That's one of the books found at the park with Swan's personals.'

'Best shot of the killer?' Callanach asked, reaching past Lively and getting the CCTV footage back up.

'Don't touch my computer,' Lively grumbled, brushing Callanach's hand away and taking control of the keyboard. 'We've got no definition around the face. No hair showing, no eyes, nothing. But we've got a pretty bloody good view of the profile.' A screen grab appeared of a single frame containing a shadowy profile. What was very clear was that the carrier of the books had a defined bust. 'It's a woman,' Lively said unnecessarily. 'The legs are thin too. Jacket is covering the waistline so we can't see much else, but there's no real doubt.'

'And she picked up that dropped book with her left hand,' Callanach said. 'That's our homicidal maniac. Can we get any more detail from the remaining footage?'

'We should be able to work out her height in comparison to some of the building features in the shot,' Lively said.

'One hour for that, Sergeant, then compare it with the footage of Sim Thorburn. I want the best stills you've got and an analysis to see if there's a match. I'll be in my office.'

Callanach swung past the coffee machine and grimaced as he took a swig of caffeine with a hint of melted plastic. He sat at his desk and dialled Lance Proudfoot's number, getting voicemail.

'Lance, Luc Callanach. I need your help tonight. I have to access your work emails and I need somewhere to do that. Could I bring someone to your office? And I know I need to repay the favour. I have an idea about that too. Call me.'

He was replacing the receiver as Superintendent Overbeck walked in.

'Callanach, update me,' she said, sitting down and stretching out long, nylon-clad legs. Ideal for tripping him up, he thought.

'Michael Swan's murderer was female. We're doing a comparison with the Sim Thorburn case. The body types are similar, and the forensic pathologist already had a theory about the same batch of blades being used,' Callanach said.

'Good, because I need to get the squads better organised. You'll cover the Swan and Thorburn investigations. DI Turner will run the Lott and Balcaskie cases. Limit the overtime, Callanach. I don't want bureaucrats on my back about the overspend.'

'This is an unusual case, ma'am. We need as many officers and as many hours as—'

'It's the same case you were trained to do, and that you're supposed to be doing competently. Don't start acting like it's all impossible just because someone's actually been killed. And it just got markedly easier now that you've two lots of evidence pointing towards one killer. Can you hear the clock ticking, Detective Inspector? Because it sounds pretty frigging loud to me. And if the alarm goes off before you're out of bed and ready with some spectacularly good news, pack your fucking bags. No more officers. Minimal overtime. Do the job you're already being paid to do.'

She walked out. Callanach pondered what was required to be promoted to such a rank. It took him the time to lift his coffee cup from desk to mouth to realise he'd never cut it. His phone buzzed with a text from Lance Proudfoot.

'Come to my home. 7a St. Thomas Road. 8 p.m. – bring beer. Expecting return favour to be substantial. LP.'

Callanach quickly confirmed, then went looking for Ava who was in her office, on her mobile. He waited while she hung up.

'How's Natasha doing?' Callanach asked. She was the only friend of Ava's he'd come to know since moving to Edinburgh.

'Enjoying New Orleans, perhaps too much to bother rushing back,' Ava said. 'It's her birthday today, did you know?' Callanach shook his head. 'We usually have a sleepover on her birthday. It's a throwback to when we were kids. We'd stay up all night watching bad horror flicks and eating junk. This is the first year for a decade that we won't be together.'

'She must be missing you too,' Callanach said.

'I'm glad she's not here. One less person I have to worry about.'

Callanach felt differently. In the months he'd known Natasha since Ava had introduced them, he'd seen how much she and Ava relied on one other. They filled in the gaps that family and work left behind. The two of them communicated as only childhood friends could – a kind word, an embrace, honest advice, a joke, even a reprimand when it was called for. He'd been thrown together with Natasha when she'd become entangled in a previous case. Her steadfastness and stoicism had impressed him then. Now he longed for her to return and have the conversation with Ava he felt uncomfortable even starting.

'Look, tell me it's none of my business if you like, but you and DCI Edgar. He seems an odd choice. When I first came here you were the one person I could count on not to be influenced by rank or class. He's everything I thought you despised.'

131

'You of all people should know that life isn't as simple as we want to believe. I thought I could rely on you not to be judgemental,' Ava said.

'I'm not judging. I just don't get what you think he can offer you, besides the obvious,' Callanach replied.

'Besides the obvious? You think I'm in this for the social and professional gains? Jesus, Luc, I never had you pegged as quite that insulting. Is that what you think of me?'

'Ava, don't. I'm trying to understand what's going on, that's all,' Callanach said.

'Okay, he's from a good family, he's got a good job, and he can order from a menu in French almost as well as you. He may not be a former model, and perhaps he doesn't skydive, but I'm not going to write him off for that,' Ava responded.

'I don't understand why you're making this personal,' Callanach said. Before joining Interpol seven years earlier, he'd spent every weekend with friends enjoying whichever costly leisure activity took their fancy and met their adrenalin-pumping needs. It was a period of his life he considered wasted, surrounded by people whose primary interests were themselves. Since then he'd used sport only for fitness and escapism. His last skydiving trip just a few months ago, however, had earned him a ban from a Scottish drop-zone when he'd elected not to open his parachute manually, relying on the automatic system to save him. He'd been living through some dark days at the time and Ava knew better than to remind him of it. 'You know what? Forget it. I misjudged, that's all.'

'Everywhere I go people load different expectations on me. I'm just trying to find a bit of bloody peace. Is that too much to ask?'

'Not at all.' Callanach stood up. 'Our investigations have been separated. I've got Thorburn and Swan. You've got Lott and Balcaskie. I want Tripp and Salter on my squad. You can choose your guys. No reason for us to overlap. I apologise for whatever I've done to offend you.'

'You can apologise to DCI Edgar as well. You've been out of line,' Ava snapped.

'You want to climb the ladder with your boyfriend, Ava, be my guest. But don't expect me to follow suit. There must be better positions to see the top than from on your back.'

Ava was on her feet in a second. The slap was hard and she didn't flinch when she delivered it. Callanach didn't oblige her with putting his hand to his reddening cheek.

'Get the fuck out of my office right now,' Ava whispered.

'My pleasure,' he said, tearing the door open. Lively was in the corridor, making no secret of the fact that he'd been there some time, leaning against the opposite wall. 'What, Sergeant?' Callanach shouted.

'Same woman, both murders. Matching frame and height. No facial details, she's good at hiding what she doesn't want anyone to see. You all right, sir, only your cheek's a wee bit red?' Lively smirked.

'Prepare a statement. Get as many details together as you can, excluding the book titles so we can eliminate time-wasters. Call the media liaison office and tell them I want a press conference at the end of the day.'

'Should I get you an ice pack first? Only that may look a bit strange on camera. Truth be told, looks like someone just gave you a proper hiding. Will you be making a complaint, sir?'

Callanach leaned in and spoke into his sergeant's ear.

'If you don't get moving right now, I'm going to give you grounds to have me fired, Detective Sergeant Lively. And you'll be making that complaint from a hospital bed.'

Lively started to smile, pulled back to get a better look at Callanach's face, then opted for making no further comment.

★　★　★

Two hours and two ice packs later, Callanach was in front of a roaring crowd of reporters, cameras and microphones. The difference this time was that a second layer of media personnel was in the room. There were translators everywhere, testament to the spread of the story of Edinburgh's rising mortality rate. Callanach wasted no time getting the facts out.

'We don't have a facial photofit, but the woman we'd like to speak with is estimated to be in her late twenties or early thirties, five foot six, slim build. In the footage we have, she's been wearing hats. We have two profile shots we'd like you to circulate please.' As he spoke, the images appeared on a projector. 'Copies will be provided to each of you later. Please include the crime-line number. This is a substantial step forward in the investigation.'

'Detective Inspector, was this woman known to either of the victims or their families?' a journalist shouted, the formality of waiting for questions abandoned.

'Not to our knowledge,' Callanach replied.

'So she just picked them out at random?' another reporter joined in. 'What advice do you have to the people of Edinburgh about staying safe?'

Callanach sighed. He hadn't wanted to get into this, but it was a question he couldn't fail to answer. The graffiti lead was still a live part of the investigation and he didn't want to give it away.

'Our advice would be to only go out around the city whilst accompanied. Avoid The Meadows area. Avoid being out late at night. Take care with personal safety both in public and at home. Check the locks are engaged on your doors and windows. Use alarms where you have them.'

'That's it?' a voice called out. 'Your advice to people is to lock their windows? Detective Inspector, four people are dead. One at home, one at work, one at night and another in the

134

middle of the day in a crowd. Is there anywhere that anyone is safe in Edinburgh at the moment?'

The press liaison officer stood up before Callanach could be dragged to the bottom of that particular public relations mire. 'Please see me on your way out for written copies of the press release, crime-line number and stills for distribution. All other questions via email in the usual way,' she said.

Callanach took his cue and exited through the rear door of the conference room. His mobile was buzzing before he'd even made it back to his desk.

'Monumental fuck-up. No more press cons without me present. Last warning.' Superintendent Overbeck was a delight. Callanach grabbed a folder from his desk and retreated to his car. It was time to make some proper progress.

He stopped on his way to Lance Proudfoot's to pick up a Chinese takeaway and beer. It was worth keeping people's stomachs full when you were asking favours.

He was surprised to find Ben Paulson already inside and working away on Lance's laptop when he arrived. Lance disappeared off to fetch plates and forks while Callanach got comfortable.

'I'd assumed you'd wait for me outside,' Callanach said to Ben, who was typing furiously into a laptop that he'd attached to the journalist's machine.

'I'd rather not be left hanging around on street corners, if you don't mind,' Ben replied as Callanach opened a bottle of beer. 'And I thought you didn't want to be seen with me. Or is there something else going on here?'

Callanach offered Ben a beer which he accepted but put down without drinking from it.

'I don't understand,' Callanach said. 'What else do you think is going on?'

'I need your email password!' Ben shouted to Lance who was clattering in the kitchen.

'Mooncat129,' Lance replied on his way into the lounge. 'I take it I can trust this man, Inspector, only I've just given him the key to my online chastity belt.'

'I'm in,' Ben said. 'It'll take a while to transfer the files to my machine. So tell me, Callanach. Why me? I mean really. That had to be more than a quick hunt through CyberBallista's website.'

'It was exactly that,' Callanach said, piling a plate with noodles and tipping unidentifiable protein strips over the top. 'CyberBallista is supposed to be the best in Scotland for this sort of thing. How did a boy from California end up here? I'd have thought Silicon Valley would have offered better career prospects, not to mention the weather and the cars.'

'Do I need to record this conversation as well, DI Callanach, or shall we just get on with the business at hand? And by the way, this laptop is clean. There'll be nothing on here except this project. No access to anything else of mine,' Ben said, one hand poised on the lid of his laptop as if preparing to close it.

Lance interjected. 'DI Callanach, may I call you Luc? You seem to have a policeman's knack for asking too many questions. This young fellow seems to want to help, so why not stick to discussing the price of eggs? I still have very little idea what's going on. Would anyone care to enlighten me? And that favour you promised isn't going unforgotten.'

'I'm backtracking the path the email took to reach you,' Ben said.

'Surely that's something the police have already tried,' Lance noted. 'Not that I don't appreciate being part of the action, but didn't your boys seize my hard drive for precisely that reason?'

'Between us, they did and they failed. I figured it was worth another go. Was I right?' Callanach asked Ben.

'Your in-house team wouldn't have had a hope in hell,' Ben answered, laughing. 'Did they outsource it?'

'Some company in London had a try. They got further, but said finding any firm information was impossible because of the number of times the email had bounced around the world. I asked for more funding and it was made clear that I was wasting my time.'

'There's no such thing as impossible in computing,' Ben said. 'It's like saying that numbers can be finite. There's always one more. This has been wrapped up tight though, no doubt about it.'

'I love this stuff,' Lance announced, abandoning his plate and sitting down next to Ben. He leaned forward staring at the screen as if the answers were about to appear. 'Explain what you're doing.'

'You can't print my name,' Ben said. 'Not who I work for, nothing. You get it?'

'Let me get this right,' Lance said. 'Neither of you are in my house, drinking beer with me, talking to me and conducting this investigation through my computer. And although I'm a journalist you still both somehow thought this was a fair set-up.'

'I'll leave if it's a problem for you,' Ben said.

'Just pulling your leg, son,' Lance grumbled. 'You were never here. Help me understand how this works.'

Ben pressed a few keys and the screen was suddenly filled with scrolling data. He sat back, hands behind his head, as the programme worked its magic.

'Every email comes marked, a bit like leaving your DNA on an envelope when you lick it and stick it. The problem these days is that you can create false email accounts, steal identities, use throwaway phones – everything is disposable and virtually untraceable. But the email itself is ultimately linked to one IP address – an internet protocol number that's unique to a computer – no matter how many different routes it takes to get to its destination. That's how we know that certain scams originate from Russia, Nigeria, Ireland or wherever.' The laptop pinged. Ben disconnected his machine from Lance's.

'What software are you using?' Callanach asked.

'Nothing you can buy online or pick up nicely packaged in a shop,' Ben answered. 'This guy is good. The email was bouncing around the globe a while before it landed in your inbox, Mr Proudfoot. And it wasn't sent by an amateur. The original sender data was destroyed as soon as the file was opened. Clever trick.'

'*Fils de pute*,' Callanach swore. Son of a bitch. 'So it is a dead end.'

'Not necessarily,' Ben said, tapping away on the keyboard again. 'There may be some geographical markers. I can't get you any personal details, but it was definitely sent from Scotland.'

'Given that the photos were of a dead girl's body in Edinburgh, that's not really news,' Callanach said, head in hands.

'You mentioned something else. Another lead to follow,' Ben reminded him.

'Autopsy details were leaked,' Callanach said. 'But that could have been anyone, either an insider with a grudge, or a hack.'

'Give me a minute,' Ben said, typing at a speed Callanach had never witnessed before.

'I can't give you access to the forensic pathologist's intranet,' Callanach said. 'I'd have to go a long way up the chain of command for that.'

'You seriously think I need permission to get through this pathetic firewall?' Ben asked. 'I'm already into their database.'

'Aren't the files encrypted?' Lance asked.

'They are, but they've used a standard encryption software. That's the problem. Once a code has been written to break down an encryption, you just have to apply the correct code to it. Takes minutes to get into files like this. Governments are the worst offenders for having sloppy digital guards in place. You should see how much more money private corporations spend protecting their data. Here you go. I can see a list of all autopsy reports for the last twelve months. What's the name?' Callanach hesitated. 'It's a bit late to be coy now, Detective Inspector. A twelve-year-old with a half decent brain could have hacked in here. Who's report was it?'

'Helen Lott,' Lance answered. 'There were details about her I haven't seen for any other victims, right Luc?'

Callanach nodded.

'There's an access with no username here. No changes logged. It looks like a computer glitch, but that would've been the entry point.' Ben tapped away again as Callanach joined the two men peering at the screen. 'There you go. It's not evidence, but it is proof. The same identification destruction has been used here. Follow the trail back and you hit a point where the file wipes itself clean like a booby trap, so you can't get a user ID.'

'In plain English?' Lance asked.

'It's not a coincidence. Programming at a certain level never is. Both the leaking of the photos and the hack into the mortuary reports end in the same way, when you chase the original IP address. There's a point when the software recognises that it's being inspected and self-destructs. It's intelligent design. We pushed the self-destruct button ourselves by following the trail.'

'How many people are capable of designing something like that?' Lance asked.

'Globally? Plenty,' Ben said. 'But in Scotland? You're looking for a murderer who has the ability or the connections to do this, as well as the desire and motivation to kill. That's quite some combination. There can't be that many people who fit the description.'

'I need to speak to DI Turner,' Callanach said. 'These two cases were assigned to her this morning. Would you mind meeting with her to explain what you've just told me?' Callanach asked.

'Detective Inspector Ava Turner?' Ben asked.

'Do you know her?' Callanach countered.

Ben slammed down the lid of his laptop, took his first and last swig of beer, and zipped up his coat.

'You know, I came here because I genuinely wanted to help. I gave you the benefit of the doubt through all the questions and I checked you out. Interpol, a fabricated sexual assault charge, an understanding of how the system works against the little man. I thought you just might be genuine. But here you go, using the murders of innocent people to help some big faceless suits. Well, good luck with that, Callanach. You can tell DCI Edgar that it didn't work. I'm not going for a cosy chat with his girlfriend and I'm done being drawn in. You'll have to find a different way. And I have a member of the press to back me up if you start getting creative with anything I've told you tonight, so good fucking luck using that in court.'

He stormed out, banging the door behind him, leaving Callanach and Lance with their mouths gaping. Lance reached for a fresh bottle of beer and popped the top.

'That's quite some talent for pissing people off you have, Luc,' Lance said.

Chapter Eighteen

Callanach drove directly to Tripp's address, needing to ask a question he couldn't put into words. More importantly, he needed Tripp not to attempt to answer it.

It was after ten when he arrived. The door was answered by a man in his early twenties, maybe a year or two younger then Tripp.

'Good evening, I'm Luc Callanach . . .'

'I know who you are,' the man said. 'You'd better come in. Max! Your boss is here.'

Tripp dropped something loudly in another room, looking sheepish as he emerged.

'Sir, is something wrong? I didn't know you were trying to get in touch with me. I'm sure I left my mobile on.'

'I didn't call. I apologise. To you both,' Callanach said.

'Oh, this is Duncan. I normally flat-share with my brother but he's away on business so Duncan's staying a while.'

'You don't have to explain. I have no right to intrude.' Callanach looked over at Duncan who was watching protectively. 'And I apologise for asking this, but could I please talk with you privately?'

'Of course. Duncan, sorry, could you?' Tripp asked.

'Headed for the kettle,' Duncan said. 'Do you want anything?' He looked at Callanach.

'No, but thank you.' Callanach paused while Duncan left then looked straight at Tripp. 'You warned me not to talk to anyone from CyberBallista, only I was too busy worrying about the murders to consider the reasons behind your warning.'

'You mustn't, sir. It's a very close-knit industry and any approach by the police would get around . . .'

'Ben Paulson,' Callanach said. Tripp's eyes widened briefly. Callanach knew the name was exactly the one his detective constable had been hoping not to hear. Tripp began to stutter. Callanach held a hand up to stop him. 'Not one word. You've done nothing wrong. I just had to know. I haven't asked you anything and you've said nothing except that I should stay away from CyberBallista. If there's a backlash, it'll be mine alone.'

'Sir, I might be out of line here but DCI Edgar's a balls-aching bastard. If he finds out you've made contact . . .'

'I've done nothing, Max,' Callanach said. 'So don't worry about DCI Edgar. Forget I was here and apologise to Duncan for me. I'll see myself out.'

Callanach drove slowly, considering whether it was better to go home or detour to Ava's and explain what had happened, risking seeing DCI Edgar. The see-saw landed in favour of keeping Ava out of it, not least because it seemed unlikely he'd get a sympathetic hearing. The slap she'd delivered earlier had been more than justified. He hadn't meant what he'd said. Edgar was just one of those people who wound him up and he'd taken it out on Ava.

Back in his apartment, Callanach kicked off his boots and opened a bottle of wine. He'd had to stick to a driving-appropriate amount of alcohol at Lance's, but not now. Enough was enough. He'd stumbled into the middle of Scotland Yard's hacking investigation, requesting help from the very man the Cyber Crime Unit had pinned as their prime suspect. Tripp's face had made that abundantly clear. More than that, Ben Paulson plainly knew all about it, however clever and quiet Edgar and his squad thought they'd been. Ben was keeping tabs on both the investigation and DCI Edgar, extending to his newly rekindled relationship with Ava. Callanach wondered how much Ben knew about it that he didn't. Had he hacked their emails, their texts? Could he listen to their telephone conversations?

Callanach's mind began to wander, bringing up images of Joe Edgar with Ava. He pushed the thoughts away. It was none of his business what Ava did, or who she did it with. Even if Edgar was the last person on earth he'd have chosen as his friend's partner, that was her business. Callanach downed the glass of wine and poured himself another, halfway through it he heard the voice calling.

'Luc! Are you in? It's Bunny. I thought I heard your door slam, only I've got a package for you.'

Callanach gritted his teeth and opened the door. Bunny was wearing shorts and a T-shirt designed to save on the cost of material. She smiled warmly.

'I haven't seen you for ages!' she said, handing over a large brown envelope. 'I left you a note about a party I had. Sorry you couldn't make it.' She looked over his shoulder into the apartment. 'Have I called at a bad time?' she asked. 'I saw you on the news tonight. I felt awful for you with those reporters giving you a hard time. Honestly, they've no idea how hard you must be working. Did you eat? Only I could fix you something in a couple of minutes. It's no bother.'

'I was just off to bed,' Callanach said. 'Perhaps another time.'

'I've got no plans tomorrow night,' Bunny said, leaning against his doorway. 'And I don't mind cooking. What's your favourite? I do a mean steak and chips.'

'I can't make plans in the middle of an investigation,' Callanach said, glancing at his watch, wanting only to go back to his wine. 'I never know what time I'll be home. Maybe when this is over.'

'Sure, that's more sensible. But if you need anything, I can always grab you a few bits from the supermarket, or put the vacuum round for you. You can leave a key at mine if you like.'

'I prefer my privacy,' Callanach said. Bunny's cheeks reddened. It had come out as a reprimand and he was in no mood to bother trying to retract. 'Thanks for the package. I'll see you some time.'

He took a step backwards and shut the door. A couple of seconds later he heard Bunny's slow footsteps as she went back to her own apartment. He dialled Ava's number, thought better of it and cut the call off, then grabbed the wine bottle and took it to his bedroom. However much he tried to drink his memory blank on the subject of his clash with Ava, alcohol wasn't a strong enough drug. Remembering it was Natasha's birthday, Callanach did the next best thing to speaking with Ava herself and called Natasha instead.

The dialling tone wasn't what he'd expected. Too late he realised he was phoning her in New Orleans with absolutely no idea what time it was in the southern USA.

'Luc?' Natasha said. 'What's happened? Is Ava okay?'

'How did you know it was me?' he asked, wondering why it was such an effort to speak and sit up straight.

'Your name came up on my mobile. I'm pretty sure yours works the same way,' Natasha laughed. 'It's 11 p.m. in Scotland. Are you all right?'

'Just wanted to say happy birthday,' he said, rubbing his eyes.

'You're slurring. Are you drunk? Is Ava with you?'

'No,' Callanach said. 'Ava's with Detective Chief Inspector Dickhead, did I say that right?'

'Your Scottish swearing has improved, then,' Natasha said. 'I'd forgotten Joe was around. You're not a fan?'

'I hadn't even noticed him,' Callanach said, finishing what little was left in the bottom of his glass.

Natasha sighed. He could hear her taking in a slow breath.

'Have you spoken to her, Luc?' she asked.

'Not since she slapped me this morning, no. I don't think she's in the mood for me right now.'

'She's under a lot of pressure at the moment. I think this thing with Joe is just a symptom of that.'

'Four dead bodies, Tasha. Terrible murders. Ava's right, I'm glad you're away from here too. I just called to wish you a happy birthday.' Callanach let himself fall back onto the pillow. He was finally ready to sleep.

'You already said that, but you need to listen to me. I can't speak for Ava – she's very private about what goes on in her life. Give her some time. She needs you, Luc. And I know how you feel about her.'

'Doesn't need me any more, made that totally clear today. Forget it. Stay away until this is over. The city's not safe.'

'I appreciate the concern, but I'm more worried about you. Shall I speak to Ava? She'd hate it if she knew you were this upset,' Natasha said.

'No,' Callanach murmured. 'There's nothing to sort out. I'm glad she's found someone.' He ended the call, threw his mobile onto the floor and rolled over. Next to him on the bed was the envelope Bunny had delivered. Yet another apology he'd need to make tomorrow. He was amassing enemies much faster than he was making progress on the case.

Ripping the paper apart, he pulled out a slim cardboard box, inside which was a plastic and foil press-out board containing long blue pills. He pitched them against the wall and closed his eyes. The tablets that were his last-ditch attempt at over-coming his impotence had finally arrived, and he had absolutely no idea why he'd ever bothered ordering them.

Chapter Nineteen

The next morning brought little relief from the media storm and public pressure. A man seen pulling a young woman into a car had been badly beaten by vigilantes, his injuries not life-threatening but serious. On arrest, his attackers claimed the man fitted the description of Emily Balcaskie's murderer and that they were thwarting another killing. To be fair, at 6'3" and heavily built, the man did fit the general description released by Police Scotland to the press. What his attackers didn't know, was that the man in question was pulling his incredibly drunk, underage daughter into his car before she disappeared off for the night with a man twice her age, who was a known pimp. Callanach suspected there would be a reasonable amount of post-incident discussion between the victim and his daughter once he was fit enough to talk again.

Panicky reports were being called in at all hours of the day and night. People who thought they'd seen someone carrying a knife. Those who lived alone and heard noises in the dark. Workers staying late in offices who saw a strange face at the window. No pattern to the crimes meant that no one felt safe anywhere, and the amount of mistaken reporting was making real progress all but impossible. There just weren't enough ears for the phones or boots for the groundwork.

As much as Callanach wanted to stay out of Ava's way, he'd blundered into her investigation and had facts that might help. He'd put off seeing her as long as he could, but by 11 a.m. there was nowhere left to hide. He knocked her door.

'Come in,' she called, looking up. Her face said it all. 'Not in the mood. And if you're expecting an apology for the slap, then you can—'

'I should buy you dinner for slapping me,' Callanach said. 'It was a fraction of what I deserved. A less restrained woman would have followed it up with a knee.'

Ava glared and bit her bottom lip, fighting the upturning corners of her lips.

'I'll remember that for next time,' she said.

'I'm not sure when we stopped being able to have a civil conversation but I'd like to think it's not irreversible. This thing that's happening, it's getting to everyone. My squad are tense and defensive – it feels as if Edinburgh's streets are under attack. I called Natasha last night,' he said.

'What did she tell you?' Ava leaned forward.

'Only what I already knew. That you're under tremendous stress with these cases. That's why I'm here. I have a source, a journalist. He's investigating the murders and has shared some information. The software used to stop the Emily Balcaskie email being traced ran on home-made code, signature work. The same code was used to prevent anyone from tracking whoever got into Helen Lott's autopsy report. And that report was definitely hacked, rather than leaked.'

'How do you know all this?' Ava asked, walking to the whiteboard on her wall.

'I told you, I know a journalist . . .'

'Who did the journalist get it from? That's not readily accessible information.'

Callanach had reached a decision about what he was prepared to say well in advance. He didn't skip a beat. 'The source is anonymous and will remain so, but it's from an expert. I've no reason to doubt the veracity of the claim.'

'We've had people analyse this, Luc. No one else could confirm that it was the same person involved in both incidents. You'll have to disclose your source to verify.'

'I don't have the information to give. I was just trying to help. How's Joe's hacker investigation going, by the way?' He'd promised himself he wouldn't ask. He wasn't even sure he wanted to know, but now that the box was open Callanach found himself incapable of closing it. 'Have they named any suspects yet?'

'I think it best we steer away from the subject of Joe, don't you? It's not exactly common ground,' Ava said.

'I've been an idiot about it. I think I was feeling protective. And maybe a little jealous of having my drinking mate stolen.' Callanach delivered a smile he didn't feel. Ava didn't return it.

'This thing with Joe – it's complicated,' she said. 'I know you don't think he's my type and it's sudden, but the timing's right. Anyway, Joe doesn't speak to me about his investigation so you shouldn't feel out of the loop. Security on this one's tighter than MI5's Christmas party list.'

'Really? They've managed to keep a team here with no information getting spilled at all? That is impressive,' Callanach said.

'The usual generic info is out. The hackers they're looking for, The Unsung, seem to be an international group. It's only their main man who's based here. No names yet though. Joe's paranoid that they're even able to get into internal police communications. No arrests yet and this was supposed to have been a done deal by now.'

'That's tough,' Callanach said, fraudulent sympathy on his face. 'Still, at least it means he'll be around longer for you.' He stood up.

Ava scribbled a couple of notes on her board, a shorthand version of the information Callanach had shared, then put the pen down.

'Do you mean that?' she asked. 'Only I thought you might . . .' her voice trailed off into a distracted silence.

Callanach prompted her. 'You thought I might what?' he asked.

'Um, I thought you might feel like a movie late tonight. If you're okay with the Joe thing now. I'll text you the details later, okay?'

'I'd like that,' Callanach said, making for the door. He couldn't escape the feeling that he and Ava were avoiding having a real conversation. They used to find it easy to talk. Nothing fake. Nothing formal. Lately she'd been different in a way he couldn't put his finger on. Perhaps it really was the stress of the investigation. Or maybe Joe's appearance had made Ava view her own life differently. At least later he'd have the chance to see if they could salvage some of the closeness they'd once shared.

An hour later Ava sent a text with details for them to meet that evening. Callanach slogged through a few piles of paperwork, issuing orders to keep momentum on the investigations, but everyone knew they were flagging. So many murder cases involved perpetrators and victims who were known to one another. That was the well-trodden path that usually led the police to an arrest. Violent deaths involving strangers were rare, and unless there was a DNA match on the database or an eyewitness, it was hard to make ground.

At 11 p.m., Callanach found himself waiting outside the cinema where he and Ava watched occasional reruns of old movies. Only late at night, of course, when most of the viewing public was either in bed or in bars. Tonight's offering was Alfred Hitchcock's *North by Northwest*.

'No popcorn tonight?' Callanach asked as they sat down.

'I'm not hungry,' she said, pulling out a hip flask and separating two metal caps. She handed one to Callanach and kept one herself. It wasn't like her to be drinking midweek, mid-case. Callanach had been amazed at her self-discipline since he'd joined Police Scotland. Tonight, she filled each cap with single malt and began sipping hers as she settled back with her feet up on the seat in front, the absence of any other viewers meaning they wouldn't get any complaints about either the whiskey or blocking anyone else's view.

Cary Grant had witnessed a man being murdered in a restaurant, and unwittingly made himself a suspect, when Ava leaned over to whisper in Callanach's ear.

'Why are these people being killed?' she asked.

For a moment Callanach wondered if she was referring to the film or to their respective cases. It was Ava's golden rule that no one spoke during the movie. He'd never known her break it and he'd been told off by her a few times for doing the same.

'You mean why now, in Edinburgh?' he asked. Ava nodded. 'I don't know. Your killer is male. Perhaps it's a sexual thing. Power, dominance, woman-hater. The amount of force he's using suggests a level of psychosis.'

'But your murderer's female,' Ava said. 'She's choosing diverse victims, making an art form of it. The graffiti about the victim being a primary school teacher in my case was there before the killing. So it was what? An assassination? Doesn't make sense. If you want a specific victim dead, you name them. You pass an envelope of used notes to a person whose identity you never really know and you leave them to do their job. Was this the killer boasting, or trying to get caught before he did the act?'

She sank back down in her seat. Callanach didn't have the answers. The same questions had been rolling around inside his head in a constant cycle. They returned their attention to the screen. After a train journey and some intimate moments between Cary Grant and Eva Marie Saint, Ava refilled their caps and began drinking again.

'Two killers appear at the same time. Two victims each. This damned graffiti making such a public display of it all. Is this some new form of domestic terrorism? Keeping it in our faces? Undermining our internal security?' Ava said.

'If it was an organised group someone would have claimed it by now, although it's psychological terrorism at its best. We can't keep up with all the calls, people offering information which has no link to the crimes,' Callanach responded.

Ava sighed. She sounded lost. Callanach wished the burden they were sharing was going to be an easier one to shift, but there were four dead bodies in the city mortuary. Wishing was an exercise in futility.

Setting her whisky down, Ava shifted in her seat and leaned her head against Callanach's shoulder. He had to stop himself from flinching, not from the contact with her, although for a long time after the rape allegation he'd struggled to let anyone physically close. It was her. Ava was the definition of independence and self-possession. She'd never leaned on him at all, neither literally nor figuratively. Not when she'd had difficult days at work, not when she'd been suspended during disciplinary action, not even after she'd been abducted by a deluded psychopath. Her chosen way through all of that had been to show even more steel, even greater humour and self-sufficiency. This one tiny act, as trifling and momentary as it was, was unlike her to an extreme. Callanach closed his eyes. Ava's head was heavy on his shoulder. He felt strange, as if one weight was lifting while another was settling. She lifted her head and looked at him.

'And the victims,' Ava carried on as if there'd been no pause in the conversation. 'All exemplary people, not so much as a driving conviction between them, unless they're all members of some bizarre secret cult. The killers went out of their way to choose the most righteous people, not just to be murdered, but to be murdered as hideously and violently as they could possibly conceive. It's like they're competing with each other, for Christ's sake.' In the silence Callanach tried to shake the image of Ava's head on his shoulder. She picked up the cap and tossed back the remnants of her single malt.

'So the graffiti is what then? A declaration of their next target?' Callanach asked.

'Could be,' Ava said. 'Stating their chosen victim type, so there's no mistake about whose work it is. Come on, we can't do this here. Let's go back to mine.'

They left James Mason losing his temper and hustled out of the door. A taxi ride later and they were at Ava's house. She went directly to the kitchen and poured more whisky. Callanach put his down untouched.

'So either they're communicating somehow, or they already know each other on a personal level,' Ava said.

'Two psychopaths agreeing a plan? There'd have to be a more substantial link. They could have met through the Probation Service? Or a therapist?' Callanach suggested.

'There would be records, a professional who knew them both. If a probation officer or a psychiatrist suspected anything, they'd have come forward by now. And we have Helen Lott's killer's DNA. He's not on the UK database. What are the odds of a killer this violent having no police record at all?'

'About the same as the odds of two murderers being in the same city at the same time and communicating,' Callanach said.

'You think maybe it's a couples thing? That they work together? A modern day Brady and Hindley? I didn't think I'd

153

ever see evil like that first-hand.' Ava kicked a couple of pairs of trainers out of the way and shifted a pile of washing so she could lie on the sofa. Her place was a mess. Not that she normally put tidiness before getting on with living, but there was a lack of care about the place. As if she no longer did anything but walk in and out occasionally.

Perhaps that was because she was spending her time at DCI Edgar's, Callanach thought. Between her new relationship and the demands of the current caseload, it wasn't really surprising that nothing seemed normal. The thought of Joe Edgar made Callanach uncomfortable again. He stood up.

'Don't move,' he told Ava, picking up a blanket from an armchair and passing it to her. 'You look comfortable. I'll see myself out. Let's think this over tonight. See if we can't move it forward tomorrow. I enjoyed what bits of the film I saw, by the way.' He was in the hallway before she called to him.

'We're right though, aren't we? It's about the killers surpassing one another in some sick, twisted way.'

'Yes,' Callanach said. 'I think that's exactly it. Goodnight Ava.' He made sure the lock clicked into place, certain she'd fall asleep without bothering to get up to double-lock it.

Callanach needed either a taxi or a patrol car to pick him up. He wasn't going to sleep any time soon – there was too much going on in his head – so going straight back to the station seemed the obvious choice. A takeaway wouldn't go amiss either, he thought.

The blow to the back of his head was hard enough to send him reeling. He'd have hit the pavement face down had two pairs of hands not caught him. Callanach did his best to stagger away, catching his breath sufficiently to try to scream for help, but something soft and spongy was shoved in his mouth seconds before a bag was pulled over his head. His assailants folded his arms behind his back, pulling them up tightly and leaving him no choice but to walk forwards when pushed. They didn't speak. Within seconds he was shoved into a van, head held to the floor as his ankles were tied together. His mind was already conjuring the image of Michael Swan's body. He tried to thrash, realised the uselessness of wasting vital energy, and did the only thing left to do. Callanach waited to see just how bad it was going to get.

Chapter Twenty

Time was either rushing past or dragging intolerably, Callanach wasn't sure which. He wanted the rolling and bumping to be over and to get the sack off his head. At the same time he knew that when the journey finished he would be facing an unknown enemy on their terms. He was powerless until he knew if he had anything to bargain with. His head was throbbing, but adrenalin had kicked in and he'd begun to formulate a scrap of a plan.

He would tell his assailants that he was a police officer expected back at the station imminently. He could bargain with offers of prosecutorial clemency. Then again, he could just plead for his life.

If he concentrated, Callanach could hear whispering. A couple of male voices, one giving orders, from the tone of voice, another asking questions. No hint of a female on board, which seemed to rule out Michael Swan's killer in spite of his initial panic. Breathing slowly, he tried to get control of his body and his flitting mind. He needed to think. This was a well-organised assault. The men who'd abducted him were professionals. He hadn't seen them hiding or noticed a suspicious vehicle. And he was certain this was no random street crime. Whoever they were, they'd been waiting for him.

People who knew him then, who were aware of his profession, and who presumably were undeterred by the potential consequences of their actions. Callanach cast his mind back over years of investigations. If he had to list the names of everyone with a grudge, the journey would need to be a long one. There were plenty of criminals who'd be happy to see him take a bullet, and a fair number who'd be pleased to deliver it to him personally.

As the van swerved to a halt, hands hauled him first to his knees then to his feet.

'Out!' a man commanded, cutting his ankle ties and pushing Callanach forwards. Another pair of hands stopped him from falling out of the back. Gravel crunched beneath his feet. What he registered was the lack of noise, the city centre's constant low level hum – traffic, people, businesses, homes – faded. The ground changed to soft and yielding as he walked, then a solid step and the sound of a door opening. This was some door though. Callanach could imagine the weight of it by the creak on the hinges. The tone of the echo as it slammed shut was metallic. Inside now, and he was walking on concrete. The sound of their footsteps rattled closely off walls, ceiling and floor. Callanach estimated himself plus at least three others. Blindly navigating a distinct downward slope, he breathed in hard, tasting the air, listening for ambient sounds, sniffing. It was dank, stale, the temperature inside markedly colder than out.

At the end of the hallway another door opened. This time someone held Callanach's head down as he entered, slamming the door behind him. The room was freezing. The bag, finally, was pulled from his face. There was no chair to be strapped to, no bright light shone in his eyes. By the light of a small hand lantern Callanach saw that there were four of them dressed in similar black clothes, gloves, boots, and balaclavas to complete the look. Callanach leaned against a rough, unpainted wall in the low-ceilinged, windowless room. He said nothing. They would let him know what they wanted in their own time. It turned out that what they wanted first was to remind him that they were the ones in control, and that his fate lay entirely in their hands.

The first punch smashed the wind out of him. He crumpled, gasping for breath, his solar plexus spasming uncontrollably. A kick followed to the side of his left thigh, connecting hard with his bone, shooting pain down into his ankle and up into his hip. When the third strike came he managed to block it, winning himself several extra hits to the face.

'*C'est assez. Qu'est-ce que vous voulez*?' Callanach spat blood to one side, his tongue bleeding freely. A hand slapped the back of his head hard enough to jar his neck.

'Speak English, you fucking Froggie,' one of the men ordered.

Callanach hadn't been aware that he'd reverted to his primary language. His brain was all instinct.

'What is it?' Callanach panted. 'You've made your point. You obviously want something from me. Why not just tell me what it is?'

Ever so slightly, three of the men turned towards the fourth – the one who hadn't punched or kicked yet. He was stood in the furthest corner, arms folded.

'You've been keeping strange company,' he said. 'Do you want to tell us about that?' Callanach couldn't quite place the accent. The man's English was fluent but there was an unfamiliar lilt to his pronunciation.

'I have no idea what you're talking about,' Callanach said. 'I'm a police officer . . .'

The fourth man moved in, grabbing Callanach by the hair,

ripping it upwards, dragging him away from the wall and standing behind him.

'I'm well aware of that, boy. You even had yourself a little work-related accident recently, did you not?' He drew back a boot, then planted a kick squarely in Callanach's coccyx. The pain silenced him completely. Whatever healing had begun was well and truly undone. It felt as if he'd been split in two. He hit the floor and rolled onto his side, curling into a ball, gritting his teeth against a tidal wave of blackness, desperate to remain conscious.

The fourth man sauntered back to the corner he'd originally inhabited. 'Plenty of coppers take the odd backhander to make some money on the side. Or they just go bad. I've seen enough of that in my time. Which is it with you, Detective Inspector?'

It took Callanach a while to fight the nausea and speak without throwing up.

'I have no idea what the fuck you're talking about. I haven't taken money from anyone.'

After a quick nod from the fourth man to his crew, a photo was shoved in front of Callanach's face. It took a few seconds to focus and recognise where he was when it was taken. The picture showed him entering Lance Proudfoot's house the evening he met up with Ben.

'Any bells ringing yet?' the fourth man asked.

'It's a journalist's house. He shared some information with me. Nothing that hasn't gone on the record. Why were you following me?'

'Who else was with you?' one of the men asked, stepping forward, fist raised, to stand over Callanach. Fourth man held up one hand and the blow was delayed.

'Who do you think was with me?' Callanach asked, doing his best to sit up and get in a position where he could defend himself.

'The man who organised the theft of more millions than the frigging Securitas Depot Robbery, my boy, that's who was there.'

Another photo was produced. This one showed Ben entering the property. They'd been following him, not Callanach. These were police officers. Callanach didn't know whether to be relieved or even more scared. These people were the law, and clearly also considered themselves to be positioned well above its normal reach.

'It's a coincidence,' Callanach said. 'I had no idea he was a person of interest. This is a misunderstanding.'

'Oh, is it?' Fourth man asked, walking forward and pinching his fingers hard in the flesh at the base of Callanach's throat. 'Because we're having some difficulty keeping track of what young Mr Paulson is up to. He's never where his diary says he's going to be, always one step ahead. Is that because he's getting a bit of unofficial help from someone on the inside?'

'This is about my case, not yours. I understand you're investigating a serious offence, but that's nothing to do with me. Paulson's name had never come to my attention,' Callanach said.

'Is that right? Not even courtesy of that little faggot in your squad who thinks he's so bloody clever?'

'If you're talking about Tripp, he never said a word. Quite the opposite. He made it clear that he was under strict orders to maintain full silence, even to me.'

'So you asked him about our investigation then? Did you ask him about Paulson?' Fourth man asked.

'Tripp refused to comment,' Callanach shouted.

'You're sure about that, are you, *sir*?' the emphasis from one of the lower ranking goons was on the last word. 'Only we understand that DC Tripp has a bit of a thing about pretty men. Can't believe he hasn't got a crush on a piece of Euro-ass like you. He must have been desperate to win brownie points with his precious DI. You gay as well, are you? Do you encourage your men with special treats?'

'He's not gay,' Fourth man cut in. 'He was only a hair's breadth away from being a convicted rapist, weren't you, lad?'

Callanach stood up, fear gone, replaced by what might turn out to be either homicidal or suicidal rage, depending on how the fight went.

'Who ordered an investigation into my squad?' Callanach demanded. 'You have no fucking right to go prying into Tripp's personal life. Mine either. And that rape charge was false, as you well know, given the access you seem to have had to my file.'

Fourth man stepped up so that his breath was going directly into Callanach's mouth. The man wanted the fight, and Callanach knew it. Only there was no way it was going to end with just the two of them going for it.

'Tripp said nothing. It was an unfortunate coincidence. Paulson was tracing a hack which might lead to a murderer,' Callanach reiterated, keeping his voice calm.

'And what did you promise Paulson in return?' Fourth man asked.

'Nothing,' Callanach spat.

'He was just helping out of the goodness of his heart, was he? And you believed that?' another man asked. They all laughed. It was Callanach's first moment of self-doubt, now that he'd had his suspicions about Ben confirmed. Why had Ben agreed to help if he knew the police were following him? Unless he was waiting for a better moment to ask a return favour.

'Well done, Detective Inspector,' Fourth man clapped him on the back. 'You're finally putting two and two together, by the look on your face.' He slid a hand around Callanach's throat and pushed him back against the wall. 'I don't know what you've done and what you haven't, but that streak of American

161

piss stole from some very powerful men and women. He got into their bank accounts, their emails, their private correspondences. I don't need to explain how nervous that can make those sorts of people. He's going to prison for the rest of his natural, understand? And if you fuck up our investigation, you're going to be sharing a cell with him. Stay away from Ben Paulson. No phone calls, no emails, no texts. No more help.' He pulled Callanach forward in order to shove him hard against the wall again. His already bruised skull struck brick. 'We'll leave the door open for you. I suggest you stay here and lick your wounds for a good twenty minutes. You might want to let the stink of fear settle off your clothes before you walk home.'

They all laughed big fake belly laughs that lasted too long. They were each as scared of the fourth man as he'd been made to feel, Callanach realised. With a man like that, you knew he could be your friend one minute and your worst enemy the next. The fact that you thought you were playing for the same team was irrelevant.

They began walking towards the door, one of them picking up the bag that had been over Callanach's head and shoving it in his pocket. No evidence left behind. The three lower ranks went first, leaving the fourth man to issue one last threat in the semi-dark.

'There'll be no more late night rendezvous with Ava Turner, or next time DCI Edgar might send you a more permanent message. Not a word now, DI Callanach. Joe Edgar has friends in places so high, they could spit on you and it would take a week for your hair to feel wet. And if you go down, your squad'll go with you. That's quite some responsibility, son. Ease your pain with the knowledge that silence makes you a martyr.'

His footsteps took an age to cease their echoing through the hallway. Only when certain they had all gone did Callanach allow himself to sink to the floor and assess his injuries. His jaw was throbbing, the back of his head was badly bruised. Too shaky to stand for five minutes, he did his best to rest while his abductors created some distance between him and them.

When he finally emerged from the room he saw that the corridor was an arc of metal-lined tunnel, ribbed with steel. Long since defunct electric panels spewed out their wires where rats had made homes. He plodded upwards towards the dim light at the surface. At least, as promised, they had left the door open.

A nearby signpost directed visitors to the bunker entrance. That explained where he'd been. He followed the directions towards a main gate. Edinburgh's old nuclear bunkers had been converted into a visitor attraction, although they hadn't opened all of the tunnels. Some had been reserved for less educational purposes, although it was fair to say he'd learned quite a lot in the relatively short time he'd been inside. Finally Callanach came out onto Clermiston Road. He was about three miles west of the city centre, not far from Murrayfield. Any taxi would take one look at him and disappear, and he didn't want to run the risk of being recognised from his recent televised press conference. If he called a police car to pick him up, the rumour-mongers would run riot. He walked – sore leg, head pounding, stomach so bruised that eating would be out of the question for a couple of days, but the fresh air helped.

He understood that many successful people, in business as in the police, were simply well-dressed sociopaths. It fed their ambition, their intellect, the ability to adapt and to overcome opponents. So he didn't know why he was so surprised to find a gang of them operating on his patch. Scotland Yard had certainly put some resources into taking Ben Paulson down. Perhaps that was what the men with the money had insisted on. Perhaps that was why they'd put Joseph Edgar in charge. Callanach wondered if Ava knew what her lover was capable of, dismissing the thought immediately. Ava might be blinded by Edgar, but if she really understood what lay behind the charming English mask, Callanach knew she wouldn't tolerate him for a second. She had a right to be told, of course. Did being a good friend mean letting her work it out on her own or intervening now? No conversation with Ava about DCI Edgar had ended well. And Callanach had a team to protect. There was no doubt in his mind that the threat to discredit both him and his squad was real. How could he balance that responsibility against his friendship with Ava? He still hadn't figured out the answer to that question when he stumbled into his apartment. The sun was rising as Callanach fell into bed and a darkly disturbed sleep.

Chapter Twenty-One

There was a hammering sound, inside his head at first, then beyond its bruised and swollen skull as he came round. Glancing at his clock, he discovered it was after 1 p.m. The hammering was rapidly followed by shouting as he shuffled towards his apartment door, hastily pulling on jogging bottoms and a T-shirt.

'Sir, sir, are you in there? Are you all right?' Salter's voice boomed. Callanach winced.

'I'm here, Salter,' Callanach called. 'And I'm fine. What's going on?'

'Um, could you open the door, please?' Salter said. 'Only I'm in your corridor shouting.'

Callanach stared into the mirror next to his door. His face resembled a failed example of patchwork quilting, purple, red, patches of grey-green, the bruises blackening at their centres. There was no way of hiding it.

'What's up, Salter?' he called through the still-closed door.

'No one could get you on the phone. Superintendent Overbeck issued an order to get you to her office within the hour. Could you let me in? Next step might be to break your door down if one of us can't confirm face-to-face contact.'

'*Merde*,' Callanach swore under his breath, opening the door enough that Salter could confirm it was him and that he didn't have some unwanted visitor holding a knife to his throat. He stifled a laugh at the irony of that.

'Ruddy hell, sir,' Salter said. 'Do you need a doctor?'

'No, I'm fine. I overslept, that's all.'

'You have to let me in, sir. Right now. Or I'm calling Overbeck and telling her everything.'

Callanach tried rolling his eyes, realised even that small action was going to cause too much pain, and caved in.

DS Salter pulled Callanach by the sleeve into the window light. She whistled as she inspected his wounds.

'You'll need a heavy dose of arnica, not to mention witch hazel. We can stop at the chemist on our way to the station. What other injuries are there?' Callanach lifted his shirt, more out of his own curiosity than to show Salter. His ribs were black and red tramlines of contusion, and the tip of a boot was marked plainly on the skin over his stomach. He wasn't prepared to think about the pain in his lower back. The kick to his coccyx had made the fracture worse even than when he'd first done it. 'Painkillers?' Salter asked. Callanach pointed in the direction of the kitchen. 'If you don't mind my suggesting, sir, you should take a shower. I'll make coffee and dig out some paracetamol.'

'Are you not going to ask what happened, Salter?' Callanach asked.

'Not my place. Unless you want to tell me. Just so long as you're okay.'

Callanach nodded.

'I'll get that shower,' he said. 'Call in and tell them I'm sick and that I'll work from home today, would you?'

'Not sure that'll wash with the evil superintendent overlord. There was a reason she sent me to get you.' Callanach stopped on his way to the bathroom. 'There's some new graffiti. A uniformed officer called it in early this morning when he passed it on his regular beat.'

'What does it say?' Callanach asked.

'It says, "Lollipop lady". I'll get you that coffee now.' Salter headed for the kitchen.

Callanach was resigning himself to comprehensive lying over the next few hours when Salter appeared with her handbag as he was tying his shoes.

'I thought you might like some help with, er, you know. Your face,' she said.

'Sorry Salter, not with you,' he said. She held up a variety of brushes and tubes.

'You think that'll work?' Callanach asked.

'Can't look any worse than you do right now. No offence.'

'None taken,' Callanach said, feeling the painkillers he'd taken starting to breach the surface of his discomfort. 'Give it a try. Anything to reduce the amount of time I'll have to spend explaining myself.' He allowed Salter to dab and brush him with themes on beige.

'Best I can do,' she said. 'Are you sure a doctor wouldn't be wise?'

'What's wise and what I've got time for are two different things,' he said. Salter held up a small mirror for him to inspect his face. At least it looked more credibly like a minor car accident or as if he'd stumbled off the treadmill at the gym. Before, it had virtually screamed fist fight. 'Thank you,' he said. 'Woman of hidden talents.'

'Best get going,' Salter smiled. 'The Super will be spitting nails by now.'

'Never mind Overbeck,' Callanach said. 'Drive straight to the site of the new graffiti. I want to see it first-hand. Have we had forensics out there yet?'

'No, that's your call. DI Turner thought you should be consulted before we touched it.'

'Have we set up surveillance?' Callanach asked.

'From a building opposite. Local CCTV's being checked. There's been some interest from residents, although it hasn't sparked any sort of outcry yet, so we're assuming that the public haven't clocked the relevance of it. They will soon, though, if the next victim matches what was spray-painted there. It's on a previously clean wall, so no chance of it blending in with other tags this time. Once the public realises messages are being sprayed by the killers, anyone in Edinburgh with a paint can in their pocket is likely to get lynched,' Salter said.

Northumberland Place off Nelson Street was residential and relatively quiet. It was a through road to other housing, featuring Edinburgh's trademark brown-bricked, four-storey, castlesque structures. There was a humble-looking bar opposite the graffiti, but no witnesses to what would have seemed a trifling offence, probably done late at night, well after closing hours. It wasn't a heavy footfall part of the city. There would have been few passers-by after lights out. Callanach found it difficult to understand how the location fulfilled the murderer's need to claim their next kill. Here, it might never have been noticed.

'How does each killer know where to find the other's graffiti?' Callanach muttered. They were keeping their distance from the wall, having passed it once in the car, now parked down the road, staring at the tourist book Salter kept with her as an excuse to hang around.

'You think they're announcing to each other who their next target is?' Salter asked.

'DI Turner has a theory that the killings are competitive. Choosing the most perfect victim to make the crime resonate all the more effectively through the community. I think the graffiti may be a way of tagging the kill,' Callanach said.

'So they're communicating to get additional gratification from it. A sense of winning,' Salter said.

'I guess,' Callanach shrugged. 'Unless it's all about the reaction from the press. And given that the global media is branding Edinburgh hell on earth, I suppose they both think they're winning at the moment. Get photos of the graffiti over to the handwriting expert. It may not hold up in court, but I want to know if we can liken it to any of the other graffiti at the original sites. Keep surveillance on it twenty-four hours for the next week. I want to know who passes by, reads it, adds to it. Best photographic evidence we can get. Anyone matching the descriptions of our murderers to be followed immediately and call in back-up.'

'Got it,' Salter said. 'Sorry, but I'm bursting. Did you need to do more here, or shall we head for the station?'

'Let's go,' Callanach said. 'I'm way overdue a disciplinary hearing. Perhaps we should stop on the way so I can buy the superintendent some chocolates. Maybe try putting her in a better mood.'

'Do you not think she's sweet enough already?' Salter grinned.

Overbeck was less entertaining in person. She managed to rant without visibly pausing for breath for several minutes. The only blessing was that her obsession with her own public status completely overrode any careful inspection of Callanach. He blamed an ongoing problem with pain in his coccyx for the need to take additional painkillers and thus fail to wake up or hear his phone ringing. That was at least partially true.

'So given that your slipshod investigative powers have led us to the point of simply waiting for another murder, and the victim's profession has actually been identified, what's your plan of action? Keywords for whatever you're about to say to me are – foolproof, fast and inexpensive. Go.'

'If we release this publicly there'll be panic. Probably more false alarms, resulting in assaults on innocent people. But if we don't act and a lollipop lady is harmed, we'll be accused of incompetence,' Callanach began.

'What are the numbers?' Overbeck asked.

'One hundred and fifty-eight lollipop persons working for Edinburgh City Council. One hundred and two of those are female,' Callanach said, thankful he'd made the relevant call before the meeting. 'We will approach the potential targets privately. Sooner or later it'll get out anyway. Someone will speak to the press, whether we ask them to or not. Couple that with the issue of people asking for protection, demanding around-the-clock officers outside their address, the investigation will grind to a halt while we try to prevent the next crime.'

'Not we, Detective Inspector. Don't drag me into your logistical nightmare. This is your investigation. Yours and DI Turner's at any rate. Do we know which of the murderers graffitied the wall this time?'

'We don't. It's still only a theory, and with the exception of the "Primary School Teacher" graffiti, we can't identify what other scrawling might belong to a suspect. The handwriting expert says there are similarities between the two samples, but this is spray-painting not penmanship. We're never going to be able to draw definite links.'

'One hundred and two potential victims. Bravo, Callanach. You may as well inform Police Scotland's lawyers of the impending negligence suit right now. Perhaps I should complete the job by writing a few incompetence headlines for the popular press and save everyone's time. What a sodding mess. And where's Turner?'

'No idea, ma'am,' Callanach said. He'd been wondering the same thing himself, not that he was keen to see Ava. She wouldn't fall for the make-up and lies, and he had no intention of telling her the truth, a decision he'd made overnight.

'Find her and light a fire under her equally lukewarm arse. Make an arrest, Callanach, and hand the file over to the Procurator Fiscal. I want someone in the dock being charged with these crimes before I face my next professional review, and that's not far enough away for my liking.'

DS Lively was at the coffee machine when Callanach went in search of sustenance.

'Bless my bollocks, sir,' Lively said. 'Is that make-up you're wearing?'

'Where's DI Turner, Sergeant?' Callanach asked.

'She was called to the hospital about an hour ago. Did someone throw you a blanket party? Only they made substantial improvements to your face.'

'Not DI Begbie again?' Callanach asked, ignoring the inquisition.

'Do you think I'd be standing here if it was? I do respect a few of my senior officers, you know,' Lively laughed. Callanach bent down to take his coffee from the machine, wincing as he went. 'The Chief's flown out somewhere sunny to recuperate, from what I hear. Looks like you should do the same.'

'And be parted from your delightful company, Lively?' Callanach asked, taking a sip of what tasted like hot, caffeinated bracken water. 'Why would I do that?'

Callanach texted Ava to let her know what was happening, shortly before a senior administrator from Edinburgh City Council turned up at his office.

Fours hours later, Callanach was stood in front of eighty-six lollipop ladies. It wasn't a bad show out of the 102 they needed to locate. Some were on leave, others weren't contactable. Uniformed officers had been sent out to make contact with the missing sixteen.

'We have reason to believe that one of you may be the target of a crime,' Callanach began. There were some jokey whistles which he ignored as he carried on. 'You've been asked to attend because there may be a link to other murders recently in the city.' He paused. No jokes or amusing noises issued from the crowd this time. The shock was plain on their faces. 'We may be wrong and we very much hope that this is an error or a misreading of the evidence. But we've taken the view that you are better forewarned.'

'Are you saying that one of us might be killed?' a woman in the front row asked. The following barrage of questions was inevitable. In their position Callanach knew he'd be reacting the same way. The thing to do was head it off and keep the crowd calm. Staring across the sea of faces, he supposed there wasn't a collective noun for potential murder victims.

'It is only a possible threat. There's nothing concrete. You do, however, need to be vigilant. You shouldn't go anywhere alone. Avoid public places where you might be vulnerable. Keep a mobile phone and personal attack alarm with you at all times. Make sure your homes are secure. Lock your car doors when driving. Do not open your door at all to people you don't know.'

'For how long?' another asked, standing up. 'We're supposed to hide away until when? The rest of us'll be safe once one is dead, is that it?'

'Aye, is that the best you've on offer? What are you gonna be doing to make us safe?' the first woman asked before turning around to address the crowd. 'This isn't on, is it ladies? Why are we being left to protect ourselves?' That started a riot of heckling.

'We can't take you all into protective care,' Callanach said. 'Our advice would be to leave the city if you have relatives elsewhere. No one is obliged to attend for work, the Council has made that clear. The precautions we're asking you to take are the same as have applied to everyone in the city since this began. It's just that you need to exercise a special level of awareness about your circumstances.'

'That's it?' a woman shouted. 'Special level of awareness! For goodness sake, is my husband supposed to give up work to stay home and look after me?'

'I'm not running scared,' another responded. 'They can try me. I won't be a prisoner in my own home.'

'It's important that you tell as few people as possible about this. I can't insist on it, but it might make matters worse if any of you speaks to the press. These people seem to be courting publicity. I'd prefer not to give it to them.' That went down about as well as he'd expected.

Callanach listened to another hour of alternating anger, fear, confusion and insults then called time.

He phoned Ava from his car, curious when she didn't answer her mobile, leaving a brief message about the crossing guards and asking her to call when she was available. A text came through as he was finishing the voicemail.

'30 Broughton Street. 1 hour.' Callanach checked the number. It was sent from Lance Proudfoot's phone. He considered the possibility that it was some new fun that DCI Edgar had planned for him, but it seemed unlikely in such a public place. He went home and changed, then walked the two minutes from his apartment to the given address. It turned out to be a wine shop Callanach frequented, although he'd not been aware of the precise address before. It was filled with enough shelves to allow privacy from the window view, and to enable a private conversation.

Lance was wearing a hoodie, with the hood pulled over as far as it would go and glasses Callanach hadn't noticed before.

'Lance,' Callanach sidled up to him. 'Are you in disguise?'

The journalist gave him a wary look, checked the aisles either side, then handed him an envelope. Callanach opened it as Lance busied himself studying labels. Inside was a disposable mobile, with a piece of paper and phone number attached. He read the note.

'I underestimated you. I know what they planned to do and I hope they didn't find you. I couldn't warn you in case they were tracing your calls. Hence the enclosed gift. Use it only to phone or text the number attached. You need help and the level of programming involved is beyond your police force. Tell no one. Especially not DI Turner. Let me know what evidence you've got. I'll do what I can. The police aren't all bad. Same goes for my people.'

There was no sign-off, but it wasn't required. Ben had proved that his access to police communications was way beyond what DCI Edgar had even contemplated, and he had to have accessed either their phone or email communications to have known what Edgar's men had planned for Callanach. That meant there was a trail, which also meant he could prove they'd conspired to abduct him. Callanach considered taking it all to the super-intendent, exposing Edgar for the maniacal thug he was. Of course, that would be the last thing that Overbeck would tolerate at the moment – a scandal involving Scotland Yard's golden boys in the midst of a double killer crisis. Then there was the fact that Callanach had given unauthorised people confidential case information. Overbeck would have none of it. It would be hushed up as quickly as possible, probably with a resulting transfer to the Outer Hebrides. Reporting Edgar would do no good and might well be playing into the man's hands. Callanach decided he'd bide his time. It wasn't as if he had nothing else to think about. He looked at Lance who was glancing at his watch.

'Where did you get this note?' Callanach asked him.

'Courier dropped it to my door. Not a company I recognised though. Ben put a note in for me too. Told me to watch my back and yours. Said I was being watched. Turns out an unfamiliar car has been coming and going outside my house for the last twenty-four hours. And now you turn up with a face that looks like it's auditioning for a part in a prison soap opera. I feel as if I've stumbled onto the best story of my career and it's going to be entirely off the record. So am I in real danger or are the men watching my house there for my protection?'

'They're police,' Callanach said.

'Oh thank God,' Lance breathed out heavily. 'I was actually getting rather worried.'

'About that,' Callanach said. 'It's not that you should be worried exactly, but be careful. We're all too quick to ascribe positive qualities to people in uniform. They don't always apply.'

'In plain terms?' Lance asked.

'Don't let them in your house. Tell them nothing. Stay away from Ben.'

'Easier said than done. He planted some sort of software on my machine that auto-encodes whatever I send from it. For your convenience, presumably. I appear to be the go-between. Tell me I'm not going to end up on some trumped-up charge . . .' his voice grew quieter and his words slowed. 'They did that to you, didn't they? Sorry, I was being obtuse, but these are policemen . . . is that why Ben told me not to meet you anywhere openly?'

'The less said the better, is that the phrase?' Callanach responded. 'Lance, it was you who first spotted the graffiti pattern. Another has appeared in a new place. We think the killers are boasting to one another about their next target, that

175

it's part of some sadistic game. Almost like tagging the kill. Does that make sense to you?'

'Yes and no. You're suggesting that the two killers have set this whole thing up. Why the need to communicate so publicly then, if they're just taking turns?'

'This graffiti's at Northumberland Place, just off Nelson. If you have a look, do it subtly. There's twenty-four-hour surveillance in place. Let me know your thoughts. This is between us.'

'You've told the potential victims though, right?'

'We have,' Callanach said.

'So when this leaks, and it will leak, I get the exclusive. Whatever whitewash the official police line is, it comes to me first?'

'I won't argue with that,' Callanach said. His phone buzzed in his pocket. Tripp was calling. The line was bad. All Callanach could get was intermittent fragments of speech and what sounded like screaming and yelling in the background.

'Come now . . . DI Turner . . . couldn't find you . . . Hemma . . . Holyrood Road . . .' What little mobile reception there was gave in and the call ended. Callanach pocketed the envelope and turned back to Lance.

'Something's happening across town. Thanks for this, Lance. Keep your head down and I'll be in touch.' Callanach didn't wait for a reply. He ran to his car. Holyrood Road was only a few minutes away if the traffic was light. He put his foot down and went.

Chapter Twenty-Two

Callanach was expecting to hear sirens long before he reached the scene, yet there wasn't a police car in sight. Whatever had happened, Police Scotland was keeping its presence covert. He parked his car in a neighbouring street and made his way towards Hemma, a Swedish bar he'd passed several times but never entered. The frontage was all glass panels through which slanting white columns could be seen. He tried to figure out what he was missing. There was a mass of bodies inside, the noise pervasive from some distance, but the reflections on the glass veiled a detailed view. What was missing was any sign of the incident Tripp had been warning him about. Callanach kept his head low and opened the door, doing his best not to look like a police officer until he'd figured out exactly what was happening.

A cheer went up as he entered. It wasn't your usual Friday night Edinburgh crowd. About half the station was there, from uniforms to support staff, his own squad, even DCI Edgar's crew. Tripp pushed through the crowd to reach him. The doors were locked as a glass of champagne was pushed into his hand.

'What's going on?' Callanach demanded. 'We've got more than one hundred potential victims out there and we're already short of manpower. Who in God's name organised this?'

Tripp didn't need to answer. DCI Edgar climbed onto a table holding a bottle of champagne aloft.

'Thank you all for coming to the most last-minute of celebrations,' Edgar began.

'God, Tripp,' Callanach said, grabbing his detective constable's arm. 'Tell me they haven't arrested Ben Paulson – he may be the only one who can help . . .'

'Under circumstances stranger than I'd ever have imagined, I would like to introduce you to my fiancée!' The crowd moved back unprompted from Ava and raised their glasses in her direction.

'We got a phone call, sir. DCI Edgar insisted that everyone finishing a shift should come. I assumed you'd heard,' Tripp said.

Callanach stared at Ava who was smiling uncomfortably at the sudden attention, sipping champagne and staring glassily at the well-wishers. She tapped the toe of one foot against her other shoe as Edgar continued his self-congratulations.

'You want a seat, sir?' Salter asked.

'I'm not that shocked, Salter,' Callanach responded.

'I was thinking about your injury,' she said, leaning against a table and taking a sip of Coke. 'I'm driving,' she explained. 'Going straight back to the station after this. Don't know when I'll next sleep in my own bed.'

'This party has to end. I've had enough,' Callanach said.

'Sir, don't do anything rash,' Salter replied quietly.

Callanach grimaced. It wasn't enough that Joseph Edgar had ordered him beaten, and fooled Ava into believing he was good enough for her. Now he was putting innocent people's safety at risk. He strode forward as Edgar was climbing down from the table.

'I want my squad and any uniformed officers back at the station immediately,' Callanach announced to the crowd. 'Whatever you've got in your hands, put it down. Report to the incident room and . . .'

'DI Callanach,' Edgar shouted. 'Everyone's on their way back to work right now. I simply borrowed my friend's bar for thirty minutes. Scotland Yard is well aware how little progress is being made in the murders and of how much help you need. Your team could do with a morale boost. They're all still on call. I've got it under control, don't worry yourself.'

There was an embarrassed silence as Callanach figured out how to respond. Ava was already nowhere to be seen.

'Phone call for you, sir,' DS Lively called from the back of the crowd, waving his mobile in the air. 'Urgent. Sorry to interrupt.'

Callanach pushed between bodies, grabbed the phone from Lively and barged out onto the street. The phone was dead. Sergeant Lively appeared behind him, holding out his hand for the mobile.

'What was that about, Sergeant?' Callanach asked.

'Thought you might like some fresh air,' Lively replied.

Callanach took a few calming breaths. 'Thank you,' he said eventually.

'Didn't do it for you. That one's a right wanker. You'd better do something about him, sir. From what I hear, DCI Begbie's not planning on coming back. There'll be a vacancy, and we don't want Lord Edgar applying for a transfer to Police Scotland. That may be the first thing you and I have agreed about since you arrived.' He walked off, leaving Callanach feeling more alone than he had for a very long time.

The chief was leaving, Ava was starting a new life with a man who would make absolutely sure that Callanach was strictly a former friend, his own mother had failed to respond to his final email to her, and DS Lively had turned out to be his saving ally. Callanach took a last look at the party beginning to wrap up inside the bar. He'd made a fool of himself, behaving like a fun-killing prig. Edgar must have been absolutely delighted. Ava would have been humiliated. The Major Investigation Team must have been thoroughly embarrassed. It was a disaster. He seemed to be leaving a trail of dislike in his wake and there was little he could see in his future that would make it any brighter.

He drove home faster than he should have, banishing the image of the diamond on Ava's finger from his mind. Back in his flat he took out his laptop and began compiling a document containing all the information about the murders so far. They could be certain that the man who had killed Emily Balcaskie and leaked Helen Lott's autopsy report either knew his way around coding or had help from someone extremely skilled. And those murders were without a doubt linked to the Thorburn and Swan cases. If he had to ask for help below the radar, so be it. And if Ben Paulson was a suspect in Joe Edgar's case, then Callanach could live with that.

He fired off the document to Lance with a note to forward it, not mentioning any names. Lance would know what to do. Then he followed it up with a text to Ben.

'Document on way. Your help appreciated. Can't give any in return.' Callanach wondered again about the programmer's motivation for helping, then decided it wasn't his problem. A reply buzzed through in less than a minute.

'Will take a look. Wasn't expecting return favour. Be less cynical.'

Callanach laughed out loud. Be less cynical. How was he supposed to do that? The only people he felt able to confide in were a journalist and a suspect. Ava's judgement was off. Everything about her life was alien – even the choice of bar for the impromptu engagement party, so unlike her preference

180

for pubs with fireplaces and overused leather sofas. Had she changed so dramatically, or had Callanach never really known her at all?

He tried to settle with a glass of wine, flicking on the television to drown out the din in his head, but all he could feel was the ghost of Ava's head on his shoulder. Fragments of conversations from when they'd first met. Times she'd joked with him, sided with him. When he'd opened up to her and found someone utterly without judgement or bias. Long nights spent talking about nothing, sharing treasures from their childhoods. A day fishing when she'd taught him to cast a line. He'd flicked it clumsily and caught it in her hair, spending the next half hour getting the hook out and patching up the scratch below her ear. He remembered the slender curve of her neck, her lightly tanned, smooth skin. And the moment when he'd brushed his fingertips downwards releasing her hair, both of them silenced in the midst of their chatter by the unexpected, intimate contact. Ava had shaken her head suddenly, as if waking up, reaching for the rod and busying herself with clearing up. But she hadn't met his eyes for several minutes after that.

The glass of wine he'd been holding flew from his hand and smashed against the wall before he'd even realised he was going to throw it. He stormed across the room away from the shards of glass, slamming his fist down on the desk. The drugs he'd been intending to throw away were still there. He pushed two tablets from the plastic and swallowed them.

The shower was cold when he stepped in, the shock welcome. Comfort wasn't what he was looking for. Conscious of how wrong his plans were, he dressed and walked across the hallway. Bunny opened her door almost immediately.

'Luc, I was wondering if you'd come in yet. Are you hungry? I've got loads of stuff in my freezer. And my new couch has arrived. We should toast it with something bubbly. You all right?'

Callanach stepped through the doorway, his eyes locked on Bunny's. She was wearing a denim shirt, tied at the front, with a miniskirt. He reached one hand out slowly, flexing his jaw, breathing in deeply as the first wave of liberating endorphins hit his system. Hooking one finger inside the knot of her shirt, he tugged it hard, both loosening the knot and pulling Bunny towards him. She raised an eyebrow and laughed nervously, but allowed herself to be pulled into his arms.

'I never thought you'd be interested,' she said as he began kissing her neck, pushing his hands into her hair, running the tip of his tongue along her collarbone. 'Did you want to go somewhere more comfortable?' she asked.

'Okay,' he said, letting her lead the way into the kitchen where Bunny took a bottle of Prosecco from the fridge and grabbed two glasses. Callanach poured the drinks and walked into the lounge, getting comfortable on the couch. Bunny clinked her glass against his and smiled.

'I've been hoping this might happen,' she said. 'I did wonder the day that lady came to your door. It was the way she looked when I talked about you. I figured you two must have had something going on.'

Callanach realised she meant the day Ava had come looking for him. Ava never had explained what she'd been doing there.

He took Bunny's glass from her hand and kissed her, crushing his lips against hers, sliding one arm around her shoulders. Silencing her, and forcing the image of Ava from his mind. Tilting her head to one side, she ran her tongue around the edge of his lips. He pushed the shirt off her shoulders, undoing the few buttons that held it in place, dropping it to the floor as she peeled his shirt from his body. He wrapped his legs around hers, shifting their bodies sideways and moving his hand to her groin. She closed her eyes, lifting her chin, tipping her head over the arm of the sofa, panting softly as he touched her. He could feel the drugs working, reigniting the maleness he'd grieved for so long. Bunny ran a hand down the outside of his jeans and clutched the hardness there. This time he wouldn't fail.

Bunny lifted her head back up as he began to undo his jeans, putting her hand lightly over his.

'Shall we slow down?' she asked. 'We've got all night. And this isn't really very comfortable.' She picked up their glasses, handing Callanach his and sipping from hers. He did his best to mask the frustration on his face and smiled as they drank. 'So what made up your mind?' Bunny asked. 'I was about to give up hope that you'd noticed me. That first night when you got my power back on, I couldn't believe I was living opposite you. My mates joke about stuff like this happening – you move into a new building, the guy opposite just happens to be gorgeous and has an amazing job. And he's single. I've been telling everyone about you.'

Callanach sat up, feeling his coccyx and ribs complain. He'd been able to ignore the pain until now, the sensation of grinding in his lower back, the stabbing around his lungs when he rolled over.

'Do you think you could make it to dinner Friday night? There'll be eight of us. We could have a takeaway here then go to a bar.'

'I don't know,' Callanach said, downing the overly sweet liquid and placing his glass on the table. His groin was throbbing as hard as he could ever remember, as if a spring had coiled and was building up an unstoppable force. But his head was thumping. There was a growing itch inside him, accompanied by a rising tide of panic that he might end up out of control.

'Shall I put some music on?' Bunny asked. 'What do you like?'

He knew he had to leave. Bunny was a good person. Not his kind of person, but sweet and well-intentioned. He'd come here without thinking it through. The shameful truth was that he'd come here to use her.

'I have to leave,' he said, head hammering and lower back protesting as he got up.

'You could stay here tonight,' she said, reaching for his hand.

'I can't. I have work early in the morning.'

'Stay a while longer. We could watch a movie?' she asked. Callanach saw the plea in her eyes, the disappointment. He'd been a complete bastard. The least he could do was let her down gently.

'I shouldn't have come,' he said. 'It was a mistake.'

'Friday then? With my mates. It'll be a laugh. You'll like them.'

'I think I'll be working. You know how it is.' He put his shirt back on, not bothering to button it up. His body was burning, as if it had become one single organ, pulsating, ready to burst. He kissed Bunny on the cheek.

'I understand,' she said quietly. 'I'll be here if you change your mind. That's what good neighbours do, isn't it?' She tried a smile, failed and hid her tears by pouring herself a fresh glass of Prosecco. Callanach left.

Inside his flat, he headed straight back to the shower cursing his selfish destructiveness. Bunny hadn't deserved to be the target for his attempt to repair himself. She'd been more graceful in defeat than he'd had any right to expect. And now he'd made life awkward where he lived. Don't shit where you eat, wasn't that the rule?

He was left with the crawling sensation that his body had been invaded by a creature demanding to be fed. It should have been cause for celebration. His body was working again, and yet he couldn't face the prospect of having sex with Bunny. She was attractive, bubbly and sweet, but not what he wanted. He'd imagined, after all that time, that the prospect of having sex at all would have been sufficient. But it was a false god.

He hadn't arrived there through free will and the power of his mind. He'd overwhelmed his body with chemicals, tricking his brain. And now he was stuck in pharmaceutical limbo, waiting for the drugs to wear off before he could rest. There would be no easy resolution to his impotence. Drugs had fixed his dysfunctional body but the root cause was in his mind and he wasn't a single step closer to fixing that.

Chapter Twenty-Three

He awoke at 7 a.m. tasting chemicals, and went straight to make coffee. Last night was a half-drawn sketch in his mind and he chose not to fill in the blanks. Some things couldn't be mended.

He checked his messages to make sure there had been no attacks overnight. It seemed Edinburgh's lollipop ladies were safe. There had been extra units on duty overnight in case of any incidents. Superintendent Overbeck wouldn't like accounting for the overtime, but that was her problem. Once the murders were resolved, if the chief wasn't coming back, Callanach had already decided that he'd be looking for a post elsewhere. Anywhere in the world that would have him. Except France, of course.

When he heard buzzing, his first reaction was to check his phone for texts. Only when that came up blank did he remember there was a second mobile in his flat. He hadn't realised it was still switched on.

'I have something. Will call at 10 a.m. Pen and paper ready.'

Ben had obviously spent his night more productively than Callanach. He checked his watch. He had two and a half hours to kill.

★　★　★

186

The answer to filling that expanse of time was waiting in an almost feral pack outside the police station. The cameras were set to roll as he walked in, questions were fired, lights flashed. No hope, then, of concealing from the murderers that they'd figured out the role of the graffiti.

Every major newspaper and television channel was represented. What sickened Callanach was the sense that what they needed now was an actual lollipop lady victim to complete their story. He liaised with the press office and composed a statement. As he left the Police Scotland media team to deal with it, he recalled his promise to give Lance the first reveal when the story broke. It was close to 10 a.m. Lance would have to wait a few more minutes until he'd finished speaking to Ben. Callanach grabbed a notebook, then retreated to his car and waited for the other mobile to ring.

'Where are you?' Ben asked.

'In my car,' Callanach said. 'Do you have something?'

'Only numbers, as yet,' Ben said, 'but it's a start. I'm sending you an image now. Have a look.'

Callanach opened it, not that it made much sense.

'La 55.95741075489907/Lo -3.19568574178561.'

He put the phone back to his ear. 'Got it, but I have no idea what I'm looking at,' he said.

'Those are GPS coordinates. That location is exactly where the lollipop lady graffiti appeared,' Ben said. Callanach scribbled notes. It hadn't occurred to him to look up the GPS coordinates. The positioning of the graffiti had always seemed more casual than that. 'I typed in every possible description of the graffiti sites and trawled the net for road names, GPS, any search term I could think of. The only match was the coordinates,' Ben continued.

'For all the graffiti sites where the victims' professions were listed?' Callanach asked.

'I found coordinates for four of the graffiti sites in the city,' Ben said.

'In what context?' Callanach clarified. 'Was it a website or search engine?'

'Nothing so simple,' Ben laughed. 'I was trawling chatter on the darknet. The part of the internet that exists only for people to do things unseen. Most computer users don't even know it's there. Precious few are able to access it.'

'So you've found the people sharing the coordinates then?' Callanach stopped writing, closing his eyes. This was the moment he'd been waiting for. A real break. The point where he could finally be sure there would be no more victims on the mortuary table.

'All I have at the moment is a heavily encoded website, with restricted access and invitation-only usability. The reason the GPS coordinates got a hit is because they're numerical. My software picked up the fact that the numbers had been bounced around in exactly that order. It'll take more work to get in deeper.'

'You have to show me,' Callanach said. 'If this turns out to be the only evidential trail, then I need to be able to follow it myself.'

'Too risky,' Ben said. 'You know I'm being followed and what they're capable of. You have a career to think of, Detective Inspector. I can't believe DCI Edgar's boys left you without issuing some sort of threat.'

'That's not important. You need to explain this to me in detail,' Callanach said.

'It's easier to slip out unseen during work hours. Meet me in three hours. I'll text you the address. Tell Lance to bring his laptop so I can leave you any files I find in the meantime.' Ben hung up. The text came through immediately. It was a city centre address in an area Callanach knew, although he didn't recognise the name of the cafe.

Back in the incident room, Callanach found his squad watching the television. On the screen, an elderly lady could be seen regaling an interviewer with tales of her former career as a lollipop lady outside one of Edinburgh's largest junior schools. The graphics at the bottom of the screen declared her to be Gladys Talthwaite, eighty years of age. She had retired years earlier but her brain was obviously as active as it had been in middle age. The interviewer was milking it for all it was worth.

'So how do you think they'll be feeling now, Gladys, those women who spend their working hours making the city roads safer for our children to pass?' the interviewer asked.

'I should think they'll be terrified, dearie, don't you?' Gladys said. 'In the war, we faced these sorts of enemies and we rallied. Of course back then, we had communities where everyone knew each other. A stranger in your road stood out a mile. Nowadays no one has a clue what's going on in the house next door.'

'What was it like being a lollipop lady? Can you describe the most difficult aspects of the job?' the interviewer continued, keen to get her tear-jerker back on track. Any more talk of the war and they'd be losing their audience.

'The proper terminology is crossing guard, in fact,' Gladys corrected the interviewer. 'I suppose the drivers could be impatient. Some didn't want to slow down. I once saw a woman drive right over a duck who'd had the temerity to be crossing the road with her ducklings. She didn't even stop.'

'And did you ever feel threatened or as if your job might have made you a target?'

'No, my love. Who would want to hurt a lollipop lady?' Gladys replied with a slight giggle.

'And what would you say to the man or woman who wants to hurt one of your former colleagues, if they were listening now?'

'I'd tell them to do the decent thing. If they want to spill blood, they can spill their own. Turn the knife on themselves,' Gladys said. The interviewer looked off to one side, putting one hand to her earpiece.

'Bet she wasn't expecting that answer,' a uniformed officer chipped in.

'Or their gun, or whatever they've got handy,' Gladys continued. Callanach stared at the screen. Gladys was tiny. The enormous interviewee armchair made her appear child-sized. Her hair was entirely white, her knuckles bent. And the vitriol she was venting illustrated exactly how most of Scotland was feeling at the moment.

Finally the interviewer cut in. 'And the police. What advice would you give them about dealing with these offenders? Detective Inspector Luc Callanach gave a press conference just this week. What suggestions do you have for him?'

'Oh I know who he is, pet. He's French. And look how they behaved during the war. Rolled over and let Hitler walk all over them for the most part!'

A black frame appeared followed by an unscheduled advertising break. You could almost hear the panic in the broadcast control room. Advising the murderers to kill themselves was shocking, but the anti-French racism was a step too far. Tripp switched off the television.

DS Lively stood up from the desk he'd been perching on.

'I rather liked her,' Lively said grinning. 'I'm getting coffee while DCI Edgar's cyber-wank crew are out on their raid. Last time I tried to approach the coffee machine, I found one of those tosspots putting coconut oil into their cup. I asked if it was for laxative purposes and the wee pish gave me a lecture on fat absorption.'

'How long are they going to be here, sir? The sergeant's right. They're a pain in the arse to have around,' Salter said.

'As long as it takes, I guess,' Callanach said.

'No more than another week, I heard,' one of the uniforms called out. 'One of them was on the phone to the place they're staying last night.'

'Never mind the cyber crime unit,' Callanach said. 'Start running searches for any crossing guard who might be of special note – won an award, been celebrated by their community – that sort of thing.'

'Already tried it, sir,' Salter replied. 'Got hundreds of results. Children drawing their local lollipop person in competitions. Schools nominating their lollipop person as an outstanding community member. Any crossing guard who had been in the job for more than a decade was invited to a special ceremony last year. You wouldn't believe how much Edinburgh celebrates its road-crossing safety technicians.'

'So no shortlist, then?' Callanach asked, rubbing his eyes. Nobody bothered to answer. He left his team to their work and went back to his office.

Edgar's squad were closing in on Ben Paulson who was just starting to prove useful. Callanach had a straightforward choice. He either warned Ben about the raid – completely illegally, of course – thereby protecting his own investigation, or he kept quiet and let possibly his only lead disappear without a trace. He tried to keep the memory of what Edgar had done to him out of it. Instead, he wondered what advice he'd give a colleague who came to him with the same dilemma. He knew very little about Ben, and there was still a question mark over his motives. Perhaps this was exactly what the hacker had banked on – Callanach feeling beholden or reliant so that help would be available whether he asked for it or not.

After an hour of staring at paperwork, issuing orders, and going over and over the same ground in his head, Callanach did the thing he'd sworn he'd never do having left France.

He picked up the phone and dialled Interpol's headquarters in Lyon.

Jean-Paul had been his best friend. During their years together at Interpol, they'd shared holidays, an apartment for a while, more meals than Callanach could count, and a host of memories that ranged from taking down an international paedophile ring in New York to trekking the Sahara as a bet. Then Jean-Paul had arranged a date for him with Astrid Borde and so started a chain of events that ended in a rape allegation. Jean-Paul had slipped away from him, as had so many others. But of all his colleagues and friends, it was Jean-Paul's disloyalty that had hurt the most. No doubt it had been hard for him, too. His best friend, the rapist. Did people tar them with the same brush? Did Jean-Paul suffer for their association? He certainly hadn't lost his job or his country as Callanach had. When Astrid had decided not to proceed with the trial, their friendship had been too wrecked to salvage. Now Callanach needed a favour and Jean-Paul owed him a lifetime of them.

'J-P,' he answered. Callanach hadn't thought how he might feel hearing his voice. He pushed the memories away and focused on what he needed.

'Hello Jean-Paul,' he said. 'This is Luc Callanach.' He chose to speak English, knowing his friend spoke it equally fluently. Callanach wanted to pretend that it was automatic for him now, but the truth was less noble. He was making a point. This was his new life. Even his language had been stolen from him. There was an audible intake of breath at the other end of the line.

'Luc,' Jean-Paul said. 'How are you?'

'Busy. We have a situation in Edinburgh. Four murders and we're bracing for more.'

'I've heard,' Jean-Paul said. 'So this is an official enquiry?'

'Not exactly,' Callanach replied. 'After all these years, does it really need to be?'

There was a long pause. Callanach heard a door slam. He could imagine J-P's office, his friend with his feet up on his desk, reading or writing notes. If the door had ever needed closing, he had stretched out a foot to kick it. It was as if he was right there in the room with him.

'I can't do anything without the proper authorisation. You know what procedure is like here.'

'You can if it's your own research, rather than an intelligence request. You'll find a way to link the name to one of your own investigations,' Callanach said, refusing to be put off. He could hear the shame in J-P's voice. Hopefully that shame would be enough to close the deal on an unofficial background check.

'And if that name also happens to be linked to a major crime in Scotland?' Jean-Paul asked.

'He's an international player, not a Scottish national. Ex Silicon Valley. Make it work.'

'Why did you call me?' Jean-Paul asked. There was an edge of whininess to his voice. Callanach felt a surge of irritation. If anyone deserved to be feeling sorry for themselves, it wasn't his former friend.

'Maybe I was missing you. Or perhaps I need to get a job done because lives are at stake. Does it matter? I need the background check. Everything. Family, work, education, criminal investigations, known associates.'

'How long do I have?' Jean-Paul asked. Callanach was relieved that he hadn't wanted to dwell on the reasons why he should play ball. It was as much recognition as he was going to get that his friend felt some guilt for what had happened.

'Now, on the phone. I have a meeting shortly,' Callanach said.

'The name?' Jean-Paul asked.

'Ben Paulson, US citizen currently residing and working in Edinburgh. He may be flagged in relation to cyber crime.'

'Working on it,' Jean-Paul said. 'So why is this off the record? It wouldn't have hurt to come through formal channels. Sounds like a legitimate request. What are you avoiding?'

'The cyber crime is someone else's investigation. Unfortunately myself and the officer in charge have conflicting interests.'

'You never make things easy, do you?' Jean-Paul said with a small laugh.

'The easy way was an option I lost when I had to start my career all over again,' Callanach said. He hadn't intended to say anything, but there it was – the bitter pill – still in his mouth, after swallowing so hard for so long.

'Luc, I didn't know what to do. I had no way of knowing what had really happened that night. You never mentioned a thing. How could I have known that you were innocent?'

'How could you ever have believed I was capable of it?' Callanach asked.

'Please, what you went through was terrible, but you have to believe I would do anything to turn back the clock,' Jean-Paul said. Callanach wanted to believe him, but it was easy for such declarations to be made on the telephone from so far away. And it was too little, too late.

'All I want is information. Find your own way to live with what happened. I have enough to worry about,' Callanach said.

There was silence. Callanach could almost see his friend's face. When Jean-Paul was worried he used to take a packet of tobacco from his pocket and roll a cigarette. His eyes would be closed as he did it, his hands so practised at the motions. Perhaps it was only his imagination, but Callanach thought he could hear the rustle of a cigarette paper beneath Jean-Paul's uneven breathing. He felt a rift within himself and wondered how it could be possible to feel such fury and such longing at the same time.

'Got it,' Jean-Paul said quietly. 'Benjamin Samuel Paulson, born July 29th 1987, believed to be part of an international hacking group. Mother and father both died when he was thirteen. Car accident. Moved school multiple times, lived with various of his parents' relatives. At fourteen he hacked into the school computer and erased students' disciplinary files. His IQ was noted to be extremely high but his behaviour was challenging. Arrested aged sixteen in San Francisco during a peace march that got out of hand, but only received a warning. He was taken on by a start-up in Silicon Valley, then fell in with some known Greenpeace activists. No other criminal proceedings on record. Lived in New York for a while, working for tech companies. Looks like Paulson's at the top of his game in programmer terms. NASA ran a background check on him with a view to offering him a position. He turned them down. Since then he's worked for a number of blue-chip companies all in the tech sector. There's mention of a group, The Unsung, but nothing concrete in the files. Someone else ran a background check on him recently – must be the investigation you mentioned. Known associates are other hackers. A couple of them have faced trial, but the charges weren't proved. They're left-wing anti-establishment.'

'Do you have anything else about The Unsung?' Callanach asked.

'Some suggestion that they were involved in the British politicians' expenses scandal last year. There's a suggestion The Unsung might have hacked into emails, leaked some documents. Nothing confirmed.'

That was the key, then. Whoever was putting pressure on DCI Edgar to make arrests had their own agenda, and it might be nothing more than simple revenge. A lot of important people still had mud on their faces and it was going to take a while to wash off.

'Any more about Paulson on a personal level?' Callanach asked.

'Not much. He was born in California. Had one sister, but there's nothing here about what happened to her. Mother was a teacher, aged forty-one when she died. Father was a couple of years older. He was a serving police officer. That may explain why Paulson got away with a warning after the disturbance at the peace rally. Those guys protect their own,' J-P said, his voice fading away, the irony of his words sinking in.

'That'll do,' Callanach said. 'Thank you J-P. And don't worry. I have no intention of making a habit of calling.' He put the phone down.

Below Par was underground. Not in the hacking, secretive sense of the word, but quite literally. The streets were busy with workers on lunch hours, shoppers and tourists, but even so Callanach was careful to check he wasn't being followed. He walked past Below Par twice, crossing the street and watching from other shops before committing to going in. Callanach walked down some old, stone steps, peered through the dusty, barred window a moment, then entered. The cafe, situated beneath a wedding dress shop, turned out to serve only decaffeinated tea and coffee, an array of herbal options and a variety of organic soft drinks.

Callanach was stopped at the door by a girl with more piercings than he could count, and an English accent that was all East End London. She looked him up and down before asking what he was after.

'Just coffee,' Callanach said. The cafe was only half full, mostly occupied by singles staring at screens.

'We're a bit busy at the moment,' the girl said. 'Perhaps one of the larger chain coffee stores would have the sort of thing you're after.'

'I'm supposed to be meeting someone here,' Callanach said, realising he was being bounced by a suspicious twenty-something who was probably half his weight. She was smiling and polite, but it was clear he wasn't going to be allowed entry. He guessed there was a lot more going on than the service of healthy, carbon-footprint-friendly beverages.

'And who might that be?' the girl enquired, raising a pencilled eyebrow.

'I'd rather not give a name, if you don't mind,' Callanach said.

'Then I'm afraid we're too busy to seat you.' She folded her arms.

Callanach had no idea what to do. He wasn't about to show his badge, given the circumstances, and the girl had done nothing wrong.

'Look, it's really important. My friend gave me the name of this place. If I leave now I might miss him,' Callanach said.

The girl put her hands on her hips and looked towards a door at the far end of the coffee shop. It opened.

'You can go on in,' the girl said. Callanach stepped past the counter towards the back of the cafe. 'Hold on, your mobile stays here. Next time, make sure your friend tells you the rules before inviting you.' She held out her hand. Callanach paused. There were numbers and details on his phone that shouldn't fall into other people's hands. He considered arguing, until Ben poked his head out of the rear door and nodded at him.

'It'll be fine,' Ben said. 'Polly's bark is worse than her bite.' A couple of the other cafe users laughed. Polly ignored them all, took the mobile from Callanach's hand and slid it into a drawer beneath the cash register.

'Thank you. Can I get you anything to drink?' she asked, as

if none of the previous conversation had taken place and he'd just walked in off the street.

'Espresso, please,' Callanach said.

Polly turned round, picked up a jug of coffee, poured a mug and handed it to him.

'Decaff is better for you,' she said.

Callanach knew when to give in. He thanked her and made his way to the back of the premises.

Lance was already there. He and Ben were grinning as Callanach entered.

'You must have a suspicious face,' Lance said. 'She let me straight in. No questions asked.'

'Polly's just looking out for me,' Ben said as he wired Lance's laptop into his own. 'She wasn't all that keen on the idea of me inviting a policeman for a meeting here.'

'She's your girlfriend?' Callanach asked.

'Necessary disclosures only, if you don't mind. Personal questions make me nervous.' Ben glanced at his watch. 'I've a client consultation back at the office in an hour so I can't be long. Let me show you what I've found.' He tapped through a series of passwords and logins at a pace Callanach couldn't follow, and landed on a page with a green flashing tab in the top left-hand corner. The only other graphic on the screen was a tiny yellow bottle at the bottom. The bottle slowly disappeared from sight. When it had gone completely, Ben refreshed the screen and it appeared again.

'What is this?' Callanach asked.

'This is where the GPS coordinates for your graffiti turned up. I suspect they're within chat folders, but I can't get in at the moment, so I can't give you the context.'

'What's the website? Can you not just give us the internet address?' Lance asked.

'It's darknet,' Ben said. 'Like Silk Road, the online drug

marketplace the FBI shut down. It's all encoded. You need the right software and to know how to use it. And most people who try only succeed in getting their own computer hacked. The majority of darknet websites are traps or scams.'

'So there's no way to find out who's posting or visiting the website?' Callanach asked.

'There's no such thing as "no way" when you're talking about the internet. It's just that some hacks take longer than others. This site is set up for specific users who will have been identity-checked by a moderator. The thing is, I can't find any information on what type of site we're dealing with. It might be pornography, paedophiles, drugs, even arms dealing.'

'So you need to set up a profile as the sort of scumbag who might genuinely be interested in this stuff? A generally violent, evil pervert,' Lance said.

'Exactly,' Ben replied. 'The problem is that you can't just create that person from nowhere. A moderator capable of setting up this site would have a new applicant checked out in minutes. A newly faked identity would stand out a mile.'

'Not if he's real,' Callanach said. 'What if we use someone who already exists, whose background I know? Someone who might genuinely want access to this sort of material.'

'That's identity theft, DI Callanach. We'll need to give real details. If you have someone in mind, I'll need to hack them first. Are you willing to take responsibility for that?' Ben asked.

Callanach sat back in his chair, hands behind his head. 'I'm sharing confidential information with a journalist, having lunch with someone who . . .' he didn't finish that sentence. 'I'm off the record and chasing leads I'm not sharing with my squad. If this gets out, borrowing a criminal's identity will be just one small charge among the many I'll be facing.'

Ben grinned and opened a new page on his laptop. 'You've got someone in mind, I take it?' he asked.

'Absolutely,' Callanach muttered, remembering his first case with Police Scotland. 'Rory Hand. He has previous convictions for some nasty sexual offences. Nothing serious recently, so he's in the community and will have access to the internet. He falsely claimed responsibility for a couple of murders last year in order to have access to the autopsy and crime scene photos. This is exactly his sort of thing. Identity checks will come back positive and make sense.'

'I'll need details – date of birth, last known address, passport number if he has one, that sort of thing,' Ben said.

'Not a problem,' Callanach said.

'But won't Rory Hand be sent an access code or password by email?' Lance asked. 'Hand will know something's going on.'

'I can control his emails, like putting a fishing net in front of everything that goes in. Whatever we don't need, I let go to him. Anything of interest to us he'll never see,' Ben said.

'And even if he suspects anything, the police would be the last place he'd go for help,' Callanach added. 'He's on the sex offenders register and still having to report to probation. Hand's no threat to us. I'm more concerned about the timing. We're at the mercy of the person in control of the website – the webmaster – as to how quickly he checks Hand out. I've got more than one hundred women waiting for a murderer to turn up and I'd sooner meet him or her before one of them does. Is there nothing else we can do to speed things along?'

'One thing at a time,' Ben said. 'We need to become Rory Hand, type his email address into the box you saw flashing on the website. Access will be denied, but the webmaster will check out the attempted entry anyway and then we wait for an invitation. No shortcuts, I'm afraid.'

Polly put her head round the door, passing in a plate of biscuits and three small cups with a glass teapot containing a green liquid.

'Anything else I can get you, Ben?' she asked.

'No thanks,' Ben replied, pouring a cup of herbal tea. Polly remained as Lance began to speak.

'Sorry, but this conversation can only be for the three of us,' Callanach said, trying not to look at the girl, keeping his voice friendly.

'You're safe with Polly,' Ben said. 'You keep us safe from the prying ears and eyes of the world, don't you babe?'

'Bloody Americans!' Polly said, smiling. 'Think you can call me babe and get away with it. I'll leave. I know when I'm not wanted.'

'I don't suppose you're free Friday night?' Ben called after her as she turned to go.

'Supposing's for idiots,' Polly replied, shutting the door after herself.

'So, not your girlfriend then,' Lance smiled. Ben glared and Lance slurped tea before beginning to speak again. 'I've been thinking – the emailed photos of Emily Balcaskie and leaked autopsy report are about publicity. But the police have kept the details of Michael Swan's death very quiet.'

'I ordered Swan's details to be kept offline after Helen Lott's autopsy report was hacked,' Callanach said.

'Exactly,' Lance continued. 'Which may be why Emily Balcaskie's murderer had to go to the lengths of taking photos and emailing them himself.'

'We kept the details of Michael Swan's death quiet for a reason,' Callanach said. 'What the killer did is too awful for public consumption. It'll have to come out if there's a trial, but for now his family shouldn't have to deal with any more press coverage.'

'I'm not suggesting you let those poor people suffer any more than they already have. I may be a journalist but I'm not a sadist. But why not release the wrong details? Issue a formal statement, through me, stating that Mr Swan died painlessly, swiftly, and that he wouldn't have been aware what was happening.'

'You want to see if the killer will make contact to put his side of it across?' Ben asked.

Lance nodded.

'Man, you've got some balls. I wouldn't want one of those guys coming round to correct my copy,' Ben said.

'Might it give us another chance to trace them, if we were waiting and watching?' Lance asked.

'It's possible,' Ben said. 'But I can't guarantee anything.'

'Possible is better than waiting for the next corpse,' Callanach said. 'Let me warn Mrs Swan what we're doing first, Lance, then we'll agree the wording.'

The door opened, this time with no warning.

'Ben,' Polly said. 'You'd better get back to your office. We got a call. The police are there asking questions and your name has come up.'

Callanach ran a hand through his hair.

'Did you know about this?' Ben asked Callanach. 'You know what, don't answer that.'

'Ben, even if I'd told you, there's nothing you could have done. If you'd started wiping files off your computer they'd have known . . .'

Ben leaned down to whisper in Callanach's ear. 'DI Callanach, I'm not asking you to protect me. If Edgar thinks I'm stupid enough to have anything on my work computers except work, then he's even more moronic than his school records suggest. But they'll have put maximum surveillance on today, meaning this may not have been the best time for us to do lunch, for your sake, more than mine. I already have people watching my back. Who's got yours?'

Chapter Twenty-Four

Callanach drove directly to Craigentinny to visit the widowed Mrs Swan. It was a difficult thing to explain – that he had gone there not to give her answers, but to open more avenues of investigation, involving a substantial lie being told very publicly.

'What then, Detective Inspector?' Mrs Swan asked. 'When your killer decides that they want the truth to be known? Will they post photos of what they did to Michael? Is that what you expect?'

She broke down into tears, as Callanach had known she would. Police work wasn't always about sparing people pain. Sometimes it was about knowingly causing it, in the belief that the end would justify the means. Callanach let her recover before answering.

'I don't believe the killer has a photographic record or they'd have released it before now. They're more likely to give a written account of what they did. We need them to do that so we can trace their communications. I would hope that the press would be careful in publishing details, especially as they won't be able to verify the source. It's a risk, though. And one I need you to be aware of before I take this any further.'

'And if I say no? If I say that my husband being taken from us is terrible enough, without my family suffering further? Will you accept that and reconsider?'

'Mrs Swan, you've seen the papers. There are other people under threat now. The whole city has been overtaken by a sense of panic,' Callanach said.

'As well it might be,' she replied. 'Did you know the pathologist thinks my husband might have taken an hour to die. An hour! You should be going door to door, checking every single person and asking what they were doing that night. Writing a new press report and hoping the murderer will give herself away? My God, if that's the best you've got then the people of Edinburgh shouldn't just be worried. They should be fleeing!'

Callanach could do no more. Nothing he said was going to soften the blow. And Mrs Swan was right – Callanach wasn't going to change his mind. They were running out of options.

Driving back through the city, a marked police car passed him at speed. Callanach took no notice until another followed, then two more and an emergency response team in a van. He checked his phone but there were no texts or missed calls. On instinct he followed, chasing the blues and twos south through the traffic.

The parade of police cars stopped at the corner of Findhorn Place with Grange Loan, in the Blackford area of the city. These were quiet streets with a mixture of old and new housing, front hedges kept neat, on-street parking, and an orderly plainness to it all. At the corner was a three-storey seventies-looking block of flats, sealed off with crime scene tape. Callanach's phone rang as he was climbing out of his vehicle. He could see Lively before he heard his voice.

'I'm already here, sergeant,' Callanach said, ducking the tape and flashing his badge at the guarding uniforms. 'What is it?' he asked, sliding his mobile back into his pocket.

'One of the lollipop ladies, sir. A woman from a flat on the ground floor was due to meet her this morning. They always get the bus into town together, she says. When her mate didn't arrive at the bus stop, the friend went to find her and saw her front door was busted.'

'Where's the body?' Callanach asked.

'That's the thing. No body this time. You'd better come up.' Lively was already pulling on shoe covers and an overall. Callanach followed suit, making the forensics team aware of his presence and grabbing a pair of gloves.

'What's the missing woman's name?' Callanach asked.

'Julia Stimple, aged sixty-four, divorced, lives alone. One son, one daughter, but no one's been able to reach them yet. She doesn't own a mobile. It's a one-bedroomed flat on the second floor.'

Callanach stood on the front step of the flats, looking around. This was the sort of neighbourhood where people knew each other. Beyond the crime scene tape was a growing wall of faces, united in their silence, some wrapped arm in arm, others standing respectfully with heads down. All expecting the worse. The juxtaposition from the stillness of the onlookers to the business of the forensic team was jarring. The other flats had been cleared, the residents moved elsewhere to have statements taken.

Callanach climbed the stairs. It was not lavish accommodation by any stretch of the imagination. The internal doors had lost their former blue and were now a mottled grey. The walls were stained nicotine yellow. There was an obvious lack of recent redecoration. It was more functional than comfortable, but within the affordability range of a woman living between state allowance and the top-up wages from the few hours spent seeing people safely across busy roads.

The door to Julia Stimple's flat stood open. Callanach took his time walking through, trying to imagine it without the ant-like procession of white-suited technicians inhabiting the place now. Not one piece of furniture had been left upright. A small dining table was on its side, both chairs tipped over, one of which had a leg snapped off. Mismatched, threadbare armchairs were on their sides, a coffee table smashed to pieces. One curtain had been ripped from its pole, the other hung limply from pulled hooks. Crockery and glasses were smashed on the floor and the remains of a half-eaten dinner lay in a congealed trail across the kitchen linoleum. Callanach went into the bathroom. A swing seat that should have helped its owner in and out of the bath had been broken. The contents of the bathroom cabinet were scattered over the sink, the floor, the windowsill.

In the bedroom, sheets and an old patchwork quilt had been dragged from the bed, twisted, then left hanging where they'd been tucked in at one corner, as if they'd clung to the bed in terror. Drawers were tipped out, the wardrobe door left open to show an array of deserted clothes. It was as if a tornado had ripped through. Nothing had been left untouched.

Callanach walked to the bedside table and picked up a framed photograph that had fallen on its face. In it was a woman he estimated to be in her fifties, wearing the sort of hat you could only get away with at a race track, holding up a glass of champagne and smiling as if she'd won the lottery. Her hair was bouffant, surrounding her head in massive, hairdresser-constructed curls. But it was dwarfed by the size of the woman herself who filled the shot in a pink and green ensemble, flowing across her frame like a waterfall. At her size, even the single set of stairs up to her flat would have been a daily struggle. It was a wonder that she was still working at all. Her health must already have been failing if the bath seat was anything to go by.

'Blood, sir,' Lively said, poking his head round the door.

Callanach handed him the photo by way of reply.

'Bag the photo and tell forensics we need to take it with us once it's been logged. If we can't get hold of a family member soon, this will be the only identification we'll have for a press release. Where's the blood?'

'Kitchen,' Lively said, grabbing an evidence bag from a passing crime scene officer.

Callanach retraced his steps, watching the progress forensics were making. The blood was a stream of drips rather than the dramatic pooling found at the previous murder scenes. It ran from the dinner table to the kitchen, as if she'd been trying to stem the flow as she'd walked. Samples and photographs were taken as a blood spatter analyst marked the pathway and plotted it on a plan.

'Anyone found a weapon?' Callanach called. There was a ripple of negative responses. It wasn't a surprise. No weapon had been found at the other crime scenes, save for Emily Balcaskie's scarf, and that had been left for effect.

In the doorway the chain was hanging off, the screws that had once held it to the frame abandoned on the floor. Julia Stimple had been persuaded to open up and see what her visitor wanted, but not trusted them enough to have opened the door fully. The question was how they'd gained access through the main door. There was a buzzer but no camera feed. Either her visitor had persuaded her to let them in, or waited and followed someone else up the stairs.

'Anything obviously missing?' Callanach asked the nearest officer.

'Her purse isn't in her handbag and it hasn't been located anywhere else in the flat. Other than that, it's hard to know what we're looking for. It was a hell of a fight though. I'm not sure how they managed to create so much devastation in every room,' the technician replied.

207

Lively stepped back through the door as Callanach was getting ready to leave.

'What a bloody mess,' Lively said. 'You'd think someone would've heard something, wouldn't you?' Callanach stared at him. 'Nothing. Quiet as a poxy church mouse. Everyone was in, and I mean everyone. Residents above, below and opposite. No one was aware of a stranger in the building, no one saw her being taken out.'

'Give me a break,' Callanach said, stretching his neck and rolling his shoulders.

'Too much even for a genius like yourself, is it sir?' Lively asked, although his usual grin was missing. 'To be fair, these are people who go to bed early, some are hard of hearing, probably have their TVs turned way up. But this . . .' He gestured around the room. The chaos was quite an achievement.

'We've two murderers out there,' Callanach said. 'One's quiet, almost ghostlike. She leaves no trail, no trace, even in broad daylight. Her work is surgical and planned. Helen Lott's killer is all strength and brutality. Nothing subtle there. But how could this invader have been neither heard nor seen, given that he or she kicked the door off its chain?'

'And then cleaned off the bootmark,' a forensic technician replied from behind them. 'There's nothing here. Only the usual mixture of fingerprints around the lock, but nothing lower down that indicates a shoe.'

'Perhaps they took their boots off to climb the stairs quietly, then kicked the door open with bare feet,' Lively said.

'And why take the victim away?' Callanach asked. 'I don't see the purpose. It would have been more risky than anything they've done so far to have moved her through a multiple occupancy building.'

'That's not so difficult. Knife in her back. A promise not to harm her. It's amazing how many victims will believe whatever they're told. The friend who reported it says Miss Stimple suffers from advanced type 2 diabetes. She's on regular medication, has complications with her kidneys and her eyesight is failing. Sounds as if she was going to have to stop work pretty soon anyway. Wasn't fit enough to stand up for long stretches,' Lively read from his notebook.

'So this time they took the most vulnerable person they could find. She worked in the community, is coming to the end of her time there, becoming physically less able. Fits the pattern. I'll need to speak with her manager. Let me know as soon as we contact a family member. No press release until we've dealt with it personally,' Callanach instructed.

'Aye, and the usual work is underway. Door-to-door checks in case anyone saw them leaving, or any suspicious vehicles. There's no CCTV locally, it's all residential. Best hope we've got is an eyewitness. You off back to your cushy office then, sir?' Lively asked.

'No, Lively, I thought I'd spend some time at the gym, maybe get a quick sports massage and a sunbed,' Callanach sighed. 'Now, control the scene, get me photos of the flat ASAP and make sure none of it goes online. No leaks. And stop being such an idiot, would you? I've got enough of that in my life at the moment.'

Lively's mouth hung open as Callanach walked away. The lack of comment from him was a tiny victory, but the only one Callanach was likely to be celebrating for some time.

By the time Callanach got back to his office, Tripp was waiting with Julia Stimple's manager on the line. He handed the phone over and Callanach sat down waiting for the barrage of abuse.

'Have you found her yet, Detective Inspector?' the manager asked. 'Only we're being bombarded with requests from the press and I have no idea what to say.'

'Julia Stimple is missing from her home but there's no body, so we'd like you to say you're unable to comment. At the moment we have no idea where she is or what state she's in. Can you tell me more about Miss Stimple, only we're struggling to locate her family? I'm also trying to ascertain how she came to the killer's attention. Had there been any publicity about her, community awards, that sort of thing?'

There was a long period of quiet, punctuated only by throat clearing.

'I'm not sure how much I should tell you,' the manager said. 'Obviously we have to protect staff confidentiality. I wouldn't want this to get out . . .'

Callanach rolled his eyes to the ceiling, pleased he wasn't in the same room as the woman on the end of the line. As if four murders and an abduction weren't enough, now he was having to persuade other officials to information share.

'It'll all be confidential,' Callanach reassured through gritted teeth.

'Well, if you're sure, I suppose I can pass on what I've been told. Miss Stimple had been informed that her employment was to be terminated at the end of the month. A decision had been made to replace her. She wasn't up to the job,' the manager said.

'I'm aware of her health problems,' Callanach said, 'but I don't think that would have attracted any attention. All the other victims—'

'You don't understand,' the manager interrupted. 'Miss Stimple had been the subject of complaints from parents. She would turn up late, leave early, was often seen leaning against the wall, just waving children over the road. When a parent challenged her about it a couple of weeks ago, Miss Stimple's reply was, um, not exactly what Edinburgh City Council would hope from one of its employees. There was some language used, you see. It was only your investigation and her remaining at home that saved us from having to take more drastic action. There was a disciplinary hearing. She wasn't best pleased.'

'But there had been no publicity about it,' Callanach said, 'so no one would have known she was being fired?'

'Goodness no, none at all. These sorts of things are handled with complete discretion. Miss Stimple agreed with Human Resources that she was finding the work too physically hard and that it would be better for all concerned if she agreed to leave.'

'I see,' said Callanach. 'And has there been any other press coverage you know of that might have made her a target?'

'Only the employee newsletter from a couple of months ago,' the manager replied. 'A group photo was taken of all the lollipop team, men and women. I can email it to you if it would help.'

'It would,' Callanach said. 'Please get in touch if you think of anything else. We'll let you know as soon as there's an update.'

Callanach busied himself retrieving Rory Hand's details from the police national computer. It didn't take long. Hand had only been released from prison three months earlier. He didn't have a passport and was reporting to probation twice a week. Callanach noted his address, mobile number, national insurance number and date of birth, then sent the agreed text to Ben with no regrets at all. Rory Hand deserved a lot more than to have his identity abused.

Five minutes later, Tripp handed him a printout of the scanned lollipop person's photo. Sitting in the front row, centre stage and staring straight at the camera, was Julia Stimple. The picture had come attached to an email, revealing that the newsletter had been left in just about every public building in the city, from job centres to courts, adult education facilities to libraries. Not much of a stretch to imagine a passer-by picking it up and choosing the woman who, because of her size, would be easy to identify and locate. The sort of woman, in fact, who looked as if she wouldn't be capable of putting up much of a fight at all.

PART TWO

Chapter Twenty-Five

The Moderator – always with a capital letter in his own mind – made sure his office door was locked, left his work system uploading some new code and plugged in his laptop instead. He'd told his personal assistant he would be on a conference call and should not be interrupted. It was a reasonable excuse for having his door locked should anyone attempt an unscheduled visit.

He logged onto the darknet site of which he was creator, designer, webmaster and overseer of all things, and made sure secure encoding was enabled. He had set up six different levels of security, including twenty character passwords, randomised personal knowledge questions, a thumbprint scan and a mathematical formula that had to be solved against a countdown clock. Every aspect had been designed and built by him. The encoding software was commonly downloadable, but then he had to make sure that the site users he wanted to attract would be able to find their way in.

Today there were three new applicants requesting access to the site. More than he was expecting, but things were heating up. He had a global audience, albeit with specific appetites. In a new and braver world, had this been a reality TV show, he'd have been a billionaire by now.

He scrolled through the applicants' names: Travis Stoppa from Utah, Askel Lund from Denmark and Rory Hand from Scotland. He paused on the third name, making some cursory checks and finding an address for him in less than a minute. Was it coincidence that Hand was from Edinburgh or had he moved to be closer to the action? There was no referral username given in his application. The Moderator didn't like that. He preferred it when he knew which current user had shared the site information. It meant he would have to be that much more thorough with the background checks.

Standard internet search engines were always the first port of call, but they usually had low information yield. Not so this time. Rory Hand had been a busy boy. A variety of unimpressive sexual offences had earned him the usual prison sentences. The more interesting press coverage detailed Hand's attempt to pass off Dr Reginald King's murders of three prostitutes last year as his own. That had earned Mr Hand another spell at Her Majesty's Hotel for those who couldn't commit crimes without getting caught.

The Moderator confirmed Hand's previous convictions and checked his personal information against local authority records. The pervert certainly had the motivation for joining the group, although he wasn't as well qualified as certain of its members. There were hundreds of them now from all over the world. A fair proportion were from Russia, many from China, and the predictable crowd from the United States – large population masses, where individuals could disappear and live virtually undetected. That was where his followers liked to exist. Under the public radar, beneath the governmental administrative net, in their own little worlds. More importantly these days, the place they really liked to live in was the world the Moderator had created.

There was some bitcoin exchanged. No one used real money on the darknet. Real money was too traceable, too regulated. In fact, the site had generated more bitcoin than the Moderator had anticipated, but that wasn't the point. The point was to get all the right people together in the right place. He felt a momentary flush of embarrassment at his own pomposity, then thrust it aside. Why shouldn't he feel proud? He'd planned it, spent a punishing amount of time learning the coding, taken some risks at the start contacting the sort of people who might be interested. He was entitled to be self-congratulatory. Not yet, though. Not too soon. There was still a way to go.

The Moderator sent Rory Hand an email containing a link to click. Once Hand had done so, the Moderator would be able to look through his emails, check his internet use, see what hidden horrors lurked in his deleted folders. That was where the telling information sat. It was in the nooks and crannies of the digital world, in the places people thought it couldn't be found and seen. He could have blackmailed hundreds of people by now with what he'd found. Or become the online equivalent of a comic book hero, ridding the world of a fair selection of deviants, abusers, and sadists. Other men would have allowed themselves to become heady with the power of it. Lesser men would have taken sexual gratification from some of the material he'd seen in his site users' inboxes. His purpose was more practical than that.

He spent another fifteen minutes checking out the other two applicants then turned his attention to the site. The police had finally figured out the graffiti communications. About time too. He'd been almost at the point of sending an anonymous tip to help them out. The set-up had been simple. For every victim, each site member was entitled to suggest one profession as a target. The Moderator secretly notified the kill target to one of the players who had to graffiti it at a given location for their opponent to act upon. Grom notified Sem Culpa who her next kill was, Sem Culpa did the same for Grom, and so on. Every part of the process served a purpose. The poll gave the members a sense of drama and involvement. Impressing the members was the driver for Grom and Sem Culpa to make the kills. The graffiti, all part of the showmanship, enabled the police to see a pattern. And crucially, every part of the scheme created a world in which two psychopathic murderers could draw the world's attention. The targets were random, unfortunate, chosen courtesy of the global appetite for online media coverage. And that was where the police focus would be. Not that Police Scotland's dim-witted detectives were any closer to either of the killers yet. The selected two were better than that. The Moderator had chosen them from numerous applicants because of their track records of avoiding arrest.

There had been some game changes required along the way – what plan ever ran smoothly? Upon choosing his two players, he'd imagined that Grom would be the right choice to make the final kill with all the drama and horror he could unleash. But it was Sem Culpa who had pleased audiences most. The audacity of killing in the middle of a crowd and waltzing away. The poetic resonance of the destruction of life in a library, where the improvement of human minds through literature was the foremost aim. Sem Culpa was the cleverer of the two by far. The truth was that Grom couldn't be trusted. His smash and crush approach had its place, but the moderator needed to make absolutely sure that the final target would be successfully dispatched. It had required some rejigging of the order of things, but that wasn't the end of the world. What really mattered was getting Sem Culpa to the right place at the right time. Whatever Grom did from now on was entirely a matter of keeping the public entertained and keeping the police busy.

Last thing before logging out he posted a few online articles that would take time to rise up the search engine rankings, enabling them to be found quickly when the time came. There was always groundwork to be done. Nothing could be left to chance. His phone beeped to let him know it was time to get back to the day job. He would still need it for a while.

Chapter Twenty-Six

DI Ava Turner stood outside Superintendent Overbeck's door, twisting her newly fitted gold band complete with oversized diamond round and round her ring finger. It was fractionally too large, although that did make it easy to slip off, as she had last night once Joe had fallen asleep. She was too aware of its weight for comfort.

'Come in,' Overbeck shouted. Ava obeyed.

'Sit down DI Turner,' Overbeck said. She was being friendly. Ava's hackles rose. 'I gather congratulations are in order. Sensible girl marrying well.'

The chief, old-school though he was, would never have called her 'girl'. Coming from a fellow female officer it seemed even more offensive. Or perhaps that should have made it acceptable. Ava tried to focus. She was oversensitive and off her game.

'What was it you needed, ma'am?' Ava asked.

'How's the investigation going?' Overbeck asked. 'Any forward momentum?'

'There's a video reconstruction of the Emily Balcaskie murder scheduled for television broadcast tonight. We've been flooded with so many false alarms and wrong identifications that we're chasing our tails. I'm waiting to hear back from Interpol about the DNA found at the Helen Lott murder scene. It takes a while to process through the international database, it's so vast.'

'Speaking of Interpol, I've had a complaint about DI Callanach,' Overbeck said.

So that was why she'd been called in, Ava thought. So much for subtlety.

'Who?' Ava asked.

'I beg your pardon?' Overbeck said, handing Ava a cup of coffee she didn't want and hadn't requested.

'Who put in the complaint?' Ava said, putting the coffee cup straight back down on the table.

'That's not important. What interests me is how much you know about his current activities. He seems rather lax about reporting in and I'm concerned about what progress he's making.'

'The graffiti was Callanach's discovery,' Ava said, 'and it's been borne out by the abduction of Julia Stimple. It's the best break either of us has got in the investigation so far.'

'But that's all. One of his murders was committed in broad daylight in a crowd of festival-goers. It beggars belief that there's no lead on that.'

'None of these murders were impromptu. They were professionally planned and executed. If Callanach hasn't got anything concrete yet, that's just the way it is. What exactly was the complaint against DI Callanach about?'

'A variety of things. I'd appreciate your input. There are some changes coming and I need to know where all the pieces fit in the puzzle.'

Ava frowned. It wasn't like Overbeck to be anything less than brutally direct. She was even more dislikeable in pleasant mode than when she was being deliberately harsh.

'If you don't mind my saying, ma'am, you should be asking Callanach himself about this. It's not for me to comment. Was there anything else?' Ava asked.

'Are you in a particular hurry?' Overbeck arched an eyebrow. 'Tell me what your plans are once you marry. Will you remain in Edinburgh or move to London?'

'I hadn't thought that far ahead,' Ava said, her face reddening. 'It's all happened so fast.'

'DCI Edgar has a bright future ahead of him at Scotland Yard by all accounts. I'd have thought you'd be excited about an opportunity to move to London. It would be easy for you to find a post. And then I suppose you'll be thinking about children.'

'Do you have children then, ma'am?' Ava asked, her tone harsh enough to earn a glower from Overbeck.

'I don't,' Overbeck said, 'but I know Joe is keen to start a family. I'd assumed you two would have discussed it.'

Ava stood up. Overbeck could order her to remain and talk work, but she couldn't be forced to spill her guts about her private life.

'I'm needed in the incident room. We're already short-handed. If there's nothing else?' Ava said.

'One more thing about Callanach. Are you aware who he's been spending time with lately, or what channels he's pursuing?' Overbeck asked.

'No,' Ava said. 'We communicate professionally and that's it.'

'Oh, I thought you two were friends outside of work,' Overbeck said. 'Some people seem to attract trouble wherever they go, don't they?'

'Has something specific been raised about DI Callanach's private life?' Ava asked.

'I thought you were in a hurry, DI Turner. Your squad will be waiting.'

Ava had been dismissed. She made her way back to the incident room, passing Callanach's office on the way. She wondered if he was in, considered knocking, reconsidered, and went to her own office instead. Callanach had been absent from the station a lot lately. Somebody had it in for him though, and if Ava were in his shoes she'd want to know.

She thumped down hard into her chair. Callanach had behaved like an idiot at her engagement party, storming in and issuing orders to get back to work. Joe had been so nice about it afterwards, hypothesising that it was hard for Callanach to see her starting a new life when he'd had to leave his behind in France. That was probably right, but still . . . Callanach's reaction had been childish.

Ava considered phoning Natasha in the States. She hadn't told her about the engagement yet. It had been years since Tasha had met Joe, and Ava had been avoiding the subject of their renewed relationship, knowing that Natasha and he had never really hit it off. Joe had changed, though. He was what Ava needed right now. Natasha would understand.

A uniformed constable slid a note onto her desk, bearing an Interpol heading and a tiny font. Ava began to read. The international DNA database had come back with a hit for Helen Lott's killer's DNA. Her initial excitement morphed into frustration. It was an empty hit, meaning they had a DNA match on file for another murder, but no one had ever been apprehended. She read the summary of the related offence.

'Ljubljana, Slovenia. 4 May 2011. Corpse of male, twenty-three years of age, found in trunk of car left undisturbed in public car park for three weeks. Police alerted to scene by passer-by concerned over smell issuing from vehicle. Extreme violence. Cause of death massive brain trauma. Weapon used: hammer, found in boot of car with body. Skin scrape beneath victim's fingernail provided DNA sample. Believed defensive injury. Autopsy shows twenty-four hammer blow sites to head and torso. No DNA match on Slovenian police database. Victim had recently moved to area. No known motive. No persons of interest identified.'

So the murderer had struck once in Slovenia, twice in Scotland, and who knew where else. Without a criminal record he was free to move across much of Europe unchecked. The offences were notably similar in the degrees of violence, but in Slovenia he'd sought to cover his tracks, hiding the body to allow time for escape. And the only reason to need time to leave the area was if he had links there. It was an assumption, but a reasonable one, that Ava was hunting for a Slovenian national. She called in a detective sergeant.

'Follow up this Interpol report. I want to know if the Slovenian police publicised the fact that they had the killer's DNA. If not, our killer won't be bothering to hide the fact that he's Slovenian. Text me as soon as you have an answer. And let the media team know I may be calling a press conference tonight.'

Chapter Twenty-Seven

Grom sat opposite the lollipop lady. He'd expected her to be scared, but she had either misunderstood her circumstances or she was the bravest person he'd ever met. Then there was the dementia option. He hadn't bothered tying her up. It wasn't as if she was in a fit state to run anywhere.

His English wasn't great, and the Scottish accent made it that bit harder, but he'd been able to settle in relatively well. Edinburgh was more welcoming than London. He'd only stayed in the English capital a few months before moving on. Poland had been his first stop when he'd left Slovenia, but it had felt too close to home. After that he'd tried Paris, but found he couldn't walk down a street without people staring. He didn't blend into crowds. He was too tall, too broad. And in Paris, the fact that he wasn't French had seemed to stand out a mile. Even amidst the immigrant population, he still felt out of place. But the United Kingdom was across a stretch of water. It was as if the ferry trip had removed him from his past life. He had finally been able to stop running. And then this opportunity had presented itself. He was living in Birmingham when he'd been tipped off about the website. Birmingham was like a bowl of human soup, everyone mixed, blended, shoved together. There he'd been free to do whatever he wanted, to experiment.

Born Alfonz Kopitar, he was from the mountains originally. A country boy who had grown up with his father and brother, always the target of their jokes, always to blame for whatever went wrong. If only they could see him now – travelling the world, feared by so many, venerated by the few who mattered.

'Lollipop lady,' Grom said, spitting globules of saliva-soaked bread as he stuffed himself with a sandwich. 'You hungry?'

'Animal,' lollipop lady responded. Grom understood her better when she said only one word at a time. At first, she'd spewed endless language at him, most of which he'd found unintelligible.

'You eat if I say,' Grom said, throwing the last piece of his sandwich across the room. It hit the edge of the bin and bounced onto the floor. He didn't need to clean up. He'd be making enough of a mess of the place before the week was out. Why worry about a few stray pieces of food? He was the boss. No one could tell him what to eat, how to eat. Not like it had been with his father, dragging him across the floor if food had been spilt, making him lick it off the broken, dirty tiles like a dog.

'I have to go to the toilet,' lollipop lady said.

'You just gone,' Grom told her. He hated that aspect of having a prisoner. The need to care for them, the demands. Killing quickly was easier.

'I have a weak bladder. And my medication has a diuretic effect.'

'Not understand,' Grom said, pushing his face into hers. He couldn't allow himself to lose his temper. One punch from him and it would all be over, and he hadn't yet figured out how to kill her. It had to be spectacular. He had to win back some of the ground he was losing to that bitch Sem Culpa.

That was her username. He had a much better picture of her now that she'd been careless enough to get caught on CCTV after murdering the librarian.

Grom was Kopitar's username. It meant thunder in Slovenian. He preferred it to his given name. Grom was everything anyone needed to know about him. He was unstoppable, a crack of pure energy that would be heard across the globe. And he had thought of it all by himself.

'I . . . need . . . to . . . pee,' lollipop lady said. 'Do . . . you . . . understand?'

Grom bent down close to her ear and roared. See how much she liked his special brand of thunder. He pulled his head back to look into her eyes and witness the fear. He saw none.

'I'm a bit deaf in that ear,' she said. 'Could you take me to the bathroom now?'

Grom grabbed the front of her jumper, marching her to the toilet. The lollipop lady made it last as long as she could, then retook her chair. For now, Grom was keeping her in the lounge. He was biding his time, waiting for a sufficient build-up of press attention before showing his work to the world.

Sem Culpa had taken out her first victim in the middle of a festival – in bright sunshine, in view of thousands – and walked away, for God's sake. It was so perfect, he'd cried. Then he'd had his chance to shine, reducing Helen Lott to pulp on the floor. There couldn't have been a bone left unbroken. He had been a machine. Remorseless, untiring, bestial. And still Sem Culpa had outshone him with her next kill, perhaps not publicly, but her description of it on the website had garnered ridiculous praise. The only thing that had stopped him from giving up and boarding the next ferry out of Scotland was the fact that the press had been all but silent on the details. Sem Culpa had yet to prove her claims. His work on Emily Balcaskie had been simple but powerful, leaving Edinburgh's inhabitants scared to walk the city streets at night. And now this unexpected opportunity, before Sem Culpa had taken her next shot, not that it mattered how the game was being organised. Only that he won it. Psychologists would be arguing for decades about his mental state and motivation.

'Where're you from, then?' lollipop lady asked.

'Slovenia,' Grom replied.

'Never heard of it,' she responded with a smile.

'You know as Yugoslavia,' Grom said, picking up a notebook and trying to focus on the crucial aspects of a perfect murder.

'Damned foreigners,' lollipop lady muttered. 'Will I get myself a cup of tea then?'

Chapter Twenty-Eight

Sem Culpa, 'blameless' when translated from her native Portuguese, was meditating. She had a strict morning regime which included jogging, yoga, bathing in hot salted water, masturbation and finally meditation.

She brought herself back from her trance state, stretched and stared in the mirror. Her hair was shorter than she usually kept it, but the new length enabled her to hide it beneath hats, wear a variety of wigs, and disguise herself convincingly in male clothing as required. It was currently an unexciting shade of brown, but it matched her eyes and the overall effect was to make her appear younger than her twenty-eight years.

There was a discreet knock on the other side of her door. She wrapped a towel around herself and stood aside to allow the room service porter to deliver lunch. Scrambled eggs with chillies and avocado, mineral water and fresh pomegranate. Passing him a rolled up five pound note, she grabbed a fork. Her appetite was raging. Not that she would gain weight. Every day was about staying in shape, making sure she was strong and flexible, at her peak whether fight or flight was needed. Flicking on the television, she channel-hopped until the Scottish news appeared.

It appeared that Grom — what sort of low-level thug name was that? — had finally made his move. A lollipop lady was missing from her flat. Sem Culpa had been waiting impatiently for him to get on with it ever since she'd scrawled the victim choice on the wall. There was no corpse yet though. It wasn't like Grom to take his time. His other efforts had been like teenage sex. All hot, sweaty, clumsy, grinding and grunting. No finesse. No artistry. And as far as she was concerned, with simply no sufficiently thrilling element of risk. It had been a nice touch, admittedly, taking those photographs of sweet Emily and getting the moderator to leak them to the press.

She bristled at how little publicity she'd received for her work on Michael Swan. Certain the moderator would be able to hack the forensic pathologist's files, Sem Culpa hadn't thought to take a camera of her own. Then there was her obsession with utmost professionalism. It was cameras that hung you. No evidence was quite as damning as the police finding crime scene photos on your mobile or hard drive. She remained philosophical though. Sooner or later the reporting dam would burst and the details would cause the most hardened readers and viewers to close their eyes.

In the meantime she had only to wait for notification of her final target, and that was unlikely to arrive until Grom had finished his latest challenge. She had a while to plan. The precise details would be subject-specific — male or female, age, location — but she could dream beautiful dreams of how to present the corpse. That was her pride and joy. Let Grom chase mindless notoriety. Her goal was to create the ultimate horror.

Turning the television off, she picked up a sketch pad and pencil. Drawing was one of her other passions. Those dark lines could express so much pain, such infinite wretchedness, as if they were soaking up through the paper rather than being trailed across it. Lacking a vision for her next masterpiece, Sem

Culpa slashed lines and filled shade to recreate Michael Swan's last moments as best she could. It wasn't bad for the speed with which she'd drawn. Swan's mouth was a broad hole of agony, his clotting blood the last hurrah of his deteriorating body's efforts to sustain him. Arms spread wide like some falling angel, long legs flying behind him, graceful and lithe. Sem Culpa stared, breathless, reliving his plea for life until she'd shown him the picture of his wife taken outside their pitiable home.

After that Michael Swan had proved himself a good man. She was pleased. It wouldn't have been worth half the trouble she'd gone to if he'd been a disappointment. All those articles about his community work, his forthcoming award, his dedication to children's literacy. When he'd grasped the fact that it was him or his precious – and accessible – spouse, he hadn't uttered one word more. He'd fallen willingly on the proverbial sword. Only his tears had lessened the effect. That softness. That weakness.

Sem Culpa was not weak. She was the arrow that always found its mark. Portugal had been too small to hold her. Her parents had been too simpering, too obliging to control her. Expelled from one private school after another, they had resorted to a series of ineffectual tutors to educate her. Eventually enough years passed and the prospect of university dawned. The University of Lisbon had accepted her application immediately. Not that they would have turned her away given the funding contributions her family had made over the years. That was in her early days, when she was taking tentative steps towards her true self. Back then she had been known as Amalia, meaning industrious. In that, at least, she had proved her parents right.

University had been a drag. Timetables, deadlines, puerile children playing at being grown-ups. She had hated it. It was supposed to have been the great equaliser. Living together, studying together, exchanging ideas and enjoying the day-to-day.

And yet she was blighted by idiots teaching her, serving her, living alongside her, giggling, posing, stressing. That had been both her undoing and the start of her great adventure.

There had been poison involved. Industrial arsenic – not hard to obtain – and the university canteen's ratatouille. No one had died, disappointingly, but it had been an awakening. Her first true orgasm.

She'd left soon after that, discovering that neither a university education nor a nine-to-five routine was necessary to make money in the digital age. A year later she was running a successful social media promotions website. All at a distance from her clients, no private details required, only a sound knowledge of how the internet worked and what people wanted from it. Between the allowance from her parents and the money her company made, she could afford to stay in five-star hotels wherever she went.

Her family didn't try to contact her often. There were messages on her birthday, at Christmas, perfunctory monthly email updates. But never a plea for her to return home, to spend time with them. Almost as if her continued travels were a relief to them.

Her knowledge of the digital world had drawn her to the darknet's twisty passages years before the game in which she was now star player had been imagined. She had bought knives there unlike anything the open market had to offer, found devices for sexual play that offered uses in other, more torturous scenarios. More recently an organ marketplace had sprung up. That one offered the really big money. If she ever found herself strapped for cash, it would be a joyous way to make money. Her skills with a scalpel were something to behold.

Then the moderator had found her on a different website, inviting her to join. At first she'd been sure it was a trap. Then membership grew. Identities were tested. No one made their way onto the forum without the right credentials. The darknet had stuttered briefly when the FBI and MI5 had made their lives a bit harder, but the programmers were always a step ahead. Encoding software these days was pretty much foolproof. No communications could be traced back to an IP address. It was like being on the sea at night, shouting from one lightless boat to another, alone in the company of others who also thrived amidst the rocking and crashing of waves others found too perilous to brave.

Covering the smoke detector and striking a match, Sem Culpa sent her sketch back to the realm of simple remembrances where it could never be found, nor ever do her harm.

Chapter Twenty-Nine

Ava should have gone straight to the chemotherapy unit. She was loath to leave her mother there alone, but Callanach was on her mind and missing from the station again, his phone diverting to voicemail. The only place left to check was his apartment, not that she held out any great hope of finding him there. It was difficult to conceive what the point would be of working from home when his squad was amassed in the incident room. Still, there was the impending press conference to discuss. They might finally have a break. He ought to be told about it in person. And Overbeck was coiling to strike. Ava could feel it. Overbeck had been deliberately vague in her questions about Callanach's activities and had completely refused to detail the supposed complaint. However badly Ava and Callanach had been communicating of late, she wasn't prepared to let him sink without so much as a warning.

Ava buzzed up to his apartment. No response. She buzzed again. If he was there, he wasn't in the mood to be disturbed. Ava walked away, getting as far as putting her hand on the car door. If Callanach's apartment was 2a then logic dictated his chatty neighbour was in 2b. Perhaps there was a reason why he wasn't answering his phone. She owed it to him to check properly. Ignoring the sense that she was crossing a line, Ava pressed the buzzer for apartment 2b.

'This is Bunny. Hello?' a perky voice enquired.

'Hi, sorry to bother you. I'm trying to get hold of Luc Callanach. We met before at his door.'

'I'm not sure he's in,' Bunny replied, her voice a little flatter this time. Not too keen on having another woman calling for Luc, Ava guessed. Perhaps the sight of her new engagement ring would be reassuring. It had finally come in useful.

'Could you buzz me in? I'm a police officer. I need to discuss a professional matter with him urgently.'

'Of course,' Bunny said, releasing the door catch immediately.

Ava made her way up the stairs.

'I haven't heard anything from his flat all day and I've had clients coming and going,' Bunny called out before Ava reached the landing. 'Have you tried his mobile?'

'I have,' Ava said, giving Callanach's door a hammering. She should have left then, but Bunny was hanging around in a way that made it hard not to continue the conversation. 'Have you seen much of him recently?' Ava asked. Bunny laughed – a short, forced noise. There were tears in her eyes. 'Are you all right?'

Bunny shrugged, leaning against the wall and letting herself slide down until she was sitting on the floor.

Ava fought the urge to check her watch, knowing the girl wanted someone to talk to as the seconds slid by.

'I've been single so long, I thought I'd never meet anyone else nice,' Bunny began, 'and Luc is nice, isn't he?'

'He is,' Ava agreed, wondering whether to wait a while to see if Luc turned up or cut her losses and go, a prickle of guilt descending as she realised that continuing the conversation was likely to be an invasion of her colleague's privacy. It was just possible that the girl knew something that might help her locate Luc, though.

'We were becoming friends. We'd chat whenever we saw each other, I cooked him dinner a couple of times. He seemed exhausted, coming and going all times of the night.'

'Comes with the job,' Ava said. 'Did you ever see anyone else with him or visiting?'

'Only you that one time and the other policeman. Max something.'

'Tripp,' Ava filled in.

'That's him. Apart from that, no one. Luc seemed lonely. I'm in hair and make-up so I'm really a people person. You have to be. I offered to introduce him to my friends but he was always working.'

Not really his kind of crowd, Ava suspected, knowing she was drawing conclusions based on a stereotype. But not unreasonably. Luc was a private person, not one for bars or parties. Much like herself. Then Natasha had gone to the States, her mother had been diagnosed with cancer, and Joe had turned up, bringing with him the drinks parties and dinners that she was used to avoiding. Since then she and Luc had barely spent any time at all together. Ava's phone rang.

'Sorry, give me a moment?' She answered the call. 'Turner,' she said.

'DS Black here, ma'am. Interpol responded to your query. The Slovenian police never went public about the DNA. The killer won't be aware that he can be linked back to Slovenia.'

'Good. Do we have a time for the press conference?' Ava asked.

'Two hours from now. Media team is organising it. I've let Superintendent Overbeck know. She actually smiled.'

'Right. I'll get into uniform and be back in the office soon,' Ava said, ending the call. 'Sorry about that. It never stops, you know?' she smiled.

'Nice to feel wanted, I expect,' Bunny said, more tears forming in her eyes.

Ava finally allowed herself a time check. It wouldn't take her long to prepare for the press conference, she was too late for her mother's chemo appointment, and there was always a chance that Luc would turn up if she waited. Bunny looked truly miserable. 'I've a couple of minutes for a cup of tea, if you don't mind making me one,' Ava said. Bunny's face brightened up.

Callanach pulled into a public car park and got Lance on the phone.

'I've spoken to Mrs Swan,' Callanach said. 'She knows what I'm going to do.'

'Judging by your voice I'd say she wasn't best pleased,' Lance said.

'You'll print it?' Callanach asked.

'I'm a journalist. What do you think?'

'Great,' Callanach responded. 'I'll dictate, you type. DI Callanach has today confirmed that McDonald Road library murder victim Michael Swan did not suffer, according to the autopsy findings. Open speech marks – death was almost instantaneous – close speech marks, Callanach said. Whilst the victim suffered some trauma, he would have been unconscious throughout. Police conclude that the killer fled the scene immediately. Mr Swan's body was found on the floor of the library basement. End the piece there. That should be enough to light a fire. Let Ben know when you're uploading it, would you?'

'Copying him in now,' Lance said. 'Ben's a step ahead of you. The webmaster has already picked up Rory Hand's application to join whatever bizarre club they're running. Hand's emails and computer drives have been remotely accessed.'

'Just make sure Ben's waiting for the backlash from your

press release. If we can pick up any information from online chatter, it might just save Julia Stimple's life,' Callanach said.

'Your lollipop lady. Thanks for not bothering to give me that story first. Whatever happened to, I scratch your back, you make sure I can pay my rent next month?' Lance asked.

'If you run too many exclusives, whoever is watching will get suspicious. This has to feel real.'

'Got an answer for everything, haven't you? I'll post this to my site, make sure it's all over social media, then I've got to get going. I assume I should pretend we're complete strangers at the press conference later?' Lance asked.

'What press conference?' Callanach replied.

'DI Turner's.' Callanach didn't respond. 'Best leave you to sort that out then. I'll tell Ben to text you if anything comes up.'

Callanach ended the call then checked through the notifications on his phone. He'd had his mobile on silent at Mrs Swan's house, then been too busy to change it back, missing two calls from Ava and another from the station. He also found a text from DC Tripp.

'Overbeck ordered full uniform for press con tonight 6 p.m. DI Turner to lead. You to follow re J Stimple. Pls call DS Lively for update, sir.' Somehow Tripp even managed to be respectful when he was texting. Callanach sighed and dialled in to the incident room.

'What's up, Sergeant?' Callanach asked

'Door-to-doors in Julia Stimple's block of flats and along the road have turned up one neighbour who overheard some banging, although it's described as more like DIY than a fight, so we're not sure that's linked. Plus we have three vehicles in the road on the evening in question that aren't normally parked there.'

'Is that unusual for the area?' Callanach asked.

'Not particularly,' Lively said. 'Visitors, friends staying over, deliveries. The one we're interested in is a van. It was first noticed very late in the evening and parked badly. We've only got a partial plate but there were recognisable bumper stickers on it.'

'It's a start,' Callanach said. 'Get the description and the partial out to all officers, and alert other government agency workers. Parking attendants, dog patrol officers, street cleaning crews. Someone may have caught a glimpse of it on a driveway or going into a garage. Make it clear that no one's to approach.'

'On it, sir,' Lively said, all hint of previous sarcasm disappeared. Somehow that was all the reminder Callanach needed of just how dire the situation had become. He headed home to change.

Twenty minutes later Callanach entered his apartment block. He had time to shower and grab some food before getting back to the station, and he still had to prepare a statement about Julia Stimple's disappearance. He ran up the flight of stairs to his landing and got the key in his door when Bunny opened hers.

'There you are,' Bunny said.

Callanach wondered how brief he could be. He hadn't seen her since he'd bailed and fled back to his own apartment. She'd been upset then and he'd not made any attempt to put it right.

'You're a hard man to get hold of at the moment,' Ava said, walking out from behind Bunny. 'Thanks for the tea. It was nice getting to know you.'

'That's all right. Thanks for listening. I know you're busy, so I'll leave you to it.' Bunny shut her door. Ava stood in the corridor, arms crossed.

'How long have you been in there?' Callanach asked.

'Longer than I should've. Bunny needed someone to talk to,' Ava said. 'I tried calling.'

'It's been a busy day.' Callanach unlocked his door. 'I take it you're coming in.'

Inside, Ava loitered near the door. 'I've called a press conference,' she said. 'I wanted to talk you through it and when I couldn't get hold of you I was concerned.'

'You could have called DS Lively. I was with him most of the afternoon.'

'You left the station later on without notifying anyone of where you were going. You are accountable, you know. Your squad may be experienced but they still need visible leadership,' Ava said, feeling the tension between them rising again. They couldn't be in one another's presence these days without an argument kicking off. 'Luc, I didn't come here to give you a lecture.'

'What did Bunny tell you?' Callanach asked. He'd wanted to shout the question at the two of them as they'd come out of Bunny's door, furious that Ava could have invaded his privacy so brazenly. Was it possible that she'd been persuaded to spy on him by DCI Edgar? Callanach walked into his bedroom, throwing off his clothes as he went, leaving her standing in the hallway.

'Why are you so concerned? Is there something you want to tell me?' Ava asked, following him.

'Are we discussing my private life?' Callanach asked. 'Only you might want to be a bit more worried about the choices you're making at the moment.'

'Don't make this personal,' Ava said. 'Bloody hell! Look at the bruises on your ribcage!' She walked towards him, stretching out her fingers, running them along the red–black lines on his torso. He'd forgotten what a mess his body still was. His face had recovered faster. He'd never meant her to see it. 'What sort of trouble have you got yourself into, Luc? Please talk to me. Whatever it is, I can help.'

Callanach caught her fingers in his hand, holding them as

she stared at his body. He wanted to confide everything. To explain exactly what her fiancé was capable of. But there was a chasm between them and they both knew it.

'You don't need to worry about me,' he said, releasing her hand. 'And your fiancé probably wouldn't appreciate you being in here with me half-naked.'

Ava clinched her jaw and looked away.

'There's been a complaint,' she said. 'I don't know the specifics. Overbeck was asking what you'd been up to. I told her I didn't know.'

'Thank you,' Callanach said.

'Don't thank me. It's the truth. I haven't a clue what's going on with you at the moment.'

It was strange having her in his bedroom. All the times she'd been in his apartment – for meals, meetings, to borrow or deliver things – but never as close to him as this. He changed the subject, uncomfortable with the way he was feeling. 'What's the press conference about, Ava?' Callanach asked.

'I believe the man who killed Helen Lott and Emily Balcaskie is Slovenian. No criminal record, but Interpol has his DNA on the international database in relation to another murder. No one was ever arrested.'

'That's progress,' Callanach said. 'Now can I take my shower?'

'I'm not stopping you,' she said, crossing her arms. That was the old Ava. Too proud and fierce to be dismissed.

Callanach unzipped his jeans.

'Fine,' he said, stripping off the denim. Ava just stood there, staring at his face, immovable. He walked into the bathroom, letting the door swing half shut, throwing his underwear to the floor and getting into the shower.

'You think I'm going to run away like some stupid girl because you're naked? We're in the middle of a conversation,' Ava said, leaning against the bathroom doorway.

Callanach stared at the wall, letting the water calm him. He wanted Bunny not to have told Ava about their disastrous evening, not that it should matter what Ava knew or thought. Especially when he had so many more pressing problems.

'Why didn't you call me to the Julia Stimple crime scene? It's as if you're actively excluding me. Is this about my engagement to Joe?' Ava asked eventually.

Callanach laughed, switching off the shower and grabbing a towel. Ava turned to look down at the street from his bedroom window as he dried himself.

'You seem a bit distracted at the moment,' he said, selecting clothes from his wardrobe. 'It didn't need two of us. Why do you want to follow me around?'

'I'm not following you around. Since you joined Police Scotland we've shared every investigation willingly, to help each other and because it's easier with someone on your side. Now, when we really need to communicate, you've completely stopped.'

Callanach threw his towel down and began to get dressed. He could see the rise and fall of Ava's shoulders with each breath, her nails digging into the backs of her arms, wrapped around herself. He pulled on his uniform, did up his shirt and sat on the edge of his bed.

'Ava,' he said. 'I have a contact who could hurt you. Not physically. I mean your career and everything that goes with it.'

She turned to face him, her arms dropping to her sides.

'If your contact can hurt me, he can hurt you too. Is that what Overbeck was talking about?'

'I don't know,' Callanach said. 'This is what's going to happen. I'll tell you what you need to know, but stay away from me until this is over. I'm not trying to hurt you.'

She sat down next to him, playing with a loose thread that was hanging off her shirt button.

'Okay,' she said. 'And you can be happy for me, right? The engagement, Joe? I need to know you're all right with it.'

'Why?' he asked.

She shrugged. He watched as she bit her lower lip, her hands still fiddling nervously, her shoulders uncharacteristically hunched.

'Of course,' he said. 'I'm happy for you. Which is more than Overbeck will be if we don't get moving. I'll drive. We'll call in at yours and grab your uniform. We can figure out what we're going to tell the press on the way.' He stood up.

She reached out a hand for him to pull her up, grinning.

'I'm sorry I invaded your bedroom,' she said, trying not to laugh. He could have kissed her then. 'But the next time you get cocky enough to take off all your clothes in front of me, I'll arrest you.'

'You should be paying me, not arresting me,' Callanach said, grabbing his car keys.

'If I want to pay for a good laugh, I'll go to a comedy club,' Ava said.

'I'm not sure what you'd find there to stare at,' Luc smiled.

'I'm so glad you managed to get a grip on your massive ego all those years ago,' she said, pushing past him and marching down the stairs as he locked up.

Chapter Thirty

Sem Culpa heard her mobile ping a notification alert, ignored it while she filed her nails, then heard it go off again and again. She had set up programmes to notify her whenever the Sim Thorburn or Michael Swan murders were mentioned. All of a sudden, Swan's name was everywhere. She sat down to read the first report, delighted that her kill, which had received so little detailed attention, was once again headline news, until she realised why.

Her eyes swam over phrases – 'did not suffer', 'instantaneous', 'unconscious throughout', 'body found on floor' – and she screamed. It did not matter that she was in a hotel, that other guests could hear, that she was causing a disturbance that might well end up recorded somewhere.

She had been fucked over!

Flicking through each report in turn, she found the same source named. Detective Inspector Luc Callanach. He knew what he was saying wasn't true, so he could only be trying to call her out. After every precaution, the pride she took in her no-trace crime scenes, her skill at changing her own appearance, he actually thought she would reveal herself now? It was more than just insulting. It was disrespectful.

She grabbed her laptop and encoded a message to the moderator. Then she picked up her drawing pad and pencil once more, shifting her head forward and back, side to side, to ease the tension in her neck, and began to sketch.

Grom was sick of the old woman. She had done nothing but moan and piss for two days. Now she was hungry. He would have thought that eating would be the last thing on her mind. She should have been terrified. He'd even shown her the photos of Emily Balcaskie's body. Her response had been to request a cushion. He hadn't understood at first. She'd shouted 'piles' at him repeatedly until he'd been forced to look it up on the translator. The lollipop lady disgusted him. He couldn't understand why she had been chosen as a target. Helen Lott had been a nurse, that was a fair kill, someone worth the effort. And Emily Balcaskie in her scout uniform had been delicious. He was sure she'd been a virgin, too. A virgin in her twenties – you didn't come across those very often. She'd pleaded, tried to reason with him, begged him to stop. Then Emily had asked him if he wanted to talk. For the briefest, most perfect moment, that had made him love her, not to mention getting him off as he'd killed her. She was immaculate, caring, understanding, beautiful throughout. And she had been entirely his. Emily had stopped breathing in his arms, her windpipe crushed like a bird's. He'd tried to make it slower, to savour the moment, but the power he possessed had been unstoppable. After she'd passed, Grom had allowed himself the dangerous pleasure of sitting with her in his lap, crouched in the bushes, and he had trembled. The scarf given by her pupils had been a prize, and it had been meant for him.

He fired up his laptop and waited for the latest Police Scotland announcements. They had a press conference planned, which was always helpful for figuring out how close they were getting.

The woman in charge was skinny, tall and resembled Grom's idea of a fetish dominatrix. The sign on the desk in front of her proclaimed her to be Superintendent Overbeck. She had dark lipstick, the kind he liked to mess up and rub over women's faces. He turned up the sound.

'. . . the missing woman is confirmed to be one of Edinburgh's lollipop ladies. We have reason to believe that the man responsible is Slovenian. We are appealing for anyone aware of a Slovenian male matching the description given to contact the police. He should not be approached or tackled. We must stress how dangerous he may be.'

Grom slammed his foot on the wooden floor. How could they have his nationality? He hadn't left a trail. There were no convictions in his home country. He'd never been arrested, and another man had been convicted of that murder in Paris.

He put his head between his legs and breathed deeply. He needed to be calm. There was no trace of him here. He'd travelled under a false passport which gave his nationality as Romanian. And he hadn't exactly been socialising in Edinburgh. He bought food from large supermarkets late at night, always with his hood up. He hadn't used his real name at all. Which begged the question of how the police knew.

They had begun taking questions at the press conference, hands raised, like mutts begging for a scrap of meat from the table.

'Things seem to be moving very slowly, Superintendent, with minimal information being released. Do you now foresee a faster resolution?' one journalist asked.

'I accept that one could describe the progress as piecemeal,' the uniformed dominatrix said, scowling at the officers to her side, 'but that is due to the nature of this case. Police work is not always easy. These murders have proved particularly challenging.'

She stood up, revealing her full height and a spectacular

figure. Grom thought he would enjoy meeting her in person very much indeed. In the dark. Just the two of them. He would even play with her a while before destroying her. It was entirely possible she would enjoy it. He'd seen that supercilious look on other women's faces before, and every one of them had confessed to wanting him before he'd finished with them.

As the police officers filed out, Grom returned to his translation dictionary and looked up the word piecemeal. It meant a quantity taken one section or particle at a time. He liked the idea. That would get their attention. Sem Culpa would be all but forgotten.

He strode over to the lollipop lady who had ceased her chatter. Something about his demeanour had finally shut the old bitch up. She looked up at him, sneered, then spat in his face. This time he didn't mind. She would apologise for her behaviour soon enough. The saliva dribbling down his face was a symptom of her fear.

Grom grabbed her hand. She did her best to pull away, but no amount of resistance could have altered his chosen course. Pushing her hand down firmly onto the table, he drew a knife from his pocket and began to cut.

Chapter Thirty-One

Ben had had a busy afternoon. Polly at the Below Par Cafe had been right. When he'd returned to work, the police had been there. Not DCI Joseph Edgar, of course. He was way too important to dirty his hands with preliminary enquiries.

Ben had wandered in carrying a takeaway coffee and bagel, looking as surprised as he could bother to pretend being about the kerfuffle. It was old-school tactics – ask the boss a few barely coded questions about various employees, make the atmosphere strained, raise the spectre of rogue employees. Word about the police interest would get passed around faster than a joint in a prison cell. Even now CyberBallista's account handlers would be phoning their substantially powerful and influential clients to explain the situation. In turn, those client companies would be phoning their own lawyers to make sure none of their information was in danger of being accessed. The irony was that the multi-billion pound banks and investment companies who had insisted on DCI Edgar's investigation were the same ones who wouldn't want their private information made public in a court case, which made CyberBallista the safest place for Ben to work.

It had taken exactly three hours before Ben was back at his desk working on a new computer while his manager checked the old one for any unusual activity. He swung by Below Par on the way home to thank Polly who, in the tradition of their budding relationship, had good-naturedly refused his daily attempt to lure her out for a drink or some food.

'Got to wash my hair. You know I like to look my best for the early morning coffee customers. Off you go, back to your man-cave.' She said the same thing every day.

Ben had been working in Edinburgh since January. A friend from Glasgow had tipped him off about Below Par. Polly had begun working there three months ago, quick-witted with an acid tongue and the sort of sense of humour that could get you in trouble if it was expressed publicly. Ben liked her. The tough girl London twang, the steady appraising eye and her hatred of all things establishment. If he'd been asked to state his gut feeling he'd have said she liked him too, but try as he might, she would not go the way of dating. Some days he'd ask and there would be a sigh before her refusal, a soft smile that gave him hope. He wouldn't give up. The right woman was worth a million rejections.

Ben had finalised Rory Hand's application to the webmaster whilst drinking coffee at Below Par and contemplating Polly's habitual rebuff. It hadn't taken long before an answer arrived. He had clicked the link the webmaster had sent, knowing it would allow access to Hand's computer. Nothing to fear there. The deviant would have exactly the sort of material the webmaster was expecting to find.

An email from Lance warned him to keep an eye open for a response to their falsified account of Michael Swan's death. What arrived as a result was both exactly what Callanach had been hoping for, and way too much more. Ben dialled Callanach's number.

'Get online somewhere fast,' Ben told him.

'Ava, I've got to take this call. I'll be in my office,' Callanach said, muffling the speaker. In the background, Ben could hear another mobile ring tone followed by a woman's voice. She had a similar accent to Polly, definitely English, but all round vowels and crisp consonants. It had to belong to DI Turner.

'Is that a second mobile ringing in your pocket?' she asked.

Callanach mumbled a response, then Ben heard the echoing slap of footsteps, an opening and closing door.

'What's going on?' Callanach asked. 'I've literally just stepped out of the press conference.'

'Michael Swan's going to be the big headline tomorrow. Whatever you've just been talking about will be irrelevant,' Ben said, his blood pumping audibly in his ears as he enlarged the downloaded images on his screen. 'They were sent in the same way as the photos of Emily Balcaskie, via a link that destroys its own pathway as soon as it's opened. I've taken them from Lance's email already. If the other journalists are still travelling back from your press conference then you have about ten minutes to prepare a statement, but this is bad. Really fucking bad. I'm emailing you the link now.'

Callanach waited a few seconds, then clicked. The email came with four documents attached. He walked briskly to his door, locked it, then took his seat before opening the first.

It was a sketch, pencil-drawn then photographed, and the artist was as accomplished as she was deranged. There was no doubt in his mind that the artist was the same person as had conceived and executed the murder. The perspective was much the same as the first view Callanach had of Michael Swan from directly below, looking up into the face that was no longer a face, from which a bloodied swathe of skin swung. Even in black and white, this was a masterpiece of horror. Swan's face was enlarged within the frame, giving the impression that it was hanging towards you. Even the detail on the ceiling had been included, to leave no doubt as to the position of the body. Callanach cursed his own ingenuity in deciding to announce that the body had been left on the floor.

'Callanach, are you there?' Ben's voice sounded tinnily from the mobile. Callanach had forgotten that he was still on the line.

'Give me a moment,' he replied. Callanach unlocked his door and put his head out into the corridor. 'Tripp, get me a lawyer in here now!' he shouted. He didn't wait for a response, returning to open the second attachment. This was another drawing, but a close-up of Michael Swan's face partway through the skinning. It showed the tears in Swan's eyes, his muscles contorted, the pulling of flesh and seeping of blood an agony to see. It was no leap of the imagination to hear the sounds that must have accompanied those moments. Callanach wanted to look away, found that he couldn't, and finally became aware of Tripp peering over his shoulder.

'Oh holy shit, sir. Who's done that?' Tripp said, actually taking a step backwards before pulling himself together.

'It's been sent to the press,' Callanach said. 'I need an injunction to stop anyone from publishing either on paper or online, and I need it right now. And get a unit over to Mrs Swan's house. Send Salter to look after her. She needs to be warned.'

'So it's not gone public yet then?' Tripp asked.

'Not yet,' Callanach said, opening the third attachment and beginning to read.

'So how did we get it, sir?' Tripp said. Callanach glanced down at the mobile.

'Tip-off,' Callanach answered. 'Now move. And find DI Turner. She needs to be aware of this too.'

Tripp ran from his office as Callanach continued to read.

'Things you will need,' was the title. 'Ammonia inhalants' was at the top of the list. Smelling salts. That was how she had continued to rouse Michael Swan from unconsciousness. 'Surgical grade scalpel. Several pairs surgical gloves (these become bloody and slippery quickly). Rope. Cable ties. Industrial knife. Duct tape to minimise noise disturbance. One old librarian. One visionary.'

'Vous devez être putain blague,' Callanach whispered.

'What?' Ben asked.

'I said, you have to be fucking kidding. I didn't expect this. Can you trace it?'

'No, but what I can tell you is that the same code was used on the Rory Hand email regarding membership to the darknet site,' Ben said.

'So the coordinates for the graffiti, the emailed photos from Michael Swan's murderer and this latest email have all come from the same place. What the hell is that website, Ben?' Callanach asked.

'I don't know yet. But if our application is successful we'll be able to take a closer look. No way I can do any more before we're given a password,' Ben said.

As Ben spoke, Callanach clicked open the final document. It was a poem.

'He spread his wings and flew for me,
My scarlet Swan, my gaping muse.
Sustained me with his love of life,
Enriched me with his plaintive tears.
I plunged his depths, erased his flaws,
They were skin-deep, they are no more.
Immortalised by this sweet blade,
A man, remembered, at my hand.'

'I have to go,' Callanach told Ben. His throat was hoarse.

Ben ended the call without saying anything else. He'd felt the same the first time he'd seen the documents.

This wasn't your normal psycho. This was someone who had elevated themselves in their own mind as if they were above mere mortals, and those delusions were only going to get more powerful each time she killed.

Ben double-checked his CCTV. He had cameras set up in his hallway, looking out from above his window even though his apartment was on the upper floor, and a few recording internally. There were also motion sensors which would have alerted him during the day had anyone entered. He could see the plain-clothes police officers on the street. They changed each day, were in different vehicles, sometimes making the effort to pretend they were tradesmen, sometimes just sitting in a car reading a newspaper as if waiting to pick up a teenager from a date. But there was always someone watching. If they ever broke in, they wouldn't like what they found.

He made himself an egg white omelette – once a Californian, always a Californian – and set an alarm that would wake him if the webmaster decided to make Rory Hand a member of his darknet club.

Chapter Thirty-Two

The Moderator was tired. After a long day at work, he had returned home to find a to-do list from his wife pinned to the fridge. It included preparing her dinner (she only cooked at weekends, her days were now so lengthy), getting the washing out of the machine (primarily hers, which could not be tumble-dried because of the delicate fabrics) and changing the sheets on their bed (she had left the new bedding out for him, presumably so he didn't choose the wrong colour). And he had work to do. There truly was no rest for the goddamned wicked.

And now the police were playing games, trying to out Sem Culpa by goading her into a stupid public display. She'd reacted in an entirely predictable way, albeit with more flair than the Moderator had foreseen. But Police Scotland wouldn't be getting any more information than he chose to release. Everything he did was untraceable and he'd specifically banned site users from communicating directly with the press. If any of the users got caught, it would only take the handing over of passwords and the game would be over before it had served its purpose.

The Moderator emptied the washing machine first, hanging the clothes on the airer, letting them stay rumpled. If his wife wanted crisp linens, she could iron them when she deigned to get home. Dinner was risotto, shop-bought, although he'd put it into an oven dish, added some chicken and would pretend to have made it himself. With that in the oven (sod changing the sheets) he went into his study, shoving a chair under the door handle. There was no real danger of her coming home early, but it was the way of things that she would if he didn't take precautions.

He logged in. Lots of site traffic today. Everyone so excited by Sem Culpa's childish scribbles and dreadful poetry, made available to all the users at the same time they'd been released to the press. It only seemed fair. And Sem Culpa was entitled to rebut the reports suggesting her work had been bland and craft-less. The police may have set Sem Culpa up for their own ends, but they were also contributing nicely to the Moderator's greater plan.

Even Grom was being substantially more exotic than with his previous kills. Crushing the nurse to death with her own chest of drawers had been brutal, and the strangulation of Emily Balcaskie had made the nation weep. But this abduction, keeping a horrified public (not too horrified to stop them wanting more details though) glued to their social media feed for updates, this was brilliant. Waiting not for her to be found, not for her to be freed. No – some truth-telling was overdue – they were waiting to see what shocking, faint-inducing, protest-spawning method of murder would be used to dispatch the lollipop lady.

The Moderator prepared a few more search engine entries, some articles, a blog and some newspaper references, then uploaded them. They would only hold their high positions in the search engine ranks for a very brief amount of time. It would be unhelpful if the subject of the articles came to too many people's attention for too long. That done, he completed the membership access for a number of waiting applicants. The more the merrier, as long as they were the right kind of people. Each and every one helped fuel the fire of the necessary murders, and not one of them could run to the police without being conspirators. They were all trapped, and he alone knew every detail of their true identities. Finally he looked up an off-the-record home address that Grom had requested. Thank goodness for local government's penny-pinching cyber security.

Finished, he walked around the house. They had not moved in long ago and it still had that sense of waiting to be filled up. They hadn't created any of their own history here yet. But that would come. Not children. His wife professed to want them, but they had to be having sex once in a while for that to be possible. He suspected she thought she could order them and have them delivered to the door for all the effort she was putting in. Everyone else got a piece of her – her passion, her dedication, her attention. Just not him. He had his own dreams. Such a shame she'd never really appreciated his potential.

The front door opened as he reached the top of the stairs. It was already past eight in the evening and she walked in as if he just didn't matter at all.

'Hey honey, I'm back. Wow, dinner smells great. Have I time for a shower, love?'

Chapter Thirty-Three

Overbeck picked her nails. The tips were ragged with chipped nail varnish, the result of a childhood chewing habit which had recently made an unwelcome return. They'd been in perfect condition this morning, before another day of leaden progress and disappointing news. Then the Chief Superintendent had phoned. It had been one of those calls that felt like a professional game of snakes and ladders.

'Detective Superintendent Overbeck,' the CS had begun. Not her first name. First names were reserved for good news days. The first nail had slipped into the corner of her mouth and her teeth had begun doing their damage. 'I hope this isn't a bad time?'

'No sir, not at all,' she'd said.

'Oh, that's disappointing. I was hoping you'd be too busy to talk. Always signifies progress when you're so tied up you can't pick up the phone,' he said, a smile in his voice keeping the tone light.

She moved on to her second nail. 'Well, it's not that we're not making progress, sir, it's just that . . .'

'Excellent, I was hoping for some good news. When can we expect to see results?'

'It's not exactly a results scenario at the moment, it's more that we are steadily continuing to follow up leads, sir,' Overbeck had said.

'Goodness me, we're still at the following up leads stage?' The third nail had taken its place in the biting line. 'Do you need any help there?'

'No, sir, I've got the investigation properly managed, but it's kind of you to suggest . . .'

'You don't need help, but you can't give me a positive progress report? That's what I've always admired about you, Detective Superintendent Overbeck. Your independence,' the Chief Superintendent said loudly. 'I shall be sure to tell the board that you've refused help in spite of the offer being made. I'm sure they'll all be as impressed as me.'

'Thank you, sir,' Overbeck had said, her fourth nail tip in tatters. 'Actually, I wanted to discuss the overtime restrictions.'

'Yes, I know,' the Chief Super cooed, 'I think you're doing a great job keeping on top of them. I know you'll have it in hand and ensure that the costs are capped. Thank goodness we've got you in place to think in a businesslike manner about affordability in tandem with public safety. Good of you to reassure me about it. Progress report with an expected date of closure by the end of the week then, yes? I'm sure you've got that in hand already. And great job on keeping your face all over the publicity on this one. Always useful for the public to know who the buck stops with. Very responsible.'

And then he was gone, as were the ends of the nails on her right hand, and Overbeck was trying to grip onto the tail of an awfully slippery snake that wanted to deposit her at the bottom of a board she'd spent years playing. Piles of paperwork, endless phone calls, and three nicotine patches later she'd gone home. Several large gin and tonics after that and the state of her nails hadn't seemed to matter quite so much.

Hangover notwithstanding, she'd risen early the next morning to repair her manicure damage. It was a new day. The Chief Superintendent wanted results and a scapegoat. Overbeck would provide him with one or the other, and the latter wasn't going to be her.

The package was hanging from the letter box inside Superintendent Overbeck's front door, evidently unnoticed from postal deliveries the day before. She snatched it as she left for work air-kissing her husband in the general area of his cheek (he didn't want lipstick marks any more than she wanted her make-up messed up) and trod carefully in her stilettos. Their driveway was terribly pot-holed. She'd asked her husband several times to have it seen to, but still nothing had been done. There were days when she thought that if she weren't on top of things, he would literally die in his study reading a newspaper, or whatever it was he did in there for hours on end.

The package was marked to Ms Overbeck with their address printed on it. It was roughly the size of a packet of cigarettes, wrapped in brown parcel paper. Bloody postal worker couldn't even be bothered to push things through properly these days. She threw it on the seat of her car, cursing the pigeons nesting in the trees along her driveway. If they weren't dispatched soon, her paintwork would be ruined.

It wasn't a long drive to the police station but it was enough to have her swearing by the time she arrived. What was it with people who couldn't operate their indicators? And as for the women who let their children run up and down pavements unchecked so you had to crawl past, constantly waiting for the fateful dash into the road, well, she had long since reserved a special place in bad-parenting hell for them.

Overbeck had watched and re-watched the press conference from the previous evening online. At last there had been a break with the information about Lott and Balcaskie's killer's nationality, although the result would inevitably be policing some anti-immigrant rally. This case would make or break her, and the latter wasn't an option she was prepared to consider.

Leaving her car parked across two spaces, Overbeck marched towards her office. The first item on her agenda was an update on the lollipop lady abduction. She'd been notified that Julia Stimple's daughter had been located when she'd turned up at her mother's flat expecting to share a pizza with her. How in this day and age people didn't either turn on the TV, switch on a radio or read the news online was almost unbelievable, but apparently the forty-year-old had been enjoying a day's shopping in Glasgow and turned everything off, including her mobile.

No doubt the media would make the most of that, bleeding hearts dry with the retelling of the daughter's shock, seeing her mother's doorway sealed with crime scene tape, staring through the broken wood at the chaos and desecration within. It was almost worthy of a movie. And if that fancy piece of ass, Callanach, didn't get his French butt in gear soon, there would be Oscar nominations for the director who had the balls to dramatise the tale of Edinburgh's worst killing spree in modern history. Overbeck didn't like Callanach. It was personal, she was big enough to accept that. She'd had her own man she'd wanted to push into the Detective Inspector opening last year, but strings were pulled. A word was whispered into the right ear, no doubt a couple of meals were purchased, and up popped the man with the golden accent. Interpol were no doubt glad to get rid of him after the rape allegation. Not that she believed he'd done it. Her experience of men who looked like Callanach was that they were way too arrogant to bother raping anyone. If you didn't fall on your back with your legs open, they simply assumed you were gay. It was exactly why she had married so wisely. Her husband might be plain-looking, even dull company, but he was safe and unthreatening.

Overbeck slung her bag on her desk.

'Liz, black tea with lemon. I'm gasping,' she shouted at her assistant. The package fell out of her bag. Probably another free sample. She'd been plagued with them since spending a weekend at a spa and signing up for a variety of useless treatments. The only thing that ever seemed to make her look less frazzled was valium. The mirror was less offensive when she'd swallowed one of those.

Picking up a silver letter opener, she cut the tape holding the parcel together. Inside was a second layer of wrapping. Whatever it contained was so small it hardly seemed worth the effort of sending. Presumably that meant the product was over-priced as well as useless. She got through to the final layer of wrapping, kicking her shoes off under the desk and leaning to see if her assistant was fetching her tea yet. No, still playing with emails.

'Liz, tea now!' She wasn't really supposed to speak to her staff like that, but Jesus, did she have to give every command twice? And who the hell was going to complain? Everyone was scared shitless of her.

Overbeck peered at the thing in her hand. It was grey, with a hard upper edge, and a brown substance crusted on the bottom.

'Oh, holy fucking fuck! Liz, get off that frigging computer and get forensics up here! And get me Detective Inspector Callanach. If he's not here in the next two minutes, tell him he's bloody well fired!' Chair legs scraped the floor and heels clacked staccato down the corridor. Overbeck stared at the half finger that she'd dropped onto her update to the Chief Constable, typed and ready for signature. Now out of date already.

Inside the final layer of tissue paper had been a note with a single word printed on it. It sat in the centre of her prized and polished walnut desk. A desk she'd paid to have brought in, those she'd been offered by Police Scotland hardly the sort of furniture she wanted to stare at day after day.

Callanach appeared in her doorway.

'Stay there,' Overbeck instructed. 'No one comes in until forensics are done.'

'What is that?' Callanach asked, his eyes on the organic lump on her desk.

'It's the end of someone's finger, Callanach, and it came with a note.' She pointed at the scrap of paper without touching it. 'Technically, it says "piecemeal", but the real message is a massive "screw you!" Get a team to my house. The parcel was put through my front door.'

'Yes, ma'am,' Callanach said.

'Then find this motherfucker. Not only does he have my home address, he's planning to serve us slivers of lollipop lady for lunch and supper!'

Chapter Thirty-Four

Callanach delegated Overbeck's instructions to his squad then bolted to his office, locking the door and dialling Ben's mobile. No answer. He'd be at work by now, probably stuck in meetings discussing yesterday's police visit and the amount of work CyberBallista required to repair their corporate reputation.

There was no way Callanach could risk going back to CyberBallista's offices. DCI Edgar's men had followed him before, and now a complaint had been made to Overbeck. They'd recognise Lance, too, after taking photos of Callanach and Ben entering the journalist's home. And Tripp had been on Edgar's team. Not many options left.

'Salter!' Callanach called down the corridor. The detective constable poked her head out of the incident room.

'I'm just off to Superintendent Overbeck's house, sir. I'll phone you if we find anything,' she said.

'Send uniforms. I need you.' He stepped back into his office and waited for Salter to arrive. She was casually dressed, shirt untucked, hair down. Perhaps that was best. He needed her not to stand out in a crowd.

'Sir?' she asked as she walked in. He reached behind her,

shut the door and locked it. 'Um, is everything okay?' Salter said, her eyes lingering on the door handle.

Callanach sat down, staring at his second mobile phone, willing it to ring so he could avoid dragging Salter into such a procedural mess. It didn't, so he had no choice.

'Sit down, Salter,' Callanach said, ripping a sheet of paper off a notepad and grabbing a pen.

'I don't need to sit down, sir. I'm fine.' Salter was defensive, bordering on twitchy.

'I locked the door because no one else must overhear this conversation. I'm trying to protect you,' Callanach said.

'I don't need protecting, sir. And I have no desire to be pandered to. As soon as I'm ready I'll—'

'Salter, listen carefully because I need you out of the door in the next five minutes. Go to this address.' Callanach scribbled CyberBallista's details down and handed the paper over. 'At reception, ask to speak with Ben Paulson.' Salter took a pen out of her pocket and went to write the name down. 'No, don't do that, just remember it. Don't give your name. Don't show your warrant card. If he's in a meeting or you're told he can't be reached, tell them it's a personal emergency involving a family member. Get him to phone me straight away.'

'Ben Paulson. CyberBallista. All right, sir.'

'You can't tell anyone where you're going. Just say I'm sending you out, no questions. And destroy that piece of paper when you've memorised it.'

The door handle rattled, there was a soft cursing, then a foot hit the bottom of the wood.

'Callanach, would you open the door?' Ava sounded as if she was trying to repress a screaming fit.

'One minute,' Callanach said.

'No, right now,' Ava said. 'Whatever you're doing can wait.'

He opened the door.

'I need to finish speaking with DC Salter,' Callanach said. 'Could you wait?'

'No, I can't wait. There's a piece of recently removed finger sitting on the superintendent's desk and somewhere there's a Slovenian on a countdown until he can cut off another piece and send it to us.'

'I'll be off then, sir. Shall I phone you when it's done?' Salter asked.

'No. Stay off your phone. Get straight back here.'

'Fine. I'll grab a car from the pool,' Salter said.

'Unmarked,' Callanach said. 'Nothing obvious.'

Ava stared at Salter, turned her gaze on Callanach, then reached out a hand to stop the detective constable from leaving the office. 'Where exactly is it you're going, Detective Constable?'

'It's a private matter,' Callanach said. 'Off you go, Salter.'

'There's no privacy in police work. If it's part of this investigation then I'm entitled to information sharing.'

'Um, sir?' Salter looked to Callanach. He put his hands on his hips and stared at the ceiling.

'Salter is following up a line of investigation that requires absolute discretion. Information sharing at this point may jeopardise it.'

'Are you going alone, Salter?' Ava asked her. Salter said nothing. 'I'll take that as a yes. Is it part of the investigation into these murders?'

'Yes, ma'am,' Salter murmured.

'DC Salter isn't going,' Ava said, sitting down, 'unless you tell me where you're sending her and I can assess the risk.'

'You need to back off, DI Turner,' Callanach leaned over his desk.

'And you need to recognise when one of your female detectives is pregnant, even if she chooses for perfectly understandable career reasons not to disclose that fact. Isn't that right, Detective Constable?'

Salter's head took a dip. Callanach breathed out hard.

'Is that right, Salter?' Callanach asked.

'How did you know, ma'am?' Salter asked.

'Your skin is glowing but you look exhausted, you've taken to wearing your shirt outside your trousers, you're in flat shoes every day. And you've gone off tea. It's a dead giveaway. You should have disclosed it. You know there's an everyday risk out on the street, whatever you're doing. Never more so than during this investigation.'

'This is just an office visit. It's not like there's any danger attached,' Salter said, holding up the paper to highlight her point.

Ava had snatched it from her before Callanach even saw her get up.

Salter gasped and took a step forward.

'Please, ma'am . . .' Salter said.

'Off you go, Salter. You're on incident room duties unless I assess every call you're attending. And congratulations, by the way,' Callanach managed through gritted teeth.

Salter slipped silently out of the door.

Ava put the slip of paper in the pocket of her jeans.

'Do I want to read it?' she asked Callanach.

'You'll open a door you can't close again,' Callanach said, walking to stand directly in front of her, leaning against his desk and folding his arms.

'Is this what Overbeck was asking me about? The reason you're never here?'

'It's part of it,' Callanach said.

'Are you breaking the law?' Ava asked, lowering her voice and taking a step closer to him.

'I'm trying to stop two murderers. If I cross a line to do that, does it really matter?'

'Depends on the line,' Ava said. 'And if this is about Lott and Balcaskie's murderer, withholding information from me is not a good idea.'

'I'll pass on the information,' Callanach said. 'But you can't get involved in how I obtain it.'

Ava turned round, staring at the photos, notes, maps and diagrams covering Callanach's office wall, studying the faces of the four victims before facing him again.

'Julia Stimple is, what, hours from death? Maybe already dead. We know she's been tortured. Whatever you're doing, you have to let me in,' Ava said.

Callanach kept his voice as low as he could. 'Ava, I won't do that. Don't ask me to.'

'It's not up to you,' she said. Walking to the door Ava pulled the paper from her pocket.

'CyberBallista,' she said.

'*Mon Dieu, tu es têtue!*' Callanach said. 'Not just stubborn, but infuriating.'

'Where have I heard that name before?' Ava muttered, staring at the paper.

'Ava, you have to stop.'

'Isn't that . . . hang on, Joe said something about . . .' she stared at Callanach. 'I'm imagining this, right? You're not really communicating with someone in a company at the heart of a major hacking investigation, being personally overseen from 10 Downing Street?'

'I told you to stay out of it,' he said.

'I thought you were just being a bit of a maverick, maybe getting information from a few dodgy ex-cons. Do you have any idea . . .' Ava's face bloomed a deep shade of purple.

'Keep your voice down. This is none of your concern. It's a company name on a piece of paper. Screw it up and walk away. Perhaps now you understand why I didn't want you involved.'

'Yeah, well, remind me to buy you a drink and thank you for that sometime when we've both finished being sacked. What were you sending Salter off to do? Did you think about the sort of difficulty you were putting her in? Were you even going to warn her? You really are an idiot, I hope you know that!'

She stormed over to the door and yanked it open. He picked up the paper she'd left lying in the middle of the floor, ripped it into pieces and dropped them in his bin.

Chapter Thirty-Five

Ava managed to reach her office without screaming. The mystery of Superintendent Overbeck's questions was solved. Bloody Callanach. No wonder there'd been a complaint. She found herself twisting her engagement ring again and speculated about how much Joe knew. Surely if he was aware what Callanach had been up to, he'd have said something to her. Her head was thumping. She didn't seem to go an hour without a headache these days. If only Natasha were there, the one person who listened without judgement, who could get her through the next month.

Callanach had gone too far and the truth was there was no going back. She couldn't believe it. He was neither stupid nor reckless. What could be worth his entire career, even the prospect of facing criminal charges? Joe was a closed book when it came to his investigation. She'd only heard the word CyberBallista in passing when he'd been on his mobile as she cooked dinner one night. Whatever Callanach was after from them, it was worth him risking everything. Swallowing a couple of paracetamol, she put on her coat and walked back down the corridor. This time she didn't bother knocking.

'We're going for a walk,' she told Callanach. 'I'll see you out front.'

She took the stairs two at a time, wishing she'd found more time to exercise recently, out of breath by the time she hit the ground floor. Callanach joined her two minutes later, grim-faced. They wandered away from the police station, neither of them speaking until they were clear of other human beings, able to sit on a small patch of grass and stare at the sky.

'You're putting yourself on the line,' Ava said.

'You think I don't know that?' Callanach took a packet of Gauloises cigarettes from his pocket, taking one out, lying back and drawing air through it unlit.

'Let me try that,' Ava said, taking another cigarette from the packet and lying back shoulder to shoulder with him. She smelled the tobacco first, playing it between her fingers, getting used to the feel of it. 'I haven't smoked since I was at university. Even then I was only trying to look cool. It never really suited me.' She took it between her lips and inhaled. 'Why do you still do this?'

'Reminds me of simpler times,' Callanach said, closing his eyes.

Ava sat up, leaning on one arm as she stared at him.

'What has your source got that we can't get anywhere else?' she asked.

'I'm not discussing it,' Callanach said.

'Yes, you are. That's why you came out here with me. You knew I was going to ask. Also, if you don't, you'll leave me no choice but to go to Overbeck and spill the whole thing.'

'You wouldn't,' Callanach said.

'You may have too high an opinion of me,' Ava said. 'Let's not test it today. Come on Luc, I know you. You wouldn't be taking this risk if there weren't the prospect of a suitable reward. I don't want all the details. I sure as hell don't want to be implicated. I just need to know if what you're doing could save lives. I need to understand it.'

Callanach opened his eyes, followed the progress of a smudge of cloud being blown across the sky, and rolled onto his stomach. 'There's a coder inside CyberBallista. He's hacking into a darknet website to which both murderers have links. We've assumed the identity of the sort of person who'd be interested in the killings and we're waiting for a password so we can get in.'

'But we had one of the top London cyber companies look at this stuff and it was locked tight. There were no leads,' Ava said.

'It's down to the skill of the individual hacker. And the guy I'm dealing with is one of the best in the world.'

'Is he also responsible for the banker thefts?' Ava asked. She didn't want the answer, but not asking the question seemed like cowardice.

'Are you asking if he did it, or if your fiancé thinks he did it? I can't answer the first question and I won't answer the second.'

'God, Luc, what have you done?'

'I've found possibly the only person in the UK who has the ability to trace these murderers. I'm doing my job. We should get back. If I can't send anyone else to speak to him, I'll go myself.' He stood up, extending his hand to Ava and pulling her up too.

'Don't be stupid. You're already the subject of a complaint and it's obviously all wrapped up in this. What is it you need?'

'I need Ben Paulson out of his office and trying to get into that website. We're pretty sure his work phone line is not secure and he's not picking up his mobile. I need someone there now.'

They began to walk back, brushing grass off their backs, squinting in the sunlight. Even the Edinburgh wind had died down in response to their low moods.

'Look, Luc, why don't I just speak with Joe? If he knew what was at stake, if I could make him understand, I'm sure he'd see sense.'

Callanach laughed. Ava watched him, genuinely unable to stop, clutching his sides. She crossed her arms and waited until he'd pulled himself together.

'That was rude,' Ava said, walking away.

'I'm sorry. It's just that you have no idea who Joseph Edgar is – what he is – and yet you want to spend the rest of your life with him? I've already been warned off. Closing his case is a guaranteed step up the ladder, skipping a few rungs on the way. He's not going to let anything ruin it. Not even a few dead bodies.'

Ava drew breath to speak. She wanted to defend Joe, to deny what Callanach had said, but even if she'd been capable of speaking, the pretence of making Joe out to be something better than he was, wasn't worthy of her.

'I'll go,' she said. 'They won't be looking for me. You can't put anyone else from the squad at risk. If he finds out, I'll tell Joe I was following up a lead of my own and that I had no idea what was going on at CyberBallista. He's not going to make a complaint against me, is he?'

Callanach checked his watch. They were both thinking the same thing. They were out of time. Julia Stimple was waiting.

'I'm going,' Ava said, pulling out her keys as they reached the station car park.

'Would it make any difference if I said no?' Callanach asked.

'Only to the extent that I'd enjoy defying you. Other than that, not a bloody bit. Give me twenty minutes.'

Ava drove as fast as she could without breaking any laws or drawing attention to herself. She parked round the back of CyberBallista's offices, went through the car park to the reception area for the office block and asked to use their phone.

'I need to talk to Mr Paulson,' she told CyberBallista's receptionist, who had announced himself on the phone with no small measure of self-importance.

'Not going to happen, missy, he's in with the boss.'

'Please, I'm his girlfriend. I'm downstairs in reception.' Ava forced a slight sob into her voice. It was sympathy or threats. She started with the least offensive option.

'Then Mr Paulson should've told you no personal visits at work. Company policy.'

'But I've been . . .' Ava made her voice catch in her throat. 'I can't talk about it.'

'Are you all right? Perhaps we should call the police?' he said.

'No, there was a break-in, you see, at our flat. The police have already been round. I'm just shaken up and I need to know where to find the insurance details so I can get the front door mended. I feel really vulnerable about going home when I can't lock up securely. I only need to see him for a minute. Could you ask, please? And say I'm sorry.'

His voice softened. 'I'll see what I can do. You just stay where you are.'

Ava put the phone down, walking away from the ground floor reception desk, grateful that it was summer and she had an excuse for wearing dark sunglasses and a hat. She looked exactly like every other tourist wandering around the city in her faded jeans and white T-shirt. Even so, she moved out of view of the front windows.

It took a while, but eventually a man in his twenties, tanned with long hair and an attitude, came out. Ava raised a hand, mindful that the receptionist had heard her telephone tale of woe.

Ben took Ava's arm and walked her through the door that led to the car park.

'Unless I'm mistaken,' he said, 'you're not my girlfriend. Honestly, you're a bit old for me.'

'Callanach needs you to phone him,' Ava said. 'Straight away. It's urgent.'

'I have no idea who you're talking about,' Ben said. 'And I think proper procedure dictates that you introduce yourself and explain what you're doing here.'

Ava gritted her teeth. Callanach hadn't warned her that the boy was such a pain.

'I've passed the message on, and you do know who I'm talking about. This isn't a game. If you can help, then we need you to help right now.'

'DCI Edgar is stooping pretty low using you to get to me,' Ben said.

'What?' Ava said, stepping away. 'So you know who I am?'

'For the record, as I'm guessing you're taping or filming this, I haven't been read my rights and I've no idea who Callanach is. Tell Edgar he'll have to do better than that. Excuse me.'

'Ben,' Ava said as he walked away. 'I get it. And I have no desire to be dragged into whatever you're doing. Check your mobile. There have been developments and you'll find missed calls. When DCI Edgar gets his case together you'll be arrested. Until then, you might want to consider helping as a way to make up for those thefts. For some reason Luc has faith in you. He's taken a monumental risk. Don't screw it up.'

'Whatever. Thanks for the pep talk, lady. Give your fiancé my love.' He let the door fall shut as he walked through, the slam echoing between the concrete pillars. Ava cursed. That could have gone better. Computer genius he might be, but he was also a jumped-up little sod.

Chapter Thirty-Six

When Callanach got back to the incident room, DS Lively was waiting.

'There's a woman in your office,' Lively said.

'Bit more information, Sergeant, or am I supposed to guess?'

'Name's Leigh-Anne Hoskins, born Stimple if that gives you a clue. She wants to know what the progress is with locating her mother. And she's upset.'

'Of course she's upset,' Callanach said. 'Have someone bring a cup of tea and ask Salter to come in. It'd be useful to have another woman in the room.'

'I'll get the tea,' Lively said. Callanach wondered if he'd heard right. Lively had never been known to make a drink for anyone other than himself. Salter came through holding a notebook.

'You won't be needing that,' Callanach said. 'I've got to break some bad news to Julia Stimple's daughter and I thought you might be able to, you know . . .'

'Hold her hand?' Salter asked.

'Exactly,' Callanach said, walking through to his office.

Leigh-Anne Hoskins was startlingly like her mother, size and all. Not just large, but tall. She sat stony-faced, bag clutched on her lap. Callanach introduced himself and Salter, and sat down as Lively entered with the tea. The detective sergeant didn't leave as Callanach had expected, choosing instead to lean against the wall and drink his coffee. None had been brought for Callanach or Salter, naturally.

'Miss Hoskins, we're doing everything we can to find your mother,' Callanach began.

'It's not enough! My poor old mam, God knows what she's going through. Have you got any idea where she is?'

'Not yet, but we're getting closer. We believe the man holding her is Slovenian and we've circulated a good description of him.'

Leigh-Anne pulled out a handkerchief and began wiping her eyes.

'But you definitely don't know where he's taken her. Is that right?'

'I'm afraid not. There is some other news, though. I'm sorry to have to tell you that the man holding your mother has taken action to persuade us how serious he is.'

'Really?' Leigh-Anne asked, eyes wide, cup of tea frozen half way to her lips. She looked from Callanach to Salter to Lively. 'What?'

'There's no easy way to break this. A section of your mother's finger was removed and sent here. It was left with a note referring to our recent press conference.'

'What are you talking about?' Leigh-Anne asked. Her face was taut, eyebrows pulled high, mouth open. Callanach had no desire to explain in any more detail. 'How is that possible?'

'Ms Hoskins, is there someone we can phone for you? You'll need support,' Salter said, putting a gentle hand on the woman's arm. Leigh-Anne shook the hand off.

'This isn't right,' she shouted. 'I need to get out of here.' She stood up, sending her teacup flying, spraying liquid across Callanach's desk.

'Don't worry about that, I'll clear it up,' Salter said. 'Shall I organise transport to get you home? You probably shouldn't drive. We appreciate how much of a shock that was.'

'What about your brother?' Lively asked. 'We haven't been able to speak with him yet, but if you have a mobile number, we could ask him to pick you up.'

'He's working away and doesn't want to be contacted. Too upset. We all are. So what happens now?' Leigh-Anne said.

'We're working on some leads. Hopefully we'll have answers soon. You'll be the first to know should anything change,' Callanach said.

'I'll be speaking to the press,' Leigh-Anne said. 'You people should never have let this happen. You knew she was at risk. My mum should have been moved to a safe house.'

'Ms Hoskins, giving a statement to the press at this stage might make things worse. Specifically, you should avoid referring to the information I've just given you. The murderer is craving attention. Any wrong moves might push him to do something more drastic.'

'The public has a right to know what's going on,' Leigh-Anne said, blowing her nose loudly. 'I'll get myself home.' She walked out.

'Do you want me to go after her, sir?' Salter asked.

'That's all right, Salter, I'll go,' Lively said. 'Put your feet up. You'll be no good to that baby if you don't.'

'You told them then?' Callanach asked when Lively had gone.

'Aye. Figured it was time. I just didn't want to seem to be asking for special treatment or have people acting differently around me. It's hard. I like being a detective. The pregnancy wasn't exactly planned,' Salter said.

'Maybe that's the best way. You'll be a great mother. And your career will be waiting when you're ready to come back.'

'It took a while to get used to the idea,' Salter said, cleaning up the tea. Callanach fought the urge to take the cloth from her. Salter was right, his immediate instinct was to treat her differently. 'But now I spend every free minute imagining the first time I'll hold my baby, thinking up names, worrying, feeling ecstatic. Strange how you can love the idea of something before it's actually there for you to touch.'

Salter had tears in her eyes. Callanach felt a surge of protectiveness, glad that Ava had burst in when she did, however complicated that had made things.

A phone rang – the one Ben had given him. He looked up at Salter.

'It's all right, sir. I was just going,' she said. Callanach locked the door behind her.

Chapter Thirty-Seven

Ben was in no mood to help the police. Callanach had sent DCI Edgar's girlfriend to him, for Christ's sake. Like that wasn't a set-up from the start. That was on top of the fact that his boss at CyberBallista was deeply, deeply pissed off with him. He'd had a whole morning of interrogation, putting strategies in place, and resetting their internal security system. He wouldn't get fired, he knew that. He'd been head-hunted to CyberBallista when a former colleague from his Silicon Valley post had mentioned Ben's unique talents. There were very few people who could do his job. That was the only thing saving him at the moment.

Now he had to disappear off for another lunch hour when he should have been at his desk tidying up yesterday's shitstorm. The police hadn't found anything. He wasn't that sloppy. They'd have to get into his apartment whilst his computers were logged on to get anywhere near evidence, and that was never going to happen. He'd even prepared for the prospect of a police raid. If they barged in, he had only to hit two keys in combination and everything got wiped. It was foolproof.

There was no way he would risk going back to his apartment straight after a visit from DI Turner. Callanach may have been an idiot to have trusted Turner, but he was a well-intentioned idiot, doing police work for the right reasons just like Ben's dad had. Promotion was irrelevant to a good cop, so occasionally the rules became irrelevant too. All that mattered was catching the bad guys and protecting the innocent. His dad had always expressed a simple view of life. Now that his father was gone, the things he'd stood for seemed to be all that mattered. Justice, equality, standing up to the wealthy upper classes who contributed so little to those they looked down upon from their penthouses and corporate skyscrapers.

Ben grabbed his laptop, repeated Ava's lie that his place had been broken into and began the walk round to the Below Par cafe. On his way, he texted Callanach to meet him for coffee. He'd know where to go. Polly met him with a smile.

'All right, Ben? Didn't expect you in today. You need the back room or are you here for the pleasure of my company?'

She was wearing a cut-off T-shirt and denim shorts, her hair tied up in a pink scarf. The emerald stud she always wore in her belly button cast a green light back on his own white shirt. He wanted to reach out and touch it. That would be dicing with death. He'd seen Polly cut more than a few men down to size when they'd taken liberties. She shot from the hip. It was one of the reasons he liked her so much.

'The room, please, Pol, if no one's in there.'

'Ham on sourdough and a coffee?' she smiled, walking ahead to open up.

'You're an angel,' Ben said. 'There'll be a guest, same as before. Let him straight in, would you?'

'Killjoy,' Polly muttered. 'It was fun last time. But seeing as you asked nicely.'

'I always ask nicely, in case you hadn't noticed. Maybe that's it, has my accent been hard to understand? It would explain why you always say no when I ask you on a date.'

'Maybe it's just about persistence,' Polly said. 'A girl needs to know if she's just a quick fix or a long-term deal. Sounds like you're about to give up already.'

'Nope. Not going anywhere. Especially not now I've been given something that feels a bit like hope,' Ben smiled at her.

'Don't hold your breath,' she said, laughing as she walked off, hips swaying ever so slightly. Ben watched, conscious of the fact that she knew he was watching. Even so, looking away was impossible. Below Par belonged to a friend of a friend, someone sympathetic to The Unsung and their work. The cafe was a meeting point, a safe house away from prying eyes. You came and went, and whatever you'd done there went with you. When Polly started working there, Ben had become a more regular visitor. He was so used to Californian clone girls – golden tan, white teeth, size zero, blonde hair – that Polly had seemed like a cure-all to what he hated most. The establishment. Conformity. Society was the gossiping neighbour peering in next door's windows, jealous of success, quick to point out failure. The earthiness of Scotland had been an antidote to all of that.

Ben fired up his laptop, ready for Callanach to join him. The five-minute security sequence finished, he opened the email to Rory Hand from the webmaster. There were instructions with it. You could only access the site if your machine was running encryption software. Standard stuff for the darknet. A username had been provided that Ben would be able to change once he was in. The password was a random series of twenty-one numbers, capitalised and small letters.

Callanach opened the door and walked in without speaking. Polly followed him and left coffee and the promised sandwich on the table.

'You ever pull a stunt like that again and we're through,' Ben said.

'It was complicated,' Callanach said, 'involving the theft of a piece of paper, a pregnancy and a threat.'

'Spare me,' Ben replied. 'I take it there's been a development.'

'A delivery from the killer. We're out of time,' Callanach said. 'What do we have?'

'Rory Hand's history was enough to convince the webmaster that he was eligible for membership to the club. I'm just about to enter the password.' Ben typed for a few seconds then waited. A menu of options appeared.

'Where first?' Callanach asked.

'Ignore User Profile, we don't want to add details. The less attention we draw the better. Your choices are Polls, Forum and Gallery.'

'Gallery seems the most obvious way to check we're in the right place,' Callanach said, shifting his chair closer to the table.

There were four sections within Gallery labelled Thorburn, Lott, Swan and Balcaskie. Callanach didn't want to open any of them. It wasn't what he would see that bothered him – chances were that the files held few surprises. It was more the sense that he was stepping into a world he had always opposed, tainting himself with the bloodlust of people who had no place in society. Ben clicked on the first window.

There were photographs of Sim Thorburn stolen from social media, a sign of an age where the populace was so addicted to recording everything that a few had taken snaps of the young man bleeding out. There was a copy of the autopsy documents, the press coverage, links to video news reports. It wasn't dissimilar to the incident room wall. This was here for very different purposes though. Callanach knew what they were going to get on the other gallery pages. There was little point reminding himself how bloody the deaths had been.

'Go to Forum,' he told Ben. The click moved them to a list of threads, complete with user numbers and the date of the last posted comment. Some were discussions about the crimes, others were general conversations about killing techniques, more on serial killers in different countries and various conspiracy theories. There was a thread dedicated to recommended snuff videos, and another detailing weapons purchasing from knives and guns to poisons and chemicals. 'How many users, do you think?' Callanach asked, scrolling through the list of people posting.

'Hundreds. The site must have been running a while. It'll be attracting global traffic.'

'And we can't trace any of the users?' Callanach asked, doing his best not to fixate on any one aspect of what he was reading. If he started, he had a suspicion he'd never stop.

'No, the encryption software is too good for that,' Ben said.

'So where the hell do we start?'

Ben clicked on the final link. The polls section was split in two halves. The first was entitled 'Next Kill', although it had no other information available.

'It's disabled at the moment,' Ben said. 'I should be able to click in the box and type but I can't. I guess there's no poll open now. Let's try the other one.' He tapped his mouse button over the heading 'Kill Grades'.

An instruction box opened up. Ben read it aloud. '"One vote per user, per kill. Vote cannot be changed once posted." I don't get it.' He scrolled down and found each victim's name. When he rolled the mouse over the name, three new boxes appeared to the side. 'Proficiency. Originality. Fear. It allows you to enter numerals up to 100.'

Callanach put his cup down. His temples were throbbing. 'That's what this site is about? They're grading the kills?' He lowered his head, trying to combat the dizziness he was experiencing with additional blood. It didn't work.

Ben said nothing, just stared at the screen.

'How do we catch them, Ben? Now we know exactly what they're doing. This whole thing is a fucking game. What good is this if we can't get any closer to them?'

'The killers will be in here somewhere,' Ben said. 'This is how they're being given instructions. I need time to go through the threads, see what I can pick up. I've got to get back to work this afternoon though. I'll start as soon as I get home tonight.'

'You'll need help,' Callanach said. 'We could ask Lance.'

'I'll call him,' Ben said. 'You don't look well. Can I get you anything?'

'You can get me the address where they're holding Julia Stimple,' Callanach said. 'Because as soon as her abductor figures out how to score maximum points for killing her, we'll be too late.'

Callanach left first, followed a few minutes later by Ben. Neither of them noticed Ava Turner across the street. She saw them though. She saw Callanach looking scared and exhausted as he exited, then Ben hurrying out, checking his watch. And she saw the girl who put a closed sign up in the window afterwards.

Chapter Thirty-Eight

Lance phoned Callanach. His hands were still shaking. He wasn't quite sure what he was looking at, but he knew it wasn't good. The morning had started positively. A quick jog before work to get the heart pumping, some leads on a few stories, and a birthday card from his son who was travelling for a year but who'd managed to remember. It had been a pleasant ride in to his tiny rented office – little traffic, bike running smoothly, no rain. Then the post had been delivered and he'd had the misfortune to open the package whilst eating a late lunch.

'Hey Lance,' Callanach said. 'I was just dialling your number. I'm going to need your help this evening. Ben will contact you to . . .'

'Someone's sent me a piece of someone,' Lance said. 'Sorry, that didn't make much sense. I mean, I've just opened a package and it contains what looks like human flesh. A soft part, not sure what.'

'Julia Stimple,' Callanach said. 'Where are you?'

'In my office. I don't know what to do.' Lance looked down at the blob that had once been a healthy pink and which now resembled an uncooked prawn.

'Don't move. Literally not a muscle. I'll have a team there in minutes. Don't touch anything at all, especially the packaging. I'm on my way.'

Lance wasn't ordinarily squeamish. He'd patched up friends over the years, carried his fellow rugby players off the pitch in his youth, helped at his fair share of accidents. He'd even delivered his second child himself when things had moved faster than he and his then wife had anticipated. But this was infinitely worse. It was the knowledge that someone had had to endure having a piece of themselves cut off.

When the first crime scene investigator came in, she was already suited. Lance felt as if he'd been caught in the middle of a science fiction movie. The officers checked he was all right, photographed him with the flesh on his lap where it had fallen, inspected it, bagged and tagged it, then repeated the process with every piece of packaging. Finally Lance was allowed to leave the room, fingerprinted to eliminate his prints from the packaging, and taken to a quiet place to give a statement.

Callanach arrived as Lance was being brought a cup of tea by a uniformed officer. 'Lance, what happened?'

'Envelope must have been put through the front door. These are shared offices. They get hundreds of items of mail each day and bring them round just after lunch.'

'I'm sorry this happened to you,' Callanach said.

'It's not your fault,' Lance responded.

'If I hadn't used you to leak the false report about Michael Swan's death the killer would have chosen a different outlet. Forensic pathologist says it's a piece of earlobe, by the way. Nothing life-threatening if that makes you feel any better.'

'Good God, poor woman,' Lance said.

'I didn't know this was your office, Lance,' DS Lively said from behind Callanach's shoulder. 'I'd fetch you a dram of single malt, only I suspect the DI here would frown on me so much as handling the stuff during working hours. You all right?'

'I've been told I'm free to leave, although I'm not sure I should get on my bike yet. Can't hang around in this corridor any longer though. Any chance I could grab a lift home?' Lance asked.

'Suits me, if the boss doesn't get all huffy about health and safety. You know what these managerial types are like, mate. I've been asked to get you back to the station for a briefing, sir, so we can drop Lance off on the way,' Lively said.

'Is there anyone in Edinburgh you don't know, Sergeant?' Callanach asked.

Lively shrugged his shoulders in response. 'Lance and I played rugby together back in the days when they splashed a bit of cold water over a broken bone and sent you back on the pitch. None of this running on with a physiotherapist to give you a wee cuddle better.'

'I had to stop when my son was born,' Lance said. 'Too many Sundays ruined with post-match hangovers. Don't worry about the lift if it's a bother,' he directed towards Callanach.

'Of course we can drop you on the way,' Callanach replied politely. 'What's the briefing about, Lively?'

'There's been a sighting of a van matching the description of the vehicle outside Julia Stimple's house at the time she disappeared. A marked car tried to pull it over but it sped off. Unit couldn't pursue at speed as it was in a busy pedestrian area. We've lost the van for now, but we've got a team on the cameras out of the city and we're hoping to pick it up again.'

'Let's get going, then,' Callanach said.

Lance settled himself into the rear passenger seat and closed his eyes. 'So you've got a break?' he asked.

'It may yet prove to be nothing,' Lively said. 'I just hope to God we haven't lost our only chance to catch this scabby bastard.'

'Can I quote you on that?' Lance asked.

'I forgot you're a journo. One step up from bloody lawyers, you lot. Quote me and you'll never be able to park in the city again without getting towed, understand?'

The radio burst into life a second before Callanach's mobile began beeping. The radio won.

'All available units to Moffat Road, Ormiston. Silent approach. Officers already on the scene and awaiting backup. Confirm positions.'

Lively swung the car round, put on the lights and sped up as Callanach called Tripp.

'I was just trying to phone you, sir,' Tripp said.

'Ormiston, right? Lively and I are in a marked car and on our way. What's happened?' Callanach asked.

'We've picked up the progress of the van believed to have been parked outside Julia Stimple's. It was seen leaving an off-licence earlier. We lost it for a while but CCTV caught it again. We got an unmarked vehicle to pick up the route, and they followed it back to a property which is looking more than a little suspicious,' Tripp said.

'Where's Ormiston?' Callanach asked Lively.

'A few miles east of the city. It's a mainly residential area,' Lively said.

'Describe the scene,' Callanach directed back towards Tripp.

'A single white male parked the van and entered a property. Officers noted that all the curtains were drawn, upstairs and down. He was carrying a bag of booze and a few items of food, hood up, gloves on in spite of the heat. And the licence plate doesn't match the vehicle.'

'What do we know about the house?' Callanach asked, texting Ava the details.

'It belongs to a Mrs Ellen Lavery only she's been in a retirement home for the past four months so it's unoccupied, has a for sale board outside. Shouldn't be anyone in there,' Tripp said.

'And the van?' Callanach asked.

'Not registered, no tax, no insurance. Looks like the plate has been tampered with.'

'We've got him,' Callanach said. 'Where's the armed response unit?'

'Two roads out and waiting for you or DI Turner, whoever gets there first. Paramedics are on standby. All units are on a no lights, no sirens warning,' Tripp said. 'They're ready to move on your command.'

Chapter Thirty-Nine

Grom changed the bandages on the lollipop lady's hand. He'd taken the finger as cleanly as he could – her bleeding to death was not part of his plan – but it was leaving a sticky trail of half-congealed blood everywhere and frankly it was starting to stink. He'd had enough of that with her toilet habits. He still wasn't sure if she really couldn't make it to the bathroom to piss or if she was just torturing him by letting her bladder go whenever and wherever she felt like it. Either way, the air in the house was taking on the thickness and dampness of his father's stables. If air could hold a colour, then this was ochre.

He boiled the kettle as she slurped the glass of water he'd got her, letting most of it dribble down into her lap, and tipped a fistful of cooking salt into a jug. He'd learned this in the stables too. It seemed now that most of his education had taken place there. Sex, birth, death. How to end life as painlessly as possible. And how to drag it out so that the end, when it came, was as great a relief as it was a defeat. The first time he'd cleaned and packed a wound had been on his father's horse. The mare had refused to jump a river during a hunt, enraging Grom's father enough for him to rip a bough from a tree and flay her hindquarters with it. She was lame within two days. It had been Grom's task to clean the wounds and heal them. Grom intended to do the same with the old woman as he had with the horse, only he'd felt markedly more sympathy for the horse.

He waited until the hot saltwater was at a temperature where it wouldn't cause burns, then held the stump of her finger in the saline. The lollipop lady moaned and twisted but his grip was inescapable. Then he packed the wound hard with a clean bandage he'd found in a bathroom cupboard and wrapped it back up. The horse had survived another year, which was a better fate than the old woman had coming. The same mare had kicked his father in the chest one December morning when he'd been dragging her out of the stables. There had been a second when Grom had felt close to elated, watching the big man fly through the air helpless, seeing him crash to the ground clutching his sternum, unmoving. Just a few utopian moments in which he'd believed his father was dead, then the bastard had groaned and lifted one arm, and Grom's world was as bleak as it had always been. His father had lived to tell the tale, albeit with a horseshoe-shaped bruise on his chest. It was the horse who had suffered.

His father had taken the mare out into the woods, tied her to three trees – one noose around her head, a rope around each back leg – to make movement impossible. Then he'd lit a fire under her. It had begun gently enough, some smoke, the crackling of twigs, the wind battering the flames down so that Grom had felt sure it would simply go out and his father would return to his senses. But the old man had thrown on more kindling, then a log, and suddenly the horse was bucking and jumping, unable to shift to either side to avoid the heat, bashing its head on the branches above, slamming its hooves into the tree trunks around. The fire took its time rising, fighting the icy winter air, and the smoke took off down the mountainside, affording the animal no chance of unconsciousness before the flames began licking its flesh. It was the smell that Grom remembered most clearly. The acrid offence of burning hair, replaced only seconds later with charring meat, sooty, coppery with a sauce of running blood. And his father had roared with laughter.

Grom stared at the old woman. He knew now what he was going to do and it was genius. It would make Sem Culpa's past efforts look like childish crayon drawings of a halloween party. He would cremate the ancient bitch alive, limbs stretched out above the pyre. He just needed to find the perfect location. Somewhere he could film it without the authorities being alerted until he'd completed the task. It would take a couple of days to research and buy what he needed, that was all.

A flicker of movement out on the road caught his attention. He shifted to the curtains to see what was happening. The old woman called out to him. She needed to piss again. He threw his head back, tempted to use his fists and end it all there and then. But he had to wait. Now that he had his masterpiece in mind, he was within a stone's throw of victory.

Chapter Forty

Lively pulled the car into a street parallel to Moffat Road. Callanach jumped out as Lively parked, a huddle of men and women drawing around him. One of them passed him a stabproof vest and a helmet, another handed over an earpiece. An enforcer had been leant against a wall, big enough that few doors would withstand its force, and a perimeter had been established to stop vehicles entering or leaving the road.

'You're to stay in the car,' Lively told Lance. 'Stay down, stay still. No getting involved and no taking photos. I'll come and find you once the scene's secured, then we'll make sure you get home.'

'Got it,' Lance said, looking around as Lively disappeared into a huddle of bodies.

The area was defined by its greyness, not only the roads and pavements, but the pebble-dashed houses in semi-detached rows. It dripped decline. The ideal place to hide in relatively plain sight. Easy access to the city for the killer's recent deliveries. Part of Lance was hoping the police would mess the bastard up good and proper. The more rational half, who occasionally attended human rights rallies and wrote about public justice, knew that a trial and a lifetime of incarceration was the only option that separated men from beasts.

Lance scribbled notes as he sat in the back of the car, taking out his mobile and drafting a news release. He hadn't been told not to write anything, and all he'd promised Lively was not to quote him or take photos. He might have been helping Callanach but he was still a reporter, and it was definitely in the public interest to know about this. So much the better if he got there first.

Lively had left the car windows down for him. Lance stuck his head out as far as he dared without being too obvious, and listened in on the briefing.

'We're going in the front and back doors simultaneously. We'll have officers in position covering neighbouring properties to prevent him entering those and taking alternative or additional hostages. Police marksmen will cover all window and door accesses to the property, so open curtains as you move through each room.' Lance decided the officer talking was from the Armed Response Unit. Callanach was taking a back seat for now. Lance had rather taken to the detective inspector. In spite of his ridiculous good looks, the woman-charming French accent, and his vaguely distant air – all reasons Lance felt he probably should have disliked him – he was all right. Even for the police.

'I'll knock and announce,' Lance heard Callanach say. 'The priority is to secure the victim safely. The suspect will have weapons, so disable him as quickly as you can. Julia Stimple is likely to be in shock. We know she has injuries to her hand and one ear, possibly more. No heroics. This man is extraordinarily strong, so high levels of control may be necessary.'

Lance continued to type, giving a brief description of the scene. There were multiple vehicles, at least twenty armed officers, concerned residents being ordered gently but firmly back into their houses. You'd think the inside of the buildings had come alive, so twitchy were the curtains. He saved his draft until he had the final details, and settled back to watch the drama as it unfolded.

'Right, get in position,' Callanach ordered. 'We move on my go.' He secured his body armour then jogged with the Armed Response Unit to the house in question. The property was deteriorating, paintwork peeling, windows unwashed. There were no lights on that he could see. The officers carrying the enforcer went in front, holding the ram either side. Everyone was in place. There was a momentary silence.

'Police, open the door immediately,' Callanach shouted.

Inside a woman shrieked, followed by the sound of furniture turning over, a door slamming.

'Go, all units go,' came a voice from within his headset. The enforcer was pulled back, thrust hard forward. Wood splintered but didn't quite give. It took only a second battering to have the door flying open as the lock went. He heard the back door smash at the same time as the front. From both directions, police stormed the property. There were yells from upstairs, a woman screaming hysterically, sobbing. Police were shouting orders. Callanach took the stairs in a few bounds, pushing through the crowd to see Julia Stimple lying on a bed, covering her face with a pillow.

There was an overwhelming moment of relief that at least this life had been spared, that they'd been able to get to her in time. Whatever she'd suffered, she'd escaped the worst of it.

He made his way through to the next room, seeing drawn weapons and at least three police officers on top of a large male struggling on the floor.

'Is he armed?' Callanach asked.

'Haven't found anything yet, sir,' the response came.

'Right, victim out first to the paramedics, then bring the van to the front and get him straight out. Blanket over his head. I don't want any photographs appearing on the internet. This needs to stay quiet until we've prepared a statement, and Julia Stimple's children must be the first to know.'

'I'll phone the daughter now,' Lively shouted from the hallway.

Callanach followed the procession of officers helping a hysterical Julia Stimple safely down the stairs.

'It's all right now, Julia,' an officer said. 'The paramedics are waiting. Your kidnapper is being restrained by officers and he won't be on the streets again while there's still life in his body.'

With that Julia let out a tremendous wail, screeching and babbling. Callanach looked around as she was escorted out. The place was warm enough and there was little sign of disturbance. On a table in the kitchen were newspapers with stories about the missing lollipop lady cut out. A small television set was still playing a daytime soap. It looked almost domesticated. The remains of several pizzas were lying on the countertop and there was crockery in the sink waiting to be washed.

Callanach decided to wait outside. He could do nothing else until the murderer had been arrested and processed.

'One down, one to go, eh sir?' Lively commented. 'I got the daughter on the phone, told her the news and she hung up. I'm waiting for her to phone back so I can let her know where her mother's been taken.'

From the car, Lance watched the unmistakable figure of Julia Stimple being wheeled from house to ambulance, still screaming and crying. He finalised his headline, adding more sensational language than he usually would, and pressed send. Edinburgh could rest more peacefully with one less psychopath on the prowl tonight.

★　★　★

This was it. The Moderator had waited so long for this moment. It was finally time to open the poll for the next victim. All he'd needed was confirmation that Grom's part in it was over, and the news channels had been more than forthcoming with that. True, it hadn't gone the way he'd anticipated, but that didn't matter now. The stupid Slovenian had fallen into the hands of the police and his lollipop lady victim had apparently survived. The media reports had made it sound as if the police had been utterly heroic. The reality was that Grom must have been incompetent beyond belief to have been followed all the way to Ormiston and caught with the lollipop lady still alive. All the more reason for Sem Culpa to complete her trio of kills and prove herself the ultimate killer. She wouldn't run scared, he was certain of that. Insane bitch would no doubt have something even more devastating than usual planned, just to taunt Grom as he settled into his prison cell. Their egos were what had made his chosen pair so easy to manipulate. Wanting to kill was a private matter for most, but there were a select few who needed to kill and craved admiration for it. The Moderator had discovered that there were many more candidates for his competition than he'd expected.

The first thing he did was lock down Grom's access to the website, cancelling his password entry. After that he scrolled through the member details, wiping every mention of Grom from the site – his application, his email address, every communication that had passed between them. Not that he was particularly concerned that Grom would give anything away to the police – it certainly wouldn't reduce his sentence in the circumstances – but better safe than sorry. As for the new poll, he would make it the shortest voting period he could get away with. There was no point waiting any longer. He'd been patient for so long. Months of planning, the hours of work he'd put into bringing everyone together at the right time. All that was left to do was email site users to announce that the final poll was running.

This time there would be no need for graffiti, which was just as well with Grom out of the picture. It had been a useful tactic – getting Sem Culpa and Grom to leave messages around the city, notifying each other what the next kill target was – heating up the competition with the added benefit of publicity. And it had proved vital in assisting the morons at Police Scotland to figure out what was happening, but there was no way he could run the risk of the next victim suddenly leaving town. That wouldn't work for him at all. This target was to be notified to one person only.

He checked his watch. If he rushed the shopping, he could get back to his beautiful house and spend a couple of hours enjoying it alone before his wife ruined yet another evening. The Moderator uploaded the new poll and set off to find smoked salmon.

Chapter Forty-One

Ava hadn't made it to Ormiston in time for the raid but she was waiting at the hospital door to meet the ambulance carrying Julia Stimple. It arrived flanked by police cars. She could hear the bellowing of a female voice before the ambulance doors had even opened.

'I want to see my son! Let me call my boy!'

Ava prepared herself for a long evening trying to calm Julia Stimple down enough to take a statement. At least this meant that the murders of Helen Lott and Emily Balcaskie had been resolved without any further need to collaborate with the criminal at the centre of Joe's investigation. Ben Paulson had made her deeply uneasy. The whole furtive set-up, that cafe with the girl who looked like a caricature of a twenty-something 'don't give a fuck' female, closing as soon as Paulson and Callanach had exited. It was all way too professional for Ava's liking. Callanach was in over his head, not that he'd be told.

The ambulance doors finally opened and the trolley was wheeled out. Ava walked straight up, showed her badge and did her best to sound both authoritative and reassuring.

'I'm Detective Inspector Ava Turner. Can I confirm that you are Julia Stimple from Findhorn Place?'

'I am,' the woman cried, holding her head in her hands. She was trembling, obviously in need of some sedation.

'It's all right, Ms Stimple. We'll get you straight to a doctor and leave a police guard with you. We'll need to take a statement but not until you're feeling calmer.'

Ava looked at the woman's hands as she raked them madly through her hair. It didn't strike her at first what she was looking for, but it wasn't long before it dawned.

'Could you hold out both hands, please?' Ava asked.

The woman did as she was told, the extent of her shaking causing Ava to grip both hands with her own.

'Turn your head right then left,' Ava instructed. The woman complied, obviously terrified. It suddenly occurred to Ava that Julia Stimple might not have been terrified for the same reason they had all been expecting.

'Ms Stimple, the man with you in the house, the one the police arrested. Can you tell me who he was?'

'That's what I've been trying to tell everyone!' she shouted. 'That's my boy. He didn't mean any harm! We were only going to stay there a while then he was supposed to drop me off in the city again.'

'So you left your house voluntarily?' Ava's voice was gravelly. She was aware that she wasn't hiding her rising temper particularly well. One of the paramedics tried to intervene. Ava stuck out her hand and made it clear that would be a really bad move.

'I was going to lose my job!' Julie Stimple screeched. 'Some nosy git complained about my language and about me leaning against a wall while supervising the children for crying out loud. I got disciplined! And there's no way I'll get a new job with my health problems.'

'And you have had absolutely no contact with anyone who has threatened or hurt you?' Ava asked, her fingers curling fistward.

'No, I tried to tell them at the house, he never hurt me. We just needed a bit of spare cash. Those magazines'll pay anything for a good story. No one got hurt, did they? Did you not see what they did to my boy? Treating him like some bloody criminal. They had guns. Real guns. I thought they were going to shoot us!'

'And you have no physical injuries that need treating?' Ava checked.

'No, I keep telling you. My boy would never hurt me. It was just a wee bit of a ruse.'

Ava dug deep into her self-control in spite of the heat rising in her cheeks and the bile high in her throat. She had a call to make to Callanach, but before that there was one thing she was going to do personally.

'Julia Stimple. You are under arrest,' she said.

A few minutes later Ava left uniformed officers to transport the wailing woman back to the station. Ms Stimple would still have a story to sell to the magazines. It's just that she'd have to wait until she'd been released from prison before she'd be free to organise it.

Callanach took the call as he was striding towards the cells. He very nearly didn't answer it, except that the prisoner was opting for silence as he was booked in, slowing the process down.

'It's me,' Ava blurted before Callanach had said anything. 'Don't waste your time with an interview. Get Lively to take it. That's not our murderer.'

'What? How do you—'

'Julia Stimple's fingers and ears are intact. She and her son cooked the whole thing up. They decided the publicity would mean easy cash, only no one was supposed to find her.'

'Oh Jesus, that means—' Callanach sank onto a nearby chair.

'We still have no idea who the hostage is,' Ava finished for him. 'I'll get the squad checking to see if any of the other lollipop ladies is missing. We need to find the real victim. Whoever that is, is running out of time.'

'I've got to go.' Callanach ended the call. 'Where's DS Lively?' he asked a passing constable.

'Already in the interview room, sir. Suspect has just been taken in.'

'Right,' Callanach said, slamming open the door. Lively was just getting started. Julia Stimple's son was crying. 'Wrong man,' he announced. 'That's Stimple junior on a money-making scheme. Charge him for wasting our time and whatever else you can throw at him.'

'I bloody knew it,' Lively said. 'Your sister was in on it too, wasn't she, pal? Her face when she was told her mum had lost a finger. She'd not a bloody clue! Cry all you like, mate. You'll have reason when you're stuck inside a cell twenty-three hours a day.'

'We didn't mean to do anything wrong,' the man blubbed.

'Aye, like you didn't mean to make your mum's flat look like a crime scene and divert police resources away from a real investigation,' Lively said.

'I don't want to do time. It wasn't even my idea,' Stimple junior snivelled.

'You need to stop talking,' Callanach said, 'or prison will be the least of your problems.'

Back in his office Callanach was flooded with requests to answer questions about Julia Stimple and her abductor. The worst of it was that Emily Balcaskie's parents and Helen Lott's family had already been in contact. The press were a step ahead again, only this time they'd picked up a disaster story. It hardly seemed possible, given that he'd only left Ormiston forty-five minutes earlier.

'Lance,' Callanach said. 'Shit.'

The reporter had been dropped home while Callanach sped back to the station. It hadn't occurred to Callanach to tell him not to report, he'd just expected him not to. His own mistake. Nothing like taking a journalist to a crime scene to ensure a nightmare ending.

He dialled Lance's phone, but a different voice answered.

'Hey,' the Californian twang came. 'I'm at Lance's. He's getting beers. Sounds like you guys have one less lunatic to apprehend. Good work!'

'Ben, you have to come up with something. Lance's story was a mistake. I'll explain later, but you have to keep going with the website. Read every thread you can. I'm right back at the start and reduced to waiting for body parts to be delivered.'

'Already on it,' Ben said, sounding remarkably unfazed. Callanach heard the clink of bottles next to the phone. 'As soon as Lance posted his article about the arrest, a new poll went live on the website. I got an email saying I had two hours to vote. Let me read it to you. Lance, hold the phone,' Ben said.

'You not out celebrating, Luc?' Lance asked.

'We got the wrong man, Lance, and you posted the story before we realised it.'

There was a pause long enough that Callanach could have filled a kettle and boiled water.

'I'm finished,' Lance said. There was a fumbling as Ben grabbed the phone back and began to read.

'Okay, it says that voting rules for all polls are as follows. Each user is entitled to make only one submission. Once submissions close, the poll will become inaccessible. Your submission must be for a worthy victim, by employment or status description, whose death society will rightly be entitled to mourn. Do not enter names. The identity of the victim is for the competitor to choose. All entries must be in English. The suggestion with the highest number of like submissions will be selected and notified to the competitor.'

'Is that everything?' Callanach asked.

'There's a box to type in,' Ben said. 'You know we're going to have to make an entry. I've logged in, there'll be a record. Having applied for membership, if we don't make a submission it'll be an immediate red flag that something's not right about Rory Hand.'

'Put in something ridiculous that they're not going to go for,' Callanach said.

'Any preferences?' Ben asked.

'Just make it a profession obviously repulsive to normal human beings.' He could hear Ben typing. 'How long until the vote closes?' Callanach asked.

'Seventy minutes,' Ben said.

'Keep watching,' Callanach said. 'And see if you can trace anything else to do with Grom. He's still out there somewhere and he's holding someone hostage. Right now I have no idea who or where they might be.'

'Got it. There's another call coming in. I'll get back to you.' Ben hit end on Callanach's call and opened the new line. 'Hello?'

'Ben, it's Polly. I know you're busy but Big Dave gave me your number and asked me to call. He said to stay out of the cafe tomorrow. Lots of police on the streets, the city's gone a bit crazy. He said to say sorry.'

'Not a problem, Pol. Thanks for letting me know. And I don't mind you having my number,' Ben said. 'Would be nicer if you'd used it because you wanted to speak to me, but I'll settle for second best.'

'Really?' she laughed. 'And you're not even going to ask me out now that you've finally got me on the phone?'

Ben tapped at a speed Lance couldn't even focus on properly, only pausing when he realised that Polly wasn't following up with a joke or a jibe. 'Okay, well, is there any chance at all that I could tempt you to spend some time with me? No cafe, no customers, no one except us, some beer and some food?'

'All right then. I'm free this evening,' Polly said. Ben flushed under Lance's stare.

'This evening? Um, great, yep. I'm just finishing something up then you could come over to mine. I'll text you the address.'

'Sure. Your place it is. And don't get any big ideas. You know it's just because you wore me down, right?' she laughed.

'Never thought it could have been for any other reason. See you in an hour.' Ben hung up, allowed himself a grin, then began typing again. 'Gotta speed this up, Lance. I have somewhere to be.'

Chapter Forty-Two

The news had been full of Grom's disastrous failure and capture. Typical of his clumsy nature, and he hadn't even finalised the kill. Sem Culpa had won, subject only to completing her last task and remaining free. Not that her destiny lay behind bars. She was a free spirit. Free within the world at large, free from normal societal constraints, free from the conscience and fears that kept lesser creatures bowed in compliance with laws and regulations. Her wings were not for clipping.

Opening the email, she scanned it with only slight surprise. This target was more interesting. She fed the internet the appropriate search term and began to read. Edinburgh was home to remarkably few such targets. How Grom had managed to screw up his task with so many options was laughable. Still, the reduced field dictated that her research could be done fast and her next victim identified quickly. Sem Culpa was bored of Scotland, longing for an endless stretch of sandy beach and plates of food where protein was served with more delicacy.

In fact it took her no more than an hour to find the perfect target, having obtained enough information to know where they worked, lived and preferred to dine. The only task left was to conceive of a fitting death – one that would leave people gasping at her ingenuity and cruelty – even as she boarded a plane for some less populated place. Articles read, websites perused, addresses memorised, she turned her attention to choosing her next destination. Somewhere in South America would be nice, she thought, selecting a passport for the booking and matching it with a credit card. It was almost time to become someone else again and rest enjoying the memories of her victory.

Grom stared at the screen in disbelief. He had read and reread the news article, certain that it was simply his English letting him down. He hadn't been caught. The lollipop lady had not been rescued. What would the moderator think? And that arrogant witch Sem Culpa would believe she'd won. He tried to log onto the darknet site to let the moderator know it was a mistake. His password failed once, twice. He retyped it, reloaded the site, checked his network connections. He'd been locked out, of course. As far as the moderator was concerned he was in custody.

He went to look out of the windows of the house. It had been a risk, staying at the old woman's place, but he'd watched the address for two days before making his move. Not a single person had come up the drive. No milk or post were delivered, no family or friends had come to visit. She'd once taken a bus, arriving home two hours later with a bag of food shopping, but she would hardly be missed by the supermarket staff. Her bungalow was out of the city, on the outskirts of a village, with little in the way of passing traffic. Even now the crossroads beyond the overgrown garden were deserted. Moving her had seemed even more treacherous with everyone in the city looking for him. He'd needed the time to plan, to think, to perfect the kill. Now he was starting to wish he'd simply driven up the motorway throwing her severed limbs out of the window into the paths of other cars.

Back in the kitchen, the lollipop lady was cramming baked beans into her mouth. She'd given up speaking to him and he was grateful for that. He was still having to keep her alive though, stupidly assuming he could draw this out to his own timetable. Not now. This required immediate action to prove he was still very much in the game.

'Put down plate,' Grom said, picking up his favourite knife.

The lollipop lady ignored him, shovelling tiny orange ovoids into her mouth, strings of sauce seeping from the corners of her lips and diverting into the wrinkles running down her chin. He brought a fist down into the plate and it skittered across the floor, leaving a mess in its wake that he would have to clean up later. No matter. There would soon be more to clean up than just that.

Looking up into his face, she spat her as yet unswallowed mouthful so that it spattered his eyes and forehead. She stared, laughed hard, her hands flying into the air with the delight of it, and that was when he caught the first whiff of urine. She hadn't even bothered telling him she needed to go. He should have known. It had been at least an hour since the last bathroom break. Her waning pelvic floor muscles were no match for the ageing process. He grabbed her by the hair, pulling her up from her seat, his face a knot of disgust. She dangled before him, a wet, withered puppet, wiping herself with the material of her skirt, still cackling occasionally in spite of the pain he was inflicting on her scalp.

'Hold out your arms,' he ordered, releasing his hold and letting her drop.

'Make me,' she said.

Grom did.

Chapter Forty-Three

Ava had to speak to Joe. It had all become so overwhelming. The endless consultations with medics, the hours spent in waiting rooms, the way that time seemed to liquify, each drop bloating slowly until the weight became too much and it fell. Like the drip that was feeding chemicals into her mother's arm, an unwinnable attempt at saving her. A life-shortening cocktail of embarrassment and pride had kept her mother from seeking medical help at an earlier stage and now the cancer destroying her bowel had marched its poisonous army to other places from which they would never be made to retreat. Buying time was the best they could do.

Regret was a massively understated word in Ava's humble opinion, and yet she could find no better synonym. She did not feel remorse for the years she and her mother had not been close. It wasn't in Ava's nature to rewrite history. Her mother had set her own agenda and it hadn't included Ava for most of her formative years. Little wonder that her daughter had embraced independence early and rejected later efforts at maternal closeness. Lamentation was too strong. She was not reduced to weeping nor dramatic scenes anticipating the loss to come. It was simple, clean regret. Mainly that she had not been a better daughter. Also that she hadn't been able to forgive her mother's failings. Largely that she had not applied the same detective skills to her family life as she did to the cases she worked every day. Consequently, Ava had failed to join the dots between her mother's own childhood and her resultant inability to forge the sort of close bond between them that Ava had craved.

A career in the police had been the result. Ava's choice had been part rebellion, and part desire to get her hands dirty after the sterile English public school that had polished her accent, her dress sense and her fingernails. Her parents had wanted her to follow a pathway into something beautifully bland and suitably upper class. A fashion designer, high-end of course, would have been acceptable. Or a corporate lawyer, if she really felt she couldn't hide her outspoken, confrontational traits. Her father had encouraged her towards the diplomatic service which her mother had seen as the perfect way to find a husband one would be proud to announce in the national newspapers.

Ava had viewed their suggestions with disdain, making it her mission to pursue the opposite of what they had planned for her. Police work offered her endless hours in rough company, seeking out the bloodshed and human misery from which she had always been shielded. Her parents had tried for months to dissuade her, reasoning at first, refusing to allow it when reason failed. Desperate, her mother had threatened to cut her off from the money that could have bought Ava top-of-the-range cars and luxury apartments. Ava had walked out, content to make ends meet on her own. She had never stopped talking to her family. She wasn't spiteful or vengeful. But there was an unspoken rule that the world's filth should not be referred to in her mother's presence. Ava was to leave her casework outside their door. In her attempt to align her life with the reality of other people's, she had created a false relationship with her parents. Now her mother was dying. All those wasted years playing a game that had served neither of them.

Ava was making it better now though. Her mother was softening. Over the last few weeks she had been able to hold her mother, slide a hand over hers as she sat shivering but stoic in the chemotherapy suite, and feel a real connection. How dreadful that it had taken the knowledge of the loss to come to jolt her from her arrogance. But it wasn't too late. Not quite yet. She could stop playing games and start being honest. With her mother, with herself, and specifically with Joe.

She was starting a new life with a man she was already deceiving. Joe would understand when she explained just how much good Ben Paulson was doing, and without a request for a return favour. She just had to get her fiancé at a good moment, free of the stress of an investigation with so much top-down pressure he was inevitably feeling crushed by it.

Joe had been the same way at university. Always needing to be a leader. Had to be captain of the rugby team. Fought to head up the debating society. Ever keen to go shopping with Ava to ensure she had the most beautiful dress for whatever ball they were attending. The amount of detail he'd put into everything had been overwhelming and part of the reason she'd closed their relationship down. But her mother had liked Joe, and Ava's decision to break up with him had been another thorn in the already sore flesh of the mother/daughter relationship. Joe had always been ambitious, both socially and professionally. And now, having promised to marry him, Ava was putting his whole investigation in jeopardy by keeping secrets.

She drove to Joe's short-term apartment rental to see him driving away towards the city centre. She contemplated having the conversation by telephone and knew that it would play out worse if she couldn't look him in the eyes and explain what had happened. As much work as she had to do, the conversation just wouldn't wait. Ava kept his car in her sights and followed as he headed out towards Murrayfield, taking Roseburn Street and starting to slow down. Ava reduced her speed, the sense that she shouldn't be following gnawing her insides, but not so much that she turned around. To the best of her knowledge, Joe knew no one in this part of the city. He'd not mentioned this trip when they'd discussed their working day over breakfast, not that she always knew where he was going, but it seemed strange. Joe pulled into a parking space. Ava searched for her own. There were none immediately visible so she drove past Joe's car to find somewhere to park further up the road.

She noticed the figure running as she passed the rear of his vehicle, dashing from another car to dive into Joe's passenger seat. The person had moved as fast as they could, collar up, sunglasses on, slamming the door shut. Ava kept driving, wishing she could unsee what she'd seen, furious with herself. She didn't park her car, making her way towards the stadium instead then turning left at the junction with West Approach Road back into the city.

Putting on the radio, she sought external noise to drown out the din of her thoughts. She had recognised Joe's visitor in spite of the brevity of the sighting. Ava thumped her steering wheel and cursed.

Chapter Forty-Four

Ben spent an hour reassuring Lance that his journalistic mistake was not worth a long drop from a tall tower, as he simultaneously flung code into the black space of the internet. His attention was elsewhere though and the reason for that was due to arrive at his apartment in thirty minutes. On his laptop from Lance's flat, he remotely checked his home cameras, wishing he'd spent less time programming and more time decorating, wincing at the dirty dishes in his sink and the clothes on the sofa. He was so used to shutting people out of his private space that he wasn't really prepared for a visitor.

Fifteen minutes later he had done all he could, said goodbye to Lance, and made his way home. The apartment wasn't luxurious – he disliked shows of money and tried to lead a simple life, but it was warm, clean and comfortable. He turned off the overhead lights in favour of a few lamps, decided the effect was too suggestive and put all the overhead lights back on, then realised he hadn't chilled the wine and didn't have any ice. The doorbell rang. Even expecting someone, he checked his security cameras before answering. Such ingrained habits even dominated his dreams.

Polly gave up with the doorbell and began knocking. Ben wiped sweat from his forehead and opened the door.

'Finally!' Polly said, walking past him into the lounge. 'I brought beer, organic of course, and my sparkling company. Shall I . . . open them?'

'Yeah, wow, sorry,' Ben said, rushing to take the bottles from her. 'You want one now?' he asked.

'That would be the general idea,' Polly laughed. 'It's funny. All those times in the coffee shop and you've never seemed like anything could faze you.'

'I just haven't done this for a while. Not that we're doing anything. Shit. Listen, let me open these beers and drink at least half the contents, then I'll try speaking again, okay?'

Polly followed him to the compact kitchen, leaning against the door frame as he grabbed a bottle opener.

'What happened with the police?' Polly asked.

'Nothing, predictably. All they did was piss off my boss and make our clients twitchy.' Ben handed Polly a bottle and knocked his against hers. 'Cheers.'

'Cheers? That's a bit British for you.' Polly walked back into the lounge.

'I'm not the only one who's moved country. How did you end up in Scotland?'

'It's a bit boring really,' Polly said, throwing herself into an armchair. 'My parents got divorced, had to sell the house, buy two small flats. Not enough space for me. It was time to move on anyway. I was seduced by the lochs and highlands. All the stuff I never leave Edinburgh to see. So are we going to compare past lives all evening or are you going to offer me some food?'

'I'll have to call out, if that's okay? To be honest my culinary skills are pretty much limited to breakfast,' Ben said.

Polly laughed. 'I'll remember that,' she said, 'but for now

Chinese would be great, if you know a good one. Could you point me towards your loo while you phone?'

'Sure, second on the left. The lock's a bit dodgy.'

Polly giggled and left Ben riffling through a drawer full of take-out menus. His mobile pinged as he was trying to remember if Polly was a vegetarian or a vegan and wondering what he was going to order if she was the latter.

He grabbed his mobile, conscious that he shouldn't check the alert, wanting only to enjoy a normal evening with a girl. It was his finger that betrayed him, swiping at the flashing icon. Ben looked at the notification. There was information available that might help Callanach. It wouldn't take long, just a few minutes to check and he could continue his evening as if nothing had happened. Polly was still in his bathroom, hopefully not spending her time figuring out how to let him down gently. In spite of his looks, he'd never been lucky with girls. The geek label was the first and last thing most of them saw, and he wasn't great about socialising. He'd had a more successful long-term relationship with his laptop than anything else in his life. He certainly didn't want to blow this opportunity. As Polly came out of the bathroom, Ben made the decision not to blow his chance with her by staying attached to the screen, closed the notification and dialled for take-out, choosing a selection of vegetable and noodle dishes.

'That sounds good,' Polly said sitting down before picking up her beer and Ben's iPod, flicking through his music collection with the odd grin and raised eyebrow.

He tried to settle, scrabbling around for things to talk about, before sighing and shifting forward in his seat to look Polly directly in the eyes. 'Pol, I'm sorry. I need to do something and it won't wait. The food will be here in twenty minutes. I'll be back with you in five. Please don't leave. You have to promise.'

'All right, don't freak out, of course I'm not going to leave.

Can I help? I mean . . . I'm interested. In you, your life, what you do.' Polly smiled, her various piercings sparkling, giving her the appearance of an urban fairy-tale princess.

Ben knew he shouldn't let anyone in his study. The things he did there, the information he had, were for no one's eyes but his own. But Polly had proved her loyalty at the cafe. And Big Dave, a long-time friend of The Unsung, was no fool. He had taken her on, made her part of their circle. And the tiny corner of the universe Ben inhabited was starting to feel bleak, like travelling through life in a one-man spacecraft, always talking to mission control without ever making physical contact. It was time to let someone in.

'Would you wait while I run my opening sequence?' Ben asked. 'I need to be alone for that.'

'Right you are!' Polly gave a mock salute. She offered Ben her hand to pull her up. He gripped it, thinking he should take the opportunity to kiss her, missing his moment while he considered how she might react. 'Lead the way. I'll stand guard until you give me the word.'

Ben walked into the hallway, taking a key from around his neck and opening his study door. Polly stood back, giving him space, keeping her eyes on a black and white photo of the Big Sur coastline.

'Is this California?' she asked as he withdrew the key and punched a six figure number into a keypad.

'Yeah, not far from Carmel. I never got bored of taking that drive. Give me a couple of minutes.' He relaxed for the first time since she'd arrived.

'Get on with it then, or the food'll be here before you're done, and if there's one thing I hate it's my dinner going cold.'

Ben closed the door behind himself. His computer wouldn't fire up unless the door was properly shut. It was another of his obsessive security moves. He ran through his login routine and only then allowed Polly to enter. There was only one chair in the room – he'd never needed a second. Polly perched on the arm.

'It doesn't look much,' Polly said. 'I thought it'd be like the Starship Enterprise in here.'

'All the magic happens in there,' Ben pointed to a line of computers on the floor.

'And I thought it all happened in here,' Polly said, tapping Ben's forehead with her finger. He flushed, suddenly aware how small and windowless the room was, switching on the air-conditioning unit while he recovered from his ridiculously teenaged reaction to her touch.

Ben clicked open a file, expecting nothing more than a data dump, wanting only to exclude the possibility that there was something useful there. He typed a few lines of code, searching through the scroll of symbols, frowning at the screen, the sense that he was wasting second after second as he tried to comprehend what he was seeing.

'Out,' he said, wanting to move Polly out of his way without letting her see how panicked he was. 'I need to get out, right now.'

Polly jumped through the door ahead of him and he dashed down the corridor without even stopping to turn off the computer. What he needed to do wouldn't wait for anything. Ben grabbed his mobile and ran to the bathroom, slamming the door, landing on his knees.

'Callanach,' the voice said on the other end.

'It's me,' Ben said. 'It's all gone wrong. I didn't think they'd do it, but they have and I got the data back. I got an alert and—'

'Ben, slow down. I can't understand what's going on. Take a breath,' Callanach said.

Ben took several, clenching his core muscles against their threat to eject the beer upwards.

'I've unscrambled communications from the webmaster to other users. There are repeated references to two people and I only have usernames, but given the context it's clear that they're the murderers. One is called Grom and the other is Sem Culpa. I haven't got any more details about them, but I do know the target for the next kill. I'm sorry, Luc. I wish I could take it back.'

'You're not making sense. Do you need me to come over?' Callanach asked.

'No time,' Ben said. 'You have to stop her, whoever Sem Culpa is. You have to find the target. I didn't think they'd choose it.'

'Ben, just give me the information. I need to get working.'

'It's the one I submitted, Luc. You told me to choose a profession most people disliked, only they took it and changed it.'

'*Baise-moi*,' Callanach muttered. Fuck me. 'Ben, what did you write?'

'I'm sorry, I never thought . . . lawyer. I wrote lawyer. And Sem Culpa is going to choose one to kill if you don't find her first. You have to stop her, Luc. I can't be responsible for what that crazy bitch does.'

'You said they changed it. What did they do?'

'They chose the only type of lawyer that most people would regard as sympathetic. It'll be a human rights lawyer. And you don't have much time. The email to Sem Culpa gave her just twenty-four hours to complete the kill.'

Chapter Forty-Five

The news desk editor, known mainly to those around her as Eddie, was literally running from desk to desk. It had been the same since the murders started. Almost every bulletin and item, broadcast and online, had included some mention of it. Every statement from a family member, every theorist, every potential witness, their words recorded, reported, rehashed. The truth was that Eddie (often mistakenly thought of as a nickname from her job, but in fact from Edwina which she hated) had had enough of it. Not from any lack of empathy, but from sheer repulsion. Privately she longed to join a team debating politics, economics, or philosophical arguments with a real world edge. Her career was impressive, yet she still had days when she felt she hadn't done her job if there wasn't at least one shocking news report. It was draining.

The package arrived looking innocent enough. It was no more than a slightly bulky brown envelope, typewritten address for the attention of Ms E Kitt. She got several pieces of post each day. Sometimes people sent images of their child winning a gymnastics competition. More often, people were after free publicity about a new restaurant/bar/club opening up. About ninety per cent went straight into the bin.

The receptionist called her name and threw the package over to her. Eddie celebrated her one-handed catch given that she was holding a steaming cup of hot chocolate in the other. She allowed herself that one sugary vice each day, never until after 8 p.m. when the worst of the crises were usually over.

Eddie sat listening to the banter, preparing for the late broadcast, wishing she hadn't been so stupid as to wear new shoes, or to have tried online dating. Life was much easier when you trod familiar ground. So much less scope for blisters or unwanted attention.

'What are we leading with?' someone shouted, one hand over a phone receiver.

'Julia Stimple's arrest and the police failure to apprehend the real murderer,' Eddie replied. 'And we'll be ignoring the thousands dead in Africa, hundreds illegally imprisoned in Asia, and the grotesqueries of human trafficking in South America, like we always do,' she muttered, ripping open the envelope one-handed by holding it between her legs as she sipped her drink. The package was too tight to get her fingers in and pull out whatever was wedged at the bottom, but she plucked out the note easily enough.

'A gift to put some flesh on the bones of your reporting. Your lollipop lady is not talking any more. Grom.'

'What the hell is this now?' Eddie said, tipping up the envelope to inspect the contents. They fell onto her lap. Onto her cream trousers to be precise. She'd just had them dry-cleaned, that was her first thought. Strewn across Eddie's thighs sat two matching circles of shrivelled flesh, the edges blackened with dried blood, each about an inch in diameter with a marked dimple in the centre. She poked one with her fingernail, realising too late that she should have called someone over the second she'd read the note. Eddie's body had jerked before she could stop the cup from flying into the air and crashing down in her lap, over the amputated flesh, burning her and making her earlier concerns for her trousers entirely irrelevant. 'Oh shite, no!' she screamed. 'Get them off me, get the bloody things off me!'

By then the team had rallied, grabbing the cup, dabbing her burning legs, none of them seeing what she'd seen, treading on the chunks of flesh that the police would need for evidence.

'Pick them up,' she shouted. 'They're on the floor, you're treading on them. Oh Jesus, my legs.' She stripped off her trousers, not caring who saw her supermarket underwear and unshaved legs.

'Call the police. Get either DI Callanach or Turner here right now. Tell them one of the murderers has sent in some slices of their current victim. Step back, all of you. Look around on the floor.'

They did as they were told, journalistic instincts kicking in. They were part of the story now, and it had just got bigger.

'What are we looking for, Eddie?' the receptionist asked as he dialled the Major Investigation Team number.

'That,' Eddie said, pointing to a squashed grey-pink lump on the floor, a heel mark visible on its surface. 'Only there were two of them. And I'm pretty sure that's the skin off someone's elbows.'

Callanach rang Ava not really expecting her to pick up. When she spoke, it wasn't in the whispered tones he'd anticipated calling so late at night. Clearly Joe wasn't in the room.

'There's been a delivery at BBC Scotland from someone called Grom. Another body part, or parts to be precise,' he said.

'Oh god,' Ava groaned. 'What this time?'

'Forensics have confirmed a large section of skin has been

removed from two elbows, both from the same person. As long as the bleeding was stemmed, the wounds would have been painful but not life-threatening. The greater risk is from infection setting in, although given the position this hostage is in, I'm guessing that's not their main concern at the moment. On top of that, we have the next target. Where are you? I can pick you up.'

'No need,' Ava said. 'My car's right outside. I'll meet you back at the station. Are you planning a press release?'

'No,' Callanach said. 'I think that would be the worst thing we could do. I've called the superintendent in. Can you be there in fifteen?'

'I can,' Ava said. 'Before you go, Luc, how did you get the information?'

'Are you with Joe?' Callanach checked.

'He's at work. I get the impression his squad are about to make their final sweep. They seem to be getting some good intelligence.'

'Ben Paulson,' Callanach said.

'You know I can't tell you who the target is,' Ava said.

'I wasn't asking you, I was giving my source. Ben has hacked part of the website. He got into their communications portal. That's where this information's from. It's reliable and recent. I'll see you at the station.' He hung up.

There was little Callanach could do for Ben if DCI Edgar's squad were ready to make an arrest. If he was convicted and sentenced, the assistance Ben had given in the murder cases could be taken into account – not that it would make a dent, given the political clout of the people The Unsung had hacked and humiliated. And if Callanach warned Ben now, the leak would inevitably lead back to Ava. He couldn't do that to her.

He parked his car and strode into the station. His squad was beginning to assemble, but he needed to brief Overbeck and

Ava first. What he wasn't sure about was precisely when the twenty-four hour period had started, nor how far the geographical net might be thrown. There were still two killers out there. Grom was holding a victim who would be in shock, possibly already dead. The other, Sem Culpa, had a stomach for atrocities the like of which he'd never seen before. If she took another victim, her only aim would be to excel at her craft in previously unimaginable ways. Salter met him at the incident room door holding out a sheet of paper.

'Here you go, sir. Names of all lawyers in the city known to be practising in human rights or civil liberties. About twenty names in all, so the field isn't too wide,' Salter said.

'It's still too many to protect,' Callanach replied. 'I'll be in with the superintendent and DI Turner. Have everyone ready for briefing and make sure there are vehicles available. I want boots on the street.' He made his way to Overbeck's office knowing he wasn't going to be popular. It was a sensation he was getting used to.

'Send Callanach and Turner in,' Overbeck boomed through her assistant's telephone speaker. The superintendent didn't wait for them to sit down. 'So you've got one hostage, location unknown, who has been tortured causing multiple injuries, and also a new target the identity of which you cannot precisely confirm. How accurate is your source on the human rights lawyer?'

'Very,' Callanach replied. There was a long pause.

'If your intention is to make me beg for the details, Callanach, you're in the wrong office. I need to know substantially more before we go off on another wild-goose chase. I'm still getting pelted with crap from the Julia Stimple debacle.'

'I can't give you the name of my source, ma'am. It's intelligence. I don't have any doubts about its veracity,' Callanach said.

'You're not a fucking journalist, Detective Inspector. We don't have undisclosable sources here. We have evidence and disclosure and rules, so you'll tell me or you can whistle for your frigging resources today.'

'Then the lawyer will die, and we'll have done nothing to stop it,' Callanach said.

'It was an anonymous tip-off,' Ava said. 'By phone. I picked it up.'

Overbeck stared at her, eyes wide, chewing her bottom lip. 'That's where we're at, is it? You're going to bullshit me in the middle of the worst case this city has seen in living memory,' she said. Callanach and Turner stood silent. 'You realise this is tantamount to blackmail, do you? If I don't give you the go-ahead for your operation and someone dies, it's on my head. And if this turns out to be a cartload of bollocks and we waste all our time and resources, it's also on my head. So I'm only going to say this once. Get out of my goddamn office and don't let anyone else get fucking murdered!'

They didn't speak until they got into Callanach's office.

'Paulson's information is really good, right? Only I just lied to a superior officer and we're playing Russian roulette with our careers,' Ava said.

'It's data. It doesn't lie,' Callanach replied, hoping like hell he was right.

'Is Paulson really so good that he can hack his way into an encrypted darknet site?' Ava asked.

'Your fiancé seems to think so,' Callanach said. 'You run the briefing. We have to catch Sem Culpa this time. Overbeck's right. We can't let anyone else die.'

Chapter Forty-Six

The incident room was bursting. Uniforms had been called in to swell the ranks. Anyone making the mistake of thinking they might be on leave the next day had been rudely disabused of the notion. Ava took her place at the front.

'We have intelligence that the next target is a human rights lawyer. Could be male or female, any age. The only thing we're sure of is that they live or work in Edinburgh. There's a list circulating now and you've been assigned partners. Understand this. You are on a watch-only brief. We're not speaking to any of the people on this list. Your job is to make sure your assigned lawyer gets through their day alive.' The muttering started. Ava pre-empted questions with an explanation. 'The attempt will be carried out by a woman with the internet username Sem Culpa.'

'Is the username relevant at all, ma'am?' Tripp asked.

'All we know is that the words Sem Culpa translate as blameless from Portuguese which might be an indicator of her nationality or relate to something else in her past. We believe she was responsible for killing both Sim Thorburn at the rock festival and Michael Swan at the McDonald Road library. Images of her have already been circulated, although there is little by way of facial definition. We estimate her to be between twenty-six and thirty-two years of age, slim, five foot six. She is dangerous in a way that makes her unpredictable. If cornered, there's a risk that she might take hostages, kill bystanders and use whatever weapon comes to hand. Do not underestimate her. She is a psychopath who has everything to lose by getting caught.'

'All the other victims seem to have been chosen because they received media attention for their work. Can we not identify the most likely victim in this case in the same way?' a uniformed officer asked.

'We have a team allocated to that already. If we can cut down to a shortlist of likely targets you'll all be notified,' Ava said.

'Why not tell the potential victims, ma'am? Seems crazy not to give them a heads-up,' someone called out. Ava didn't catch who had spoken and it didn't matter. The whole team had obviously been thinking the same thing.

'We notified potential victims last time and that didn't work out. In fact it may have worked in the killer's favour. If we put potential victims on notice, they'll change their normal patterns. They won't go to work. They'll use alternate means of transport. Right now, our best chance of finding Sem Culpa is by catching her in the act of stalking or attempting an abduction.'

'And what if she uses a sniper rifle or runs the victim down in a car? We can't protect the targets from that and we still won't have an arrest,' Sergeant Lively said.

'I understand your concerns and this isn't foolproof, but we have reason to believe Sem Culpa's desired kill method will be elaborate, something that takes time. If Sem Culpa gets away this time, we may not have another chance. If all the targets start acting unusually, she'll know we're onto her. The target will change. We'll be back to square one. I want you out on the streets within thirty minutes and there won't be anyone to relieve you for the next eighteen hours as we're stretched to capacity. Eat and drink now. All plain clothes activity. Keep in contact. Armed units are on high alert. And let's not forget that there's another victim out there right now who has suffered a further amputation of skin. Forensics are currently running tests to see if we can pick up anything from the pieces of flesh sent through to BBC Scotland. You'll be updated on that as soon as we have more, but be vigilant. There are two lives to save and right now we're not closing in on either of them. Off you go.'

Salter sidled up to Ava. 'I'm not on the list, ma'am,' she said.

'That's right, you're not. Someone has to be here to co-ordinate,' Ava said.

'I'm pregnant, not useless. You need every pair of feet you can get out there. Communications can be handled by civilians.'

'DC Salter, at risk of you accusing me of sexism, I don't want you putting that baby in harm's way. Some things in life are too precious to be exposed to unnecessary danger. Even if it's a thousand to one chance, I'm not taking it.'

Salter's hand went to her stomach. She was hiding it well, but soon there would be no disguising the bump beneath her baggy shirt.

'Is it a boy or a girl?' Ava asked.

'A girl,' Salter whispered. 'We don't want to announce it. Nice to keep a bit of a surprise.'

'Good for you,' Ava said.

'Will you and DCI Edgar be starting a family? I think you'd be a great mother.'

'I hadn't really thought that far ahead,' Ava said. 'I'd better get moving. Make sure everyone is on their way out then get some rest. It's going to be a long one.'

Ava caught up with Callanach as he was leaving the station. It was dawn. The city's lights were switching on and traffic was still light. Edinburgh was contemplating its day. Tourists would meander up and down the Royal Mile. Joggers would punish themselves on the city's hills. Parents would take their children to the open spaces to picnic and play ball. And Police Scotland would be watching nearly two dozen innocent people, one of whom was practically ticking with the imminence of their destiny.

'Did you speak to the news editor about holding back the story of the body parts delivery?' Callanach asked.

'I called the director to make sure they weren't going to run it. To his credit, he sounded appalled at the suggestion. Has Ben not come up with anything on that one?'

'Not yet,' Callanach said. 'And I think we should agree not to talk about him. You're in a difficult enough position as it is.'

'I didn't like him,' Ava said. 'But that doesn't mean I'm not grateful for what he's doing.'

'He doesn't like you either, but that didn't stop him helping. Maybe neither of you should be judging.'

'Spare me it,' Ava said. 'You've broken every rule in the book, including a few that no one had thought of before.'

'I certainly have this time. We'd better catch this bitch. I'm not sure I can carry on if this doesn't work,' Callanach said.

'What are you talking about?' Ava asked.

Callanach stopped mid-step, pinching the bridge of his nose between finger and thumb.

'There was a vote for the next target. Under our username, I told Ben to input a profession no one would feel any sympathy towards.'

'Oh God,' Ava said.

'And here we are, waiting to see just how clever Sem Culpa really is.'

'It's not your fault,' Ava said. 'You didn't know what other suggestions were being made. And we've had no joy making a shortlist of likely targets from internet searches. The problem with lawyers is their case reports, there's loads on the internet about all of them. We have hits for almost every human rights lawyer in the city. There's no single person who stands out. Even if your vote did have some sort of impact, there's no way you can be responsible for the ultimate choice of victim.'

'Thanks, but I'm not sure you and my conscience are going to agree about that,' Callanach said opening his car door. 'Stay safe today.'

She waited as he climbed in, motioning for him to lower his window.

'Luc, why don't you like Joe?' Ava asked as he started the engine.

'I think the more relevant question is, what do you like about him so much?' He pulled away gently. The hunt had begun.

Chapter Forty-Seven

The clock showed 4 a.m. and Alexina O'Rourke had been awake for more than an hour with the sort of headache that started slowly and settled in behind her eyes for the long haul. She'd done her best not to wake her husband but there was no avoiding getting up to fetch water and the strongest pain-killers she could find in the house.

'You okay, darling?' he asked as she slid from between the sheets, grabbing her dressing gown and stepping softly towards the bedroom door.

'Just a headache. Sorry I disturbed you. Go back to sleep,' she said.

He managed to catch her fingers as she passed him, pulling them lightly back towards the bed.

'Oh no you don't,' he said. 'Get back in. I'll go. And don't argue. How long has it been coming on?'

'About an hour,' she said, lying gratefully back down.

He kissed her forehead, brushing her hair away from her face and pulling the duvet up to her chin. 'Give me a minute.'

'Wes?' she muttered as he pulled on a T-shirt. He leaned over her. 'Thank you.'

★　★　★

Two hours later Alexina awoke from a brief sleep to a throbbing that ran from her right eye around her skull, ending in a screeching that matched the pulse in her temples. She ran to the en suite, dry-heaved over the toilet, plodded back to bed with her water and gave in to the migraine that she knew was going to be her companion for the next twelve or so hours. She groaned. It couldn't have come at the weekend when she had time to feel sorry for herself and stay in bed. No, it had to be on a weekday when she had a new brief waiting on her desk and a client conference in the diary. Wesley was absent from their bed. He was always the same. Once awake, he never could get back to sleep.

Alexina slipped out of bed, padding downstairs quietly, needing an ice pack and more water. Wesley was on his computer. Always working when sleep eluded him. She could hear him in his study tapping away on the keyboard. She looked around at the white walls. Next weekend, she promised herself, they would both put their laptops and mobiles in a cupboard and leave them untouched until Monday morning. Somewhere there would be an antiques market or an auction, anything to get them out together, focusing entirely on one another again just like when they'd first met. A pair of warm arms slid around her waist and Wesley's head rested gently on her shoulder.

'You should have called me,' he said. 'I'd have brought the ice up to you.'

'Didn't want to disturb you,' she said, closing her eyes and leaning against the strong bulk of his chest. 'I'm going to phone in sick.'

'I should think so too,' Wesley replied, reaching out to pick up the kettle. 'They'll have to manage without you for one day. Can I bring you a cup of Earl Grey?'

'I'm fine with water,' she said. 'Listen, this weekend, let's go out and buy something great for the house. A painting for your study or a coffee table for the lounge. Something we both love. It'll be fun.'

'Way ahead of you,' Wesley smiled. 'How about we do that then find a hotel, have dinner in a country pub, lock the rest of the world out for a while.'

Alexina knotted her hands together behind her husband's back, breathing out into his chest. 'God, yes, let's do all of that.' She winced and shut her eyes.

'Right, back to bed with you. I want you in a fit state to be spoiled rotten on Saturday morning. I'll lock up as I go. You try to get some more sleep.' He kissed the top of her head, put the bag of ice in her hand and sent her towards the stairs.

He was already dressed and ready for work. Better to get in early, establish a firm head start on the day's tasks and get home early. Making a quick chicken mayonnaise sandwich, he left it on a plate in the fridge covered with cling film and folded a tiny note on top. 'Lexy, Try to eat. The migraine will get worse if you starve it. And NO work today! Love you more, W xxx'

Chapter Forty-Eight

Ben rolled over, studying the woman next to him. Polly was asleep, her hair falling across her face, particles of dust dancing around her in the sunlight. Last night had been awful and joyful in equal measures. He'd expected her to leave after his outburst, having declined to explain his telephone conversation with Callanach as much from shame as from the knowledge that no one else could know what they'd done. Still Polly had stayed, making coffee and insisting that he ate some of the food he'd forgotten in the aftermath of his discovery. He'd relaxed a little with the help of several bottles of beer and Polly's tales of travelling and narrowly missed disasters. But eventually he'd lost the will to make small talk and she'd asked if he was all right. When he hadn't answered she'd slid a cool hand round the back of his neck, kissing him gently, teasing him with her tongue, shifting her body to sit on his lap. The rest, unexpectedly, unbelievably, was history. And Polly had stayed – that was the best thing about it. There had been no rush, no awkwardness. She'd even had to remind him to lock his study door.

Ben slipped quietly out of bed to check if anything in the

fridge might pass as breakfast. His phone showed only one text message from Lance half an hour earlier. He was glad there was nothing from Callanach. As the cliché went, no news had to be good news. Lance had apparently not heard the latest update. Ben called him.

'Hey buddy,' Ben said.

'Ben? You all right? You sound . . .' Lance faltered.

'Yeah. No. It was kind of a weird evening. Have you spoken to Luc?' Ben asked.

'I tried his mobile a couple of times but he keeps switching it off. I was worried that something was wrong, hence the text. Apologies if I woke you.'

'You didn't. Hold on.' Ben closed the kitchen door. 'Luc's going to be busy today. The entry I put into the website . . . I wrote lawyer, Lance. They made it the next target. I had no idea . . .'

'You did what Luc told you to do. If you've spent a sleepless night sweating that one, you wasted your time. Anyway, it was supposed to be the most popular suggestion that became the target. I know why you chose lawyer, but other people doing the same thing? Makes no sense.'

'It doesn't matter now. I got the data back late last night. He only gave the killer twenty-four hours to hit her mark. That's why Callanach's not answering. I guess they've mobilised.'

'It feels wrong, Ben. A lawyer? Really?' Lance said.

'A human rights lawyer to be precise. I guess even the webmaster thought that your average lawyer wouldn't be a sufficiently endearing target to capture the public's imagination,' Ben said.

'I appreciate how much you've already done, but could you come over?' Lance asked.

'Actually I was kind of making plans. Catch a bit of sunshine, try to think about something a bit more, well, just anything but this.'

'I can't do this on my own, Ben, you know that. And after the way I messed things up announcing they'd caught the other killer, I think I owe Callanach. Just one hour. If I haven't come up with anything by then, you're free to go and do whatever you like.'

'Morning, gorgeous,' Polly said, walking into the kitchen wearing a pair of Ben's boxers and not much else.

'Ben, I'm sorry. You have company. What time is it?' Ben could hear the rustle of Lance's sleeve. 'It's only half past six. I'd lost track. Listen, about this morning, I wouldn't ask only . . .'

'I get it. I want to help him, too. I'll be at yours by seven thirty, okay? You'd better be able to cook eggs,' Ben said.

'That I can, son. However you like them.' Lance hung up.

DCI Edgar had his squad primed and ready to go. That evening would be their final move, and this time they would get all the evidence required to put the leader of The Unsung away for long enough that his Californian drawl would have faded beyond recognition on his release. As would his looks and his arrogance. Prison had a miraculous way of reducing everyone to the basest level. No more hiding behind an oversized IQ or that ridiculous Robin Hood-styled excuse for criminality.

His briefing over by 8 a.m., it was time to ensure that nothing went wrong. For that he needed one final meeting, although it couldn't take place at the station. He was well aware that in spite of clearly communicated warnings, DI Callanach had continued to correspond with Ben Paulson. Edgar hadn't expected much better. A long evening spent reading Callanach's file complete with documents relating to the rape allegation had given him all the background he'd needed. Callanach was a risk-taker, a bit of a maverick, more comfortable with the lower ranks than with his superiors. The idiot had a death wish going back a number of years – either that or a hero complex, Joe Edgar didn't really care which. Callanach would be finished at roughly the same time Ben Paulson was getting his first taste of prison food. What had made more interesting reading was Interpol's psychologist's report, compiled as part of an obligatory process once Callanach's trial had collapsed but before he'd transferred to Police Scotland. The former agent might still be sporting his movie star looks, but he hadn't emerged unscathed. Edgar should never have gained access to such personal documentation, of course, but the report had been released to Police Scotland during the assessment process and Ben Paulson wasn't the only person who could get his hands on well-protected information. Life was easier with friends in the upper echelons.

At 10 a.m. Edgar walked into the Augustine United Church in the city's Old Town, admiring its blackened brick facade and lofty arched windows, but he wasn't there to pray any more than he was to study architecture. Every August the church transformed to allow two performance areas for the Fringe Festival as well as a conveniently crowded and anonymous coffee shop. Edgar had no time for the Fringe. He recalled his one trip there in his early twenties when he and Ava had been dating and combined it with a visit to her parents. What had passed as comedy had been pitiable and he'd endured a mind-numbing three-hour play on the theme of feminism. The crowds of strangely attired, easily pleased audience members had been much too comfortable with invading his personal space. Leaving had been the best part of his experience. Ava, to his endless mystification, had loved it.

His contact arrived soon after him.

'You all set for tonight?' DCI Edgar asked.

'All set,' was the simple reply.

'The computer has to be running, all the security has to have been bypassed. If Paulson gets an opportunity to close it down . . .'

'We've been through this.'

'We're going through it again,' Edgar said. 'If he shuts the system down, we'll never get it started again. And if he presses his alarm keys, all the drives will be irreversibly wiped. He has to be away from the computer when we get there. Restrain him if you have to.'

'It's not the first time I've done this. You just get there on time. I understand the technical details.'

'Do you understand that my career stands or falls on tonight's outcome?' Edgar asked, finishing his watery coffee and grimacing. 'We've got several other suspected members of The Unsung being watched. Two more in the UK, three in China, and twelve in the USA. The CIA are watching our every move. If this gets screwed up then every major power in the world will be given my name as designated scapegoat.'

'I know all this. You do remember it was me who got the first solid information on The Unsung? Until then all you had was rumour and suspicion. When you get your man, I expect an equal share of the credit. Have the squad there at 7 p.m. sharp. And keep Callanach out of the way.'

'The Detective Inspector has more than enough to keep him busy for a while. That's why we chose tonight. There's an attack imminent related to the recent murders. Callanach won't have a clue what's happening to Paulson. Silver lining to every situation, I suppose.'

'And I have your word I'll get recognition for what I've done?'

'Of course,' Edgar said, putting sunglasses on before walking out into Edinburgh's too-brief summer sun. Not that he'd have to worry about seeing in the autumn in Scotland. When Ava's mother passed away, which wouldn't be too long judging by how fast she was fading, Joe was certain he could persuade Ava to move to London. He sure as hell wasn't prepared to contemplate living anywhere else.

Chapter Forty-Nine

By 11 a.m. every team had phoned in to report on their potential target, save for two. Five teams had made enquiries and confirmed their target as being away from Edinburgh. Two were in Strasbourg, one was on a prison visit in Spain and a further two were holidaying long-haul. It reduced the field a little, but not enough to provide substantial additional cover, and that was without accounting for the teams they had out visiting each known lollipop lady in person to verify their safety. Every officer in the city was trying to do three jobs at once and there still weren't enough hands on deck.

Callanach's phone rang. 'Sir, PC Singh here. The lawyer Richard Blaines is taking holiday leave but remaining in the city and residing with his girlfriend at her house in Murrayfield. We're on our way there now.'

'Stay posted outside the property until you receive notification that this is over,' Callanach said. 'And follow Mr Blaines if he leaves the house.' Callanach ended the call and dialled the only other outstanding team. 'This is Callanach. What's going on your end?'

'Nothing much, sir,' PC Rivers said. 'Alexina O'Rourke was

expected to leave home this morning and travel into work but her car was still there at 10 a.m. The husband left at half eight, so we called her place of work. Apparently she rang in sick and won't be available today.'

'You haven't seen anyone else enter since the husband left?' Callanach asked.

'No movement at all, sir.'

'And have you had eyes on her at all?'

'We saw her walk past an upstairs window earlier but it was less than a second's view and from a distance. It's a huge house, long driveway. One of those new executive homes. Must be at least six bedrooms. There's an alarm system and a CCTV camera on the outside overlooking the driveway, so I'm guessing she's pretty safe in there,' Rivers said.

'Keep running observations. If there's been no further movement by noon, send someone in to ring the doorbell. Ask for directions or something, but don't scare her. Just make contact.'

Callanach reported in to Overbeck who, for once, seemed to have run out of expletives, then he called Ava.

'Nothing?' she asked.

'Nothing yet,' he confirmed. 'Waiting is always the worst part. Are you with DC Tripp?'

'I am,' Ava said. 'How do you cope with his enthusiasm?'

'I give him endless tasks. He's never complained yet. Don't be fooled though. Somewhere inside that perky, irrepressible exterior, there's a Sergeant Lively just waiting to get out. A couple more decades of police work should grind him down,' Callanach said.

'Maybe I should introduce him to Natasha? She's dry enough to sap anyone's exuberance.'

Callanach laughed. 'Have you told Natasha your news yet?' he asked.

'I'm waiting to see her in person. She'll be back soon. I

think some drinking may be in order. We should fix a date to get together.'

Callanach bit his tongue. If Joe Edgar had anything to do with it, Callanach would be the last person invited for drinks.

'There's another call coming in. Keep me updated,' Callanach said, hitting one icon and swiping another on the screen. 'This is DI Callanach.'

'Luc, it's Lance.'

'Lance, I can't speak now. I need to keep communications open.'

'So I gather. I spent an hour with Ben this morning. He told me what happened. That's why I'm calling. Ben's gone to work but I'm going to meet him again this evening. I can't get hold of him on his usual mobile number. Do you have any other contact details?'

'Not unless you go to his office, which I don't recommend. He's still under surveillance. Is it really that urgent?' Callanach asked.

'The whole lawyer thing feels wrong to me. I mean, more than one person choosing such an unpopular profession? Ben tried to access the data regarding the number of entries and break them down. He couldn't take his laptop to work so he rerouted the emails to me. I've had several alerts come in, none of which make any sense to me at all.'

'Lance, I know you're still feeling bad about releasing the information about Julia Stimple, but you can stop now. We're on top of this, I promise. Ben is often uncontactable at work. Wait until the end of the day. He'll check his messages when he finishes. I'm not sure how figuring out how many people voted for a lawyer as the target will help, but I appreciate the effort,' Callanach said.

'All right. If you're sure,' Lance said. 'Once this is over, I'll take you for a ride on the bike. See if we can't find something in common other than human misery.'

Chapter Fifty

Sem Culpa was ready. She had struck gold finding an abandoned tannery that still had the basic infrastructure she needed. The trick was ensuring that she gave herself enough time. Last night she'd bought a new webcam and some basic lighting, together with a generator. Sadly the previous tannery owners had remembered to turn off the power. She was happy to trade that, though, for the fact that there was a water source and good enough mobile reception to stream the kill online. All she needed was a water vat with a hook and pulley system overhead, and the tannery provided both. Boiling a human to death had been a celebrated art centuries ago. It was a shame, she thought, that the world had forsaken so many of its old ways. Such inventive punishments were art forms. Forget sketches and photographs, leaked autopsy reports. The only sure way to secure her place in history was to broadcast her work in progress. Specifically with access to audio as well as visual – for her audience to hear the victim plead, argue, bribe, hate. And scream. When there were no words left to say, all anyone would hear were the screams. Sem Culpa felt the heat of it, making her face flush, her hands sweat.

Now all she needed was to lure the victim out of her bedroom and into her back garden. Her plan, luckily fluid, was relatively simple. She loaded the gun, picked up a rock, and threw it from her position in the bushes into a pane of the greenhouse.

The anticipated curtain twitch came seconds later, then the window opened and a face peered out. Sem Culpa couldn't see the facial expression, but she imagined a frown, followed by a rolling of eyes. One more thing to take care of in the never-ending to-do list of life.

She waited, gun sight to her eye, body tensed to absorb the kickback, but the back door never opened. It was unacceptable. She couldn't fail now. Not when so many plans had been made. This hadn't been easy. Negotiating her exit point had been the most difficult thing, especially given that she hadn't known until this morning that Alexina O'Rourke wasn't going to work today. Sem Culpa had had a route planned, intent on following Mrs O'Rourke until she could overtake and brake, causing the lawyer to crash into the back of her vehicle. After that, it would simply have been a question of inviting Alexina into the car, or climbing into hers, to exchange insurance details and producing the gun. It was supposed to have been a clean abduction. Now this. In some ways it added to the story. Her brilliance on her feet, whatever the circumstances. How unflappable she was. How superior. And she'd put too much work into it to be screwed over now.

Sem Culpa picked up a stray branch and hurled it at the same pane in the greenhouse, enlarging the hole and making a noise that no one could reasonably ignore. No curtain movement this time. But she waited.

It took only seconds – perhaps Alexina had already come downstairs – but this time the lady of the house came out into the garden. Sem Culpa didn't hesitate. She waited for Alexina to step clear of the back door, breathed out, in and out again, then fired. The shot was perfect. Straight into the thigh as planned, the dart sinking into the fleshiest part of the muscle to deliver its load of paralytic agent. The drugs would work on her vocal cords as well, preventing screaming almost immediately.

Alexina let out a gasp as the tranquilliser dart found its mark – more shock than pain in the first instant – and after that everything was glorious slow motion. Her hand moved gracefully downwards, her fingers finding the dart, wasting precious seconds as her brain decided whether or not to pull it out. By then her eyes had been upward looking, searching for the source of the attack, her head starting to nod, her legs slowly caving in. It was a tragic ballet.

Sem Culpa moved in. The house was huge, the garden designed for the sort of socialising that only up-and-coming, motivated people bothered doing. Had Sem Culpa not intervened, this garden would have been the scene of drinks parties, attempts at recapturing youth by building a firepit, some idiot thinking their guitar skills were worthy of an audience, caterers sheltering discreetly in the kitchen until required. Now the landscaping would forever be the place of a disappearance. Tragedy. Mystery. Devastation.

Alexina's eyes stared up from the ground, confused and questioning. Sem Culpa rolled her onto her side while she prepared to exit. It would be beyond ironic if the woman choked on her own tongue whilst paralysed and en route to her execution. There had been a wheelbarrow in the shed, not that either Alexina with her illustrious career nor her equally suited, briefcase-hugging husband would have dreamt of lifting a finger. That shed would be strictly the gardener's domain. It had been Sem Culpa's only concern – that a groundsman might suddenly appear – but not today. Today the gods were with her.

She took hold of Alexina under the arms, careful not to

damage her. The neuromuscular-blocking drugs would prevent Alexina from moving, but she would still feel pain, and Sem Culpa was saving that for later. Once Alexina was in the wheelbarrow – after some folding and shoving – Sem Culpa covered her with a tarpaulin, threw the gun on top, and wheeled her to the side of the property, returning only to shut the back door. The more time she bought herself the better, should anyone turn up later in the day.

The normal side gate was too risky as it shared a passageway with next door, but at the rear of the property was a wire fence which led into a different garden. From there Sem Culpa could exit through that neighbour's back gate. She had already checked that they'd left for work. The fence was high, designed with security in mind, but wire could be cut, which was how Sem Culpa had got in earlier. She pulled the wire aside, pushed the wheelbarrow through, and carefully pulled some covering branches back in place. She'd even piled up some foliage to layer over the top of the tarpaulin, disguising the body shape. Sem Culpa pulled her cap down firmly over her ears. Her rented four-by-four was parked two gardens away. As she went, she heard a distant doorbell ring, twice, three times, but by then she was opening the boot of the car and shifting the contents of the wheelbarrow inside, looking to the world like nothing more than a casual worker disposing of garden cuttings.

Chapter Fifty-One

Callanach knew something was wrong from the wobble of the man's voice, that hadn't been there during the earlier telephone call.

'PC Rivers again, sir. We've tried the doorbell at Alexina O'Rourke's house. She's not answering. Also, we've obtained her home telephone number and she's not picking that up either.'

'Do you have her mobile number?' Callanach asked.

'We're currently contacting her law offices to obtain that.'

'Forget it,' Callanach said. 'Straight in. Smash a window if you have to. It's 12.13 p.m. by my watch. Call me back within ten minutes to update me.'

'Will do, sir,' PC Rivers said.

Callanach got in his car and began to drive.

By the time he arrived at the O'Rourke's address half a mile north of Murrayfield golf course, there were two marked police cars and a forensics van at the scene. The house was new, one of a handful on a site where an older property had been demolished. It had an austere luxury that indicated a house not troubled by children, hobbies or carelessness. Callanach found PC Rivers in the kitchen at the rear of the house.

'What do we know?' Callanach asked.

'She's not here, sir,' Rivers said.

'I got that,' Callanach said. 'What else?'

Rivers pointed to a cup next to the kettle. In it was a teabag, spoon ready and waiting to stir. Callanach put a hand to the side of the kettle. It was lukewarm, boiled a while ago now. To the side of that, with the clingfilm peeled back and a single bite taken, was a chicken sandwich next to a scrap of paper. Callanach opened it up and read the note which could only have been left by Alexina O'Rourke's husband. He set it down again, gently, almost wishing he hadn't read the contents. It would be hard enough to break the news to Mr O'Rourke without having just read what might prove to be their last precious communication.

'Her mobile?' Callanach asked.

'By her bed. Her laptop was on the duvet and switched on. Looks as if she came down to make a drink then just disappeared,' Rivers said.

'No signs of a disturbance?' Callanach asked.

'Forensics are going round now but we can't find anything.'

'Doors, windows?'

'None broken or damaged. All the doors were shut, although the back wasn't double-bolted. The husband's been contacted to return home. Should be here any minute,' Rivers said.

Callanach went upstairs. The master bedroom was vast. Its carpets looked scarcely walked upon, the tiled en suite had underfloor heating that Callanach could feel rising up his legs. A television screen large enough to have hosted a dinner party on had it been horizontal dominated one wall. Prominent on the dressing table was a picture of a grinning newly wedded husband and wife. Alexina O'Rourke was staring adoringly at her husband, who was raising his glass at some unseen friend or relative, the scene so idealistic it could have been a stock photograph.

Callanach walked to the window that looked out over the back garden. The grounds had received less attention than the interior of the house, the greenery still in the process of flourishing. Some trees and bushes had been planted, a few beds still more earth than stem, and a greenhouse. He opened the window to get a clearer view, staring at the roof.

'Rivers!' he shouted. 'In the garden.'

PC Rivers was out there before Callanach could get downstairs, giving orders to avoid the slivers of glass on the patio.

'No blood, sir,' Rivers said. 'I can see both a rock and a branch on the greenhouse floor. Looks as if they went straight through.'

'From where?' Callanach asked, looking up. The nearest tree waved from halfway down the garden. 'That was no accident, and it might have been enough to disturb Mrs O'Rourke from her tea-making.' He walked further into the garden. The ground was hard from the summer sun and a remarkably un–Scottish lack of rain. 'We won't get footprints,' Callanach said. 'Have your team check the perimeter. What about the CCTV?'

'Playback is password-restricted. We're hoping the husband will assist when he gets home.'

The front door slammed and fast footsteps echoed through the house.

'Where is she?' a voice called. 'What's happened to my wife?'

A police constable reached the husband before Callanach could, talking calmly, asking him to stay out of the areas being checked by the forensics team.

'Mr O'Rourke, I'm Detective Inspector Callanach. Do you have any idea where your wife might have gone unexpectedly?

A neighbour's perhaps, somewhere that she wouldn't have taken her car.'

'No, we haven't lived here long. Why are you here? I don't understand. Who called you? Alexina was feeling unwell today. She was working from home.'

Callanach led him into the lounge, asking PC Rivers to make tea.

'At this stage we have no clear idea what's happened. It would help if you could show us the CCTV. Is it working?'

'Then you'll answer my questions?' Mr O'Rourke asked. He was shaking, gulping. Callanach felt the pressure of needing to demand speed and compliance without being unsympathetic.

'I will. And please call me Luc. I know this is hard, but the sooner we figure out where your wife is, the better.'

'I'm Wesley,' he replied, standing up. 'The CCTV is controlled from my study.' He walked through the hallway to the door opposite the lounge. On the study wall was a keypad, above which was a black monitor. 'It's off,' he said. 'Has one of your people touched this?' His tone was accusatory, frantic.

'No. We wouldn't have turned it off. We were waiting for you to get home to help with it.'

'For God's sake, Lexy,' he yelled, slamming a fist into a mahogany desk. 'She must have turned it off. She hated it, always argued that we shouldn't live watched by cameras. I'll bet she did it the second I left the house.'

'Can you tell me what time the last images were recorded?' Callanach asked.

Wesley O'Rourke reset the system, went to playback and the screen lit up showing four different cameras, three outside the house at different points, and one revealing the downstairs hallway through which they'd just walked.

'There, 8.30 a.m.,' O'Rourke said, pointing at the lower right-hand side of the screen. 'Then it all goes blank.'

'Did anyone else know your wife didn't like the CCTV? Would she have discussed turning it off with say a cleaner, gardener? Even a relative?'

O'Rourke shook his head, lowering himself into a leather chair at the desk and putting his head in his hands.

'We didn't socialise much, to tell the truth. We've just bought this place. Alexina is career-driven. Works a sixty-hour week. I'm not much better. Neither of our families are local and we don't have staff. We're not at home often enough to make much mess. What is it you think has happened, Detective Inspector? I'd rather know.'

Callanach gave the briefest explanation he could. O'Rourke sat quietly, unable to meet Callanach's eyes, hands gripping the arms of the chair, nodding occasionally.

'Why didn't you tell us?' O'Rourke asked. 'I mean, you were right there, outside the door. You could have just warned her. I'd have stayed at home. Kept her safe. She sure as hell wouldn't have turned the CCTV off if she'd known.'

'We had officers posted outside your house, as we have done with all the potential victims. We didn't want to scare people. There were so many possible targets,' Callanach said.

'We're supposed to be going away this weekend,' Wesley muttered. 'I've booked us into the Buccleuch Arms in St Boswells. If anything happens to her . . .'

'Sir, back fence has been cut,' PC Rivers shouted from the hallway. Callanach cursed the timing and the bluntness, stepping out and asking another constable to look after Wesley O'Rourke while he went to check the discovery himself.

A section of the fencing, four foot high and three foot across, had been cut so that the wire could be lifted and entrance or exit facilitated. The other side of the fence was a neighbouring property's garden. Callanach stepped through onto the pristine lawn, greener and springier than the O'Rourkes', obviously tended with an efficient but utter disregard for the need to preserve water through the height of summer.

'It has sprinklers,' Callanach said, walking further into the grounds. 'Stay back,' he told those following him, stepping carefully to the side, away from the natural route to the back gate. From the side view, it was easier to see where the blades of grass had recently been pushed down, sporting a single line of indentation from the fence to the back gate. 'Someone came through this way recently enough for the grass not to have sprung back up yet.'

'That's a wheelbarrow track, sir. The garden shed's been broken into. Makes sense now,' Rivers said.

'Organise door-to-door enquiries, constable. Whoever has Mrs O'Rourke, and we must now assume it's our murderer, isn't taking her through the streets in a wheelbarrow. Someone must have seen a vehicle. Reduce the other teams to only one per potential target, get the spare officers here following this up. I want every person in the area interviewed. Sem Culpa drove through these roads, parked nearby, and came out pushing a goddamn barrow with a body in it. Somebody saw something.'

Callanach phoned Ava. It was a brief call, neither of them having the time or inclination to expend excess words. Every potential target would continue to be watched in case Sem Culpa had additional plans, or on the off-chance that it hadn't been her work at all. In the wake of the Julia Stimple mistake, neither Turner nor Callanach was willing to risk having their heads turned while a different target was left vulnerable. Between Grom and Sem Culpa, the city resources were stretched to their limits, and still they were being outsmarted.

Salter rang as Callanach was giving instructions to officers at the O'Rourke home to ensure that Wesley O'Rourke was not left alone, and that someone stayed near the home telephone line in case either his wife or her abductor made contact.

'Sir, been checking out your abductee. Got a few hits on the search engine. Some reports on her newest cases, it seems she had recently started writing a human rights blog, and it looks as if she was shortlisted for some legal award. Sem Culpa would have been able to find the articles relatively easily, although it's right to say there were a number of other possible targets more prominent than her. Looks like she was really unlucky.'

'You found nothing to indicate that Mrs O'Rourke might have had any other reason to suddenly disappear, I suppose?' Callanach asked.

'No. She and Mr O'Rourke have been married four years. Moved from another area of Edinburgh recently. Financials are stable. Big mortgage, but then they're young, both professionals, good income. She's from quite an affluent family. Public school, mother alive, father deceased but he was a judge. Seems to be carrying on the family line,' Salter said.

'The husband is very shaken. I've posted a constable to look after him but I'm worried he might do something unpredictable.'

'Do you want me to head over to the house and wait with him, sir? I'm happy to.'

'Going stir-crazy already, Detective Constable? I think you're better off where you are. I need someone I trust managing the incident room.' There was a disappointed sigh from the end of the line. Callanach lowered his voice. 'Salter, is DCI Edgar there or have his men moved?'

'Still in the building. Do you want me to let you know if there's any change?'

'Would you? Only keep it quiet. And don't pass that on to anyone else,' Callanach said.

'I won't, sir. It'll be nice to perform at least one useful task today,' Salter said.

'Looking after that baby is performing a useful task. We'll all need something to look forward to when this is over. You're carrying the first baby born under my chain of command. The very least I expect is to have it named after me.'

'I'm not sure how that'll work if it isn't a boy, sir.'

'Put a "y" on the end. Call me if there's anything else.'

Chapter Fifty-Two

Ava took the call straight after Callanach had finished briefing her about Alexina O'Rourke's disappearance. She was in her car in seconds, flying towards the Royal Infirmary, ignoring the speed restrictions, fingernails cutting into the steering wheel, concentrating only on getting breath in and out of her body.

Leaving her car diagonally across two parking spaces, she ran. Accident and Emergency was surprisingly quiet. Ava was given immediate access, her only delay was waiting for the doctor to update her before she could see her mother. Dr Nkiru Adisa was tall, elegant and extremely dark-skinned. She reminded Ava of a warrior waiting for a storm. When Dr Adisa told Ava to sit as she explained what was happening, Ava felt tiny and childlike, clumsy in her seat, wanting to fidget, unable to concentrate. Dr Adisa repeated herself three times without frustration or rush, as if that was the way it always was.

'Did you want to wait for any other family members to go in with you?' Dr Adisa asked.

'My father's on his way but he went down to Newcastle last night for a board meeting. Some charity thing he does. I'm not sure how long it'll take him to get here. We thought we had so much more time,' Ava said.

'I understand. These things are unpredictable, I'm afraid. There's no way your mother's consultant could have anticipated this,' Dr Adisa said. 'I'll make sure a nurse is close by in case you need anything.'

Ava waited for her to leave before entering her mother's cubicle, forcing back tears before talking. The machines on either side of the bed delivered pointless news. 'I'm here, Mum,' she said. 'Can you hear me?'

Ava's mother's eyes flickered restlessly for a few seconds, her hand juddering beneath Ava's as if she were swimming to the surface. Then she awoke.

'Ava, my darling. Has your riding lesson finished already?'

'No, Mum. You're in the hospital. The doctor called me. Do you remember the paramedics bringing you in the ambulance? You were taken ill whilst shopping in the city,' Ava said.

'Oh, silly, I just felt a little dizzy. Stupid fuss. Did I dirty my coat when I fell?'

'Not at all,' Ava said, brushing hair away from her mother's eyes. 'Your coat's fine. How do you feel?'

'I have rather a headache, I'm afraid. My own fault. I ate cheese last night. It always ends in a migraine. Should you not be at work, sweetheart?'

'My day off,' Ava lied, feeling the weight of her mobile in her pocket, praying silently that it wouldn't ring and drag her away. 'Can I get you anything?'

'Oh Ava, look. What a beautiful ring!' her mother said, running her fingertips over the alien engagement ring. 'You didn't tell me.'

Ava wanted to remind her of the evening they'd spent celebrating, of the promises Joe had made that the wedding would be in Scotland. And of the conversation she'd had with her mother about where they would shop for a wedding dress. But a blood clot in her mother's brain, a rare but known side-effect of the chemotherapy apparently, had caused her to collapse, stealing those memories and bringing with it a tide of pain.

'Yes, I got engaged,' Ava said. 'You'll have to choose a new outfit for the wedding.' Ava smiled, swiping at the side of her face with the back of her hand.

'Oh yes, we'll have so much shopping to do. I have cancer, don't I?' her mother asked.

'You do,' Ava said, the words a gulp in her throat. 'But you're coping with it well. You, um, you've been really strong.'

'Don't cry, darling,' her mother said, gripping Ava's fingers for a second before the effort sapped her strength. 'It's not so bad, you know.'

'Oh God, Mum. I'm sorry. I've been so stubborn. I pushed you away when I still needed you, and now . . .'

'Do you remember when you were seven and you sang a solo in front of the whole school? That little scoundrel Jock Young ran up behind you and lifted your skirt. Any other child would have run off sobbing. You looked at him as if he'd crawled out from under a rock, neatened your skirt and instructed the music teacher to begin the introduction again. The headmistress called me later to say that Jock had a received a black eye but was too scared to reveal its source.'

'How do you remember that?' Ava gasped, letting the tears run free as she stared into her mother's smiling face.

'It was the day everyone else realised what I already knew. You're a force to be reckoned with, Ava Turner. You took my breath away that day, as you have done ever since. I always wanted a gentler life for you, but I was wrong, you were made of sterner stuff. I'm proud of you. Don't cry for me, my love. Life goes on.'

Her fingers fluttered, and her mouth slackened momentarily

before regaining its proper shape. The machine gave a warning beep then settled again.

'I'll get the doctor, Mum,' Ava said.

'Are you engaged to that nice man?' her mother asked, taking hold of Ava's hand once more.

'Yes, Mum,' Ava said. 'He is nice.'

Her mother was breathing more rapidly, her shoulders tensing, the tendons in her neck like guy-wires between head and body.

'Let me go, Mum,' Ava whispered, pulling her hand from her mother's grip. 'I have to get Dr Adisa.'

'Nothing she can do,' her mother replied. 'Take my coat to the dry-cleaner, would you, dear?'

'I will,' Ava promised, as her mother shook beneath her hands.

'So glad you aren't marrying that Joe boy. Pompous twit. Never liked him. You were right to choose that other one. The way he looked at you.'

'Dr Adisa,' Ava called. Her mother's eyes were rolling, her chest heaving as she struggled for breath. 'I need help in here!'

Dr Adisa burst through the gap in the curtains, followed by two more nurses, moving Ava aside with practised speed, ushering her out as a stream of medical terminology flew between them. She stood mid-corridor, listening to the movement of machinery, the short bursts of activity, the bullets of instructions flying. The final blow, when it came, was the silence. Then a voice delivered the time and the first of the medics reappeared from inside the curtained cubicle. Ava fell.

DCI Joseph Edgar was in a telephone conference with the Crown Prosecution Service in London, in anticipation of the arrest due to take place that evening. When he'd finished that, he had another telecon diarised with an advisor at 10 Downing Street. The PM was keen for some news to placate a selection of elite party donors who had been targeted in The Unsung's monetary diversion. Everyone was waiting for him to deliver. Then there was the need for some publicity, and to that end one of his men had ensured that a photographer, as coincidentally as they could convincingly be, happened to be in the right place at the right time. Joe Edgar intended to be the one leading Ben Paulson out in handcuffs.

Ava was calling. He considered answering it. There were still a few free minutes before he needed to make his next call, but she would want to chat. It was bothersome. He hated having his focus dulled when he was at work. He switched her call to voicemail. He could call her back in the evening and invite her out to celebrate. He took the next call, reassuring a surly Prime Minister's advisor that all would be well, then listened to his messages whilst walking to brief his technical team. That was part of the problem with heading up an active arm of the Cyber Security Department. It wasn't just basic follow the clues and find the bad guy stuff. When you found the bad guy you had to retrieve the data, be able to understand it, present it in a comprehensible evidential form and secure a conviction. The technical element of his squad were the ones who made or broke cases. It didn't matter how good the investigative policing had been if there was nothing to show for it at the end of the day. There were two messages from members of his team confirming acts completed and positions secured. The last message was from Ava.

'Joe,' her voice was scratchy. He had to strain to hear properly. 'It's my mother. She passed away this afternoon. I know it's bad timing, but could you call me back? Please?' Joe could hear her tears, her voice fading as she ended the call.

He glanced at his watch as he put his phone back in his pocket. There was no time to call Ava now. There would be paperwork for her to fill out and other family members would have gone running. If he returned her call at this stage, he'd get caught on the phone for who knew how long. It wasn't as if the death had been a shock. Sooner than expected maybe, but inevitable nonetheless. And it would allow Ava to be free of Edinburgh, to start a new life with him. He brought the phone out of his pocket briefly, wondering if he could just phone and explain how busy he was, then decided against it. Ava's mother would still be dead later in the day, and he could offer the shoulder Ava needed to cry on then. For now, there were more pressing matters for him to attend to.

Chapter Fifty-Three

Callanach sprinted into Accident and Emergency. Ava had called twenty minutes ago and he'd found it impossible to decipher what she was saying, only that she was at the Royal Infirmary. He'd taken a marked car from the team he'd been briefing and flown across the city with lights blaring.

'DI Ava Turner?' he shouted to the reception assistants, one of whom showed him through to the treatment area. 'Is she hurt?' he asked.

'She's through here. The doctor wanted to give her a sedative but she refused.'

'Thank you,' Callanach said, walking in. It was a day room, no more than a small waiting area, all pastel shades and mismatching wipe-down chairs. 'Ava,' he said. She looked up at him from a yellow plastic chair, her face its own tale, tear-stained, her eyes glassy.

She held her hands out to him and he knelt before her, letting her wrap her arms around his neck then fall against him. He knew better than to expect her to speak before the crying was done. A year ago he would have shied away from such close physical contact, cringing every time a woman laid a hand on him, creating a barrier around himself he'd thought impenetrable. But Ava had softened him again through friendship, honesty, and sheer bloody-mindedness. Eventually she lifted her head and took a tissue from the table where they were no doubt regularly restocked.

'My mother died,' she said. 'Here. This afternoon.'

'Was there an accident?' he asked.

She shook her head, blowing her nose then plucking at the edges of a new tissue as she spoke.

'She had cancer. A blood clot went to her brain. It can happen with chemo.'

'I'm so sorry. I had no idea . . .' Callanach said, realising Ava should have been confiding in Joe instead and that what she probably needed most was for him to fetch her fiancé. 'I'll get the station to locate DCI Edgar. It won't take long.'

'He's in a briefing,' Ava said. 'I left a message on his mobile an hour and a half ago. It's a big day for him.'

A number of different responses fought to be spoken aloud, but in the end Callanach let only the simplest of them out.

'It is,' he said.

'I need to go and see her. To say goodbye. They've taken her body downstairs, but I'm allowed one last look. Would you come with me, Luc? I don't think I can do this alone.'

He took her hand. They followed the signs to where a blank-faced attendant allowed them entry. Callanach let Ava dictate how much of him she needed, happy to let her leave him behind at the final moment if she wanted a solitary goodbye, but she wrapped his arm around her waist and leaned against him as they walked.

They had both been through the same procedure so many times. Steel bed palettes, a single sheet covering the body, the cold that was necessary to slow degradation, the air-conditioning required to make working there feasible. And they'd seen many worse cases than a natural death. But love was the most brutal and destructive of emotions, Callanach was all too aware of that. And the loss of it, the easy slipping away, was a torture whatever the circumstances.

Ava ran gentle fingers over her mother's face, doing her best to control the sobs she was internalising that made an earthquake of her body. Callanach barely recognised her mother. He had met her only once, at a party Ava had insisted he accompany her to. As protection, she'd said. When he asked from what, she'd claimed it was from the wealthy bachelors her mother would have invited for match-making purposes. Callanach had found the evening pleasant, if something of a spectacle. He himself had been the subject of plenty of speculation, but Ava's mother had been kind, made conversation. He'd avoided the specifics of his work and any topics likely to cause offence. The food had been good, the wine plentiful, and Ava had shone in spite of her reticence about attending. She had been able to talk to anyone, without a moment's hesitation. Callanach had watched her making her way round the room greeting old friends, making new acquaintances, before returning to him and declaring it was time to make their escape. The woman laid before him now was almost emaciated, the cancer eating more than its fair share of her, the treatment no match for its voracious appetite.

'We can go now,' Ava said, winding her fingers through his, gripping as if she were walking a tightrope across an abyss until she reached the safety of the corridor beyond the double doors. 'Oh, God,' she cried suddenly, covering her face with her hands. 'Luc! What are you doing here? I forgot. I forgot everything that was happening. You have to go. You have to find Alexina O'Rourke.'

'Every single police officer in the Edinburgh area is looking for Mrs O'Rourke. You needed me here,' Callanach said.

'If Overbeck finds out . . .' Ava said.

'Fuck Overbeck,' Callanach cut across her. 'You're more important than my career.'

Ava stared at him, her fingers still intertwined with his, until a porter coughed politely and waited for them to move.

'You have to go now. I couldn't bear the thought that you stayed with me when you could have made a difference. My family is on its way. I'll wait for them, then head back into the city and find you.'

'You don't need to do that,' Callanach said. 'Go home. Take the time you need.'

'I need to be useful. That's what I chose. And my mother told me she was proud of me. I got here in time for that, at least. I think she'd be most proud if I carried on and did my bit. Now get lost, okay? That's an order.'

'I had no idea you were my boss,' Callanach said, kissing her gently on the cheek.

'You wish!' Ava managed a small smile. 'But I think we're stuck with Overbeck.'

Callanach looked at his watch as he jogged back to the car, wheel-spinning out of the mud he'd parked in, and putting the blues and twos on when he hit the road. It was five o'clock and there were no messages on his phone. The trail had gone well and truly cold. Hopefully the same wasn't true of Alexina O'Rourke.

Chapter Fifty-Four

Lance had spent the day feeling as if his guts were being gnawed by an undernourished rat. Something had struck him as wrong since he'd spoken to Ben that morning, but he'd been in no position to do anything about it until Edinburgh's nine-to-five workforce had taken to the streets clutching their gym bags, skinny lattes and overpriced bottles of wine to accompany dinner. Ben finally answered his call at half past five.

'Jesus, Lance, what's happened? I've twelve missed calls from you,' Ben said.

'Apologies. Are you home yet to check the information we were looking for this morning?'

'I'm three minutes away,' Ben said, puffing in time with his footsteps. Lance fought the desire to tell him to walk faster. 'I'll call you back when I'm in. It'll be faster that way. Takes me a while to get though my security set-up. Hang cool, okay?'

'God almighty,' Lance said aghast into his phone. 'We're pinning our hopes on a boy who says hang cool. Please let this not have been some dreadful mistake.'

Lance put the kettle on, switched it off again and got a beer from the fridge. He'd almost finished it when his phone rang.

'Did you get it?' Lance asked before Ben could speak.

'Give me a minute, would you? I've got some data back but it's still decrypting. What is it specifically that you're trying to deduce from this?'

'Just take me through the votes. They should speak for themselves.'

There was some beeping, the click-clack of keys as Ben's fingers flew over them, accompanied by the whirring of computer unit cooling fans. Lance began tapping his foot and counting the seconds.

'Got it. This list is only visible to the moderator, not to other users on the site, listed chronologically according to time of entry. Wow, there's loads, really diverse. Greenpeace activist, disabled support worker, counsellor, dinner lady, podiatrist although that's spelled wrong so it could have been intended as something else, foster carer, alcohol and drug dependency worker, seniors carer, probation officer, gardener, prosthetics designer – someone really thought about that – soldier, police officer although that only had one vote . . .'

'Stop, stop,' Lance said. 'Just look for lawyer. How many times does it come up?'

Ben muttered as he surveyed the screen. 'Once,' he said. 'That can't be right. It's definitely ours. I have time codes for each entry, and I know that's when we were online.'

'Do any of the other suggestions have more than one entry?' Lance asked.

'Some do,' Ben said. 'Foster carer was input by at least four different people. Counsellor had three votes. Quite a few had two. So why the hell did he pick up on ours, unless the webmaster was onto us. Maybe he'd been in touch with the real Rory Hand and was teaching us a lesson.'

'Occam's Razor,' Lance said. 'The simplest explanation is that it had nothing to do with us at all, and everything to do with the person controlling the game. After all, why amend it to specify a human rights lawyer if he was making a point to us? We might never have realised that we were the only ones who had made the relevant suggestion.'

'I don't get where this takes us,' Ben said.

'I'm going to find Callanach,' Lance said. 'Stay where you are. There may be more we can do. It's nearly six o'clock now. Give me an hour – I'll come to you. See if you can get any more information from that website. We need to get into the webmaster's communications files. He gathered a lot of detailed information about Rory Hand before allowing membership. Somewhere he has the same information about the killers.'

'It'll be heavily encrypted, and that's if he doesn't dump the information once he's finished vetting applicants. You're going to have to come up with something more reliable than my hacking skills given what little time we have left,' Ben said.

Chapter Fifty-Five

DC Salter was in the incident room where she'd been manning the phones all day. Callanach burst in first, demanding a full update. She'd wished there had been more to report, but the person who had seen a large four-by-four behind the O'Rourkes' hadn't been suspicious enough to take a licence plate, or notice the make or model. Randomly following the progress of dark-coloured four-by-fours in Edinburgh was a bit like spotting a fish in a loch and trying to figure out which way it was going to swim.

Callanach had explained DI Turner's absence, instructed Salter to keep the pressure off Turner unless unavoidable, then disappeared off towards his office. He was avoiding Superintendent Evil Overlord and Salter didn't blame him. The super had darted into the incident room several times during the day, each visit more furious than the last, demanding random useless snippets of information as if Salter were personally responsible for the lack of progress.

An hour after Callanach's sudden reappearance, another man hurtled down the corridor accompanied, or rather chased, by PC Biddlecombe from the front desk, puffing to catch up.

'He's signed in and I've check his credentials,' Biddlecombe called desperately, 'but he's press.'

It was as if the man had been carrying an infectious disease, Salter thought.

'I've got it,' Salter shouted, rising to head the man off. 'Can I help you, sir?' she asked.

'Where's Callanach?' the man asked. 'I'm Lance Proudfoot. He's not answering his calls. I tried his mobile but it went to voicemail.'

'That's because he's a wee bit busy, and to be honest he's not in the mood to talk to journalists. Perhaps you could tell me what's happening and then I . . .'

Salter had found that as her years in the police went by, her ability to be surprised was waning. She'd expected the man before her to insist on seeing Callanach personally, to get huffy, to refuse to speak to an underling, or all of the above. Instead, he took her gently but firmly by the shoulders, looked her straight in the eyes, and spoke clearly.

'The human rights lawyer target wasn't chosen as the most popular suggestion. It was planted by whoever runs the website communications. Someone had a motive for choosing this particular target. If Callanach wants to find the target, he needs to figure out who chose her.'

Salter spent no more than three seconds staring into his eyes before breaking into a run.

'Stay there, Mr Proudfoot. Right where you are,' she shouted.

It took no more than the same length of time again for Callanach to come striding back down the corridor.

'Lance, you're sure?' he asked.

'Aye, Ben retrieved the data,' Lance said.

Callanach shushed him, pushed him into the incident room, beckoned Salter in to follow, then shut the door.

'Quietly and don't say any names,' Callanach said, watching

the internal windows and hoping none of Edgar's men walked past. Lance had been observed with Callanach entering Ben's flat. Now wasn't the time for him to be seen in the police station.

'We found the list of all the target suggestions submitted to the webmaster,' Lance whispered. 'Lawyer definitely wasn't the most popular choice. Foster carer was suggested by four different individuals. And human rights lawyer wasn't mentioned at all.'

'You're saying it's a set-up?' Callanach asked. 'But the other victims, the whole competition between Sem Culpa and Grom, that wasn't faked. This lawyer thing must just be an anomaly with the data.'

'No, it's felt wrong to me all day. The data didn't come to us rigged, it was too well protected for that. I can't tell you about the other victims – if they were chosen at someone else's whim or under the guise of a user vote – but this target is deliberate and specific. It sure as hell had nothing to do with that vote.'

Callanach looked at his shoes, waiting for the answer to come. It made no sense. It was bad enough when it had seemed to be some sick game, but the thought that the whole thing had been rigged . . .

'Salter,' Callanach said. 'You found articles on a search engine that could have suggested Alexina O'Rourke as a victim. I need to see them.' Salter brought them up on her computer. 'Here you go, Lance, this is what we found. Even if the category of a human rights lawyer was a set-up, these articles seem to be what prompted Sem Culpa to choose Alexina O'Rourke. It's the same as the other victims. Someone within a specified profession who had received public attention for doing good work. Maybe whoever runs the site is cheating a bit. Taking a suggestion from the list without worrying about the maths. There could be any number of explanations. Perhaps a lawyer seemed a more visible target, get a bit more press, attract extra attention. Assuming the human rights lawyer category was set up, without naming a specific victim this doesn't take us any closer to finding her. There were other lawyers with similar press reports, so there's a randomness to Mrs O'Rourke being selected. It may simply be that she was just the easiest victim to locate.'

Lance rubbed his temples and sat down.

'I'm sorry, Luc, you're right. I'm wasting your time when you've got a thousand other things to do. The webmaster didn't specify Alexina O'Rourke. I'll leave you in peace.'

'Sometimes the pieces don't quite fit together,' Callanach said, 'but if you hadn't noticed the graffiti to begin with, we wouldn't be here now.'

'I hope you work it out,' Lance said, clapping Callanach on the shoulder. 'And thank you, too, Detective Constable Salter. Sorry to have caused such a stir.'

'No problem at all, Mr Proudfoot. It was nice to have met you,' Salter said.

Lance smiled at her. 'Old-fashioned manners in a time of crisis. That's the rock that Scotland's built on,' he said, raising a hand as he plodded away down the corridor.

The phone rang. Callanach motioned to Salter that he was headed back to his office, and she picked up the line.

'DC Salter, MIT,' she said.

'It's PC Biddlecombe. We've got a lady just phoned in, worried about an elderly neighbour. They live quite remotely. Says she normally sees her once a week but the neighbour isn't picking up the phone. She walked to her house to check on her, neighbour didn't answer, and the lady has no known family. I can't get hold of anyone. Every uniformed patrol is in the city because of the operation today and DCI Edgar has taken all the other spare bodies. I'm literally out of officers. I saw

370

you earlier and I wondered, if I divert your phone to me on the front desk . . .'

'I'm reduced to driving miles to wake up old ladies who can no longer hear their doorbells,' Salter sighed. 'Fine, anything to get me out of this chair.'

'I'll email you my notes and an address. Sorry to drop it on you, but I can't leave the desk unattended,' Biddlecombe said.

'Just us wallflowers left,' Salter said. 'We can commiserate with cake. I'll pick something up on my way back. Any preference?'

'I'd rather have a meat pie, if you're swinging past the bakers. Any flavour as long as it's protein,' Biddlecombe laughed.

'Right you are. Email's come through. I'll call in and let you know what I've got.'

Salter picked up her badge and a set of keys to an unmarked vehicle. If nothing else, she could take it slowly, wind down the windows and enjoy the sunshine for a while.

Ben was watching television and waiting to see if any of the code he'd thrown at the webmaster's communications network was going to get him in. The clock was ticking. He'd had confirmation by text from Lance that another woman had been taken. If he could identify an email address or mobile number for Sem Culpa, the police stood a much better chance of finding the latest victim alive.

His doorbell rang at 6.47 p.m. and he found Lance clutching a bag inside which, judging by the smell, was fish and chips.

'Dinner,' Lance said, holding up his prize.

'Come in. Beer's in the fridge. Do you want a fork or not?' Ben asked.

'Not,' Lance said. 'And don't worry about the code now. I saw Luc. There were a few search engine hits about the current abductee and her work. It was enough to have put her on the killer's shortlist. No one could have controlled the choice of victim just by suggesting a human rights lawyer.'

'How do you know?' Ben asked, pulling hot newspaper parcels from the bag.

'I read them. They were definitely about her, with plenty of detail about where she works and the people she's represented. It would have taken about thirty seconds to have found her address and phone number. Poor woman didn't stand a chance,' Lance said, opening a beer and landing heavily in a chair.

Ben switched off the television and picked up his mobile, flicking through screens and typing one-handed. 'No credited author on the first piece I've found,' he said.

Lance sat with his head back, eyes closed, nursing his beer and ignoring the fish and chips on his lap. 'It's not unusual for web pieces to lack an individual author's name. They're often just linked to a website,' he replied.

'Yes, but it's not like this is coming from a newspaper, established blogger or a legal society,' Ben said. 'And it's halfway down the first page of search engine results. Not sure why that would have attracted Sem Culpa's attention particularly.'

'Your point?' Lance asked, opening his eyes and grabbing a handful of salt with a small amount of potato attached.

'My point, and the point about the internet in general, is that it's too easy to simply believe what you read. Come on,' Ben said, walking into the hallway.

'I'm being invited into the Great Unknown this time, am I?' Lance asked.

'You need to show me all the articles,' Ben said, inputting the entry code into the pad at the side of his study door before also unlocking it with a key. 'And leave your beer in the lounge. No liquid near my hard drives.'

'Does that include ketchup?' Lance asked, following Ben into the study. The doorbell rang again before he could pick up another chip. 'I'll get that for you,' he said.

'No, I'm not expecting anyone. I don't like people calling unannounced. You stay in here but keep the door locked. I'll shout when it's okay to open up,' Ben said.

Lance looked down at the computer screen which was a sea of shifting graphics.

'You've accessed your computer though, right? I'm just wondering if I should touch anything or not . . .'

'Not if you value your life,' Ben said. 'Just wait right there.'

Chapter Fifty-Six

Alexina O'Rourke vomited. The purge came whilst she was on her back and it tasted like death. Vomiting upwards was perhaps the best metaphor for hopelessness. In the moments waiting for the heaving to begin, she couldn't believe it had never occurred to her before how bad it would be. Her body's only desire was to get onto her side, yet she could not move. She fought the eruption, knowing physics was the enemy, her throat closing against its wrong-way invader, but her stomach's need to flush her system was too strong an opponent. When it came, it caused her such blind panic that she feared she would pass out and choke. She smelled the bile before it was even out of her mouth, bitter, cloying, with an overtone of spoiled dairy. Then her mouth was flooded. She couldn't breathe in to spit it out, and she couldn't move her tongue to force the vomit upwards because when she did that, it slid back down her throat. It was like gargling in puke, that was her last thought before everything turned a squirming grey before her eyes as her oxygen-depleted system began to give in. Her stomach saved her with a final gigantic heave that erupted the stationary contents of her mouth into the air with such force that she was able to clamp her jaws shut and close her eyes before the ejecta hit her, hot and stinking, full on in the face.

Her hands were tied behind her back, her ankles bound together with their prominent bones bashing one another. There was nothing except fear and it crawled inside through every pore, cramping her muscles, shrinking her. Alexina was wishing for oblivion long before she came to look her captor in the eyes.

Her face was stinging from its stomach acid mask, her eyes on fire with it, nostrils still full. Only as she was pulled from the back of the vehicle onto a makeshift trolley, bumping heavily, did she dribble out the last of the vomit. She was suddenly shivering violently, her teeth chattering. Rough material scraped her face, leaving her skin sore in its wake, but anything was better than the foul veil she'd been wearing.

Fingers pressed hard against the inside of her wrist, then her head was propped up whilst she was given a sip of water.

'You'll feel better in a minute,' the voice said. 'Try to breathe. You were sick because of the tranquilliser leaving your system.'

Alexina drank a few more sips and felt herself returning to normal, relief flooding her system, the fear flowing away with the kind words.

'Thank you, thank you so much,' she said. 'I was so scared. Could you cut the strap around my wrist? I'm not sure what happened.'

'I can't do that, I'm afraid. I don't have the time to go running after you if you try to escape. I'll turn you onto your side in case you're sick again. That should help.'

'Aren't you . . . I don't understand. You have to untie me. Someone shot me and I fell . . .'

The woman leaned down by Alexina's side, stroking sticky hair from her forehead with rubbery blue fingers.

'I shot you. It was nothing personal. I read the articles about

375

your work. You've done a lot for prisoners' rights. So misguided. If they're stupid enough to get caught, they don't deserve sympathetic lawsuits.'

'You're not rescuing me,' Alexina said. The woman had begun fiddling with a tripod, positioning a tiny camera on the top attached by a lead to a laptop. 'If you want money, I'll call my mother. My father died last year. He left me enough to give you whatever you want. It won't take long.'

'I have plenty of money,' Sem Culpa said, walking to the side of the room and repositioning a generator. 'What I'm running out of is time. Twenty-four hours really wasn't long enough to accomplish so much.'

'Twenty-four hours? Then what? Who are you? Is this revenge for a case that's gone wrong? I can have another look, lodge another appeal. Please, just tell me what you want!'

'Save your voice for later. We'll be recording sound. Now I have to get on. It took too long to get this set up, and the generator's not as powerful as I'd hoped,' Sem Culpa said.

She returned to Alexina, her cropped hair blowing in the wind that billowed through the broken glass of the windows. Alexina tried to focus on where she was. It was an old factory, once heavily industrial but now abandoned. She'd been unconscious for most of the journey, losing track of time with no idea how far from the city they'd come. There wasn't much noise though – no obvious traffic, certainly no footfall. The only other feature was the smell, noticeable even through the reek of her own skin and drenched hair, sulphuric but meaty, both heavy and acidic at once.

'You want information about what is happening?' Sem Culpa asked.

'Yes,' Alexina whispered.

'All right. I killed a boy at a rock concert, in broad daylight in the middle of a crowd of thousands. His name was Sim

Thorburn. Then I murdered an old man in a library basement. Michael Swan. Him, I skinned alive. Does that tell you all you need to know or should I go on?'

Alexina O'Rourke began to scream. The hopelessness that followed was caused by Sem Culpa's lack of an attempt to silence her. She didn't even bother to tell her to stop. That was when Alexina knew for sure that she was beyond help.

Chapter Fifty-Seven

Polly was at Ben's door holding a bottle of wine in one hand and a small plastic bag in the other.

'Cabernet Sauvignon, Californian to make you feel at home, and the finest weed on sale north of the border. I thought after your rapid exit this morning, coupled with your non-appearance at Below Par to visit me today, you could do with a pick-me-up.'

'I so totally could,' Ben said, 'but there's someone here right now. I'm sorry, Pol. Could you maybe come back later?'

'Of course I can. I'll leave the red, but I'm taking the hash. A girl's got to have something by way of compensation. Call me when you're done.'

She stepped forward and kissed him, sliding the tip of her tongue along his bottom lip, pressing her body against his. Ben was aware that Polly wasn't wearing a bra and that he didn't want Lance to stay very much longer.

'You know what, we won't be long. Come in, put the TV on. There's food, beer, I'll find a corkscrew from somewhere . . .'

'It's a screw top, but I'm not going to disturb your time with your mates,' Polly said.

'Are you going to make me beg?' Ben asked. 'Twenty minutes, no more. Say you'll stay.'

Polly rolled her eyes, walking in slowly and drawing a pack of cigarette papers from her pocket.

'D'you want one?' she asked, rolling up the paper.

'Maybe later,' he said. 'I'll just go deal with this. Pour me a glass of wine?' he called as he walked into the hall. 'Hey, Lance, do you want a glass of wine or are you sticking with beer?'

Lance frowned as he unlocked the study door for Ben to reenter.

'Who's here?' Lance asked.

'Polly,' Ben said. Lance raised his eyebrows. 'You know, from Below Par? She was here this morning when you called . . .'

'I see,' Lance said. 'Are you sure now's the best time? This could take a while. It might be better if it were only the two of us.'

'Polly's cool,' Ben said, pulling a stool out from under a pile of magazines and settling himself next to Lance in front of the screen. 'Let's get on with this. Here you go. None of these articles can be traced back to where they were uploaded.'

'And from that we can infer?' Lance asked.

'We can infer that the writer or writers of the articles didn't want to be traced,' Ben said, bringing up a search engine and typing.

'What's that?' Lance asked.

'It's the awards longlist that Alexina O'Rourke was supposed to be named in.' The two of them sat reading.

'She's not there,' Lance said. 'Could have been a mistake, or perhaps she was under consideration and didn't make it.'

'Oh yeah? Whatever happened to that guy's razor?'

'Occam,' Lance said. 'Never quote a journalist back at themselves. It's undignified. But none of this explains why Alexina was chosen. These articles are all some way down the search engine lists. A couple are even on page two of the rankings. If someone went to the trouble of faking each article, there was no way they could be sure it was enough to lead Sem Culpa to Mrs O'Rourke as the obvious choice.'

Ben tapped keys without speaking as Lance concentrated on his chips.

'Rankings history,' he said. 'Jesus, this is . . . wow, Lance, you have no idea how right you were. Look at this. Last night, for just sixty minutes, every one of these articles was ranked top in the search engines. Every single goddamned one of them. And that hour started from the time the website vote for the next kill target ended. Straight after that someone altered the relevant search terms, causing them to slip down the listings.'

Lance paused, a chip halfway to his mouth, his face drawn into a frown. 'Why would, sorry, I'm being a bit slow . . .'

'Last night when Sem Culpa was told to find a human rights lawyer to kill, these articles would have been the first ones she found. It left an obvious trail to a very specific target. And with only twenty-four hours Sem Culpa had to make a fast decision. She'd have done her research, chosen Alexina O'Rourke, and got on with her planning. Later in the evening those articles were well down the list . . .' Ben said.

'So to anyone else the articles about Alexina O'Rourke wouldn't have stood out at all. DC Salter must only have found these articles after Alexina O'Rourke was taken. It made her abduction resemble the others – there had to be some plausible press coverage available – but there's no way the police could have anticipated it was her who was going to be taken and stopped it. If we're right, then all the other murders were simply a ploy to make this one look like part of a series. Four innocent people died to ensure Alexina O'Rourke didn't stand out. We've got to get hold of Callanach,' Lance said, grabbing his mobile and beginning to dial.

'So, taking all we know, someone with substantial skill put together a darknet website. The same skill, in fact, that was employed in placing articles within a search engine to lead a killer to one particular target and then moving them to cover the trail. Someone with a grudge?' Ben hypothesised.

'Or with something to gain,' Lance added, listening to the ringing on the line. 'I'll explain it to Luc. Find out all you can about Alexina O'Rourke.'

It took only two minutes to get Callanach up to speed.

'So there is someone else involved. God, Lance, I'm sorry. If I'd listened to you earlier we might have found her by now. I'm heading back over to the O'Rourkes' now to see if her husband can think of anyone who might have a reason to want her dead. I'm not sure how the hell I'm supposed to break it to the poor man that his wife was the reason for so many deaths,' Callanach said.

'Whoever set this up had us all sucked in,' Lance said. 'If it weren't for Ben . . .'

'I know,' Callanach said. 'Tell him thank you. Keep working, would you? We may be a step closer to Alexina but we haven't got long left. And Grom's still out there with a victim who must have given up hope of ever being found alive.' He hung up.

There was a gentle knock at the door. 'Can I come in?' Polly called.

'I don't think that's a good idea,' Lance said.

'It's fine,' Ben replied, immersed in working his way through what information the internet was offering up about Alexina O'Rourke.

'Ben, we have to get this finished. You don't need any distractions,' Lance said.

'I need a life. Something other than a computer that responds when I touch it. It's okay, Lance. Open up,' Ben said.

Lance opened the door, doing his best to smile at the girl standing there with a half empty bottle and a joint.

'What are you two up to?' Polly asked.

'Motive hunting,' Ben muttered. 'Apologies for the lack of furniture. You could grab that crate from back there to sit on, if you don't mind a bit of discomfort,' he pointed behind himself. 'Just put those hard drives on the floor in the corner. Now, where to start?'

'Her emails,' Lance said quietly, glancing over his shoulder at Polly. 'She's bound to have both personal and work email accounts. Work is a law firm, so I'm guessing those will be pretty well protected.'

Ben tutted. 'It's almost as if we've only just met,' he said. 'I'm already in her work emails. No encoding. Ancient security. Simple password and she's replicated it for her personal email account. I can't believe people still do that after the amount of warnings there've been.'

'To us mere mortals, the idea of trying to remember a different password for every email, social media, bank and other type of account is bit overwhelming. You're not going to tell me you have different passwords for everything you do online,' Lance said. Ben raised his eyebrows at him. 'Right, of course you do. What are we looking for in that lot?'

'I'm searching keywords, but it's an uphill battle. Normally you wouldn't find many offensive terms in a person's email text but she has statements, pleadings, all sorts of court cases relating to some fairly serious criminal offences. I'm never going to be able to filter through all this.'

'What about looking for today's date?' Lance suggested. 'Someone asking where she'd be, what she was doing, requesting a meeting? Trying to tie her movements down.'

Ben tapped away as Polly leaned her head on his shoulder and stared at the screen.

'Did I miss something?' she asked. 'Whose email is this?'

'Just helping out a friend,' Lance said, leaning over to point one particular email out on the screen. 'She was supposed to have lunch with her mother today but cancelled it last week to see a client instead.'

'You think her mother is involved?' Ben asked. 'That's got to be a bit of a stretch.'

'What's the statistic?' Lance replied. 'I wrote an article on this last year. On average only one in eight females is killed by a stranger. Couple that with the fact that the evidence points to it being someone with a close vested interest in her, we need to be looking at her nearest and dearest first. Her email is too wide a net. I'm texting the broken lunch plan to Callanach anyway. No harm in getting him all the facts.'

Callanach read Lance's text then put in a call to a team of officers visiting a house near Aberdeen.

'This is DI Luc Callanach. I'm the officer in charge of Alexina O'Rourke's abduction. Are you with her mother now?'

'Yes, sir,' the attending officer said. 'But we've only just broken the news to her and she's very distressed. Can we give you a call back in, say, quarter of an hour when we've given her a cup of tea and let it sink in a bit?'

'If a vehicle is travelling at an average of sixty miles an hour, how far does it get in fifteen minutes?' Callanach asked her.

'Um, I'm not sure what the relevance—' the officer stuttered.

'Another fifteen miles. That's how much further away a psychotic murderer will be with Alexina O'Rourke in the boot while I wait for it to sink in a bit. And it's fifteen miles further for us to rescue her, even assuming we figure out where she is. So shall we wait?'

'Handing you over right now,' the officer said, introducing

Callanach in muffled terms. There was a pause then a new voice came onto the line.

'Sorry to have to ask you questions at such a difficult time but we're trying to get a fuller picture of your daughter's routines and life. We understand that you were due to have lunch with her today,' Callanach said.

'That's correct. She called me to cancel some days ago. An urgent case came in I think,' her mother said.

'And who suggested lunch in the first place?' Callanach asked.

'I'm not sure. Does this matter? I can't see how it helps to find Alexina,' her mother said, her voice hitching at the end of the sentence, a ruffling noise at the receiver, almost certainly a handkerchief, Callanach thought.

'I need to know if it was her making plans then changing them, or if it was beyond her control. Was there a restaurant booking?'

'We always go to a tapas bar opposite her work building. You don't need to book. It's very informal. Do you have any idea at all why this has happened to her? Alex really is the nicest person. She's always been popular. She's a hard worker, dedicated to her clients . . .' The voice faded into sobs and Callanach could hear the officer whispering consoling words in the background.

'One last question. I know this is difficult. Had there been any marked changes in Alexina's life recently? Please forgive me for asking, but did you perhaps suspect her of having an affair? Had she become withdrawn? Was there anything you thought she was hiding from you?'

'No, not at all. She was devastated by her father's death, naturally, but she'd even put a positive spin on that. All the money she's inherited is going to be invested in a charity. Alex was spending every spare hour setting it all up. And it's not in her nature to even contemplate having an affair. She prided herself on her loyalty and honesty.'

'All right. Thank you. We'll do everything we can to find your daughter as quickly as possible. In the meantime the officers will remain with you. If you think of anything else that might help, have them call me,' Callanach said.

'So Alexina's husband works full-time, wouldn't have been around during the day today,' Ben said. 'There's some press coverage of their wedding. Looks as if it was a big event. She's pretty. Could it be an attempt to hide an abduction? A stalker-type thing, maybe, or an ex-boyfriend?'

'Possible,' Lance said. 'But wouldn't she have been aware of someone following her, contacting her, especially if it was a persistent ex?' His phone buzzed. 'That's Callanach,' he said. 'Apparently Mrs O'Rourke inherited some money that she was putting into a charity. He wants us to see what we can find.'

Two minutes passed before Ben spoke again. He had been typing ever faster and was holding his breath. 'She inherited close to eleven million,' Ben whistled. 'The money came from some shrewd property investments her father made a couple of decades back. It's all pointing back towards Wesley O'Rourke. They don't have children. No one else stands to profit from her death.'

'Actually that doesn't explain it,' Lance interrupted. 'The husband could just divorce her to get his share of the cash. Their marriage might not have been long enough for him to get the full fifty per cent, but he'd still be extremely wealthy. No need for anything as dramatic as murder.'

'Alexina O'Rourke was in the process of setting up a charity to fight female genital mutilation. It was in the preliminary stages, but there are emails to and from other concerned parties. Maybe a divorce was going to take too long,' Ben said.

'As long as he issued divorce proceedings before the money went into the charity, Wesley O'Rourke would have been entitled to his share. The law is on his side. He could have issued proceedings today and she wouldn't have been able to move a penny of that money to the charity. It's another dead end,' Lance said. 'I'll update Luc. Go back to the darknet site. It looks as if we'll have to track Alexina O'Rourke that way.'

Lance left the room, dialling Callanach. Polly moved onto his chair and closer to Ben. 'What was all that about?' Polly asked.

'Just doing my bit for society,' Ben said, leaning across and planting a kiss on Polly's lips. 'I need to let this software run a while – see if we can't get any more information about Sem Culpa. Ten more minutes and I'm all yours,' he said.

Lance wandered back in, dragging the crate Polly had been sitting on to the edge of the desk near the door. 'I got hold of Luc,' he said. 'I told him what little we know. I think he feels as if he's just chasing his tail.' He looked at Ben and Polly, their hands linked under the desk. 'I guess you two have plans for the evening. Will you be able to do a bit more work on finding Alexina?' he asked.

'I'll leave the programme working. There's not much more I can do at the moment anyway. Sorry to chase you out Lance, but Polly and I . . .' A mobile phone rang in the lounge. 'I'd better get that,' Ben said. 'Give me a minute.'

'Shouldn't you . . .' Lance said as Ben dashed through the door.

'So how did you meet Ben?' Polly asked, sitting in Ben's seat and putting her feet up on the desk. In the lounge, Lance heard Ben's voice drop from normal volume to a whisper. 'Only you two don't seem a natural choice for playmates.' She began running her hand over the keyboard.

'I don't think you should do that,' Lance said, standing up and peering out into the hallway.

'God, this bottle is already empty. You couldn't be a love and fetch some beer from the fridge, could you?' Polly asked.

'I don't think I should leave the computer. Something might come in,' Lance said.

'I'll watch it. You'll only be a second. Only I've been on my feet in the cafe all day.'

Ben yelled something garbled from the lounge. There was an explosion of shouting and the thud of a massive weight crashing against wood.

'Ben, what's going on?' Lance shouted.

'I said, lock the study door and don't let . . .' Ben screamed as the front door shattered.

Lance jumped backwards into the study, hitting Polly who was already trying to close the door with him in the way. He threw himself to one side, kicking the door shut then reaching up to turn the internal deadbolt, collapsing against the reinforced wood, his chest ready to explode.

Chapter Fifty-Eight

Callanach pulled up outside the O'Rourkes' house, wondering how Ava was doing and if she might have any better ideas than him. The sparse information from Lance about Alexina O'Rourke took the investigation no further forward. All he could do was check if scenes of crime had found anything useful at the scene and reassure Wesley O'Rourke that they were doing everything possible to find his wife.

A constable opened the O'Rourkes' front door just as Callanach was about to go round to the back.

'Where's Mr O'Rourke?' Callanach asked.

'In his study, sir,' the constable said.

Callanach knocked and tried Wesley's study door, finding that the handle wouldn't budge. 'Mr O'Rourke,' Callanach called. 'Could you open the door please?'

There was a shuffling inside, the click of a laptop being shut, then footsteps in the direction of the door.

'DI Callanach,' Wesley said as he opened the door. 'Have you found Lexy?'

'Not yet, I'm afraid. We're conducting enquiries with local residents, checking CCTV for all routes to try to pick up the car based on its description and the timing, and I have people following Sem Culpa's online trail in an attempt to figure out where she may be going,' Callanach said.

'What about the media? Couldn't you use them to maybe, I don't know, have people call in whenever they see a four-by-four with a woman driving, or parked somewhere unexpected. Just something, just . . . you need to be doing something more,' he said, falling back into the chair at his desk.

'I know. What I want to do now is recreate today to make sure I haven't missed anything. Do you mind if I look at the CCTV footage again please? It might be that there's something on there. I only had a brief look this morning.'

'That won't help. We know it was turned off well in advance of Lexy being taken. Is that really the best you can do? Do you have no idea at all of what that monstrous bitch intends to do with her?'

'It might be that the CCTV footage shows someone passing by earlier, the four-by-four passing the end of the driveway, anything at all that might help,' Callanach said. 'In any event, we'll need a copy for evidence.'

'Your officers have been through it several times already. They've all agreed that there's nothing on there that makes it valuable. I'd appreciate it if you'd stop wasting time. What about Lexy's mobile? Have you checked her text messages? Surely there's still a chance that this is someone she knows. Maybe a client who became obsessed. She's represented enough psychopaths to fill a whole prison. Isn't that worth a look?'

'It is,' Callanach said. 'Absolutely. That's another reason I'd like to start with the CCTV footage. Whoever did this came to your house, watched, and made sure you had gone to work. There's every chance they were already here when you left, especially if they were expecting your wife to go to work too. Could you let me see the footage please?'

Wesley rolled his eyes and flexed his jaw. Callanach could understand the frustration. Paying attention to the tiny details always seemed like time-wasting. More often though, it was the key to forward movement in a case. Wesley rewound the footage, stepped back and let it play, turning to stare out of the window as Callanach watched the final moment before it was switched off, rewatching, studying the apparently empty driveway, deserted garden and the lack of movement in the downstairs hallway.

'Thank you, Mr O'Rourke,' Callanach said. 'I'll leave you in peace while I go and see what progress scenes of crime have made in the garden.'

Callanach slipped out of the study, moving into the lounge and taking out his mobile phone. Watching the forensics team in the garden through the rear windows, he made another call to Alexina O'Rourke's mother.

Ten minutes later Callanach knocked once more on Wesley's study door. On the desk, the laptop sat closed but still warm to the touch when Callanach ran his hand over it.

'Have you spoken to your wife's mother yet?' Callanach asked.

'No,' Wesley said. 'I didn't want to worry her until you were sure . . .'

'I understand,' Callanach said. 'I was just wondering if that's what you were doing, emailing her perhaps. Did you turn your computer off just before opening the door?'

'Habit,' O'Rourke said. 'I work within very strict security parameters at the bank. They insist on a locked door policy when I'm accessing their system.'

'So you were working?' Callanach asked.

'Trying to take my mind off what's happening,' O'Rourke said, turning his head away. 'Have your people found anything more?' he asked.

'Could you turn your computer on again,' Callanach said, 'in case the kidnapper emails with demands.'

Wesley O'Rourke stared at Callanach, lowered his voice and shook his head. 'I can't do that. I've already explained my employer's security restraints,' he said.

'I hadn't realised it was that serious,' Callanach said. 'Let's get the bank on the phone. I'm sure I can persuade them in the circumstances of a missing person believed in danger.'

'I don't want my work involved in this,' he said. 'I'm a contractor rather than a full-time employee. Any sort of hassle and they won't renew my contract.'

'What exactly is the nature of your work at the bank?'

'For God's sake. My wife's life is in danger and we're running through my fucking CV? I want to talk to your superior officer. Somebody needs to take charge here.'

'You're right. Your wife's life is in danger,' Callanach said. 'Does your contract matter more than that?' Callanach put one hand on the laptop. O'Rourke stepped forward, then back again. 'We'll need the laptop as evidence anyway in case your wife has used it. Might give us some clue as to her whereabouts. It's possible that her abductor has been following her on social media or made contact in some way.'

'My wife never touched this laptop. She didn't have access to the security code. I think perhaps I should phone Alexina's mother now. I wonder if I could have the room a minute to make the call in private.'

'Just before you do that, could you show me the last frame on the CCTV footage again? Right before the cameras were turned off,' Callanach said.

Wesley O'Rourke frowned and walked slowly towards the control panel. 'Are you looking for anything in particular?' he asked.

'I just need the timecode off the final frame, to make sure

we're cross-referencing it properly with our CCTV searches,'
Callanach said.

'I see,' O'Rourke said, scrolling through the timeline. 'I can
download a copy if you want, but I can't see that it shows
anything.'

'You're right. It shows nothing at all,' Callanach said. He
went to the study door and beckoned a uniformed officer over.
'Is it right that you're in charge of the bank's internet security
system? Data protection, website security, international routing
and encoding? The whole lot.'

'Yes, but I have no idea why you're . . .'

'And is it factually accurate to say that you signed a pre-
marital contract that limits your access to any money your wife
might receive, including her inheritance, in the event of a
divorce?'

There was a long pause. Wesley O'Rourke put his hands on
his hips. 'This is a disgrace. I see where this is going. You're not
putting me in the frame to protect your own back. Your officers
messed up. They failed to stop a kidnapping from right outside
my door. Now you have no idea where my wife is, so it's blame
the husband time. I love my wife, Detective Inspector. Phone
the Buccleuch Arms. I made the booking there just this morning
for the weekend. I made her lunch so she didn't have to do it
herself whilst she was ill. I even left her a note . . .' his voice
cracked and he looked away. The uniformed officer gave an
involuntary step towards him with an arm outstretched until
she caught sight of Callanach's face.

'All exactly the right things to do to ensure we wouldn't
suspect you of having been involved in her abduction,' Callanach
said. 'You don't need to admit the existence of the pre-marital
agreement. Your mother-in-law has a copy. You stand to lose
millions if the inheritance goes into the charitable trust, and a
divorce will keep the money out of your reach too by virtue

of the agreement you signed. But if Alexina dies before the charity is formed, it's all yours.'

'You've decided that a motive is all you need to arrest me? It may be my wife who was the lawyer, but I think even I know enough law to be confident that you would need some evidence of my involvement first.'

'You're quite right,' Callanach said, taking a pair of handcuffs from the officer. 'Your wife didn't turn the security cameras off,' Callanach said, taking a pair of handcuffs from the officer. 'If she had, the last frame would have shown you either in the hallway or the driveway and yet you're nowhere to be seen. Turn around please.' The doorbell rang. Callanach could hear Ava calling from the driveway. 'Let DI Turner in,' he instructed the officer.

O'Rourke turned round. Callanach pushed him face first against the wall as he cuffed him.

'You know, you're right. I forgot with the trauma of the morning that Alexina had called down to me as I was on my way out. She asked me to turn the cameras off for her.'

'That's not what you told me this morning,' Callanach said, securing the cuffs.

'This morning? When it was just you and me chatting with no witnesses? When I wasn't under caution and didn't write it down in a statement?' O'Rourke pushed his head back so his mouth was as close as he could get it to whisper in Callanach's ear. 'I don't think so, Detective Inspector. I don't think that's enough for you to even walk me down my driveway, let alone interview me.'

'You have the technical capability to be involved in setting up the website through which your wife's abduction was organised,' Callanach said. 'And I have your laptop. You really think a man worried sick about his missing wife does a bit of work to take his mind off it? I'm getting tech officers in here right now. I'm going to have every fragment of data analysed and I will prove what you and I already know.'

'My lawyer will have me out within hours,' O'Rourke hissed.

'That's all the time I need,' Callanach said. 'And you'd better pray that we find your wife before then.'

'There's no evidence against me,' O'Rourke said. 'You're running on speculation and crossed fingers.'

'I also have one of the best hackers in the world with a password to your darknet site,' Callanach said. 'And I think that's enough.'

Chapter Fifty-Nine

Lance looked at Polly who had assumed a pose usually reserved for action movies. Data was streaming onto Ben's screen as if the computer had taken on a life of its own. Lance risked a brief closer inspection without moving from his position between Polly and the door. Usernames, passwords and emails filled the screen.

'Ben!' Lance shouted. 'We're into the webmaster's files!'

'I'm a police officer,' Polly said. 'Move aside from the door now.'

Lance looked away from the information flooding the screen to stare at Polly, reaching one hand out to shield the door lock from her.

'Tell me that's not why you slept with Ben,' Lance said.

'I instructed you to move away from the door,' Polly repeated, taking a step forward.

'How could you do that? He really liked you. And isn't that against the rules when you're undercover?'

'Since when did journalists concern themselves with morality and abiding by rules? Don't judge me. You think it's easy making your mark as a woman in the cyber crime unit? It doesn't matter if I outperform every man there, they still look at me first when it's time for someone to make the coffee.'

'If that's the case, I can't see how sleeping with a suspect will improve your professional image,' Lance replied, pulling out his mobile and dialling.

'Whatever gets results,' Polly said. 'Now put down your phone and move or I will move you.'

'Can't oblige, I'm afraid. What we're doing is more important than any agenda you may have,' Lance said. He dragged a chair between himself and Polly, ignoring the insanity beyond the door. Callanach picked up. 'Luc, we've got the data,' Lance shouted against the torrent of noise outside.

'Hang up that phone immediately!' Polly shouted.

'Lance?' Callanach said. 'What's going on there?'

A blow from the other side of the door sent vibrations through Lance's back that would require the help of a physiotherapist. He took half a step forward and closer to Polly.

'Police raid,' Lance shouted to Callanach. 'Sem Culpa's email address is rainhadador@bmail.com.' Lance spelled it out, straining to be heard over the hammering.

'Put the phone down right now or I will use force,' Polly shouted.

'Did you get that? Callanach, I can't hear you!' Lance yelled.

Polly launched herself forward to grab the mobile, knocking an elbow into Lance's side and winding him as he went down. His head hit the side of the desk and the door flew inwards followed by several police officers.

'Secure the scene!' an officer shouted.

'His system's up and running, sir,' Polly said. 'We're through security. You'll be able to copy the hard drive.'

Ben appeared in the doorway, wrists behind his back, a police officer either side of him. He stared hard at Polly who turned away, focusing on the screen. Lance was being rolled onto his front, his hands in the process of being cuffed. His ankle was the only part of him still moving, circling a cord of wires running between the computers and the extension cable on the floor. Ben shook his head.

'You've done enough, Ben,' Lance puffed as his head was turned to the side and pinned against the floor.

'DCI Edgar, the subject has been secured. Shall we take him down to the van?' one of the officer's holding Lance asked.

'Don't, Lance,' Ben shouted.

'Would somebody stop those two from communicating and get them the fuck out of here!' Edgar shouted. The officers either side of Ben dragged him from doorway and into the hall as Lance began writhing on his stomach, banging his head against the floor, and screaming at the top of his voice. 'I said,' Edgar repeated, moving across the study to grab Lance by the arms and yank him upwards off the floor, 'get him the fuck out of here.'

Edgar gave Lance another massive wrench, hard enough that it should have propelled him over the threshold of the doorway and into the hall. Instead, there was the crunching pop of a dislocated or broken bone, followed by a halo of sparks under the desk and screams from Lance who rolled onto his back, craning his neck for evidence that the agony had been worthwhile.

'Um, sir . . .' one of Edgar's team managed in a small voice.

'What the fuck just happened?' Edgar asked.

'I didn't touch anything,' Edgar's man said. Even the pain couldn't stop Lance from grinning at the memory of his own son saying more or less the same words whenever anything got broken.

'Get it back on,' Edgar snapped, glaring at Lance who was gasping for breath on the floor. Lance winced as the DCI caught sight of his ankle, stuck at an unnatural angle and wrapped in a rainbow of wires, a freed plug dangling uselessly from the end. 'What did you do?' Edgar screamed at him.

'Your fault,' Lance gasped. 'Foot got tangled when I fell. If you hadn't pulled me . . .'

Edgar's face went from ghostly to purple. Twice he opened his mouth to speak, failing, making fish mouths with each attempt. In the end he pulled his boot back, took aim and delivered the blow that was the very last thing Lance felt.

Chapter Sixty

Salter parked near the ramshackle bungalow, called in to PC Biddlecombe to confirm her arrival, then climbed out of the unmarked car. The address was at the corner of a crossroads at the outskirts of a tiny village, and whoever lived here had given up gardening, window cleaning and any other form of maintenance a good decade ago. The building was a standard two front windows and door set-up, with all the curtains drawn. There was no vehicle on the driveway. Salter saw no sign of foul play at the front, the windows firmly shut and the door properly closed.

She knocked the door, got no response, then rang the bell, pressing her ear to the door to check it was working. There was the faintest of ring tones, as if the bell itself had had enough of functioning, then nothing.

'Hullo, Mrs Talthwaite, this is Detective Constable Salter. Can you hear me, Mrs Talthwaite?' There was no reply. Salter wandered around the side of the property, treading with pointed toes through the long grass, avoiding the abandoned tools waiting to trip unsuspecting visitors. The bins hadn't been put out for collection, she noted, opening one to find a mess of bin bags with flies competing for sustenance. The now regular tightening of her bladder warned her that it had been an hour since her last bathroom stop, and that she hadn't long before she'd be leaving it too late.

The back door was also secured, windows intact, and there was still no response to her banging. Salter realised her shift would be over before she could make it back to the station, but she had a few minutes to spare. Just enough time to visit the neighbour who'd reported Gladys Talthwaite missing, before clocking off. It was still a couple of hours until her mother-to-be yoga class and Salter was keen not to miss it. She was making friends, sharing the excitement and fears, and learning all the gross bits no one warned you about until it was too late to change your mind. Determined to leave immediately afterwards, Salter drove the couple of hundred yards to the next property. Mrs Talthwaite's concerned neighbour was at the front door by the time Salter had made it down the path, and enjoyed the visit and the fuss. By the end of the conversation, Salter was wishing she hadn't stopped in.

'Right then, Mrs Scott,' Salter said, edging her way towards the front door. 'I understand completely. Like I said, there's no sign of any disturbance at Mrs Talthwaite's cottage and the bin has been in use, so I think your friend has been there very recently.'

'You'll go back and check one more time, though, won't you, dear?' Mrs Scott persisted.

Salter sighed. She did her best not to lie to people. It was too easy, and too slippery a slope. Reassure, then disappear. But time was racing and she'd hoped to have tea before her pre-natal class. All she ever seemed to be these days was hungry or in need of a pee. Right now she was both. She sighed. It was hardly too much to ask to go back and knock on the door one more time.

'Of course I will, don't you worry,' she said, smiling through the tiredness that started at her ankles and worked up her spine until she fell into bed at night. 'And I hope you don't mind my asking, but might I use your loo? I'm pregnant.'

'Oh, you should have said. Second door on your left.'

Salter made a dash for the bathroom, dismayed to find that Mrs Scott was standing outside to continue plying her with information even while she relieved herself.

'I wouldn't make such a fuss normally, you know, only it's been five days since I heard from her. I did tell Gladys she shouldn't have gone on that television programme, talking about her time as a lollipop lady. I said, "Now Gladys, you don't want to give anyone ideas. You may be retired but . . ."'

Salter stopped mid-flow, her muscles clamped tight. She threw her hands under the tap as she fought for the right response before leaving the toilet.

'She was a lollipop lady?' Salter asked.

'Yes, and I thought with all that was happening, you know, and then that other lady whose son kidnapped her . . .'

'He didn't actually . . . never mind. Stay in the house, lock the door and call the police. Tell them everything you just told me. Right now!'

Salter ran to the car, still fighting her trouser button and fumbling the keys. She was overreacting, was her first thought. Gladys Talthwaite had retired years ago. She recalled seeing her on the television interview now, the name ringing bells too late. It took her only half a minute to cover the stretch of road back to Gladys' house. She picked up the radio, considered calling for backup, then thought again. She couldn't be certain yet that anything was wrong and Police Scotland's resources were already stretched to breaking point. The neighbour would have dialled the situation in. The least she should do was attempt to gather first-hand evidence before mobilising the squad.

Skidding the car to a halt she ran through the garden, this time ignoring the possibilities the front door had to offer and going directly to the back. She could hear crashing inside now, and swearing. A male voice, guttural and rough.

Salter huddled close to the ground as she made her way to the kitchen window at the rear, keeping her head down, making sure her radio wasn't about to screech and give her away. There was a scream, muffled but high-pitched, and the sound of something heavy hitting wood. She risked a quick glance through the window, seeing a tiny elderly woman huddled on a chair, her head resting on the kitchen table. The woman was barely moving, the only sign of life the waving of her wispy hair, up and down, with her rapid breaths. Whatever her captor's intentions, it was easy to see the woman had very little time left. Her thus far resilient body would take only so much more before ceding the battle. Salter walked towards her car to await backup. Then the back door opened.

Chapter Sixty-One

Ava watched as Wesley O'Rourke was bundled into a police car and taken to the station for processing. Her mother was being picked up by the funeral home first thing in the morning. No autopsy was necessary given the illness she'd been suffering. A doctor had already signed the death certificate. Ava's family was gathering to begin the process of mutually supportive grieving and planning, but her place was here. She finally knew it was what her mother would have wanted. Alexina O'Rourke's life might still be saved. Not that her bastard of a husband was going to give them any information that might help find her. Callanach was on the phone passing over the scant information they'd obtained as officers tore through the house looking for more clues.

'Get Salter on the line,' Callanach ordered. There was a pause. 'She's not supposed to be anywhere but in the incident room.' Another break as he listened to whatever excuse was being given. 'Well, you can tell PC Biddlecombe from me that my officers aren't supposed to be chasing around checking on elderly ladies who've missed the local tea party. Get me Tripp right now.'

'Where's DC Salter gone?' Ava asked him.

Callanach covered the mouthpiece with his hand. 'One neighbour reported another as missing. Not answering the door, probably a medical situation. There were no other officers available to cover it given the situation in the city.' He turned his attention back to the phone. 'Tripp, this is Callanach, I've texted you an email address. Cross-reference it with everything else we've got on today's events and see if we can get into Sem Culpa's emails.'

'No email address for Grom, sir?'

'Apparently not. His name didn't appear on the data list. We're no further forward finding him. Get working on Sem Culpa and have someone else check with forensics to see if they've got anything else from the elbow skin yet,' Callanach said.

Ava watched Callanach firing instructions into the phone. He was utterly decisive in action. Not bossy or overconfident, just focused. He'd been with Police Scotland and working with her for only nine months, yet she'd come to recognise the tiny indicators that he was worried, stressed, tired or amused. The way one side of his mouth twitched slightly before he was about to make a joke, the straightening and flexing of his fingers when he was working out a problem in his head which also meant he was itching to get out a cigarette. She'd long since stopped noticing how attractive he was, seeing it these days only in the reactions of others. Waitresses took longer than necessary checking orders when she was eating with him, people on the street occasionally did a double take. In a bar, he could create a space with just a smile. What she really liked about him was that he was largely unaware of it all. His neighbour Bunny was smitten, if a little bruised at the fact that Callanach didn't feel the same way. Ava felt herself reddening at the memory of their conversation, the woman having shared much

404

more than Ava had wanted to hear. She'd felt something else, too, during that conversation, having to listen to the description of how Callanach had held her and touched her. A niggling in the pit of her stomach, a sensation she was entirely unused to. Something she wasn't even prepared to name.

'Ava,' Callanach said. She realised she'd been caught staring. He put a hand on her shoulder and she flinched. 'You all right?' he asked.

'Sure,' she said. 'Miles away. What's happening?'

'Tripp's on it. What's happening in the house?'

'The IT specialist has arrived to see what we can get from Wesley's laptop. We should go back in,' Ava said.

The IT officer looked about fifteen. O'Rourke's laptop was wired into both a police computer and a small solid-looking block they were dismissively informed was a hard drive.

'Don't touch anything,' the IT woman said. 'I'm firing it up.'

She switched on O'Rourke's laptop. Callanach half expected it to explode or begin some sort of Bond-esque countdown. As it happened, there was nothing except a solitary beep and a flashing box asking for a password.

'Shit,' IT woman muttered, typing crazily, hitting the enter key periodically, and breathing more heavily than was healthy.

'What's happening?' Ava asked.

'The password's not limited by the number of attempts I make to enter it correctly – that I could have cheated. I bet it's keystroke-based . . .'

'Meaning?' Callanach asked.

'Meaning it'll forgive the odd slip as you type in your password, but starting with the wrong letter repeatedly, for example, will . . .' IT woman sighed.

The screen went black. The fan inside the laptop slowed to silence.

'It's all on the cloud, right?' Ava asked. 'I mean, wherever the website is, the information will still be there. We just have to find another way in.' IT woman stared at Ava as if she'd suggested that the design of the wheel might work equally well as a square. 'I take it that's a no,' Ava said.

'Ava, I need a favour and it's a big one.' He took her gently by the arm and led her away from less understanding ears. 'Could you speak to Joe? I need Paulson to be allowed access to his computer. When Lance phoned me the police raid at Ben's was in motion. The last thing he did was give me Sem Culpa's email address. If Ben got that, the chances are he also got other information. Without Ben, we haven't got a chance.'

'He'll be under arrest by now, Luc,' Ava said. 'Joe won't let anyone anywhere near him.'

'Ava, I know this crosses a line but there's a life depending on it.'

She thought about it, wondering why it felt such an impossible task. The sad truth was that her instinct was not to be beholden to her fiancé to such an extent.

'I'll try,' she said. 'Give me five minutes to make the call.'

Chapter Sixty-Two

Sem Culpa was rigging the winch. It was heavier than she'd expected and her back was already sore, plus she was having to tolerate the woman blubbing constantly in the background. She was unused to such annoyance. Sim Thorburn hadn't had time to so much as whimper. Michael Swan hadn't troubled her at all from the second he'd seen the photo of his precious wife outside their house. Alexina O'Rourke, however, had turned out to be a crier.

'Would you shut up?' Sem Culpa screamed as she hauled and tied ropes.

'Tell me what you're doing,' Alexina sobbed. 'What's that for?'

'It's a gift,' she smiled as she hooked up the massive rope sack and checked the distance she could raise or lower it using the winch handle.

'I don't want a gift,' Alexina dribbled as she shouted, the drugs not quite out of her system yet, rendering her limp on the floor. It saved having to chain her up during the final stages, Sem Culpa thought. Hadn't stopped her making a noise though, and Sem Culpa was bored of being distracted. She walked over, digging deep in her overalls' pocket and grabbing a roll of duct tape.

'The gift, stupid, is for me. A little offering to mark my going away. Something to get my holiday started. And you,' she ripped off a long section of silver tape, wrapping it around the back of Alexina's head all the way across her mouth and back into her hair the other side, 'can help get me in the mood for some rest and relaxation, by staying nice and quiet.'

Sem Culpa patted the top of Alexina's head as she walked away, leaving her whistling in and out of nostrils still clogged with the remnants of vomit. She stretched her neck and shoulders, preparing for the final tasks. There was a vat to fill with water, and it would take a while to get it sufficiently full for her purposes. Then she'd need the generator working. Nothing was going to go to plan without electricity.

Chapter Sixty-Three

'The police are on their way,' Salter said. 'There'll be units here any minute. The best thing you can do is let the knife go.' Salter glanced at Gladys Talthwaite, fearful that at any moment the kitchen knife would slice the papery skin of her neck.

'She deserve to die,' Grom said. 'She moan, she spit at me. You sit down!' he yelled as Salter tried to get up from the kitchen chair.

'All right,' Salter said, her voice not rising a notch. 'I'm sitting back down. What can I do to help you? Whatever you want, I can arrange it for you.'

'Already ruined. Everything lost,' he said, moving towards the hallway, positioning both the knife and Gladys so that Salter could not mistake the imminent threat.

'There's always something,' Salter said. 'You're here for a reason. I don't want to hurt you. I just need to see if we can find a way to end this. My name is Christie. The lady you're holding is Gladys. What shall I call you?'

He was huge, Salter saw, as he blocked the doorway from the kitchen with his sheer bulk. The crushing injuries to Helen Lott made much more sense. Looking at him, Salter was surprised he'd bothered using the furniture. He could easily have killed her with his bare hands. Probably with just one of them. Salter glanced around. Piles of wood had been thrown into untidy stacks in the hallway. Four coils of rope hung from coat hooks on the wall and below them a can of petrol sat half in, half out of a carrier bag on the floor. If nothing else, a fire would be an effective way of ridding the house of his DNA and any trace evidence of his time there. The worse case scenario was that the fire was intended for something more than just the destruction of evidence.

'Police lady, come with me,' Grom said, grabbing a rucksack from the hallway and dropping Gladys in a heap as he shoved a few items of clothing into it. Salter held a hand out to Gladys and Grom flashed the knife at her. 'No, you no touch.'

'She must be in shock,' Salter said. 'It would be better for you if she didn't die. Would you let me put a blanket around her shoulders? Or you could, if you don't want me near her.'

'She need die,' Grom shouted, allowing himself a quick kick to Gladys' legs. 'Bitch,' he added.

Salter didn't like the way the woman barely flinched. Her eyes were only half open and her head was nodding forwards. There were two large bandages around each of her arms, and a smaller one around her right hand. All were bloodied and dirty, but better than nothing. At least an effort had been made to control the bleeding. A meaty, ripe smell indicated how little washing of bodies, clothes or anything else had taken place in the last five days.

There were no sirens yet, that was all Salter could think about. It wouldn't take Grom long to be ready to leave. She tried not to think about what he was capable of, forcing herself to concentrate on the kitchen, spying out anything that might prove a useful weapon. All the cutlery had long since been hidden away. There wasn't so much as a frying pan handy.

Grom was rummaging around noisily in the lounge, casting an eye back into the corridor every few seconds. The clanking of tools accompanied his frenzied packing.

Salter took the opportunity to put an arm around Gladys and assess her condition. 'Gladys,' Salter whispered, 'Gladys, if you can hear me, turn your head to me. Don't try to get up. It'll be all right. Help will be here soon.'

Gladys turned her head a fraction and Salter could see the lobeless ear, crusted with dried blood and oozing a watery yellow fluid that had crystallised in her white hair. It was a miracle that Gladys Talthwaite was still alive. Or perhaps sheer bloody-mindedness. Like her own grandmother, Salter thought, Gladys was of a generation raised to smile through poverty and fight like hell when called upon.

'I need the bathroom,' Salter said, wondering if there might be anything more resemblant of a weapon in the loo.

'Do what old woman do,' Grom said, walking back into the kitchen with his coat on. 'Piss where you sit.'

'I need more than a pee though,' Salter explained.

Grom glared, checked his watch, and stormed towards her. He grabbed her by the arm. 'You not lock door,' he said. 'Fast.'

Salter took the few steps into the bathroom as a distant sound, almost imperceptible, hit the air like mechanical birdsong. She glanced at Grom before shutting the door, praying he hadn't heard it, but his face had tightened.

'You shit later,' he said, shoving the bathroom door fully open and grabbing Salter by the hair. He adjusted his backpack, carrying a tool roll in his free hand, rushing towards the back door. In her palm she concealed a metal nail file she'd found abandoned beneath the bathroom sink, sliding most of it up her sleeve. It wasn't much, but it was all she could find.

As Grom checked the windows, looking to see which direction they would come from, Salter tried not to think about

411

her baby. She didn't want Grom's hands on her, bringing bacteria and defilement to her skin. It took just one moment for her to dismiss any idea of pleading for her daughter's life. A man like this, so distantly related to the rest of humanity, what would he care for the innocent life inside her? And worse than that, her darker fear, that he might hurt the baby deliberately, get some perverse kick out of it. Salter offered a silent deal to the god she had long since ceased believing in, and waited for an opportunity to get Gladys Talthwaite, her unborn baby and herself out alive.

Chapter Sixty-Four

'I appreciate that DCI Edgar is busy,' Ava said, waiting for the inevitable further suggestions. 'Yes, I have tried his mobile.' She was sitting in her car outside Wesley O'Rourke's house wishing she wasn't making the call. Or at least wishing she didn't feel like such an idiot doing it. 'No, the point is that I know he can't be reached, and leaving a voicemail message won't work. I need you to go into the interview room and get him out.'

'Sorry ma'am, but I can't do that,' some cardboard cut-out version of Joe told her. 'And to be honest,' the volume of the voice dropped considerably, 'I don't think you'd want to speak to him at the moment . . .'

'Yup, got it,' Ava said. 'He's busy. I, however, have a missing woman presumed about to be pretty fucking dead, so get DCI Edgar on this phone right now.'

There was silence then the sound of a door opening, voices, the receiver muffled but not enough to drown out the string of expletives, then Joe's voice. Ava took a deep breath.

'Joe,' she said. 'I know what you're in the middle of, but I understand you have a man named Ben Paulson in custody.'

'I can't do this now,' Edgar said, his tone a shade away from fury.

'We need him, Joe. He might be able to access website files that will help us locate a missing woman . . .' Ava persisted.

'Do you have any idea what I'm going through? Do you even care?'

'This isn't about you, Joe. The man you're holding is the only person with the skills to save her life.'

'And you want me to put him on a computer so that he could potentially log back into his own files and wipe whatever evidence still exists.'

'It's not the way I'd have chosen it, but isn't that a risk worth taking to save a life?'

'Meaning that my career and my investigation are somehow worth less than yours. It's only data and numbers so it doesn't matter, is that what you think?'

'I think you're being an ignorant dick, if you really want to know. You know what's at stake here. It could have been anyone who was taken. Would you be this unhelpful if it was me waiting to be rescued from this psychopath?'

There was only a heartbeat of a pause, but it was there. The tiniest splinter of glass that would never be pulled out of the finger, Ava thought. It would always sting, no matter how many years might pass.

'Of course not,' Joe's voice came softly now. 'But you don't understand, Ava. There's a lot of pressure on me from people who won't be sympathetic if I let Paulson back on a computer. And once he's there pressing keys, we won't be able to control what he's accessing. There was an incident, a bit of a cock-up to be honest, during the arrest. It may be that . . .'

'Joe,' Ava cut him off. 'Yes or no. Are you going to let Paulson help us or not?'

'Once we've downloaded all the evidence from his files, got

414

everything backed up and checked, I'll give you access to him. You can ask him to do whatever you need at that point.'

'Hours, right? You're talking hours. Not just five minutes?' Ava checked.

'Of course hours,' Joe snapped. 'This stuff is incredibly complicated. Have you listened to nothing I've told you?'

'Alexina O'Rourke will be dead within a couple of hours, maybe less. Are you willing to let that happen while we wait for you to get what you need?'

'Ava, you need to take responsibility for your own investigation. Don't try the guilt card with me. If Ben Paulson is your last hope, then maybe you need to think about why the Major Investigation Team has so few leads.'

She hung up.

DC Tripp was trying to ignore the conversations in the corridor from various members of the Cyber Crime Unit, in order to focus on his own job. All he had to work with was one email address and vague descriptions of a woman driving away from the general area of Alexina O'Rourke's house in a new-looking four-by-four. DS Lively walked in.

'Sir, how many car hire outlets are there around the city, do you think?' Tripp asked.

'Maybe a dozen' Lively said. 'Why?'

'Because if that was our killer in the four-by-four, then it's unlikely she drove it to Scotland. This has all been impromptu depending on where she needed to go and what she needed to carry,' Tripp said, already searching a list of rental companies.

'And if she'd bought it from a dealer she'd have needed all sorts of ID and a bank account. They'd have got suspicious if she'd handed over that much cash,' Lively finished for him. 'There aren't that many four-by-fours for rental. It's mainly saloons or smaller cars. Let's get phoning.'

Ten minutes later they had a complete list of rented out four-by-fours. Tripp double-checked the details against the email address Callanach had given him and came up blank. None of the names were foreign and they had no mobile numbers for reference. Tripp dropped his head onto the desk.

'That's another waste of time, then,' Lively said. 'I'm heading back over to the O'Rourkes'. Call me if you come up with anything else.' He was slipping his arms into his jacket as PC Biddlecombe ran in, skidding as she rounded the corner and barrelling into Lively's legs. 'What the hell?' he shouted, picking her up from the floor. 'Would you mind yourself, ya dozy . . .'

'It's Christie Salter,' Biddlecombe shouted. 'I didn't take the call. There are uniformed units on their way. I didn't know when I sent her over there.'

Lively took her by the shoulders and held her still while she calmed down.

'Get a grip, constable,' Lively said. 'Where's Salter and what's happened?'

'I asked her to check a missing person report while everyone else was out. The control room got a call a while ago from a lady in the same road. Didn't make much sense. She just said the policewoman had asked her to get help.'

'The uniformed patrols are on their way, right? And we've no information that anyone's injured or in any danger. Salter'll be fine,' Lively said, letting go of Biddlecombe's shoulders. Biddlecombe wasn't ready to be released though, gripping Lively's sleeves as he turned away.

'No, sir. I made a follow-up call. The neighbour didn't mention it when she first phoned in, but DC Salter asked for backup when she learned that the missing woman is a retired lollipop lady.'

The silence began with Lively and moved from person to person like a virus until the whole office was still and staring. Tripp was the first one to break.

'Address,' he shouted at Biddlecombe. She held out a piece of paper in reply. He snatched it. Lively was right behind him. 'Let Callanach know,' Tripp yelled. 'And email him the document on my screen at the same time.'

They ran.

Ava was jogging back across the road when Callanach took the call. She'd stayed put after her conversation with Joe, having to remind herself that her mother had died earlier that day, justifying why she was at work instead of with her family. Avoiding asking herself why – even allowing for all the craziness and wrong-footedness – Joe still hadn't asked her if she was doing okay. And now she had to explain to Luc that her fiancé was more intent upon securing a conviction in a theft case than helping save a woman's life. She felt ill.

Callanach shouted to a uniformed officer, giving brief instructions which had the constable sprinting into the house, before getting back on his mobile. Ava hurried her pace, choosing her words.

'Luc,' she said, 'I spoke to Joe . . .'

'No time,' Callanach replied. 'Get in my car. Salter seems to have found Helen Lott and Emily Balcaskie's killer.' He started the car and slammed his foot down on the accelerator.

'Salter?' Ava said. 'She was supposed to stay at the station.' An officer ran to stand in the middle of the road, waving a piece of paper as Callanach performed a tyre-shredding three-point turn. Ava wound her window down and grabbed the sheet as they went past. 'He'll kill her.'

'Look down that list,' Callanach said. 'Those are details of four-by-fours matching the rough age and description of the one seen leaving the road behind Alexina O'Rourke's house.'

She knew he wasn't being cruel or dismissive, and that focusing on the job at hand was the only way to use her energy constructively, but the words kept moving in front of her eyes. Ava took a deep breath, forced herself to concentrate, started at the top again and studied each entry.

It was there in the back of her mind, the first clue that something didn't fit, and it still took another five passes up and down the list of email addresses before it hit her.

'Dot pt,' she said, her thumbs tapping furiously on the screen of her mobile.

'What?' Callanach asked, but Ava was already dialling a number, one finger against her lips to quieten him.

After introducing herself and making some preliminary enquiries, she began making notes.

'And she picked the car up when?' Ava asked. 'Last night. You use a vehicle tracking system presumably? Locate that car right now and call me back.' She turned to Callanach. 'You don't notice it in the list at first because the name doesn't stand out. I think the email address Sem Culpa used was paula@brisket.pt. The pt part indicates that the email provider is Portuguese. Paula turns out to be the surname she hired the car in, not a first name. Pretty common in parts of Europe.'

Ava's phone rang again and she scribbled down GPS co-ordinates as Callanach pulled over.

'Do you have a location for the car?' Callanach asked.

'Yes, but Salter is almost certainly in the hands of a monster. All I have is a hunch that a Portuguese email address might belong to Alexina's O'Rourke's abductor. I could be completely wrong. Either way, you'll have to decide. I have no faith in my judgement any more.'

Chapter Sixty-Five

Gladys had remained on the floor as Grom dragged Salter to the front window to check if the police were pulling up. The siren, however, had done nothing more than tail off into the distance. Salter wasn't sure if she was relieved or disheartened. At least Grom had relaxed his hold on her once he seemed certain he had not yet been discovered. Grom took one last look around and changed position to lead Salter by the wrist instead. She felt a jolt of panic before he selected the hand without the nail file. It wouldn't do much damage, but aimed correctly into an eye, up his nose, or into his ear, she could cause sufficient pain to buy her and Gladys the moments they needed to get out. After that, she had no plan. Adrenalin would do the rest, she reckoned.

'Keys,' Grom said, checking the landscape beyond the back door. 'Where?'

'In my pocket,' Salter said, one option for a getaway disappearing unless she could get them back once she had him at a disadvantage. Grom reached into her trousers and took them.

'We go,' he said, tugging open the door. Gladys had crawled into the kitchen and was in a huddle on the floor, clutching her hands around her stomach. 'You, old lady, I let you live. Is more funny than kill you.'

Gladys spat at him, a huge mouthful of saliva that sprayed down the right leg of his trousers, as if she'd been saving it up for precisely that moment. For a second he managed to maintain his motion towards the door, then he shook his head, swung his body round, took a step back towards Gladys, dragging Salter with him. He raised his free left fist high above his head, taking aim, snarling as he brought the vast flesh and bone hammer down to strike.

Salter knew that the force of the blow would be enough to end Gladys' debilitated existence. She waited until he was ready to deliver the battering, keeping her back towards him and her stomach out of harm's way, steadying her body to absorb the shock, her shoulder barging into the space between Grom and Gladys' head. She made it, too. Salter's body filled the space between attacker and would-be victim at exactly the moment Gladys Talthwaite anticipated the attack.

The old woman's arm lashed forward faster than Salter could see, harder than she would have thought possible from someone who looked so frail. In her hand Gladys held half a cat food bowl, ceramic, smashed into a spike several inches long.

The force of Grom's movement pushed Salter forward and down towards Gladys, full-tilt onto the out-held spike. Salter did her best to avoid the old woman, knowing as she fell sideways that something was wrong, but not what. Her first thought was that Gladys was hurt in spite of her efforts to save her, because the colour red had sprayed across Gladys' face and the wall either side. The bloody spray had cast a line so sharp it might have been made with a ruler, only ruined when the drips began to run. Gladys screamed, then Grom let Salter go. She fell, her legs drained of strength, her hands reaching for her stomach rather than saving her face from its inevitable meeting with the wall.

'Crazy mad bitch,' Grom shouted, kicking Gladys so hard that Salter heard the woman's thigh bone snap like kindling. 'I needed her. No good now.'

And still Salter couldn't understand what had happened. Her legs were warm and wet, Gladys and Grom's faces appeared above hers, and at the edge of her vision black stars were fading in and out. Then Grom was gone and the room spun. A car started up outside. The pain rolled in.

Gladys was on the floor next to her, their faces hard against the filthy linoleum, seeming to slip and slide against the daylight. The old woman was clutching her chest, her face pinching, whitening. Salter wondered why she couldn't remember the lady's name any more. It hurt so much. Her poor stomach. There was something she had to remember. Something she needed to protect. Only it was too late.

She tried to speak. There was a name she wanted the chance to say out loud before it was too late. A name she and her husband had chosen in the small hours, holding hands in the dark and whispering about the extraordinary love they had for a tiny life not yet fully formed. But Salter's mouth couldn't form the word. It was all she could do to breathe.

'Christie,' a man said from a million miles away and yet a face appeared right in front of her. 'Paramedics, right now!' Then there were hands all over her, moving clothing to one side, fumbling at her stomach, what sounded like a sob. Someone picked up her head, sliding legs beneath her so she was resting on his lap.

'There now, Salter, what did I tell you about staying out of trouble, girl?' She willed her eyes open, Detective Sergeant Lively's face swimming above her.

'It's that bad?' she whispered.

'What are you talking about, Constable? You'll be back at work tomorrow,' he smiled.

She shook her head as the world fell away, the only sound she could hear the swell and break of the waves of blood through her ears.

'Never been this nice to me before, Sarge,' she tried to say. It came out as the soft, slow expulsion of a breath that was too much effort. Her head slipped sideways. 'The baby . . .'

'Salter, Christie . . . stay with me, sweetheart!' Lively shouted. The nail file slipped unnoticed from her sleeve to the floor.

In the noise and tumult of the fading kitchen, one paramedic made a time of death announcement.

Chapter Sixty-Six

'This road layout doesn't even vaguely resemble what the satnav is telling us,' Ava moaned as Callanach performed a jolting three-point turn.

'Most of this is industrial land. If the GPS coordinates from the car Sem Culpa hired are right, then she's taken it off the road network,' Callanach said. He pulled over, zooming in on the satnav screen and looking around. 'It must be to the right of this road. Left takes us towards the dual carriageway and there are no turn-offs. If she'd parked along this road we'd have seen her car by now.'

'Up here,' Ava said, tapping the screen. 'You can see the outline of the buildings but there's no access road on the map.'

Callanach crunched the gears and the car jerked away, tyres protesting. Quarter of a mile later they made a right-hand turn onto a road that had long since ceased being used, its crumbling tarmac punctured by weeds and roots. An old signpost gave away no information, rust having eaten the words it once held. They bumped slowly down the track towards the cluster of industrial buildings that sat almost entirely out of sight of the main road.

'These must be the right coordinates. The car hire company

said they check all their GPS transmitters between each hire to avoid thefts. It's somewhere nearby,' Ava said.

Callanach stopped the car a few minutes' walk from the buildings.

'We'll have to go the rest of the way on foot. If Sem Culpa is here, she'll hear the engine if I drive any closer. Just let me call our position in,' Callanach said.

'You know, if I'm wrong we'll be diverting units from Salter,' Ava said.

'The rest of the team will be there with Salter. They won't let her down. But if you're right we'll need backup and para-medics,' Callanach said. He made the call, gave a lights and sirens off command, and asked for all units to be notified that they were in pursuit of Thorburn and Swan's killer. No one who attended the scene was to be left in any doubt how dangerous the target was. Then they began to jog towards the closest of the vast grey buildings.

'I can't see the four-by-four.' Ava looked around.

'She wouldn't have left it in plain sight, and we're still two buildings away. If it were me, I'd have driven round the back, even if I didn't think I was being tracked.'

It was a short run to the large red-brick building, several storeys high, that was partially masked from them by newer but equally abandoned buildings. An attempt at commencing demo-lition had been made then stopped halfway through, leaving tangled piles of steel and concrete rubble. The first sign of activity was the hum of the generator.

'Someone's here,' Ava said, switching her phone to silent and pulling a taser from her pocket. They rounded the final corner before the four-by-four came into sight. It had been reversed up to a building, its rear door left open and a large tarpaulin lying on the ground as if the contents of the boot had been tipped out in a hurry.

'You weren't wrong,' Callanach said. 'Stay here. I'll find a way in at the front. Give me exactly two minutes then move. Okay?'

Ava nodded, then Callanach was gone and she counted down the seconds on her watch, inching closer to the side of the building. Inside, the noises were industrial – clanging, buzzing, dragging – then a voice. It was female with inflection not dissimilar to Callanach's, and a laugh that made Ava recall a statement about Sim Thorburn's murder. Some Dutch woman in the crowd had talked about laughter, noted its quality as – Ava struggled to remember the exact word – malicious. That was it. And here, Ava was sure, was the woman who had danced through that crowd with a blade as sharp as the mind who'd conceived the killing.

Thirty seconds to go. Ava ducked low and edged closer to the rear door, crouching down on one knee as she peered through the crack left by a thick hose pipe that ran inwards from an outside tap. A few leaks were visible along the length of the hose, the puddles drying out quickly in the evening sun. The light was dying too, and as the last few seconds passed before Callanach was due to be in position, a flood of beams was cast out from inside the building, blinding Ava's view of what she was walking into. Ava set her left foot against the door, kept the taser in her right hand and moved in.

It was Callanach's face that stopped Ava in her tracks, the sheer horror on it.

'Stay where you are!' Ava shouted, struggling to make sense of what she was looking at in the glare of lights.

Sem Culpa – no mistaking her given the circumstances – had obviously overcome her own shock at being discovered. The smile on her face was as much information as Ava needed to see how the situation was going to play out.

'Two of you, then,' Sem Culpa said, releasing the rope in her hand a bit, causing a sack suspended from the ceiling to sway. Ava followed the line of the rope upwards to where it was fed through a winch mechanism, at the end of which was a rope sack. Ava took a step forward, straining her eyes to figure out what was inside it. 'You want a closer look? Come on in.' Sem Culpa, wearing combat trousers and a strappy black T-shirt, unholstered the gun she'd had at her side and waved Ava forward into the ring of lights. From there, everything became clear. Inside the rope sack was a woman bundled freakishly into a naked shivering ball. Steaming beneath her was a vat of water, a throwback to the days when the tannery used to process animal skins. The smell was still in the air, caught forever in the fabric of the building, reinvigorated by the water vapour.

'We've already called reinforcements,' Callanach said. 'You're under arrest. Stop now. Make it easier for yourself.'

'Oh, fuck off,' Sem Culpa said. 'The camera's running and I have limited time, so call your friends and tell them to stay away, or I'll shoot both of you as well as little miss whiny up there.'

To illustrate her point, she let the rope drop even further. Alexina screeched and jolted in the rope sack. Neither Ava nor Callanach touched their radios, staring at each other across the ring of lights and rigging.

'Okay then, this is what will happen every time you don't do as I say,' Sem Culpa said, pointing the gun at Callanach's head. 'Watch.'

Ava took half a step forward as the rope slid through Sem Culpa's hands. Alexina screamed again, sobbing hard as the sack came to a halt.

'Don't do this,' Ava said. 'You were played. The man controlling that website set the whole thing up. The woman in the sack up there is his wife. You don't have to give him what he wants.'

'Wesley?' a small voice croaked from deep within the tangled sphere of human limbs.

'They're lying,' Sem Culpa shouted in the direction of the writhing sack. 'Your husband? A middle-class man, living in a suburban house, with a wife and a greenhouse and flowery goddamn curtains! Your husband did not conceive this.'

'It was all about money,' Callanach said, taking a step in. 'The O'Rourkes have a prenuptial agreement which means he'll get nothing from a divorce. Alexina was about to donate a multi-million pound inheritance fund to charity. Her husband wanted her dead before that happened. He needed an alibi for the murder and circumstances where we wouldn't even think to investigate his private life. He used you and Grom to guarantee the police wouldn't consider him a suspect.'

Sem Culpa didn't flinch as she aimed the gun towards Callanach and shot just centimetres in front of his toes. The impact sent rubble flying off the floor towards his face. His feet scrambled, his body off balance, and he went down hard onto his back. He screamed. Sem Culpa kept the gun pointed at his head, tied the end of the rope around the winch handle and strode over to where Callanach was writhing on the floor.

'Get up,' she said. 'I need some security, and you appear to be injured. I like that.'

She pointed the gun directly at Callanach's forehead and kicked his chest. He rolled over and stood halfway up. His coccyx was a burning line of pain from the base to the top of his spine. It was all he could do to stagger.

'All right,' Ava said, keeping the hand with the taser in the air and slowly withdrawing her mobile with the other. She speed-dialled the station. 'This is DI Turner. All units to remain outside the perimeter of the site,' she said. 'This is an active hostage situation. No one is to approach. Confirm order.' The control room confirmed.

427

'Good,' Sem Culpa said, pushing Callanach to his knees between the camera tripod and the water vat. 'Now throw in your phone,' she told Ava. The water hissed as the plastic hit it, sending up a spray of boiling spit and steam. 'The taser, too.'

'No chance,' Ava said. 'If I'm going to throw it in the water, I might as well take a shot first and see what I hit.'

Sem Culpa laughed, looking into the camera that was flashing red for the live broadcast. With a finger on the trigger of the gun that was pushed into Callanach's head, she began to unwind the rope from the winch handle and let the rope sack glide towards the water.

'No, no, no,' Alexina O'Rourke began to screech, her hands grasping the upper ropes of the mesh, doing all she could to defy the gravity that was pulling her towards the scalding water below.

'Hold that rope or I'll use the taser,' Ava shouted.

'Taser me, my muscles will spasm and I'll drop the bag anyway. I will also squeeze the trigger involuntarily. You'll be killing your own colleague, and I shouldn't want to damage such a pretty piece of flesh. Are you screwing him?' Sem Culpa asked, letting the rope slide another foot before catching it again. 'I would be if I were you.'

'Please, please no, please don't,' Alexina screamed.

'Then there's the possibility of the sack dropping into the water and you missing your target. I wonder what would happen if the taser ended up in the water with the woman. I hadn't thought of that . . .'

'We can get you out of here,' Ava said. 'Safe passage, a helicopter, whatever you want.'

'You know what I really don't like?' Sem Culpa smiled. 'Being lied to.'

The rope slid, Ava dropped the taser and ran forward reaching desperately over the edge of the vat. Callanach pulled his head up to watch and was met with the whip of a gun barrel across his cheekbone.

Ava held her breath. There was a fragment of time filled with sounds that belonged only in a kitchen, of raw food meeting hot liquid, the popping, sizzling, crackling of flesh broiling. Alexina O'Rourke gave voice to the monstrous agony that was eating away at her legs.

Ava had to back away. The splashing water from Alexina's desperate kicks was burning Ava's face and hands.

'Not too fast, we need visuals,' Sem Culpa said, hauling the rope downwards in order to raise Alexina's legs up out of the water. The flesh was crimson, almost glowing in the harsh lighting, her skin hanging off in flayed strips. Ava was grateful that Alexina was now unconscious. Her head was lolling to one side, her lips crushed against a strand of the rope so her tongue could be seen bleeding and swollen where she'd bitten through it.

'Get her out of there,' Ava said. 'You've proved what you're capable of. No more.'

'One step forward and I shoot his head off. She's going to die anyway and you're boring me.' Sem Culpa stared into the camera. 'Enjoy,' she whispered, unwinding her hand from the rope for the last time, holding it only with her fingertips as she moved back, keeping her face out of range of the oncoming scalding splashes.

The man appeared from nowhere, flying in from beyond the ring of lights. Sem Culpa tripped forward, her knees colliding with Callanach's back, dropping the gun as she crashed into the side of the vat. The rope slid from her hands and the sack containing Alexina O'Rourke went into free fall towards the inevitable death waiting below. Callanach jumped for the end of the rope as Ava leapt to get her hands on the weapon skittering across the floor. The rope was disappearing too fast, slipping through his hands. Callanach put one foot on the ledge of the vat to give his body a prop for the force he needed to grasp the rope. At his feet, Sem Culpa and the unknown man continued to fight oblivious.

'I can't hold it!' Callanach shouted to Ava. She gave up her search for the gun and sprinted towards Callanach, jumping onto the ledge and grabbing the rope. He steadied her legs, too aware of what few centimetres she had to balance on with the weight of the sack working against her.

'Don't let me go,' Ava breathed.

'Who is he?' Callanach shouted, staring at the bodies writhing viciously on the floor.

The man was massive, his back rippling like a bull trying to throw an unwanted rider. As he turned, Callanach could see a multitude of stab marks across his face and chest, the dagger responsible for them clutched in Sem Culpa's hand.

'Luc, I can't hold her,' Ava shouted.

There was a roar from the male who had grabbed hold of Sem Culpa's feet and was dragging her towards the vat of water, babbling in a language Callanach couldn't understand, staring into the camera as he hauled her writhing body.

'That's Grom,' Callanach said. 'You've got to hold her, Ava. Just ten seconds more.'

'Luc, no, don't let go of me . . .' Ava's upper body tipped forward as Callanach released her legs. He sprinted into the darkness. The rope began to slip though her fingers as she shifted her weight to secure her position. Then Grom barged shoulder first into Ava's lower legs and Alexina headed for the boiling water.

Ava jumped upwards from the ledge, catching the end of the disappearing rope in her already slippery hands, burning her palms on the bristly fibres, clinging on for Alexina's life.

The rope sack stopped half in the water, with Alexina screaming as she regained consciousness, clambering upwards, lifting her body out of the water as she choked on the scalding steam.

Grom, dripping with blood from Sem Culpa's knife work, took her by the hair and thrust her head downwards into the vat as he shouted into the camera.

'You want show? Here – stronger always win – is me! I win!' he yelled, bringing Sem Culpa's head up for a second before plunging it down into the water again, this time ensuring he finished the job by planting his elbow in the nape of her neck.

Ava, swinging in mid-air, clung to the rope, her body weight insufficient to raise the sack more than a couple of feet above the water. Sem Culpa's arms and legs thrashed, then twitched, and finally lay still and useless.

'Raise your hands slowly, keep your feet still,' Callanach said, holding a gun to the side of Grom's head, 'you're under arrest.'

'No need be scared. I not fight,' Grom said. They could both hear the smile in his voice. 'I beat her.'

'On your knees,' Callanach said once Grom's hands were where he could see them. He called in the units standing by, their sirens echoing like a crying toddler through the darkness as they approached. 'Hold on Ava,' Callanach said. 'Just don't move.'

'Not going anywhere,' she whispered.

Suddenly there were police officers everywhere.

'Get DI Turner down, and make sure that rope's secured. The woman in the bag needs paramedics immediately.'

'They're on their way, sir,' a uniformed officer said, hand-cuffing Grom. Another hauled Sem Culpa's head out of the vat, far beyond the point where they needed to check her for a pulse. She was nothing more than faceless meat. Even after everything she'd done, the inhuman violence and suffering she'd caused, Callanach still found himself having to look away.

They swung Alexina back over the floor to safety, as they killed the generator to allow the water to cool. The lights died with it.

In the dark, a burning hand slipped into Callanach's and squeezed his fingers.

'Where's DC Salter?' Ava asked whoever could hear.

'DS Lively and DC Tripp are at the scene,' someone replied. 'The pathologist is there now although she's been told we need her here as soon as possible.'

The lights came on again. Ava took her hand back from Callanach's. Paramedics lifted Alexina O'Rourke onto a stretcher and began wheeling her out. Grom, no fewer than a dozen officers surrounding him, was escorted to a police car. Callanach's hand found his mobile but his fingers lacked the will to make the call and find out what had happened to Salter.

Chapter Sixty-Seven

Ava and Callanach were delivered to the Royal Infirmary shortly after Alexina O'Rourke. Superintendent Overbeck had insisted on medical examinations in a manner that was only just short of a threat that refusal would constitute actionable insubordination. No one had answered the calls that Callanach had finally had the stomach to make. The officers driving them had no more information. Ava had taken the front passenger seat, nursing her bleeding hands and staring out of the window.

Callanach had tried to sit normally on the back seat but ended up having to lie across it on his side. Whatever damage he'd done to his coccyx previously had faded into history compared to the pain he was now in. They were taken into Accident and Emergency through the ambulance entrance and seen at once. Callanach could hear Ava in the next cubicle as he was given painkillers and the standard humiliating gown to put on.

'No one's treating my hands until someone tells me what's happened to DC Salter,' Ava was saying.

'I'm Detective Constable Tripp,' Callanach heard from the corridor, 'and the DI will want to see me, even if he's in the middle of receiving treatment.'

'Let him in,' Callanach shouted. 'Tripp, I'm in here!'

The curtain opened and a pale-faced Max Tripp entered, his clothes spattered with blood. For the first few seconds he simply stood staring at the floor.

'Tell me,' Callanach said.

'DC Salter had no idea what she was walking into,' Tripp muttered. 'Once she realised the danger Gladys Talthwaite was in, she couldn't leave her. The neighbour was supposed to call for backup but didn't do a good enough job of explaining the circumstances, so the priority wasn't set high enough. By the time we arrived, Grom had already fled and both Salter and Mrs Talthwaite were down.'

'How did she die?' Callanach asked.

'Heart attack,' Tripp said. 'It was all too much for her.'

'A heart attack?' Callanach asked. 'But she was young and fit, even with the pregnancy . . .'

'I was talking about Mrs Talthwaite, sir, the medics called her time of death while we were at the scene.'

'For God's sake, Tripp, what happened to Salter? No one has told us anything.'

'She's in surgery now, that's why I'm here. DS Lively and I came in with her. We had no idea what was happening your end,' Tripp said. He sat down on the chair next to Callanach's bed, head in his hands. 'Christie lost the baby. There was a wound in her abdomen – she lost more blood than I'd thought was possible – we didn't think she'd make it here.'

'I have to tell DI Turner,' Callanach said, pulling himself up, wincing, pushing Tripp's hand away from his arm. 'Does Superintendent Overbeck know?'

'The super's just arrived. She went straight off to find a surgeon to get an update.'

★　★　★

Callanach shuffled one cubicle along to Ava who was in the middle of a phone call, giving lengthy instructions about how Grom should be processed until she could get back to the station. She took one look at Callanach's face and ended the call.

'Salter's alive but she's in surgery. It's touch-and-go,' he said.

'The baby?' Ava asked. Callanach shook his head. 'This bloody job takes absolutely everything,' she whispered. 'I should have been clearer with her. And I should have told everyone else that they weren't to allocate calls to her. If I'd just been a bit more . . .'

'She was on my squad, Ava. I wouldn't even have known she was pregnant if you hadn't pointed it out. It was one thing on top of another. None of us could have known how it would turn out,' Callanach said.

Superintendent Overbeck ripped back the curtain, stalking in and looking each of them up and down.

'Detective Constable Salter is in a critical condition. Her family has been notified. I gather you need an X-ray, DI Callanach. I've told the doctor you're to go to the top of the queue. Hands, DI Turner?' Ava held them out as if a schoolmistress had demanded a pre-lunch cleanliness check. 'Those burns are nasty, and I've never seen fingers quite that swollen. I need both of you back at the station as quickly as possible. Accept whatever treatment you're advised to take – I'm not having any lawsuits land on my table because of this – then come back in and interview Alfonz Kopitar.'

'Sorry, who?' Ava asked.

'The man who killed Helen Lott and Emily Balcaskie,' Overbeck said.

'Grom,' Callanach murmured. 'I'd almost forgotten he was human. It seems odd that he has a normal name.'

'He's the least of our problems,' Overbeck replied. 'We're

still holding Wesley O'Rourke who already has a lawyer and an attitude. I gather you reached the conclusion that he was somehow responsible for all this.'

'He is,' Callanach said.

'Then you'd better figure out a way to prove it, because time is not on our side. His lawyer says charge him or release him.' Callanach sighed. 'Other than that, I should thank you both for not fucking up so badly that Alexina O'Rourke also died. I'm afraid I can't see a way of being any more complimentary than that. Sort yourselves out, then close this case down. The station's a frigging war zone.'

Chapter Sixty-Eight

DC Tripp was making coffee when he was summoned to DCI Edgar in the Cyber Crime Unit incident room. Every desk was deserted. Tripp remained standing in the absence of an invitation to sit, as Edgar walked along lowering the blinds over the windows with a view into the corridor.

'DC Tripp,' Edgar said, his voice little more than a murmur. 'I'm going to give you a chance to accept what you did. If you tell the truth now, I'll settle for your badge and your career. Fuck with me one second longer than that and I'll have you charged.'

'Charged with what, sir?' Tripp asked.

'There's a long list. I'm not sure if you should be part of the overall conspiracy or if your end of it was merely obstructing the investigation. Either way, you've seen your last day as a serving police officer. So tell me, did you volunteer the information or did DI Callanach force you to hand it over?'

'Sir, I have no idea whatsoever . . .'

'Spare me the bollocks, Tripp,' Edgar threw the nearest chair. It spun and hit a glass pane, dragging half a blind down with it. 'Someone tipped Ben Paulson off. Polly reported that Paulson received a telephone call just as we were about to go in. Paulson shouted at his journalist friend to lock the door before we'd even knocked. There's no other way he could have known we were there. Only you had access to that information. Not one other officer from your force was involved. I told you right from the start what would happen if you breached confidentiality . . .'

'It wasn't me, sir. I knew you had an officer undercover but I never came into contact with them and I certainly didn't phone Ben Paulson,' Tripp said, aware that people going past were trying to see what the shouting was about.

'You were in the briefings, you had access to the files, you knew about the Below Par Cafe. Who the hell else could have done it?'

'It was me,' Ava said as she entered, walking over to fix the damaged blind. Callanach followed, closing the door behind them. 'I phoned Paulson and warned him. About the raid, about Polly, the whole lot. And you need to keep your voice down, DCI Edgar. The entire floor can hear everything you're saying and Tripp deserves better than that.'

'Stay out of this Ava, and don't you dare try to take the blame for this little faggot. My whole investigation is fucking ruined. Someone's going down for it, and if it has to be your band of mates here, so be it!'

'Then it'll be me,' Ava said, sitting down, keeping her voice low. 'I saw you with Polly, Joe. I wanted to talk to you so I followed you away from the station. You went towards Murrayfield, I got suspicious, saw the girl get into your car. I recognised her from the cafe and put two and two together. It wasn't difficult.'

'You're admitting deliberately going behind my back to wreck my investigation? What the fuck did you think you were doing? Is this about him?' Edgar pointed at Callanach who was staying well back. He had no intention of insulting Ava with any sort of macho standoff.

'It was about Ben Paulson. At the time he was our best lead and I was following you to discuss it. Paulson was doing his best to help catch two murderers. He doesn't deserve prison, Joe.'

'Have you completely lost your mind? Is this grief or is that what you're going to use as your excuse when I report you? Only I seem to remember you going through most of your life not giving a flying fuck about your mother, so it seems a bit of a stretch for you to play that card now.'

Ava stood up. Tripp looked away. Callanach concealed his fists in his pockets.

'If you're going to report me, Joe, then go ahead and do it. But understand that the whole thing comes out if you go down that path. I asked you for help. I phoned and requested access to Paulson to save a woman's life and you decided that your potential promotion was worth more.'

'Oh really?' Edgar said, taking a step closer to Ava, barely inches between their faces. She stood her ground. 'Only I don't recall that. There was a conversation. You were weeping, not making any sense. I told you I was concerned about you and that I thought you should withdraw from active duty immediately. You reassured me that you were fine and put the phone down.' He grinned, lowering his face the last short distance into hers. 'Don't ever threaten me again.'

'Oh Joe,' Ava sighed. 'I recorded it. I guess I knew what your reaction would be before I even dialled your number. I just needed to be able to listen to the conversation again later, when my head was clearer. To figure out if you and I . . .' she put a hand on his shoulder. 'It's not a threat, Joe. If you try to hurt me, or discredit Tripp or Callanach, I'll release the recording to the papers. And I'll take whatever comes my way for doing so. I'll lose my job, probably go to prison for revealing your undercover officer, but you'll face trial by press. And no one will want you anywhere near a public position again. It's over, Joe. You and me, this case. Move on to the next investigation. Your career will recover.'

Edgar brushed Ava's hand off his shoulder with an expression that suggested she might have some sort of disease, stepping back and looking around as if only just remembering there were other people in the room.

'You're actually choosing these two over me? Over us? I thought you had more going for you than that. The constable here is gay, and the pretty one in the corner couldn't get his dick hard if his life depended on it. Which one is it you think is going to hold your hand at your mother's funeral and keep you warm in bed afterwards?'

A silence rolled through the room like tumbleweed.

'You made this about sex?' Ava asked. There was no reply. Edgar's hands were balled at his sides, head down, breathing hard, nostrils flaring. Callanach took his hands out of his pockets and stepped forward, scared only that if he started punching he might forget how to stop. 'My best friend is gay. You never had a problem with Natasha.'

'It's different with women, that's just a bit of fun. It's unnatural for men,' Joe smiled. 'It's DI Callanach I was more interested in. Did you think I wouldn't have access to your files?' he asked Callanach. 'Your obligatory sessions with the Interpol psychologist before you'd served your notice made particularly interesting reading. Seems that girl you raped really got inside your head.'

'That's enough, Joe, we're finished,' Ava moved between them.

'Don't waste your time sticking up for him,' Joe smirked. 'An impotent rapist hardly seems your type.'

'His neighbour tells me differently,' Ava said. 'So whatever you read, you were ill informed. Now you need to leave this room, this police station and this city. Before something happens that can't be brushed under the carpet.'

'There's the matter of our engagement, in case you'd forgotten. And a ring that cost me the deposit on a new Porsche.'

'Oh bugger, yes, the ring,' Ava said, fumbling in her pocket. She held up a mangled lump of charred metal with a chunk of dull stone holding on by a couple of scraps. 'My hands got badly burned by the rope and the steam. They were so swollen that the doctor insisted that the ring had to be cut off. The stone will have kept its value though and I'm sure you can have the gold melted down. Apologies.' She picked up one of Joe's hands and dropped the mess of jewellery into it. 'You're a misogynistic, homophobic, arrogant, selfish moron. Feel free to tell everyone we know that I wasn't worthy of you, I really don't care. Just as long as I never, ever hear from you again.'

'Really? How about one more fuck for old times' sake, before I go?' Joe asked.

Callanach raised his fist, barging towards Edgar, bringing his arm crashing down towards his face. Ava turned and blocked the blow, sending Callanach off balance, pain spearing through his lower back as he sprawled across the floor.

'I'd have thought he'd have learned his lesson after the blanket party my boys threw him,' Edgar laughed. 'You didn't want him scarring his perfect fingers, Ava, is that it?'

'No, that's not it,' Ava said. 'It just seems to be my turn rather than his.' Ava ignored the throbbing in her hands, made the best fist she could manage given the bandages, and hit. The punch was dead on target, smashing into Edgar's solar plexus, driving the breath from his lungs, leaving him reaching for a chair to steady himself, staggering to the side.

'Get out, Joe,' Ava said. 'And count yourself lucky that Alexina O'Rourke is still alive. At least you don't have her blood on your hands.'

Chapter Sixty-Nine

Ava was nowhere to be found so Callanach had returned to his office and his stash of painkillers.

'Can we come in?' Ben asked from the corridor. He and Lance were stood at his door. They had the unkempt look of people who had recently been bundled into police vehicles and kept in rooms usually occupied by people with scant regard for hygiene. Lance was balancing on one leg, his other ankle wrapped in a hefty bandage.

'You'd better,' Callanach said. 'If you stand there looking that suspicious, someone will arrest you again.' They closed his door quietly. 'I assumed you were still in custody. What happened?'

'They couldn't get anything at all from my files. When DCI Edgar grabbed Lance all the wires were ripped out from my computer. I had it rigged to do a system wipe if it wasn't closed down properly. No evidence against me meant no evidence against my alleged co-conspirator here,' Ben said, looking at Lance.

'Can you retrieve anything from the darknet site, Ben? Anything at all that might help us convict Wesley O'Rourke for what he did?' Callanach asked.

'It'll be long gone,' Ben said, shaking his head. 'It's the same reason why Edgar needed to arrest me with my system up and running. Once the computer is shut down, the evidence isn't accessible. The website will be locked.'

'I'm sorry, Luc,' Lance said.

'*Vous aviez pas le droit*,' Callanach said, forgetting himself, retreating back into French as he tried not to raise his voice. 'You had no right.'

Ben took a step towards Callanach. 'That's not fair,' he said. 'You want to blame someone, blame me. If I hadn't been involved with The Unsung . . .'

'I knew what you'd done from the start,' Callanach said, 'but I expected you to think more clearly about the consequences,' he directed at Lance. 'Wesley O'Rourke organised the murders of four completely innocent people under the most horrific circumstances.'

'And the man next to me would have spent years of his life incarcerated after helping us. Alexina O'Rourke would likely be dead if Ben hadn't followed the trail her husband left. Did you want to spend the next decade visiting the man you were indebted to?' Lance asked.

'A murderer is going to walk free. We got precisely nothing from his laptop and everything else is just motive. It was all for money, Lance. He spilled all that blood for greed. Calling him a psychopath doesn't even start to describe him!' Callanach shouted.

'Do you think I'm unaware of the cost of what I did?' Lance yelled back. 'I've got to live with that every day for the rest of my life. But I'd make the same choice again tomorrow because when you get to my age, you realise the value of loyalty. Doing the right thing often comes at a cost. I'm of a generation that does not hang its friends out to dry, so find something else on Wesley O'Rourke.'

'You think it's that easy?' Callanach said. 'That there'll be a convenient bit of tax evasion lurking in the shadows, or that his DNA will miraculously pop up in relation to some unsolved crime? That's not how it happens.'

'Where is he now?' Ben asked.

'Still in custody,' Callanach said. 'We've got a couple of hours left to charge or release.'

'I have things to do.' Ben stood up. 'When this is over, maybe we could get a beer or something? All of us. Say thank you to DI Turner from me, would you Luc? If she hadn't phoned to warn me about Polly and the raid I'd be facing a couple of decades in prison. And it's not just me. There are members of The Unsung worldwide and all any of us are trying to do is a little bit of good. If Polly had got into my system, there'd be a lot of other people in trouble. Just shows what a sucker I was to let my guard down.'

'Was it Jane Austen who wrote, "We are all fools in love"? I think it was. Sorry how it worked out with Polly. You deserve better,' Lance said. 'I'll walk down with you.

Callanach took a deep breath. 'Thank you, both of you,' he said. 'I appreciate everything you did to help.'

Lance walked over to him, reaching an arm around Callanach's shoulders to pull him into a hug. 'We all did our best. You, me and Ben. At the end of the day, a life was saved. You have to try to see the positives.' He let go and retreated to Ben, who took Lance's arm to help him hobble out. Quietly, they left.

Callanach sat down wishing he had been more forgiving, wondering what he'd have done in Lance's place. There was a knock and DS Lively put his head round the door.

'Christie Salter is out of surgery. Thought you'd want to know,' Lively said.

'Is she stable?' Callanach asked.

'There's a good chance she'll survive,' Lively said. 'Her

husband's with her. He's a good man. I'd put money on her pulling through. Salter's a tough one.' Callanach put his head in his hands. Lively walked in, kicking the door shut, standing hands on hips. 'Cases go to shit sometimes. That's how this works. You can't save everyone, can't always get there in time. And no one gets extra luck just because their face should be on one of those crappy aftershave adverts.'

'Thanks for that, Sergeant,' Callanach said, wondering how things had gone so badly wrong that his bitter, sarcastic detective sergeant was offering words of consolation.

'Just sayin'. Get over yourself, sir. One murderer is dead, another's in custody. If Salter hadn't gone to Gladys Talthwaite's house, Grom wouldn't have stolen the police car and heard your location over the radio. Without him turning up, God knows what would have happened. You saved Mrs O'Rourke's life. Your team has worked every hour they could squeeze out of the standard twenty-four in a day. You owe us all a drink, is what I'm thinking.'

'Point taken, DS Lively. And I don't suppose you know where DI Turner is, do you?'

'Gone on leave, so I hear. Turns out her mother passed today.'

'Of course,' Callanach said. 'Get the team together, would you? You're right about that drink.'

Chapter Seventy

It was a Sunday when Ava rang to ask if she could visit him. Her voice was flatter than usual, and he'd had to restrain himself from asking if she was all right. How could she be? Her mother's funeral had come and gone, family and close friends only. Callanach had stayed away, giving Ava the distance she'd made it clear she needed. Even he had taken a few days off, surfacing only to pay his respects to the families of the victims as they were debriefed. No mention was made of Wesley O'Rourke's part in it, washed away into the realms of unconfirmed suspicion and speculation. Then there had been a visit to see Alexina O'Rourke, interrupting a session with the psychologist tasked with helping her come to terms with her new life. She would not walk again, the damage to her skin, flesh and tendons so severe that even with grafts the pain and stretching would make movement impossible. A lifetime of pain. It didn't bear thinking about. The disfigurement was a burden beyond what most people would find tolerable. She had asked only one question after Callanach had finished updating her about Sem Culpa and Grom. He'd expected her to want to know about her husband, or the trial process. But she'd asked something he hadn't seen coming.

'Assisted suicide's not likely to be made legal in Scotland any time soon, I'm guessing. Will my mother be safe from prosecution if she comes with me to Switzerland?'

Callanach had answered as best he could, trying to keep his responses impartial, emotionless but he'd emerged from that meeting to a world that looked grey in spite of the sunshine, cold in spite of the heat.

Voices from the hallway gave away Ava's presence and he opened the door to find her in animated conversation with Bunny.

'I'll let you go then,' Bunny said to Ava. 'And if you ever want your make-up done, just text me. We could have a girly evening together.'

'That would be nice, thank you,' Ava said. Callanach stood back to let her into his flat, waiting a moment to speak to Bunny.

'Before you go,' he said. 'I'm sorry. I didn't behave well. It's just—'

'No need,' Bunny said. 'Wouldn't have worked out anyway – I hate French food.' She managed a bright smile and gave him a kiss on the cheek. 'I can still knock though, if I have another power cut?'

'You can knock for anything at all,' Callanach said.

Ava was making a cafetiere of coffee by the time he walked back into his flat. He stood in the doorway to the kitchen and watched as she messed up every surface in a period of less than thirty seconds.

'You haven't checked your messages today, have you?' she asked, handing him two mugs which he assumed he had been designated to carry.

Callanach had been to the gym, on a strict regime of exercising only his arms until his coccyx was fully healed. His mobile had been on silent all morning.

'No one called my landline,' he said, setting the mugs on the table as Ava followed with milk and the coffee. 'It can't be that urgent.'

'Actually it's about Wesley O'Rourke,' Ava said. 'He's been arrested for possession and distribution of indecent images. They found it on his work email. Fairly serious stuff, by all accounts. He could get up to five years, and given the type of offences he'll be inside for, it won't be easy time either. He's completely denying it, Lively says. O'Rourke reckons it's a set-up, not that anyone's listening. Wouldn't have thought he was the type, personally.'

Callanach couldn't trust himself to speak. Ben was more than capable of remotely accessing another computer. More than that, it settled a debt, allowing Lance to come to terms with the decision he'd made. Callanach knew he could ask, but they'd never tell him the truth. Friends protected one another that way. He realised it was time to pick up the phone and apologise to Lance.

'Have you heard from Joe?' he asked.

'No,' Ava said, 'and I don't expect to. It was as much my fault as his. I used him to make peace with my mother when I found out she was dying. I restarted a relationship I knew was wrong for me, to be what I thought she wanted. I'm not sure how much more wrong I could have been.'

'I shouldn't feel too bad on Joe's account,' Callanach said. 'He can take care of himself. What you did was understandable. Everyone is irrational in the face of grief.'

'Actually I always knew Joe was capable of betraying me. That's why it didn't really hurt. But you, on the other hand, I thought you were my friend.'

Callanach had been pouring the coffee. He put the cafetiere back down on the table and straightened up to look at Ava.

'What do you mean?' he asked.

'I mean the beating Joe's men gave you. The one you failed to tell me about. Did it not occur to you that I was entitled to know what sort of man I was planning on spending the rest of my life with?'

'You think you'd have listened? I seem to recall you not being terribly rational, certainly not when it came to your relationship.'

'My mother was dying,' Ava said. 'Of course I wasn't bloody well rational. I had a matter of months to make up for the years I'd spent pushing her away.'

'I get it,' Callanach said. 'What I don't understand is why you didn't tell me about your mother right from the start? I would have supported you.'

Ava stood up. 'How could I ask you to help me repair a stupid rift with my mother when yours deserted you when you needed her most? Every time I thought about having that conversation with you, I felt like a spoilt brat. I've spent years not valuing the one thing you want more than anything else.'

Callanach reached a hand out to her. She took a step back in response. 'You were protecting me by dealing with it alone? No one is tough enough for that. Not even you.'

Ava bit her lip, trying to stop the tears from falling, and failing.

'I came round to talk about it,' she said. 'Then I met Bunny, and I felt like maybe you'd finally been able to move on from—'

'Nothing happened between us,' Callanach said. He stepped over the coffee table, putting an arm round Ava's shoulders and pulling her into his chest. 'Nothing that meant anything. It was a mistake. I'd just met Joe, and I thought if you were making the effort to build a life outside the police then maybe I should too.'

'What Joe said about reading your psychological assessments – I'm sorry. He was convinced there was something between us. It was jealousy.'

Callanach closed his eyes and held Ava while she wiped her face free of tears, feeling a peace he hadn't experienced for more than eighteen months. A sense of home, of finally being in the right place.

'Ava,' he said. 'The reason I stopped things with Bunny, and why I've avoided you since you got together with Joe . . .'

Her mobile rang. She took it from her pocket, frowning at the screen.

'It's Superintendent Overbeck,' she said. 'I'm sorry, Luc, I've got to take it. Give me one minute.'

She stepped into the kitchen. Callanach walked to the window and looked down to the street below. Normal life. People going out for a meal, or home to a loved one. People with a reason to leave the office and rush home. Perhaps it was time to let himself be happy. Time for some truth, and to take some risks. Ava walked back into the lounge, eyes wide.

'Everything okay?' Callanach asked.

'Um, yes,' she said. 'They've been considering DCI Begbie's replacement. Overbeck was phoning to let me know what they've decided.'

'Just as long as it's not DCI Edgar,' Callanach laughed. 'Anyone else is going to be a godsend.'

'I'm glad you feel like that,' Ava said, 'because it's me. I have no idea why, but that's their decision. They've asked me to go in now to go through the paperwork.' Callanach stayed where he was, hands in pockets, trying to find the words. 'Sorry – you were in the middle of saying something when she called – what was it?' Ava asked.

'Nothing important,' Callanach said. 'That's great news, Detective Chief Inspector. You deserve it. I'd give you a hug to say well done, but I'm not sure that's appropriate behaviour with my superior officer.'

'No,' Ava laughed. 'I'll be up on a sexual harassment complaint before I've got my new uniform.' She checked her watch. 'I have to go, Luc, they're waiting. Rain check on the coffee, though?'

'Absolutely, ma'am,' Callanach said, opening the door for her. 'Rain check on everything.'

A few words on the darknet

Given the underlying premise of this book, I thought it was worth adding a note about the darknet. For most of us in the developed world the internet has become as everyday as using the kettle or the toaster. The darknet is one of those things we hear about occasionally in TV programmes and films, very rarely in the media, and yet it is accessible with relatively little know-how. TOR software ('The Onion Router') used to get inside the darknet works by creating layer upon layer of diversions so that nothing can be traced back to the user.

So what goes on in there? I think the best answer to that is, if you can imagine it, the darknet is where it's happening. The obvious truth about the darknet is that the people who use it want to do things unseen. Rumour has it that you can book a hitman with the exchange of bitcoin – the internet's currency. You can certainly download every conceivable type of pornography, including snuff videos. It has become well known for drug and arms sales websites. And as far as this book goes, it is a well-established forum for people with a taste for the criminally deviant to communicate. Paedophile chatrooms have been around on the darknet a long time, but this also extends to people who want to talk about murder, rape, kidnapping, trafficking and terror networks.

So if it is used predominantly for illegal purposes, can it be shut down? The answer is no. It is all part of the internet as we know it, just hidden. Many of the darknet sites are scams waiting to access your computer should you get curious enough to go there. Various governmental organisations are working hard to crack TOR and gain full access to the darknet, but they are still a way off. Is it possible that a killing competition could be organised through the darknet? Yes, sadly, it is. Would we find out about it if it happened? Generally, the police are still reliant on real world clues. A murky, secretive underworld lies beneath the friendly, colourful search engines we visit every day and its true depths are only just starting to be plumbed.

Loved *Perfect Prey*? Then why not get back to where it all started with book one of the D.I. Callanach series?

On a remote Highland mountain, the body of Elaine Buxton is burning. All that will be left to identify the respected lawyer are her teeth and a fragment of clothing. Meanwhile, in the concealed back room of a house in Edinburgh, the real Elaine Buxton screams into the darkness . . .